DAUGHTER OF TIME

READER WRITER MAKER

A TIMELESS SCI-FI TRILOGY
BY EREC STEBBINS

From the future, a final plea. Out of the past, a last hope.

READER (Daughter of Time, Book 1): a science fiction adventure unlike any you have ever known. A young girl, born to die in freakish disregard. A doomed world, enslaved to forces unseen. A final hope beyond imagining. Become a Reader, because in the end, the most unbelievable step in the adventure - *will be your own.*

From hatred, Love. From many, One.

WRITER (Daughter of Time, Book 2): A love story & scifi epic about the beautiful & terrible destiny of profoundly star-crossed lovers with a galaxy's fate in their hands.

In the fabric of space and in the nature of matter, as in a great work of art, there is, written small, the artist's signature. —Carl Sagan, Contact

MAKER (Daughter of Time, Book 3): The final - *or is it the first?* - element of the trilogy. A story in which the One that was lost will be found. Where the thief will guide against chaos and time. Where all that was held dear will perish. And in that final and utter destruction - there will be a Creation.

"*Unique and altogether profound, reminiscent of Bradbury*" -San Francisco Book Reviews
"*Visionary*" -Richard Bunning, Another Space in Time

Praise for

RE∧DER

Daughter of Time
Book 1

"**Unique** and **altogether profound, reminiscent of Bradbury, haunting,** thought-provoking and surprisingly philosophical"
— *San Francisco Book Reviews*

"A gripping science-fiction epic that **will propel readers toward wonder**" — *ForeWord Reviews*

"A new and imaginative series." — *Publishers Weekly*

"An original take on various sci-fi motifs that meditates on themes of love and humanity. Stebbins does **an exceptional job. A richly detailed, compelling story about the power of love.**" — *Kirkus Reviews*

"**Visionary**" — *Richard Bunning, Another Space in Time*

"**Will stick with the reader long after the last page is turned.**" — *City Book Reviews*

"**A brilliant star** in the world of Sci-fi!" — *Tome Tender*

WRITER

Daughter of Time
Book 2

Erec Stebbins

New York, NY, USA

Only one thing is impossible for God: To find any sense in any copyright law on the planet. —Mark Twain

This book is a work of fiction. Any references to historical events, real people, or real locales are used fictitiously. Other names, characters, places, and incidents are the product of the author's imagination, and any resemblance to actual events or locales or persons, living or dead, is entirely coincidental.

Paperback CS
ISBN-10:0-9860571-1-8
ISBN-13:978-0-9860571-1-3

Hardback
ISBN-10:0-9860571-0-X
ISBN-13:978-0-9860571-0-6

Ebook:
ISBN-10:0-9860571-2-6
ISBN-13:978-0-9860571-2-0

Paperback LS
ISBN-13:978-0-9860571-8-2
ISBN-10:0986057185

Published 2014 by Twice Pi Press
TwicePiPress@gmail.com

Paperback cover designs by Erec Stebbins
Hans De Ridder for the CAD model used to create the Orb.
Images Copyright © 2014 diversepixel (Yvonne Less), Kudla, mystic_boy, 02lab, Mopic, Ociacia (Ociacia Vladislav).
Images licensed from Shutterstock.com and Pond5.com

Hardcopy Cover design by Marta Nael © 2014
martanael.daportfolio.com

TWICE PI PRESS

for Ambra & Nitin

never two part

When one being comes to know and love another, a new and beautiful thing is created, namely the love. The cosmos is thus far and at that date enhanced.

—Olaf Stapledon, *Last and First Men*

Prologue

I have seen a face whose sheen I could look through to the ugliness beneath, and a face whose sheen I had to lift to see how beautiful it was.

—The Madman of Gibran

How do you make love to a goddess?

Not to a divinity; this is not a myth. Well, maybe it is a myth. Or rather, the beginning of a myth, where facts and hopes and dreams and the madnesses of humanity and its desperations maniacally shape the story of the past and future like some child's clay. Maybe it's the beginning of a legend. The birth of a new Divine. After all that has happened, all that I have seen, I understand why it may seem so.

I come from a land where religion soaks into the very soil, where one thousand ragas encompass every mood and expression of our species, where a million theologies were born, copulated, and recombined like genomes to produce monotheists, polytheists, thirty-three and ten million divines, and the number zero. Where the stories of the gods and goddesses never ended and a child had no need of a superhero—with charming Krishna, dancing Shiva, and beautiful Parvati, there were stories uncounted. Perhaps, then, it is no wonder that we so easily worshiped her. The real wonder is that nearly all do, every nation across this blue-and-white marble pulled from the ashes.

Even these monstrosities, these aliens now positioned across our world with their own godlike technologies and cities—they hold her in awe. In the erased fragments of time, a shattered Earth she made whole. The tyranny of the Dram trembles across the galaxy as her power sweeps outward like a tide washing clean a tainted shore. She communes with the Orbs, summons their power, opens their portals. She is a Cosmic Messiah, writing anew the story of our universe.

But not to me. To me, this is only a beginning.

Standing here as the soft morning sunlight of New Earth streams through our bedroom window, I look down on her sleeping. The white sheets are nearly blinding, wrapped tightly around her seductive curves. Her naked shoulder has slipped out of the fabric. It is nearly as white as the sheets—such a contrast to my dark copper. The entire blank canvas is dramatically altered by waterfalls of red curls streaming down to her waist.

She is beautiful enough to be a goddess.

But *not* a mere goddess to me. She may be all these things, but to me she is a woman. My lover. She is my dearest, Ambra Dawn.

I was born to love Ambra. I know this from my heartbeat to the deep ache in my bones. It was my destiny made possible only by the miracle of her powers, born when she turned the first Dram fleets to dust. Had she been a normal woman, we would have never met. Never loved. Never walked hand in hand on the beaches of New Earth to feel the waves lap our ankles in the reddening sunset. Never made love on a distant world overlooking the colossus of our own galaxy as it painted the night sky like a frozen explosion.

But Ambra is no normal woman, and I, no normal man. I am abnormal in the ways I knew from childhood. Now, in this terrible darkness at the end, I see that my abnormality is deeper than could ever have been suspected. But it cannot be helped. It is not my doing. Can we who are made from the dust and the clay reshape our Maker?

As I look at the swollen—some would say grotesque—form of her skull resting on the soft pillow, I feel a deep attraction, a pull to touch, to caress. Her Writer powers churn there in the benign tumor that has changed the fate of the universe and given her insight into the inner workings of space and time. Insight into the minds of any she chooses to probe.

This every schoolchild knows and so also I was taught, but this does not explain my childhood obsession with that deformed, beautiful head. Nor how I melt to see those sensual red locks, stopped two-thirds of the way up her scalp, where her skin shines white and scarred, the hair removed by countless surgeries from a time long ago when she lived in bondage and pain.

I pause even now to dwell on the artificial bone around the enormous, grapefruit-sized bulge, sculpted, implanted by twisted scientists of Earth in thralldom to the Dram. The brain tissue inside altered to feed the tumor in her adolescence until it grew beyond anything anyone could have predicted. It gave her a sixth sense and stole from her the ability to see as we do, leaving her totally blind with perfectly healthy eyes.

My Ambra's bright-green eyes see nothing. And yet, they see everything. They haunt the corridors of Time.

Other schoolmates learned the story of New Earth's Mother by rote. I plunged my mind into the codified years like a warm sea. I took those lessons—words of her parents' death at the hands of monsters, her abuse, deformation, torture, escape with the help of the angelic Xix, her turning back of the powerful Dram, and even of time itself—I took them deep into the core of my consciousness.

There, she impaled my heart. I memorized every event, each line on her unchanging face from countless holographs, every lilt and tone and nuance of her voice from audio recordings. Before I had the hormones to be in love, I *loved* Ambra Dawn as no man, no human, no saintly Xixian has ever loved another. In the truest sense, I had no choice. At this terrible end, I see the inevitability of it.

And so now, as I walk to the nightstand and open the drawer, it is only in a state of unreal detachment that I remove the weapon. The composite metal should feel cold in my hand, but it does not. I feel nothing. The muscles tighten around the handle of the pistol, but I give no commands, feel no responses, and sense no contractions or tightness in my skin. I can only see as if from a distance, from a vantage point I cannot define in space or in time.

And this automaton, my body—or now rather some alien form that is no longer mine—pulls that weapon out, unlocks the safety, and turns toward the bed, raising the barrel to the elongated head of my beloved, nearly touching the scarred edges near her hairline.

And before anxiety or understanding can even rise within me, she opens those blind, green eyes with adoration, turning to stare directly into my own, tears trickling down her white cheeks. I hear her voice in my mind.

Don't be afraid, Nitin. I love you.

I pull the trigger.

Part 1

And I saw a new Heaven and a New Earth:
for the first heaven and the first earth
were passed away.

—Apocalypse of John

1

Courage is resistance to fear, mastery of fear—not absence of fear.

—Mark Twain

Without warning, the HUD pixelated, froze, and went dark. The view screen was blank. I was screwed.

I thought I heard a popping sound from my headset, but I couldn't be sure, and there was no time for diagnostics. Three Dram sandworms were bearing down on my team, and now I was blind.

"Control, this is MECHcore Lieutenant Nitin Ratava reporting emergency tactical failure! Display and all telemetry are down. Repeat: Enhanced combat mode is down."

There was a heartbeat of static and then a response.

"Roger that, Lieutenant. Situation critical." An American voice. It would be the new instructor. "The drill's live, son, and those captured Dram don't know time out. Switch to manual and optical mode. Continue theater." There was another brief pause. "Life through action!"

Life through action. Our motto, and likely the best advice for me in the middle of the Thar without backup and with live bugs bearing down on us. I was going to need *a lot* of action.

"Ratava, got your position. We'll try to draw hostiles until you can engage. Thirty seconds, max. Get rolling, metalhead!" *Suresh.* He would make the best captain if I didn't make it out of this, which I likely wouldn't. I was sure there were examples of soldiers whose suits shorted out on them and who made it through a triad. I just hadn't heard of any.

Triads were a nightmare. The Dram's smallest infantry modules, they were designed for close quarters, with three bugs per worm and three worms per group. The sandworms were a cross between a hovercraft tank and a flying drill bit—boring under the sand, flying over it, accelerating so fast your eyes barely kept up.

The real danger came from the firepower. The beam weapons usually weren't our worry—too much energy. The bugs would risk draining their power source with those only if they had a clear and important kill or were sure of victory. It was the flechettes that struck fear into our hearts. Ever since the Dram War began over two hundred years ago, on the surfaces of a hundred planets and moons, even with the Xix to help us develop countermeasures, those flechette canons firing out thousands of supersonic metal needles in a three-dimensional spray wrecked our most fortified attack units. Our armor couldn't stop them. A bed of nails would be comfortable compared to being filleted alive by those things.

Thank Dawn that the hydraulics on my suit were still functioning. I rolled onto my back, the thick metal of the combat chassis scraping across the desert sands like sandpaper on marble. I felt a slight pull in my stomach from acceleration, and I began sliding down the dune. At least I was on the right side and this would hide me from the coming Dram for a few more seconds.

I slowed my breathing and focused to remember my MECHcore training. It wasn't often that a suit failed like this, but it was known to happen, and it was something we all had to prepare for. Reaching over my head, I felt around with the nanofiber gloves and located the control box. Muscle memory of one hundred drills took over, and I disengaged the digital controller and flipped the latchkey to manual. Light streamed in, momentarily blinding me, as the plasma screen rolled back to reveal the Xixian glass faceplate. As my naked eyes adjusted to real light, the swirling sands of the Thar came into focus around me. That and black smoke rising from the other side of the dune.

Static broke out on my communicator. Suresh's voice was strained and I could hear the sounds of explosions and cries of other MECHcore infantry.

"Sandworms engaged! Repeat, MECHcore platoon 3351 engaging Dram sandworm triad. Sergeant Suresh Murli for Lieutenant Ratava. Commencing dance!"

The Xixian Dance Maneuver. It was programmed into each of our suits. It confused the sandworm AI and was promising to become the best tactic for defeating them. The suits did the dance, soldiers carried along for the stochastic pattern, the drivers firing weapons and dropping out if targeted. It had a 77 percent success rate from our trials. If all went well, the worms would die.

All wasn't going well.

I flipped to my feet and charged up the dune. The sounds of battle—sonic booms of flechette canons, ionization crackle of our Xixian ion guns, cries and static over the COM—assaulted me as I crested the sand.

Below me the dance was on; two worms were down, plowed into the sand and burning.

But the nightmare was just beginning. The third had found a node. That was what we called it, a place in the random-walk dance of the MECHcore suits that prevented us from effectively engaging the worm. Angles were wrong. Friendly fire was a real danger. We were exposed, and it was all happening so fast that human eyes couldn't track it, let alone fix the problem. Already I could see two suits down, glints of light from the thousands of silver needles embedded in the MECHs' armor. Whoever was inside those units was dead, sliced into hundreds of pieces.

"This is Command! You're in a death node, Sergeant! Break and reinitiate. Repeat, reinitiate dance sequence!"

Shit. In the time it would take to break off the formation and form a new pattern, we could lose most of the team to that remaining worm. I had to do something.

I charged down the dune, firing up my ion slingers, but before I got halfway down, I launched my two shoulder-mounted rockets. It was a pretty hopeless tactic. Without telemetry, without AI to parse the blindingly fast darting of the worm and the soldiers, I was risking their lives as much as I was chancing a hit on the Dram. But hitting them wasn't my goal. I needed to throw a wrench into the Dram AI, sop up some critical computing power with an attack out of nowhere before they could lock onto any more of my team.

And I sure as hell got their attention.

The next thing I knew, I was airborne, a thunderclap behind me from the superheated air exploding where their beam weapon had narrowly missed melting me into my suit. The combination of that explosion and my previous dash down the dune propelled me forward almost directly toward the worm. As I hurtled toward the Dram, crazy instinct took over.

Fifteen years of gymnastics training had left a set of reflexes I hadn't lost. Reflexes, it should be noted, that were honed for my body alone—not my body encased in several tons of advanced battle armor. I was going to see how well that training could be transferred.

Tucking, I somersaulted near the bottom of the dune, the impact even through the MECH suit knocking the wind out of me. I planted my feet at the end of the roll, felt the powerful hydraulics engage, and channeled the momentum into a leap that took me over twenty feet into the air. There was a sonic boom of flechette needles behind me as the worm tried to adjust to my unorthodox attack, and then I plunged down, firing the small positional thrusters on the suit. Intended for more controlled maneuvers—floating over chasms, jumping over obstacles—it wasn't much. But it was enough to steer me directly onto the worm itself. Or rather, *crash* me on it. As I plunged, I fired several ion pulses into the bulk of the craft and then momentarily lost consciousness as I slammed into the outer casing of the Dram warcraft.

I think I only lost a few seconds, coming to with the sounds of my COM screaming in my ear.

"Ratava! What the hell are you doing! Get off that boat!"

My face shield was cracked, and I could taste the soot and sand blowing up around me like some demonic tornado. My hands grasped the sandworm, or rather the edges of the metal that had been blown apart by my ion blasts and suit impact. The worm was careening to the side, the Dram navigation momentarily disoriented, flechettes firing off wildly in several directions at once. I was being jerked roughly along with it. Now was the time!

"Reform the dance, Sergeant!   Low complexity; no time! Dance, dance, dance!"

They listened. The remaining platoon synced and began jetting through another set of randomized Xixian movements. The worm was reorienting, the Dram recovering. But the bugs were too late.

"Lieutenant,   abandon   that   vehicle!"   barked Command. "They can't engage with you on it."

"Hell they can't!" I yelled. "Suresh, blast this thing back to Naraka."

"Ratava..." Suresh began.

"Do it! Fore and aft! Before you lose the chance!"

Maybe I'll get lucky in the middle. The worm shuddered suddenly as the Xixian ion shots slammed into the hull. They did as I asked, centering on the front and back of the worm. Now, I would complete the job. I detached two plasma grenades from the suit's side and engaged the magnets. The grenades jumped away from my suit and slammed into the sides of the worm, holding tightly.

"Plasgrens attached and activated! Clear! Everyone clear!"

Suddenly, the dancing MECHs broke formation and fired escape rockets, blasting out and away from the sandworm. I did the same, only without telemetry, I was going to have to rely on pure guesswork for the burn.

I angled upward and fired the rockets. I let them go just two seconds, or what seemed like two seconds to me. Firing manually in the adrenaline rush of combat, where time was as distorted as it was around the Daughter, was a recipe for putting your suit in orbit or through a canyon wall. My stomach was yanked to my feet, the g-forces causing my mind to blank. I heard the deafening explosions of the plasma grenades, confident that the hull-breached worm was not going to survive their discharge, and turned my attention to the ground now rushing up to greet me.

My suit was descending quickly. Way, way too fast. I had one shot before impact: to counterfire the front thrusters. But without the AI there was no way I was going to get it right. So I hit them for a full burn. Maybe too much, but then I'd gain a little height and maybe the second bounce wouldn't be so bad.

I was right about the first, painfully wrong about the second. The front thrusters fired and drained. My momentum stopped in a snap, reversed, and threw me thirty feet up. Then gravity took over. I had nothing left to stop it.

I smashed onto the desert floor.

2

Not the wind, not the flag; mind is moving.

—Kōan 29, The Gateless Gate

I stood in the middle of a cornfield.

The smell of the earth and thick growth around me was overpowering. My awareness seemed oddly distorted, slowed, unreal as I stared out over row upon row of shoots blasting into the clear, blue sky above, bright-green leaves in the sunlight sprouting out from nodes in the stems, husks large and pregnant, seemingly perched to release an avalanche of seed to flood the world.

I felt dizzy and I swayed, catching myself on one of the nearby shoots, the hard stem providing enough support as I tried to steady myself. The sounds from my mouth were ragged, quick. I tried to slow it, exhaling long breaths, inhaling in short spurts. *Where am I?*

The sky and corn gave no answer. In the distance there was the squawk of a large bird.

I began to walk, aimlessly at first, the warmth of the sun becoming a heat bath. I stumbled through the field of tasseled giants. I should have become lost in this sea of maize, but I never circled, never redoubled my position. It felt as if a soft pull was leading me forward, coaxing me to turn ninety degrees at this point, stopping me from backtracking when I felt confused. From nowhere and everywhere, I felt a gentle *guide*.

The soil was moist from frequent irrigation. Looking down, I was surprised to see bare feet, my toes squelching the mud where water had pooled. *I'm completely naked.* Part of my awareness, some distant chamber of my mind, whispered that I was now dreaming. But for all the rest of me, it was completely real.

I broke out of the corn ranks and stepped onto a manicured lawn. A small farmhouse stood across a glowing patch of grass. A cool breeze stirred, causing the corn to whisper behind me.

In the middle of the field was a tall and lanky man, his short hair hidden underneath a broad hat, his pale skin nonetheless reddened from exposure to the sun. His back to me, he crouched and lifted a bundle in his hands, which he then tossed into the air. Across the grass, I heard the high-pitched burst of a child's laughter as a red comet rose into the sky and fell back into his arms. Over and over he tossed the bundle, and again and again the little child squealed.

I stepped forward as in a trance. As I approached the pair, the farmer turned around and furrowed his brows at me. The little girl pressed his arms downward with impatience.

"Daddy, Daddy, down! Put me down. *He's* here!"

Her father acquiesced, a look of confusion and surprise on his face. The little girl turned her glowing green eyes to me and stepped cautiously forward. Red hair swirled around her head in the breeze as she looked me over. Then she smiled.

"Nitin."

The sound of my name ran through me like warm water. I found myself kneeling on the grass, equaling the level of our gazes, staring at the figure before me but unable to speak to her.

"You really came!" she said, her smile growing to span her entire face. "I missed you *so much*."

My mouth began to form a word. "Ambra?"

But before the girl could answer, the air between us began to distort, warp tangentially to the planes of space around us. The light faded suddenly, the blue and green, the red of her hair inches from my face. The wind and smells all disappeared. The figures disappeared. Time seemed to stop.

I was in the dark.

Even with my eyes open, I could see nothing. I tried to breathe, but no air would enter my lungs. Again and again I struggled. *Breathe. Breathe, damn you!* My mind panicked.

My body did not react. I did not suffocate. Absolutely nothing happened despite my frantic efforts to draw in air. Not for minutes. Not for hours. Days of struggle.

Or were they years?

Time had no meaning here.

It almost seemed that I floated unbound by the pull of mass. No planet. No starship. Only—emptiness.

Where am I?

Did I have a body? I did not know. I could not see it; all was black. I had a phantom sense of limbs, yet to move them gave only the sensation of paddling through molasses.

Is this hell?

I felt, rather than heard, a hum. A deep buzzing like some chainsaw in my teeth, rattling my skull, my spine, my phantom limbs. Soon, it felt as if I would burst from the terrible resonance.

And then—*light*.

Finally, light. At a great and terrible distance, a tunnel of light appeared, the walls iridescent. Undulating. Vibrating.

Pulling.

Pulling at me, deep inside me. And I felt myself ripped from the strange molasses, torn as from a womb, yanked through a passageway now blinding with radiance that seemed to stretch endlessly. Bent and twisted and crammed into a merciless tube of burning incandescence.

I was dragged helplessly across a forest of lights. Millions and millions of lights burning and winking and dying and being born in shrouds of hydrogen.

They were stars.

3

Life is short, and Art long; the crisis fleeting; experience perilous, and decision difficult. The physician must not only be prepared to do what is right himself, but also to make the patient, the attendants, and externals cooperate.

—Aphorisms of Hippocrates

"Welcome back, Lieutenant Ratava."

The lights continued to burn my eyes. I squinted, blinking repeatedly, trying to adapt to the brilliance around me. I could barely croak out my questions.

"Where am I? What happened?"

A calm yet otherworldly voice responded. "It is natural to be disoriented after such trauma, Lieutenant."

Slowly the lights dimmed enough that I could begin to focus on the objects around me. A strange shape occupied my field of vision, blurred so that I could not quite discern its nature. The soothing voice came from it.

"You suffered a severe concussion, multiple broken limbs, and third-degree burns across much of your back. Fortunately, all was well within the medical skills of your Xixian medics, both onsite and here."

Xixian. The tall shape came into better focus. Six-fold symmetry, four arms, two legs, forty-eight appendages including their twelve highly dexterous fingers on each of the upper "short arms," eighteen visual organs perched on darting eyestalks at the top of a conical protrusion at the top of the glimmering, multicolored torso. I could only find relief in recognizing the monstrous form of our galaxy's greatest benefactors.

The Xix. Dedicated to nearly every higher ideal humanity had ever imagined and succeeding in living those ideals to a level I could only find miraculous. Without the Xix, New Earth would still be ash, the Dram would control the galaxy, and the Hegemony would remain intact. Without the Xix, Ambra Dawn would have perished centuries ago in a smuggler's death boat.

And so I loved them. For me, everything returned to her.

"What do you remember, Lieutenant?"

I felt a stabbing pain in my scalp as my brows furrowed. "I'm not sure. Kidnapped Dram triad training session—went bad. They found a node. Had to improvise." The images washed across my thoughts almost uncontrollably. "My suit was FUBAR. Had to do a manual escape burn to clear the plasgrens. Guess it didn't go so well."

The eyestalks bounced over closer to me. "Considering you worked without AI, you are lucky to be alive."

I laughed. Or tried to, but the sudden movements made me gasp in pain. *"By the Daughter.* Maybe we should just go full drone. Not sure the point of organics out there. Too bloody fast."

"We need organics for the improvisation you mentioned, Lieutenant. AI is certainly artificial, but *intelligent* is still under debate."

Did these Xix have a sense of humor? I was never sure. All these years, trusting and dependent on them, and they were still as alien as alien could be to humanity. I certainly didn't understand them.

It continued. "A fully drone troop would have been annihilated in that engagement. We've seen it happen in the military's trials to remove organics from combat. Only your creative randomness saved your team."

For a moment it surprised me that a medic would know such things, and then I remembered that the Xix had some sort of group memory, something like the experience the Readers shared through the Daughter, that gave them access to everything that happened to their species.

"How many did we lose?"

"Three in the end," said the medic, flitting around the instrumentation in that bizarre bouncing choreography that so typified the Xixian movements.

Half my team. "Dear God."

"Two more are seriously wounded and under care here. You were all flown out after triage to Delhi, and from there to Tokyo, to the Xixian village outside the city."

Uchujin. A city created after the rise of New Earth, after the Unmade Calamity. Following the first few years of war on New Earth to remove the Dram and their agents, the Xix had settled in several locations across the globe. San Francisco, Paris, Auckland, Shanghai. *Tokyo.* Always outside the major human cities, building their own separate cities optimized for their living on an alien world. Always with the permission and collaboration of local governments.

But *not* always with the approval of the populace. That was for sure. I'd never forget my first engagement with the Earth First terrorists. Hatred for humans who looked or speak a little differently could be intense enough. Imagine the hatred toward the truly alien.

Over the last two hundred years, Uchujin had grown to a size nearly to rival Tokyo itself and served as the de facto center of Xixian governance of their population on Earth. It was the center of their technological contributions to humanity in engineering and medicine. They had taken me to the best facilities on the planet.

Which worried me.

"Why am I here?"

The Xix stopped bouncing and attending the medical equipment. Its eyestalks nearly to a one centered on me. "Lieutenant Ratava, do you remember nothing else?"

"Nothing from the engagement, I'm sorry."

The eyestalks didn't move. It was a little unnerving. "Anything *not* from the engagement, but after it?"

The dream. How could it know? Perhaps it had been monitoring my brain functions. But why would some injury-induced REM chaos be of any interest to this thing?

"Just...dreams."

"What sort of dreams?"

"Vague dreams, of being trapped, paralyzed, flying through space. Typical nonsense dream stuff. Why?"

"Your brain activity after your concussion was highly unusual."

"Wouldn't it be?"

The Xix turned a host of eyestalks back to monitors and equipment, keeping several on me. "In predictable ways, yes. Your brain scans were not like anything we have ever seen."

"I'm not a Reader, doctor, if you are wondering. Tested three times. Believe me, my parents hoped so much I'd turn out to be one like my cousins. Since the Calamity, the only thing better than a doctor for Indian parents is becoming a Reader." My smiled faded, the humor apparently lost on the alien.

"We need to understand as much as we can about you, Lieutenant. Your heroics have made quite an impression. I have been informed that you are in consideration for a special transfer."

My heart nearly stopped. *Could it be?* After two years of failed applications? After devoting myself to the MECHcore, training with a passion matched only by that of my dearest hope—*had I succeeded?*

"Do you mean…?"

"Appointment to the Temple Guardians." The Xix seemed to know what was in my heart. A few moments passed in silence. "You will receive a visit from your superiors as soon as I clear you medically. As soon as we are satisfied that your vitals are acceptable."

"And are they?" Now I really *was* worried about those stupid brain scans. I cursed the dreams and the threat that my overactive subconscious might derail my greatest hopes.

The eyestalks jumped back toward me, a small set remaining glued to the output of a floating 3D projection of my brain lit up in multiple colors.

"Probationary, Lieutenant. You will continue to have monitoring. The Temple Guards protect our most precious resource, as you know. They are screened as no one else. In two hundred years, we have never had an incident, never an unstable personality, never a traitor, an embezzler, anyone devoid of anything except the highest functionality and devotion to the Daughter. In this age of increasing threat from outside and within, I hope that you can understand our vigilance."

I did. And maybe had I been the one doing the screening, I would have rejected such an appointment— seen my rashness, my impulsiveness. Perhaps even my obsession was too much.

But I wasn't anyone else. I knew in all the galaxy, they would never find anyone so devoted to her as I.

"Continued monitoring," it repeated. "But cleared for service."

Cleared for service! The room seemed to swim. An elation wanted to explode from me. I wanted to shout, sing, dance! To serve her, so close, each day!

But I had to compose myself. Especially being *on probation*. I had to appear for all the world to be the stable, capable, and trustworthy soldier they were looking for.

"Should the Core find me worthy, I would be honored."

The alien medic stared at me in silence.

4

Be ye therefore wise as serpents, and harmless as doves.

—Jesus of Nazareth

"Kavita, please; he is not a child."

My father scolded my mother again as she practically touched the holographic projector in their apartment in Delhi. Her brandy eyes were enhanced by the crimson sari she wore, and her long and elegant fingers danced and gesticulated in the center of my Japanese quarters. The Tokyo MECHcore base was small but well outfitted. The reception from India was crystal clear—I could even see the garnets on her bangles.

I was struck once more by the combination of genes that had produced me. My mother, petite from northern India, lighter of complexion with a beautiful smile. My father, from the southern continent, nearly dark as an African, tall, thin, with a bristling mustache. I was painted in hue somewhere between the two, with my father's height and build, my mother's face and smile, and a psychology that had kept the entire family in turmoil since I was a child.

"He is *my* child, Sriram, and I will tell him when he is acting a fool!"

The anguish on her face was all too clear in the projection before me. My father simply stared upward. He knew all he could do was to wait this out.

"Are you deliberately trying to kill your own mother?"

"Amma, please..."

"First you join this army, full of these aliens and these low-life men. Just listen to you speak! Your language is foul like some American soldier! Then, you are nearly killed because of it and lay in a hospital thousands of miles away! We cannot even come to see you!"

Great. She was crying.

"Now? You tell me that you will go to the *Temple*, a place where powers from outer space will gather. A place of war with monsters. To risk your own life! Why, Nitin? Why? Because of some childish sense of romance for some woman who isn't even human anymore!"

"Amma, stop!" I had to control myself. Hot flashes of anger swelled across my cheeks. I knew she would attack her; it always came to that. Years and years, since I had been a child, growing in vehemence when I was an adolescent, and now, desperate as I made my choices as a grown man.

Grown, yet still a child. Still unable to free myself from childish fears. What was childish was not my love of Ambra Dawn, but the way my mother could still tie me in knots!

"Do you know what I have done?" her face was firm with that expression when she punished me as a child for coming home with my uniform soiled. "I have torn down the projections in your room! Yes? Do you hear? On the walls, the ceilings! I have thrown out the crystals, all the videos and images! There is now just a bed and desk. A proper room for a proper child, not some mad shrine to a freak!"

"Kavita, enough!" My father whispered, shaking his head. I was grateful for his intervention, however small it would be. It was not that he was on my side or ever understood these feelings, but he at least understood that he did not understand. In his universe, there was at least some space for his son to be something different, someone he could love and worry for and yet not control. Not so with Amma.

I tried a different approach. "Amma, this is a great honor."

She almost shrieked. "It is a shame! Your cousins are doctors or Readers! You? A *soldier*. Chasing a mad goddess!"

"I am determined, Amma!"

I don't know where my clarity of mind came, but despite all the inner turmoil of feeling my mother's harsh disapproval, hearing her ugly words about me and about her, a peace intervened through all the hurt. I can only think it was a gift of the higher powers. Suddenly, I was calm, sure of myself, of my life, of the path I was taking. I had always known where I had to be. For the first time, that surety gave me confidence before her.

"Amma, I will go to the Sahara. I will stand guard at the Temple. There are only a handful of people from across the world allowed there. The gods have chosen me. I have felt their call all my life. I know where I must be. And it is with her."

She sobbed, my father holding her shoulders, but she glanced toward me. She had heard the tone in my voice, and there was a resignation in her eyes. The sudden surety inside me gave way to insight, and I saw a path to salve her pain.

You see, while my father was a lapsed Catholic, Amma was a devout Hindu. She went to temple frequently, was faithful with Nitya at home, and was particularly devoted to Kali, the goddess whose name means Time. My mother had a special prayer shrine, rarely visited by my skeptic father, built as an addition to the house. A floor-to-ceiling icon of Kali, the Bhavatārini form of the goddess—literally "redeemer of the universe"—dominates that space.

"Amma," I said gently, staring into her projected eyes floating in front of me, her face as large as my body, "do you not see? The Daughter is an *avatar*. She is the Bhavatārini of the goddess here and now. They call her the Daughter of *Time*—can it be anything else? She delivered the world! Go and ask her icon. What better place can there be for your son?"

Her eyes widened, and I couldn't tell whether it was from fear that I was mad or fear that I might be right. Perhaps both. She buried her face in my father's chest.

"Nitin," he said, his voice rough, "We will talk later. I...I am happy you are well. We are thinking of you." And just like that, he switched off the connection.

I let out a long breath. It was never easy with parents.

An hour later, there was an alert tone from the house AI. "Visitor at the front door. Please advise."

The colonel. 6:25 p.m. He was early, as was his habit.

"Visual—external view, front door."

The holoprojector flashed back on, and the giant form of Lieutenant Colonel Brad Snowden appeared to invade my living room. Six foot five, 245 pounds, and even at fifty-seven he looked more like a boxer than a paper pusher. And he had lived up to his appearance with the distinction of being one of only three humans ever known to defeat a Dram warrior in hand-to-hand combat. For that badge of honor, he had lost an eye and gained a six-inch scar across his face. Most significantly of all, he was Texan.

"Son, you gonna ogle my old ass all day or let me the hell in?" At least he was in a good mood.

This is it. Nothing short of a court-martial or major promotion would warrant the personal visit of our regiment's leader. After the words of the overly talkative Xixian medic, I was counting on the latter.

"Allow entry."

I walked over toward the door, my limp almost gone. The bolt locks on the door retracted with loud click, and the magnetic latch reversed polarity. The door swung inward and Snowden marched in.

I stood at attention with a salute. These Americans were hard to predict. One day a superior officer would have a beer with you and the next dress you down for a sloppy salute. Best just to go overly formal and play it safe.

"Colonel Snowden, sir."

He shot back a salute. "At ease, son. You got any bourbon?"

So it was going to be informal. I shook my head. "No sir, but I've got sake."

"With ice; none of that warm shit." I tried not to make a face. *Texans.*

He paced around the room, looking it up and down while cocking his head for his good eye, and let out a low whistle. I understood. The Japanese did things well.

The room was spacious, three times the size of standard quarters. There were couches and tables sized to fit Westerners' expectations. There was that top-flight holoprojector. I even had my own modernized kitchen complete with nutrient synth.

"Didn't have such fancy digs back in my day. Least not in the desert."

I gripped the sake bottle tightly. "You were there?" I finished pouring the drink and handed it over to him. The ice cubes rang like small bells as he gestured.

His drawl thickened. "Sit down, Ratava. We need to talk."

The colonel pulled up a seat at the kitchen table, and I sat across from him. He took a sip of the sake and rubbed his temples, leaning back in his chair.

"You know why I'm here."

"My request for transfer."

"Son, I've had three—*three* soldiers over thirty years under my command who have been selected for the desert. It was always unpredictable. They weren't usually the toughest, the smartest, or the best. Don't get me wrong; they were always *good*, but that Witch has her ways of seeing things."

I suppressed a grimace. There were many names for the Daughter, not all of them kind. I had heard this one used by a lot of skeptics and rebel prisoners. And hard-asses who had seen too much to believe in fairies. Snowden wasn't a rebel—of this I was sure. He was certainly a hard-ass and probably a skeptic. It didn't matter. I'd dealt with many of those in the MECHcore. But it meant this conversation might be very difficult.

His one eye glared at me shrewdly, sizing me up. "Ratava, I understand that you have a certain fondness for the Witch."

"I prefer to call her the Daughter, but—yes. I don't suppose there's anyone in MECHcore who doesn't know. The military can't block all the anom networking."

"Pinups on your walls ain't gonna prep you for what's waiting in the desert. At the *Temple*. All your pretty schoolbooks, the propaganda in the media—that's all a fairy tale designed to keep fifteen billion souls in line."

"You sound like the extremists."

Snowden laughed. "One thing you'll learn is that what makes any rebel cause a contender is a foundation of *truth*. That I can see it doesn't make me a traitor or give me desires to be one. It makes me a better leader. If you're going to survive down there, you've got to grow up, son."

I felt my jaw clenching, my molars grinding against each other. "Yes, sir. What do I need to know?"

He waved his hand dismissively. "Way more than I've got time to tell you. Like I said, they snatch my people rarely and always unpredictably. Your *fondness* for the...*Daughter*," he said, pausing with a smile, "made you the least likely to be selected, from the analysis of many. Hell, son, I thought it was pretty unbalanced myself when I reviewed your requests for transfer."

"I don't understand."

He sighed and leaned forward, resting his massive arms on his knees. "There's too much to learn now. And it's all in flux anyway." He shook his head, an anxious look clouding his face as he gazed past me. "And times are changing. The war's goin' bad."

"We've had setbacks. The Dram are resilient."

"Setbacks? You've got to read *between* the lines of the official reports. We're *losing* this war, Ratava." He looked me in the eye. "The Dram have breached the galactic center."

My stomach dropped. The center was our defensive nexus. If the galaxy were a wheel, the center gave the most direct access to any location through the Orb Time Tree. To take back the center—it was inconceivable. It was a disaster.

"There are no reports—"

"Of course not! Do you know the panic that would result?"

"But the Daughter! She controls the Orbs and the Time Tree! How can they use the Strings to jump if she prevents it?"

"Well, that *is* where things get interesting. If they could jump willy-nilly, they'd be turning us on a spit for those damn spider pets they keep. But they haven't shown up on our doorstep, and I can only assume the Witch is the reason. But the center *isn't* holding. More and more they are gaining access, making raids. It's all hush-hush but the writing's on the wall. Ambra Dawn, even if she won't die, ain't God. And her powers are failing."

I couldn't believe what I was hearing. "Then there is something you don't understand about all this. Her powers don't fail! She reached back through time and saved us all!"

"So the story goes. But even if you believe that myth, she didn't do it alone. She's not all-powerful. She needed *Them*, these aliens. Saintly aliens we're all led to believe, and so they seem." He laughed glancing across my body. "They sure as hell fixed you up fast—three weeks after that crash? Yeah, that's alien meds for you."

"They treated me well."

"I'm sure they did. They always do. But do we really know them? Has anyone ever penetrated their culture, understood their motivations? Their *real* plans? Two hundred years on Earth now, building cities, giving us tech, plotting who knows what, and we are none the wiser!"

"They helped free us from the tyranny of the Dram!"

"Words right out of a textbook. A-plus, son." He downed the rest of his drink. "Sure, there's enough military history of the Emancipation to convince even me that it happened. But did we trade one alien tyranny for another?"

Now he was really edging dangerously close to treason. "Sir, we can't understand them. They are too advanced for us."

Again he waved his hand. "Perhaps, or perhaps that's just more smoke and mirrors to keep us from questioning."

I was feeling dizzy, lost at sea in this frightening conversation. This was my commanding officer! "Colonel, what are you trying to tell me?"

Snowden stood up and walked over to the window overlooking Tokyo. The sun was setting behind the forest of skyscrapers, their windows giving the wall of buildings the appearance of an endless checkered light board. Spacecraft darted back and forth across the darkening skies. Off to the left, the eerie green glow of Uchujin and the Xix. Snowden shook the ice cubes in his glass with one hand, his other arm behind his back. He nearly stood at attention.

"We're at a turning point, Ratava. As they used to say, 'The game is afoot.' Call it soldier's intuition, but after surviving a hell of a lot of death holes, you might want to take mine seriously. Something's gonna happen. Not today. Not tomorrow. Maybe not this year. But it's close. There's something big growing out there in between those stars, and when it comes, there's gonna be a fire raining down on that Temple in the desert."

Ambra. "With all due respect, sir, then I need to be there. Now."

Snowden turned around and stared at me. "Have you heard a goddamn thing I've said?"

I stood up as well and set my shoulders. "I've heard all of it. And if I've been chosen, then what I most need to do right now is get on a transport for the Sahara. ASAP."

His single eye bored into mine. "I don't know whether you're the biggest damn fool I've ever met or a fucking apostle."

I swallowed as he continued to stare at me. "Neither, sir, I hope. I just know where I have to be."

He shook his head again and put his glass down on the table. "They weren't shitting me when they said you were a believer." He walked toward the door and pressed the touchpad to exit. As the door swung open, he turned back to me.

"Report tomorrow at the hoverport, 0600. Pack lightly; you'll get new gear on arrival. And a new team, *Captain.*"

"Captain?"

"And, Ratava, keep your eyes open. Innocent doves end up sacrificed in the sands. The animal for the desert—it's a snake."

He stepped through the portal and it whisked shut, the bolts slamming into place.

5

I am always wandering around in enigmas.

—M.C. Escher

I didn't sleep much that night.

What little I got was plagued by parades of dreams, foggy narratives that slipped through my mind—training, childhood, Xixian medics hovering over me. In the end, I remembered almost nothing.

Except for the last one. A flashback to primary school in Delhi, standing in front of a projection of the Daughter as some angry teacher called out my name repeatedly.

"Ratava. Nitin Ratava! Answer the question!"

It was a dream reliving the first time I had seen a holo of Ambra Dawn. There she was, a life-size projection in three dimensions, the shimmer of a poor-quality lamp giving a ghostly appearance to the form. I almost felt as if I could reach out and touch the red curls cascading down her shoulders. Her eyes glowed like giant pools of fluorescent water.

I was to answer some question about her, the instructor calling on different children to recite the lessons. But I only stood there frozen, transfixed—struck dumb by her beauty and majesty. A boy of six utterly overwhelmed and unmade in an instant.

But in the dream, the memory changed. The static holograph animated and turned to me. Her bright eyes locked with mine, and I was bathed in a warm radiance. All else dimmed—the school, the instructor, the world. Only she was left. I looked up into those green pools, felt them draw me in like some wormhole in space toward another universe. I felt a slow acceleration, rotating faster and faster around her, the center of my experience those beautiful, unblinking eyes. She opened her lips and whispered.

"Nitin."

I awoke shaking to the blaring of my alarm.

I dressed quickly in my travel uniform. I still had my lieutenant bar and would have to see if the colonel's last words would include gaining another bar to the rank of captain. But the promotion wasn't so important to me. The destination was all that mattered.

I packed lightly, as instructed. My standard issue firearm, a Xixian gyrostabilized slug thrower, Hertz 744. All-carbon composite, grid synchronized workhorse of the MECHcore. As a rule, since we served most of our time suited up, they didn't get much use. But old traditions died hard. Otherwise, one uniform change, grooming gear, and a single zettabyte crystal. Small, not much for holoviewing. It carried graphs of my parents, a few of my cousins. All the rest of her.

I rushed out the door.

The hovercraft was impressive. As I walked into the hangar, barely settling my stomach after a poorly calibrated drone transport hurtled me from the barracks,

I had to marvel. The size of one of Old Earth's airships, this was the classic image of an alien spacecraft to our precontact ancestors. Disc-shaped with a protruding spherical dome on the top, it could handle a thousand troops at capacity. Not to mention cargo. Ring-bands of magneto-thrusters lined the bottom, powerful enough to accelerate the ship into orbit if needed.

Troops were already marching onboard. Most were infantry to be deployed at one of the Six Cities surrounding the Temple in the middle of the Sahara. Six Cities to house the human and alien engineers operating the massive network of power plants and more esoteric equipment used by the Daughter to commune with the Orbs. Six Cities over the six ancient aquifers below the sands, necessary water sources built up during older geological periods when the desert was a jungle. So went the textbooks, anyway. Mostly, it was a mystery that few had seen. Those who had rarely spoke of it.

Only a handful would continue from the outer circle toward the Temple. The Temple wasn't like the other cities. Shrouded in the deepest mystery of all, it was rumored to be dominated by a single large structure that served primarily to house the Dish, the great antenna that focused Ambra Dawn's psychic space-time powers. The Dish was thought to be buried under the Temple structure, deep below the sands in the bedrock. There were no holos, few reports, and more contradictions than established fact. Whatever was there, it was kept under the strictest secrecy.

Some of those lucky few who were to be granted access to the inner palace of the Daughter were waiting for me near the hovercraft. Colonel Snowden stood with his hands on his hips, a black scowl on his face that would likely turn a sandworm around. His eyes were hidden behind reflective shades. I half expected cowboy boots to complete the picture and was disappointed to find regular shoes.

"Captain Ratava. About goddamned time."

He shoved a small latched box toward me. I took it, popped it open, and saw the gleaming captain's bars.

Snowden smirked. "No time for formalities. Paperwork was cleared at light speed. Not that it will mean a rat's ass down there. They have a whole *other* way of doing things." He turned toward three other soldiers, two men and a woman, and swept his arm outward, as if to the sands and Temple. "Which all of you will be learning of soon enough. This is Captain Nitin Ratava. You've been briefed, but until you land and are put under Temple command, you'll be taking orders from him. Introduce yourselves."

The colonel stepped back, his body language suggesting I engage for the introductions. I stepped forward, coming to a stop a few feet from the three. The male leftmost from my perspective saluted.

"Master Sergeant David Kim, sir! Operations!" Our team sergeant. Korean from the name and accent, short, five foot six, stocky with thick quads that stretched his fatigues. Eager beaver.

I saluted back and turned to the middle soldier. She was tall, an inch or so taller than I at five foot eleven inches. Her eyes were sharp and intelligent, her skin a shade darker than my own. Her salute was swift and hard.

"Warrant Officer Aisha Williams, sir."

She would be my second in command in the MECH team, basically my alter ego. I would need to get to know her well.

I pivoted slightly to meet the third, a Caucasian male around my height and of moderate build. I caught a glint from contact lenses.

"Sergeant First Class Ryan Marshall, sir," he said, the most reserved of the three. "Medical."

I turned to the colonel. "What about the rest of the team?"

"Coming from other corners of the globe, Captain. They will rendezvous outside the Six Cities for your info briefing prior to your journey to the Temple."

I nodded. There was going to be a lot to learn.

The Texan jerked his head toward the hovercraft. "Why don't you three saddle up before this wagon leaves without you. Ratava, a few words before I leave you."

The three grabbed their duffels and darted off, jogging onto the transport. The pad was nearly empty now but for the service staff prepping the saucer. I turned toward Snowden.

"Colonel, I don't understand. You aren't coming with us? I thought—"

"Command and Control gets a reboot a hundred miles outside of the Six Cities. They've got their own way of doing things, and you'll get your commanding officer there. Besides, there's no way in hell I'm setting foot in the desert again. They know that."

I nodded without understanding, beginning to feel a bit isolated. New commanders, brand-new team. New rules. There was going to be *a lot* to learn.

"Last bit of intel for you, Captain." He waited as several dock workers rushed past, lugging crates and loading them into the hull.

A voice blared out over the speakers announcing the departure of our flight: "*All nonessential personnel clear the hovercraft pad. Liftoff in five minutes.*"

He didn't raise his voice, and I had to concentrate to understand his words over the noise. "I'm under the strictest orders not to be telling you any of it, but you need to know. This has *not* been a normal recruitment— hell, if any of them are normal."

"What do you mean, sir?"

"Shuttle A58L departing in five minutes. All nonessential personnel clear the hovercraft pad."

"You had a special visitor during your coma, son."

"Visitor?"

"Liftoff in five minutes."

The colonel almost looked awed. "Never happened before. Damnedest thing. Shuttle landed two days after you came in. I was summoned, and it was requested that I meet an envoy from the desert at the hospital. *Your* room."

"My room? From the desert?"

Snowden looked away. He actually seemed afraid, and his voice fell to a whisper. Fortunately, there was a brief lull in the announcements, and I could hear him clearly. "Spent hours with you, didn't say a goddamn thing. Just sat there by your bed, staring with those terrible eyes." He barked out a staccato laugh, glancing hesitantly at me. "That's why I left, you see. Put in for a transfer my third year. I couldn't take those damn eyes anymore. How do you stand in front of blind eyes that see *into* you?"

"Sir, *who* was there?" My hands were trembling.

"Isn't it obvious, son?"

"Shuttle A58L departing in two minutes. Clear the hovercraft pad."

I couldn't say anything. My brain didn't seem to work.

"Now, you think on that as you break atmo."

6

We must rise above the Earth—to the top of the clouds and beyond—for only thus will we fully understand the world in which we live.

— Socrates

The liftoff was what I had come to expect from the magthrusters—deceptively smooth acceleration that lulls you into gawking at the alien tech, followed by a whiplash onset of nausea around the time the ship reaches escape velocity.

My partial team was isolated from the rest of the passengers on the transport, tucked away toward the middle of the saucer in a private lounge outfitted for the brass or moneyed. Even the five-point restraints were plush, and you could almost enjoy it until you needed to revisit your breakfast.

The ride affects each person differently. Some find the initial acceleration disorienting—*too smooth* and unlike any natural or human technology made to get from A to B. For others, it's the switch when breaking atmo, several minutes of zero-g before the plunge back to the destination. And others find that plunge disturbing, physiologically or psychologically—if those things can be seperated—and that's when the barf bags come out.

For me, it was the switch to weightlessness. I had the palpable sense that my stomach was lurching independently of the rest of my body, and my brain didn't like that sense one bit. I knew how to control it. I knew to eat little in the morning. I just needed to concentrate. Of course, it was just at this point in the journey that my warrant officer decided to get chatty.

"Not looking so good, Captain," said Williams, a half-hidden smirk dancing at the corners of her mouth.

I decided to change the topic by going on the offensive. "How much combat experience do you have, Williams?"

The smirk was gone. "Standard basic and advanced infantry M, sir. Plus four live skirmishes on Freinzel."

"I hear that moon was pretty damn infested."

I could see the glow of pride on her face. "Yes, sir. Two thousand Dram grunts with some allied species. Three triads protecting a central hive."

"How'd you take it on?"

She paused, a shocked expression on her face. "Air support, sir. Drones. We cleaned up the soldiers. Standard procedure."

"I see." I let the silence do its job.

Williams looked toward me sharply. The wheels were turning. "But I've heard some teams are taking on triads directly."

Kim and Marshall woke up at her words and glanced over. I was going to have their full attention.

I nodded. "It's new. The Xix have developed a partially randomized movement pattern for the MECHs. It's a little scary—you hand over complete control to the AI—and your suit just flies around in ways you can't predict. Confuses the hell out of the triads—operators too. You do it right, you get lucky, they're sitting ducks, and you vaporize them."

Williams was studying me intently. "You've done this."

"I have. That's why I'm here. You're all going to learn, and I'm going to train the core troops at the Temple. Or so the plan goes."

Kim shook his head. "I don't know, man. Full AI control? Why do they even need us, then?"

I corrected my assessment—Korean American. With English the default in the New Earth forces, training ensured fluency in just about everyone. The Chinese resisted a little, but with India, Europe, and America onboard, it was a done deal. But that standard fluency could mask origins, at least until you engaged the speaker for some real conversation. Kim wasn't a native English speaker. Likely an immigrant to America. I hoped I would get dossiers on all of them in the desert. This entire redeployment was being rushed like hell.

"Because the AIs are as dumb as they are smart. When the patterns fail, they still need us to think on our feet. Improvise."

"Improvise? Sounds like a good way to get yourself killed," said Kim.

"It's dangerous," I agreed.

"We've heard the rumors." It was the medic, Marshall.

"What rumors?" I asked.

Williams only stared. Again I sensed the wheels spinning. *She's a careful one.*

Marshall continued. "Tokyo General. They brought wounded from India, only there a few hours before they transferred them to *Uchujin*. That was you, wasn't it?"

I nodded.

Williams cut in. "Word was the team got into trouble. Training exercises with *live* Dram. A fucking *triad*."

"On *Earth*?" Kim asked. I nodded. He laughed. "How'd you sign the bugs up for that?"

"The Daughter," I said. "That's what we hear, anyway. She grabs them, somehow, from somewhere. Maybe even from Dram."

Kim's jaw hung open. "*Grabs* them? What the fuck?"

I shook my head. "Wormhole snatch? Xixian raid? No idea. But they're Dram all right. Sandworm triad. Right in the deserts of India."

"That's fucking *crazy*," said Kim again. "*Jesus*. What the hell are we getting ourselves into down there?" He gestured toward the continent of Africa, now growing in size on the blue marble as we commenced our decent from Earth orbit. The Sahara was obvious even from this altitude—like a tan brush stroke across northern Africa.

I spoke firmly. "We are getting ourselves into the most important service in this war. We are learning the most advanced techniques, training against the enemy themselves to prepare, because our job will be to protect what is most important."

"The Daughter," said Williams, her smile returning slightly as she looked at me.

"Yes, of course."

The two men nodded, seeming to become absorbed in their own thoughts.

"You speak of her with awe, Captain." Williams studied me. It was uncomfortable, but I knew all this would come out, if they didn't already know from the grapevine.

"Go on, let's get this over with," I said, noticing the other two reengage. And it was Marshall who continued the conversation, as if he had never tuned out.

"You have quite the reputation as a member of the faithful, Captain. What denomination are you—not Orthodox—you don't sport the gear. Chrono Reformed?"

I looked across them. "Special forces are worse than the tabloids."

"That's part of how we stay alive, Captain," said Williams.

I sighed. Now came the part that wouldn't make sense to them. "None. No denomination. It's a...personal relationship."

"Sounds Next Agey," said Kim.

"It's *personal*. Since I was a kid. Now look, every team I've been on worries about this until they get used to it. I can tell you it's no different from any other personal beliefs or feelings every one of us has. You have nothing to worry about. I do my job, better than most."

"Except that our job's all about her now, isn't it?" noted Williams. "This isn't like any other old job. You've got stakes."

I locked eyes with her. "We've *all* got stakes. Our planet has stakes. She's what freed us and keeps us free still. Everyone on this planet, everyone in this transport—each of you—owes your life and freedom to the Daughter. Protecting her is protecting Earth. Whatever else I or anyone else feels doesn't figure in. Those are the hard facts. That's why we wear the uniform."

There was a silence. The muffled sounds of rushing atmosphere filled it awkwardly. I glanced at the floating view screen, its image of a rapidly growing northern Africa shining brightly in the darkness of the room.

Kim laughed. "Hell, Captain, what people do on their own time is their business. Local tail, boy-girl-alien threesome, bingo—not my concern. All I need to know is where those bastards are and when I need to start shooting."

Marshall laughed softly, and I smiled. Kim aimed his hand as if it were in a suit, angling imaginary ion slingers, a hard smile on his face. One thing about the MECHcore: to a one, they lived for combat. It was an addiction, perhaps, an age-old primitive drive augmented wildly by the speed and feedback of the machine enhancement. The thrill of life-and-death performance at light speed was a hell of a high.

Williams looked amused but didn't smile. She just stared at me.

7

Thoroughly conscious ignorance is the prelude to every real advance in science.

—James Clerk Maxwell

The Thar is hot, but even my training there did not prepare me for our planet's largest desert. As the transport doors opened, we were met by three things: First, a blast of sandy wind that felt like a blowtorch. Next, a tan radiance bright enough to hurt through our smartglasses. And finally, an ensemble of human and Xixian handlers who would shepherd us for the remainder of the trip.

The transfer of power was immediate and obvious. Where once we were the soldiers of the New Earth Force, our infantry and officers now stood surrounded by members of the Six Cities. These humans and Xix did not wear Force uniforms and answered themselves only to the Daughter. But they did not hold themselves like commanders. As rumored, they carried themselves more like the members of a religious caste.

The humans dressed in accordance with their personal traditions and the necessities of desert life. Over time, their clothes increasingly resembled the garb of the long-term nomads of the regions nearby, the Berber Arabs and other tribes that had long ago optimized their lifestyle under the sun and over the stinging sands. Full-body coverings were the norm, modernized with reflective fabrics that allowed thermal radiation to escape in the day, but they were temperature toggled to internally reflect infrared after sunset during the cold desert nights. It wasn't unusual to get a swing from one hundred degrees to freezing across a single evening. Clothing needed special properties if you weren't indoors with climate control.

The Xix required no coverings. Their homeworld was basically one large Sahara, nearly a complete desert, and they seemed to feel most at their element on New Earth with two of their six-toed feet in the sand. Their metabolism seemed to handle extreme heat and extreme cold effortlessly. Their skin was impervious to everything except the most violent sandstorms.

Towering over the group waiting for us as we exited was a Xix that did wear a thin covering, a cyan robe that was partially transparent when viewed at certain angles, as if it had been polarized. The robe opened near the cone of tissue that erupted upward from the midsection of the alien and was held in place by a blue-green organic-looking metal band that I recognized as their universal translator. Underneath the robe I could see across its body a spray of deep-purple spots, some large, some small, in patterns dizzying and hard to follow. Many of its eyestalks sprouting from the cone were trained on me, and I could feel the burn of its gaze, hotter than the air around us.

Standing alongside the Xix were several humans in the white robes of the Temple servants. Directly in front of them all were two uniformed soldiers, Special Forces, a man and a woman. By the MECHcore insignias, I knew they must be the remainder of my team.

Williams, Kim, and Marshall instinctively fell into a line a half step behind me as we approached the group. They were dressed as I was, advanced Force desert gear sized and provided in the saucer. Brown-and-tan camouflage clothing and hats, combat boots, and the dark smartglasses. I dialed the brightness down on the latter to better make out the faces in front of me as we approached. I stopped in front of the three new soldiers and saluted.

"Captain Nitin Ratava of New Earth Force reporting for duty. This is part of ODA 111, my assigned M-team for service at the Temple. Sergeants Marshall and Kim," I said, gesturing. "Warrant Officer Williams. Requesting permission to enter and be received into the Six Cities."

There was a long and awkward pause. The desert wind whistled around us, the robes in front of me dancing to some turbulent pattern. It was a little unnerving stepping into this bubble of governance on New Earth. Who actually held authority here? Not my team, that was for sure. One of the humans? I scanned their faces but saw only blank stares.

The eyes of the Xix drew my attention. Instinct told me the seat of authority lay with the alien. I took off my glasses and, momentarily blinded by the light and grit, squinted toward the monster.

"Is permission granted?"

The Xix spoke through the translator clasped about its neck like a necklace. "Indeed, Captain," came the fluid accent of the device. The voice was genderless but warm, the tones sharp with intelligence. "Both you and your team. Two you have not met and stand before you: Weapons Sergeant Grant Moore and Sergeant Erica Fox, your engineer."

It was odd to hear the alien speak the military jargon so effortlessly. But I had to remind myself to take the Xix very seriously and not underestimate them. They could likely handle all of our human areas of expertise and thought without breaking a sweat. Well, almost all of them. Humans could still *Read* better than any. That was why they were living on New Earth. That was why my team and I were here.

I made the introductions within the team. The two last members looked as capable as the rest. Fox was a small woman, of mixed heritage, possibly Chinese and European. There was a slight detachment in her demeanor I had come to expect from the techs. Moore looked every bit the stereotypical Force officer from a recruitment poster: tall, muscled, and tattooed. As I would find out frequently later, also a tongue loose and salty. His lowbrow British twang gave his speech a memorable character. Both instinctively grouped with the rest of the team, and we were now facing the Xix and its greeting party.

"Captain Ratava, I am called Waythrel, and I serve Ambra Dawn at the Temple."

My throat went dry. *Waythrel?* This was a figure out of the history books. This was the Xixian spy on Dram who had helped free Ambra Dawn from their dungeons, who had accompanied her on her mission to save Earth. For more than two hundred years, the alien had been her closest and most trusted advisor. By the Daughter, what was it doing here?

"Waythrel of the Xix, I am honored that you have chosen to welcome us." I spoke formally, trying to employ half-forgotten exocultural protocols from our basic Force training.

The eyestalks darted around impishly. "It is we who are honored. We have a special assignment for you waiting at the Temple, and Ambra desires that we get to it quickly. We will rest tonight and depart first thing in the morning. My assistants here will lead you to housing that has been prepared."

I could sense the members of my team stealing glances in my direction. They were likely dying to know what was behind this unprecedented visit of one of the Temple's most legendary residents.

They were also likely curious as hell about the meaning of a *special assignment*. MECH teams usually played an important if unexciting role at the Temple. Ours was to have been one of several that were charged with handling security and personal safety of the populace. Nothing like Special Forces flying around encased in alien-metal suits to make an impression. But I couldn't focus on the broader picture. My pulse had spiked. Waythrel's words were spinning in my mind.

Ambra desires.

My team was to be used for something unusual, and that plan was tied closely to the wishes of Ambra Dawn herself! We were not going to serve as some standard MECHcore unit. We were going to be used for something special, something *she* was planning. We might even soon be in her presence.

I could barely breathe.

"Welcome to the Fourth City, Captain."

8

There is one disease which is widespread, and from which men rarely escape: that every person thinks his mind more clever and more learned than it is. I have found that this disease has attacked many an intelligent person.

— Maimonides

Williams stood in front of the group with her hands on her hips. "Captain, what the hell's going on?"

We were gathered in a makeshift quarters. Despite their age, the buildings appeared ultra-modern, half Xixian design common in the Six Cities. The walls were *dynamic* inside the structure, composed of some field that could be altered for appearance, texture, and position. Need a bigger room to house a special forces team? No problem! Reprogram the damn walls. You could select anything from wood to marble to unearthly materials preferred by the aliens. Incredibly realistic.

The external structure was more permanent—some concrete composite material that performed a similar service as the high-tech clothing: heat stayed out in the day but was retained at night. It was also hard as hell too, and I didn't see a single scratch on the gleaming surface despite hundreds of years of sandstorms. The Xix knew how to build.

"Calm down, Williams."

Her eyes flashed at me.

That was the problem with elite forces, maybe especially the ones the Temple had selected. They were bright. They asked questions. They had attitude. That was what gave them the edge the ordinary soldier lacked, what made them the creative destroyers you needed to handle the hard cases.

And what made them such giant pains in the ass to command. The meeting hadn't even begun before the questions erupted.

"Captain, I'm calm, but I signed up for Guardian duty. I know what that requires. I'm prepared. But I didn't sign up for any *special assignment*. I want to know what we're getting into."

"Take a seat, Williams," I said firmly, motioning to the set of chairs set up in the center. I had a smartholo floating in the middle of the space, but I didn't know if I'd even get to use it. I'd planned to begin going over the new MECH AI that they would employ to engage the Dram. For now, that was on hold.

Williams eyed me for a moment and let out a curt breath, turning and taking a seat alongside the others. If one could passive-aggressively sit, she had it down.

The five were in a single line in front of me, Williams on the far left, my right-hand side for my second-in-command. Kim was next to her, followed by Fox and Marshall. Off slightly on his own a few feet from the others was the muscled tower of Moore, keeping to himself.

"I know as much as you all do about this, which is *nothing*. Colonel Snowden warned us that once we landed, we'd be under new management. Previous orders and protocols don't necessarily apply here. You signed on knowing this. That means we adapt or get back on that transport and bug out."

"Bugger out, mate. Maybe!" Moore laughed. "Squids ordering us to fight bugs for that lady who runs the damn world."

"Moore, you're welcome to fly back tonight," I said.

He just smiled.

Marshall interjected, "Then how do we prepare for a mystery assignment?"

I sighed and ran my fingers through my hair. "By staying flexible, informed, in shape, and ready. The bugs don't play by any rules, so there isn't any certainty in any engagement." I gestured to the holoscreen. "Not even in the new attack plans I was going to introduce tonight. That's true for standard Temple duty or for whatever they have planned."

"But you can't know that, sir," said Kim.

"Look, I don't see why we're that worried," interrupted Fox. "There's never been as much as a shot fired at the Temple. Or even in the Cities. Not in two hundred years. We go in, march where they say, do our time, and we're out with benefits. Meanwhile, just think of where we *are*."

"Maybe a tour there was simple before, Fox, but things might be changing. I suppose you've heard some of the rumors."

There was a short silence as glances were stolen back and forth. Williams spoke first.

"Losses on the five fronts. Dram raids. Supply lines cut."

"Worse," I said. *They needed to know.*

Moore looked up with a sharp expression. "So, what are the bloody bastards not telling us now?"

"The Center's been compromised."

Several sat upright. Williams hissed under her breath. "Those mother—"

"I know," I said, feeling that betrayal as well. "Some very bad news from Colonel Snowden."

Kim started waving his arms. "Whoa—time the fuck out! Compromised the Center? What does that mean? Hit and runs? Occupation? Are we going to get Dram war fleets pouring out of the Orb toward New Earth?"

"*I don't know!* I don't have access to field reports, and Snowden said it's all being hushed up to prevent a panic!" I tried to slow this down. "It can't be that it's been significantly occupied, or we *would* have bugs crawling out of the sewers here. But it's got to be bad, maybe significant penetration with intermittent access to the central time point."

Williams whistled. "Well, that ain't good, man."

"Fucking got that right," laughed Moore.

"That's why I'm telling you this. We're not part of Force anymore. We're cut off from the leadership and any communications by the Xixian defense fields. We're on our own. Maybe there hasn't been an attack here since the Temple was built, but we can't take that for granted anymore. I think Snowden was trying to tell me that. Don't assume. Don't take anything for granted."

Kim spoke anxiously. "Maybe they know something Snowden didn't. Maybe there *is* an invasion force on the way. Maybe *that's* our special assignment! A fucking meat grinder."

Great. He's panicking.

"Calm down, Sergeant," I said. "Don't you think there would be a Force mobilization the likes of which we haven't seen since the early days of the Dram War?"

I let that sink in. "We might have had some setbacks in the War, setbacks the brass don't want advertised on every wave across the allied net, but it's not that bad yet. We need to trust the Daughter. Ambra Dawn has never let us down. Let's keep our heads on straight and not lose touch with her."

Kim wasn't onboard. "Maybe you're the one a little too touched with her."

Fox looked at him sharply. "What the hell does that mean?"

"Means everyone knows the captain's a true believer."

Fox reached inside her shirt and pulled out a pendant. It was New Earth with a sunrise breaking over the edge of the planet. One of the main religious symbols of the Dawnists.

"He's not the only one, asshole."

Kim stared back. "Well, maybe you two are ready to die for her, see whatever heaven they promised you. Maybe he already knows what's coming and welcomes it. Maybe I don't."

Before I could respond, Moore cut in. "Or, maybe our new Capt's interested in more 'an being touched by the power of the bald lady. Maybe he's some touching of his own in mind—eh, Capt?"

Fox murmured something I couldn't hear. I was momentarily flatfooted by the radical shift in the conversation. Moore continued.

Moore continued. "I been watchin' you, sir, cause I wasn't goin' into this bloody assignment with some nutter prayin' to that Witch half the night."

There were a few gasps from the team. Fox cut in icily. "You ought to learn how to bite that fat tongue of yours, Moore."

Moore smiled. "You blokes make me laugh. Sure, yeah, *The Daughter* an' all 'at. Keep your pendants, fine with me. But for our DC—all those rumors about him weren't *resting* well with me."

"Yeah? *You're* starting not to rest well with me, Moore," said Fox.

This was a tough balancing act. Moore was edging up to the line of insubordination. And then pissing right next to it. But if I cut in too soon, I'd look weak for taking the bait. Too late, and we might have a brawl.

"But all's good, mates." He smiled broadly. *Mischievously.* "Been watchin' him. All that talk 'bout Ambra Dawn: our Capt ain't no choirboy. He ain't longing to take a needle blast for her. He's longing for something else! Arse over tits or I'm blind. I know when a man's 'bout to pitch his tent!"

From India, I knew the British slang, and felt my cheeks flush. I was glad I was dark enough in this light for it to go unnoticed.

"And she *is* fit, mate, long's you don't mind that head."

Fox stood up, but before she could engage Moore, he was in front of me, up in my face, and I sensed the other team members tense. I stood still in front of his bulk and didn't flinch, looking him in the eye.

He saluted. "Religion of heavenly bodies, sir! Sign me up!"

There was a pause, and some laughter followed. I smiled out of one side of my mouth. *That bastard!* This bruiser was sharp as a tack, and had with one short diversion derailed Kim's panic and lessened any threat from my personal feelings.

It was an acceptable trade, a little embarrassment for some humanization and team bonding. But I'd have to watch him and Fox. That looked like a bad mix brewing.

"You're enlisted," I said. "Now, sit your ass down, soldier."

"Yes, sir!" Moore grinned back and turned around, taking a seat. The other soldiers visibly relaxed. Even Kim let out a sigh. Fox sat down as well, her eyes smoldering.

Williams shook her head. "*Shit*. Looks like I'm in deep with a bunch of crazy-ass motherfuckers. Okay then, Capt. Why don't you light up that board and show us all this new shit the squids have handed down. Sounds like we might be needing it."

9

Any sufficiently advanced technology is indistinguishable from magic.

—Clarke's Third Law

We were nearly packed when Waythrel entered our quarters.

The humans subconsciously made a semicircle with the alien at the center, the presence of a creature so viscerally strange and unsettling always eliciting primitive responses that were hard to completely suppress.

And Waythrel did make an impression. Towering over us, limbs moving at angles impossible to the human body, the presence of a great intelligence unmistakable—the creature commanded our attention without a word.

"The caravan is prepared for you," Waythrel spoke. "There is a military-grade sandglider that will hold all of you and your items."

I stepped forward. "I was led to understand that our suits will be waiting for us at the Temple?"

"This is correct. However, these will be new suits, not those you had shipped. We have built enhanced versions of the MECHcore standard suits that are optimized both for the desert and for our latest battle training. Part of your initial exercises will be to learn to integrate with the suits and understand their full potential."

I heard some quiet grumbling behind me. New suits. Even more new training. *Don't move a soldier's cheese, Xixian!*

"The suit improvements are significant. Ambra wishes for her Guardians that they be outfitted in the best gear available."

I nodded. It was hard to argue with that. The alien gestured outside our quarters, and we followed it out into the blazing sun.

The glider was hovering silently in front of us, the only evidence of its propulsion system the undulating ripples in the sand. It was shaped like one of those old-time computer mice, but nearly as big as a bus, a sleek Xixian design with the upper portion completely transparent. It wasn't glass. Some other material the aliens had produced that was strong, more resistant to erosion than human material science could produce, and that had embedded in it numerous touch displays and control features.

We tossed our bags into the back, hopped into the central portion, took our seats, and buckled in. The cab consisted of seats appropriate for humans and Xix, and Waythrel occupied one of the larger seats for the aliens. Within moments, I felt the lurch of acceleration, and the glider darted like an arrow from the city.

These desert ships reached a maximum velocity of around four hundred miles per hour, the air displacement leaving a tunnel of swirling sand behind us. As we sped inward from the ring of the Six Cities toward the Temple, within minutes the structures of civilization receded to a blur and we were surrounded only by the colors and shapes of the deep desert.

The transport darted effortlessly over the colossal dunes, some reaching heights of several hundred feet. The glider would fly up the long windward side of the dune and then dart back down on the slip face to cruise within the valleys formed between the sand mountains. With the morning sun low on the horizon, those valleys would often plunge us into darkness and shadow, only to burst into blinding light again climbing another dune. All this happened at speeds of several hundred miles an hour. Now I understood why the Xix had designed the gliders with the viewport. It was stunning.

Gradually, even the dunes began to give way as we flew over an extended sand sheet of hundreds of miles. We were close to the middle of the Sahara, nearly equidistant from all inhabited regions outside the ring of the Six Cities. Basically, we were about as in the middle of nowhere as anyone could be on Earth outside of an ocean.

As the craft accelerated over the flat terrain, I could begin to make out the blurred outlines of a structure ahead. From my geography lessons, I knew it wasn't giant dunes or mountains—until two hundred years ago, there had been only flat sand in this region of the desert. It was something intelligence had thrown up from the desert floor. Thrown up very, very high.

"There it is, Captain," came the voice of Williams, her neck stretched to look toward the growing forms in front of us. "There's your Temple."

All my team stared at the marvel before us. As the dark shape took form, I felt a growing sense of awe. Not only for its sheer size and location, but for what this place meant to humanity. Here was the focal point in our war against cosmic forces that should have consumed us and continued to enslave our primitive species. If not for the help of the alien Xix. If not for the unexpected wild card in the history of our galaxy that was Ambra Dawn.

The medic Marshall whispered, "All that power in the middle of nothing."

Many of Waythrel's eyes turned toward us. "Many have wondered why we chose to build so deeply in the desert." The tones from the translator seemed to grow in mystery as we approached the Temple.

"Because the Xix want sand between their toes is what I heard," came the voice of Moore. He was slumped next to Williams, his chin on his massive chest, seemingly bored with the sightseeing, impervious to the spectacle before him. His eyes were hidden behind dark smartglasses.

"Yes, Sergeant Moore," came the unfazed voice of the alien. "We are certainly partial to such locations. But we do earnestly seek to work with our human hosts, and we understand that such climates are extreme for your organism."

Moore flipped his shades up and smiled. "Extreme for our organism. I like that."

"If not for Xixian comfort, then what?" Williams asked.

Waythrel's many eyes scanned my team, a few of them never leaving their focus on me. "From the beginning, after the recursive time alteration of the Calamity, New Earth has been in great danger. Greater danger than most humans have appreciated. Especially in the early years, there was the constant threat of attack by the Dram. In fact, there were several attempts—major, planetary-level assaults—to achieve again what had been undone."

This had my team's attention. This was definitely *not* textbook material. Kim broke in.

"You mean like the asteroid? They shot more at us?"

"Yes, there were multiple attempts through various strategies to destroy New Earth or render it inhospitable. Similar assaults on my homeworld of Xix as well as several other worlds harboring species important to our war effort. These were all effectively countered."

"The Daughter?" I asked.

Waythrel gestured with its hands moving oppositely from the center out. "Of course, Captain Ratava. Only by the powers of Ambra Dawn have we been constantly shielded from certain destruction."

"So, why didn't we ever hear about this?" asked Kim.

"Representatives of your many governments begged Ambra to keep silent. They feared that word of the continuing efforts of the Dram could instill a planetwide panic."

These facts sat quietly with each of us. While we all had learned as children about the Calamity—the alternative history of the planet in which the Dram had reduced it to slag by hurling a giant asteroid through an Orb—there were no such stories about additional, world-threatening attempts. Only stories of the alliances against the Dram, the long hundred years of continuous war—victorious war—in which we had broken the Hegemony, pushed the Dram back to a few systems near their home world. And of course the long work to create a safer galaxy for humans and aliens. It was a nice myth. Told across the globe in every schoolhouse perhaps for some of the same reasons the recent setbacks against the Dram were withheld.

"But because of these threats, Ambra insisted that we place the Temple as far from human habitation as possible. That way, should an attack succeed, even a minor one, the carnage to life on Earth would be minimized as much as could be managed."

"So why not just leave the bloody thing on the moon where it was built?" asked Moore.

"Indeed, that was Ambra's wish. But we had seen what isolation from your planet had done to individuals of your species, and to Ambra in particular. We convinced her that it was in the interests of our struggle that she relocate to her homeworld. The desert was her compromise." The Xix paused, its smaller fingers darting around. "In addition, we needed to build a new device to amplify her powers and integrate the Reader groups. The one on your moon was effective, but only a first draft, as you say. A prototype. We learned much from its building and use and put that knowledge into practice here in your world's largest desert."

"The Dish," I said.

"Yes. The Dish is an engineering feat that dwarfs the efforts on your satellite. Most of the mass of the Temple is contained in the device, which spans the size of some of your larger cities."

The dark blur in front of us had begun to come into focus. It was like approaching Manhattan in a low-flying airplane, seeing the expanse of the city across the entire field of one's peripheral vision. Instead of randomly placed skyscrapers, however, there was a striking order to the monolithic structure that grew toward the sky from the desert floor.

"My God," gasped Kim as he nearly stood up in his seat against the restraints.

"They said it was tall. I've seen the numbers, but nothing is going to prepare you for *that*," said Williams, her mouth agape.

Rising out of the desert sands like some webbed volcano was the great antenna of the Dish. Of course the

Xix had built it; there wasn't anything close to the scale of the structure in human engineering. It was impossibly tall, and it was impossible to grasp the size with human intuition. It dwarfed anything on New Earth. Staring up at it, I lost my sense of scale completely.

"It reaches to nearly fifty thousand feet," said Waythrel. "More than five times the height of your tallest mountain."

Even Moore perked up a little and had a look. "How'd you keep that giant todger from falling down?" he asked.

Waythrel pointed to the lower portion of the structure. "Do you see how wide the base is? It is difficult to appreciate from this distance, but it is more than five miles in diameter and anchored three hundred feet into the desert floor, which provides considerable support. The rods that curve up from the base like parabolic spokes—some one hundred feet in diameter— are fashioned from our strongest and most lightweight materials, millions of times stronger per unit mass than your best composites. Had it been necessary, the structure could have been several times its current height."

Extending radially from the huge base were much smaller buildings of recognizable height—likely living quarters and other constructions serving the needs of the Temple. But it was hard to focus on them. The antenna seized all attention.

Suddenly the ground below us transformed from the tan and rough sands of the desert to a black gloss. I recognized the planet's largest solar array in the giant circular mat that flowed out across the desert. The term *array* was archaic, as the material was more a continuous sheet rather than thousands of individual solar panels. The glider seemed to be speeding over a dark and utterly still sea.

"It's beautiful," said Fox, her eyes watery.

"Amazing," I said marveling as well. "This is what powers the Dish?"

"No," said Waythrel. "The Dish requires much more energy than that."

"It looks like those astronomy dishes," said Kim, staring up at the tall structure. "Focuses all her power like radio waves or something?"

Waythrel gestured in an oddly inhuman manner. "This is difficult to explain. While there is a superficial similarity with your radio dishes, the operating principle is very different. Your dishes are designed to handle electromagnetic waves of specific energies, or wavelengths. Ambra's manipulations of space and time occur through different physical means. That is why the Dish is so large, and also why it requires so much power to operate. In fact, to focus her powers on New Earth requires a gravitational lens that can be achieved only through the presence of a micro black hole."

"You're shitting us!" explained Kim, a nervous smile on his face. "You've got a damn black hole in there?"

Waythrel responded patiently, "Four."

"Holy *shit!* Well, I'm with you on the vote for the desert location now for sure."

"The black holes are located in strategic positions," added the alien. "One is in fact at the top of the tower, nearly ten miles above the desert surface. The space-time distortions the four create are channeled and focused by other devices to a multi-dimensional location, a three-space cross-section of which is located in structures beneath the sands, embedded in the bedrock. It is there that Ambra goes when she requires a great amplification of her powers."

"And how do you juice all that?" asked Moore. He had flipped his glasses back down.

"If you mean the energetics, Sergeant, we have an array of twenty fusion reactors built around the Temple."

"*Twenty?*" exclaimed Williams. "So why do you need all the solar panels?"

"The fusion cores are devoted exclusively to the powering of the Dish and the maintenance of the black-hole amplituhedron. Both require enormous energy expenditures. The solar sea is in place to provide energy for all the organism-related activities at the Temple: life support, communications, standard military defenses."

The antenna now towered above us, so high one would need to lie flat to stare up at it. If there was a black hole at the apex, we were going to have to take the alien's word for it. The top was so high as to be invisible.

The glider began to decelerate, and we plunged into shadow again as we pulled alongside the buildings of the Temple. Small in comparison to the central tower, they were still many stories high, blocking out the rising sun of the early morning.

The craft came to a stop in front of a large courtyard. A broad street extended from it and the outer desert into the walls of the Temple city itself. For the first time, we saw green in the Sahara. The courtyard was lined with olive and palm trees, and even some thorny bushes bearing flowers. While the plants were certainly arid species, significant irrigation was undoubtedly required to keep them alive here in this wasteland.

We released our restraints and assembled, filing out to the cargo section to grab our gear. I hoisted my duffel bag over my shoulder, waited until the rest of my team had secured their items, and then led a march in the direction Waythrel had taken.

We stepped alongside the sandglider, its bulk rising above our heads on the right. Waythrel had turned around the front of the ship and was lost from sight, a trail in the sand marking its path. I picked up the pace to keep close to the alien.

We made the same turn around the nose of the craft and ran right into a greeting party. This one was far larger and more diverse than that which met us at the Fourth City. Thirty to forty humans and half as many Xix awaited our approach. They were clothed in flowing desert garments of diverse colors, the fabrics reflecting the sunlight strongly. The alien eye-stalk clusters danced here and there above the short sea of human heads.

Waythrel had reached the crowd and had stopped, speaking to a central figure. The sun crested over the tops of the buildings, and the courtyard was bathed in light. My smartglasses automatically engaged and reduced the glare.

Compulsively, I stepped forward, my thoughts relegated to some distant portion of my consciousness. A mindless moth to the flame, I was drawn irresistibly to the figure underneath the height of the alien. Step by drunken step, I approached, oblivious to everything else.

It was a young woman, clothed in long robes of black, her skin seeming as bright as the white walls lit by the morning sun. The top of her head was bald and swollen to obscene proportions. Rivers of red curls fell from a midpoint in her scalp down her shoulders and nearly to her waist.

"Daughter of Time," I whispered.

It was Ambra Dawn.

10

What then is time? If no one asks me, I know what it is. If I wish to explain it to him who asks, I do not know.

—Augustine of Hippo

*T*ime.

Whatever that idea represents, if anything at all in the reality of our universe, it stopped. There was no sound. No movement. The sand particles were suspended in midair, and it seemed that my own heart no longer beat its rhythm in my chest.

Only the eyes. Blind eyes. Bright-green emeralds glowing before me. Only they seemed able to move. While everything else stood impossibly still, her eyes turned to me and focused, looking deeply into my own. It was like falling into warm water, a subtle impact rippling through my awareness, as if she had entered into my very consciousness.

It is said that time is distorted around the Daughter. The textbooks, physics lessons I hardly understood. The science-fiction serials waved through the datasphere— they all said something about it. She stopped time. She slowed time. She stood outside of time in some undefined *elsewhere*. While none of the writings agreed on what she did to time, it was clear to me now that those stories were much more than legends.

Standing before me, commanding all my attention and thoughts in the midst of all these creatures, was a human being who was over two hundred years old. But she did not look a day older than seventeen. No age lines, no skin discoloration, no gray hair or sagging posture. Ambra Dawn was the same biological age she had been when she came into full use of her powers.

I didn't understand it. None of my fellow students at the academy had understood the explanations of cyclically warped space-time that left chemistry intact yet her body unaged, that stopped time but permitted the formation of memories, that led her consciousness to loop in and out of her carbon-based flesh into hyperknots of space-time strings.

For me, it was all gibberish. Right now, with her gaze entering me like some vulnerable lover, the nonsense of understanding mattered little. I only wished to stay in this place, to forever have her dive into me, to be consumed by her, to experience her, endlessly in this impossible place with no time.

Right now—whatever *now* meant in this strange stasis—I only wished to tell Ambra that I loved her.

Be patient, Nitin. This is not the place.

The words rang in my mind as if I had thought them, but the voice was not my own. Her eyes held me a moment longer, and I felt tears trickle down the side of my face.

Suddenly, like a blow to the stomach, Time leaped forward again. The noises and smells returned, the sand grains rasping across my skin. Voices, footsteps. A murmuring crowd.

I stood halfway between my team and the crowd. The blowing sand had already begun to crust the tear paths on my cheeks. Everyone was staring at me, and Ambra smiled.

"Captain Ratava, please bring your team forward," she cried over the wind, motioning elegantly with her hand. The murmurs died down at the sound of her voice. The stares lingered.

I turned to look behind me and was greeted with shocked expressions from the members of my team. They seemed stunned but walked forward with me, and we came to a halt in front of the Daughter and Waythrel.

"We welcome you to the Temple," Ambra said. "For everyone at the Temple, I want to say to you all that we appreciate your service, your sacrifice for our common mission to protect New Earth."

I looked around at the crowd. Their faces—the many smiles and steady gazes—it felt as if this were not simply some political platitude, but that her words were true for everyone around us. It was the first realization I had of the earnestness of the people who served the Daughter. There was something different—*they* were different from almost any group of people I had ever encountered. The closest I could place them was with the Hindu monks I had known in my youth, but even that was a pale comparison.

Her blind eyes crossed over my form as a lightning strike, sending shivers through me, and then scanned across my team.

"I am needed urgently within, so I will not be able to be with you as you enter our city. Instead, I will turn you over to the capable hands of my counselor, Sepehr Mazandarani, who will serve as your guide. He will be your point of contact for the next few weeks as you prepare for Guardian service." She gestured behind her, and a short, thin man in dark-blue robes stepped forward.

His complexion was dark, his eyes a deep brown with a dagger's gaze, and a trimmed and sharp goatee accentuated his diabolical appearance. He shuffled forward with a casual confidence until he was beside the Daughter.

"Sepehr." Ambra nodded to him and turned around, walking beside Waythrel on the road into the Temple city.

"Hello. From me as well, a welcome to the city." He looked across my team, resting lastly on me. I felt a suspicion, a hostility in his gaze completely at odds with the welcome we had just received. He quickly looked away.

"You will be staying at the south end of the city, near the military training fields. There you will find housing, your new battle suits, and trained Earth Force soldiers who will work with you to get you up to speed. Inside the city, we walk whenever possible—it keeps us well adapted to the climate. Please follow me. Your quarters are about a half hour away."

With that he smiled an unsettling grin and turned to walk down the same entry road the Daughter had just taken. Ambra and Waythrel were now out of sight, and it was unclear where they had gone.

I turned to my team and smiled. "Okay, here we go." There was a pause, and no one moved. My smile faded. "Problem?"

They each looked from one to the other incredulously. Moore grinned and let out a bark of a laugh.

"Yeah. You might say."

I turned to Williams. "Warrant Officer Williams, would you kindly report on what is the damn problem with my team, and why we aren't marching inside?"

"Yes, sir," she said, bringing her face close to mine. "That is, if you can explain what the hell just happened."

"What happened? We were met by Ambra Dawn herself and assigned to her representative. We are following him to begin our required duties."

"No, sir. I don't mean that." She just stared at me. The others stared as well, Fox with a look of religious awe on her face.

Moore spoke. "She's a bit put out from your shimmering disappearing act."

My throat felt dry. "My what?"

He laughed again. "You know, the part where you blink in and out of existence and seem to teleport halfway to that would-be girlfriend of yours." He looked around at the others. "That about it?"

No one said anything. Their eyes were wide.

Moore nodded. "Yeah, see lads, we've not all gone bloody barmy in the heat. We all saw it." He hoisted his duffel. "But, I think we'd all like to hear your thoughts on the matter, Capt."

I just stared back at them.

11

The easy confidence with which I know another man's religion is folly teaches me to suspect that my own is also.

—Mark Twain

It was three weeks before I saw Ambra Dawn again.

I threw myself into the training and drills. My team members were hardworking soldiers, but I outworked them all. My energies burned with a zeal no one else could match, and the team worked that much harder because of my example. Because of what we would soon face, it was critical that we did.

And it was only the fire hose of information and training my team and I withstood that preserved my sanity, that allowed me to continue, to hold myself back from seeking her out after what had occurred before the gates of the Temple City. Part of the problem was that I did not even understand myself what had happened. Even after a few conversations with my team—each of which left them and me very unsatisfied—nothing was clarified.

"So, now," said Fox, staring around at us. "Now do you believe?" Half her torso was encased in the battle suit, her black hair blowing wildly behind her in the scalding wind. The composite chassis drank the sunlight, charging power reserves in the battery cluster planted in the back.

We had just finished an exhausting training session. Sweat poured down our faces and ran in rivulets into our suits, which sopped it up, filtered it, and stored the potable constituents for later use. The wind did little to cool us.

The team stood in a tight group. A wasted sandworm triad lay smoking before us. The new suits were incredible. A jump in technology of four or five generations. They combined new general battle features with eco-survival adaptations for the desert. The new AI for the worms was far more sophisticated, and my team had mastered the interface quickly. With the more powerful ion slingers, it almost made taking on the worms fun.

Kim shuffled his feet, nodding uncertainly. "Yeah," he exhaled, his fatigue evident. "Yeah, Fox. I guess so."

I could see in the eyes of the others that he wasn't the only one. But there was acceptance of the event, and then there was interpretation.

"Well, it's not anything new to hear that she can pull out her magic wand," spat Moore. "That don't mean I'm getting baptized."

Fox shook her head. She nearly chanted, "And in that age were great signs, but many disbelieved. And the Daughter said, 'If you believed not in Moses and Jesus, then you will believe not in Me.'"

Moore burst out laughing. "You think that witch actually said any of that shit?"

Fox stepped toward him.

"That's enough!" I said, engaging the hydraulics of my suit to push them apart. "Keep your beliefs and critiques private! We have one fight we need to focus on, and it's not with our species!"

"Yeah, Captain, but, you know, there's been an *event*. With the Daughter." It was Kim. I heard a growing awe in his voice. "We saw it. *You* were part of it. It's like all the legends, man."

Strange things had happened that seemed to defy the common-sense laws of nature we took for granted. But this event had centered not on New Earth or the Great War with the Dram, or some other textbook-worthy crisis concerning the Daughter and humanity's survival. It had focused on a single person out of all the swarm of humanity. *On me.*

Williams nodded. "It was one thing when you were such a fanboy, Captain. Now...what is it with you and her?"

I looked at the ground as they all focused on me. "I don't know, Williams. Nothing about her is normal, right? Well, I'm part of that. And maybe I'm the least strange part of it. Millions worship her."

"Yeah, but you don't," said Moore. Fox eyed me closely.

"Sergeant, I don't know what people should call it. I know what I feel. I'm not a Dawnist. I'm not a skeptic. But I know where I have to be, and that's here. With her."

Fox nodded her head. "I understand. You're like a monk. You're devoted to her."

"He ain't no monk," smirked Moore.

Fox glared at him. "I bet he's never been with another woman. Never been in love. He's waiting for *her*."

Kim looked straight at me. "That true, sir? Not to be too personal, but we're all getting past that line, I think. Is this thing with her so extreme? Have you ever even kissed a girl?"

It was strange. Of all the unusual aspects of my devotion to the Daughter, it was always sex that riled people up the most. I could have painted myself up like the wildest Hindu priest and chanted into the night on the top of a pillar, and it would go down better than abstinence. Or the perception of it.

"No, I've kissed girls. I've even slept with them. Once, I was engaged to be married. And I even loved her." I inhaled sharply, trying to dampen my emotions.

There was a silence broken by the smooth alto of Williams. "What happened?"

I stared out over the desert, unable to look directly at the others. "My parents arranged it all. They'd been trying to marry me off for a while. Maybe you can imagine how they felt with my long focus on the Daughter. These things were usually very awkward, pointless, and over before the dinner was finished." I suppressed a sigh. "But not the last one."

I could still picture her face clearly. Delicately boned with a Persian nose and rich black hair like a strong river, she was petite, barely five feet, absurdly elegant in her motions, and quick with her wit.

"She was a professional dancer. Classical Indian style. Her eyes caught me instantly and we had a very powerful mutual chemistry. Body, mind, all that. So, for the first and only time in my life, I abandoned the idea of that destiny with Ambra Dawn." I laughed. "Of course, I had a lot of help from my parents. They were beyond overjoyed to recognize that I was moved by this woman."

"So what *happened?*" pressed Fox.

"I broke it off."

"Why?" asked Kim.

"Because, while I had convinced myself to grow up, move beyond my life-long dream, I was fooling myself. I could not let go of Ambra Dawn. While I made love to this beautiful woman and planned a life with her, my mind, my heart was not pure, not devoted as it should have been to my wife-to-be. And she deserved so much more than that. As time went on, I saw that I would forever be haunted by another. Nothing I could do would change it. It wasn't fair to anyone, but it was more unfair to pretend. I knew that later it would cause even more pain than were I to end it early."

"Didn't peg you for a heart-breaker, Captain," said Williams.

I still stared into the distance. "It might not make sense, but there is love, and then there is another kind of love. A kind of love that seems bigger than even the two involved. And yes, maybe it's madness."

It is one thing to feel that reality within yourself, and quite another to have the external world so suddenly and dramatically seem to verify it for you. And yet another to lead a military assault squad with massive doubts about all that was taking place.

"Well, she *did* single you out, Captain," said Kim.

Marshall agreed. "Maybe there is some strange destiny going on."

And I heard her voice. This was something I could not share even with my team. Psychologists and skeptics could roll off one hundred theories and reasons why I had been delusional. Perhaps it would be simple enough to explain the entire episode as a cognitive reaction to the time distortion around her.

But I believed differently. More than that, I *knew* in my heart that Ambra Dawn had spoken directly to me. The experience was as real—more real—than many events in my life, even my own thoughts. Perhaps it was the beginning of a split personality disorder. But the Daughter was thought to be telepathic, to be able to enter the minds and even control the thoughts of others. I believed strongly that she had touched my mind.

With that conviction, and longing to receive more and to see how my own mad purpose in life was truly to be fulfilled, I felt her absence like a terrible vacuum in a space that had not existed before. She entered me, touched me, spoke to me, and in the fertile landscape of my love for her, had formed a nascent mini-universe. Yet it was empty! Only the displacement of reality around it to testify that it was there. What would it become?

And when?

I needed to get the team to move on from this. "So we've gotten some real-world confirmation of everything we've been taught about her. Not on a holo, not from our elders, but right in our faces. In the sands in front of us."

I looked around, holding each momentarily with my gaze.

"Things a lot bigger than us are going on. Let's take that to heart and let's get serious about why we're here. The myths are real."

The team looked sobered. Even Moore's smirk was gone for the moment. Of course, it returned quickly.

"Right, Captain. And you can hope to get a little more *serious* with the girl yourself, now that you've moved up to teleporting with her."

I looked away and put my helmet back on. More worms were coming.

12

All warfare is based on deception. Hence, when we are able to attack, we must seem unable; when using our forces, we must appear inactive; when we are near, we must make the enemy believe we are far away; when far away, we must make him believe we are near.

—*The Art of War*, Sun Tzu 孫子

The first information we received concerning our unusual assignment came at the end of the first week of training. We had just finished a particularly grueling skirmish. A captured triad was released on us in the sands, but that wasn't the challenge. We were to begin testing in combat the most powerful new feature of the redesigned MECHcore battle suits: space-time neutralizers. We were given no explanation for why we would even need such countermeasures, but the design of them into the suits had our minds racing.

As the worms were released, accompanying them were field distortions in space and time. Left uncountered, they slowed us down, sometimes dramatically, or displaced us physically or temporally. It didn't need to be much in the heat of battle to be lethal.

Our suits would constantly counter the fields automatically, but it required a change in our combat style, a strange rhythm, pulse in our movements, actions, even thoughts, that really can't be described. When time and space are being jerked around, the sensations and responses are very counterintuitive.

We spent an entire day in drills to master it and had just finished our first live combat experience with the technology when Mazandarani came to escort us back to the military barracks. We followed, cleaned up, and were immediately brought to a briefing room in a nearby building. There we were introduced to Major Tomoko Mizoguchi.

Major Mizoguchi was a hard-asses' hard-ass, and she seemed to step out of some ancient war holo. The older Japanese warrior was clipped in cadence, full of bluster and drama, and eager to put fools in their place. Her short salt-and-pepper hair was nearly spiked, and she wore a uniform that was pressed until the edges seemed sharpened like a knife. We had gathered from Mazandarani that the major had been at the Temple for over a decade and had personally run military engagements involving the Daughter and Xixian forces at various points in the galaxy during this time. But these roles had been kept at a very low profile outside of the Temple. None of my team had even heard of her. But over the next three weeks, we heard a lot from her. The voice that erupted from her short frame resonated through the room.

"You may *think* you know what you are up against. But let me tell you, you don't."

This was how Mizoguchi began our briefing on the first day. For a group of highly trained MECHcore special forces, most of whom had seen combat with the Dram, this was something to say.

"The tide of the war has changed," she said grimly. "We are no longer on the offensive but are now in a full-scale retreat across most of the galaxy."

There was a long silence. We sat there stunned. *Full-scale retreat?* This was far, far worse than anything Colonel Snowden had hinted at. *What the hell was happening?*

"As of last month, we no longer control the Time Tree. Dram forces have occupied the central Orb projection, and have begun to launch attacks against the more weakly defended worlds in the alliance. Most of those attacks have been devastating."

I glanced at Williams, who sat on my right side. Her eyes told the story—disbelief, shock, and fear. She held my gaze a moment and shook her head, returning her attention to the major.

"It is obvious that something has catalyzed this phase transition in the war, and what that catalyst is has become the focus of much of our current efforts. It is in this respect that you have been recruited here."

She paused dramatically, casting a withering gaze across each of us. Her eyes stopped last and longest on me.

"After you complete your training, which we expect will occur before the end of the month, there will be a special announcement during the Festival of Rebirth. The Daughter will address the faithful of the Temple City and broadcast the message throughout the world. We have notified all the major political and media leaders to expect this transmission."

She paused again, and I couldn't stop myself from interrupting her narrative. "And what will she say?"

The major nodded and turned to her right, motioning to a projection holo of the galaxy. Several bright points appeared across its expanse, and I recognized them as the location of extra-solar system Orbs. Or rather, as the Daughter had revealed and our books taught, the locations of projections of the one and only Orb. Many of the Orb locations turned from white to red.

"In red, you see those locations now occupied by Dram forces."

There were gasps. It is difficult to explain to you of another time what this meant. You, who have struggled only with the maps of Old Earth, the distances and meanings of national borders, you cannot grasp the size of the galaxy. You were not raised on the now-hundred-year-old charts that outlined the Dram Quarantine around their home planet. That galactic map had been burned into the consciousness of generations. We knew the Dram homeworld and the handful of satellite worlds that remained under their control. It was a small percentage of the systems with an Orb, a testament to our victory in the Great War.

But no longer. In the holo presented by the major, fully half the galaxy was red. She flicked her hand, and the map rotated around us, the viewpoint zooming into the galactic center, New Earth shooting behind me and to the back portion of the room. She zoomed to the central Orb.

"Their attack has been long planned. Once they seized the central Time Point, multiple attacks across the Time Tree occurred simultaneously. Nearly every system targeted has fallen."

"Oh, my God," whispered Kim behind me.

"Our forces find themselves unable to repel the attacks and hardly able to communicate anything useful about them. We only have strange reports, contradictory statements that even the Xix do not know how to interpret."

"What reports?" I asked. "What do they say?"

"You all will have provided to you the recordings and data streams we have been able to obtain. We want you to study those. To brainstorm. To prepare for the completely unexpected."

She touched several floating buttons on the holopanel and the projection filled with a poor-quality holovid. White noise and audio static clouded the projection, but the scene was one of battle. A human communications officer spoke with a look of desperation on her face in the midst of the chaos of explosions and screams.

"Freighter Centari 2-11658. Mayday, mayday, mayday. Escort battalion has been destroyed. We are defenseless and taking fire from Dram forces."

There was a bright light and deep sound, and the image disintegrated into random pixels. It flickered back, and the woman spoke from in front of a raging fire.

"Freighter Centari 2-11658. Mayday. Life support is failing. Condition unsalvageable. Initiating terminal data squirt."

A *TDS*. When your ship was going down, when it was clear that there might not be anything to recover or no way to recover it, if you had the presence of mind to send all information to relay beacons—to inform and warn—you could spend your last few moments firing off a squirt. It would likely drain whatever you had left in the ship's batteries—the signal was designed to reach the relays. It would render you helpless. It was a final act. The officer knew she was going to die and that it was imminent. It was on her face, the steely determination in her eyes.

Her hand paused in the air. She had not yet sent the signal. She had something she needed to say directly and set her jaw, her expression grim.

"This is Operations Specialist Emma Sung. Look for the *shadows*. The *ghosts*. I can't explain any better. They are coming."

Her finger moved. The image froze.

Mizoguchi gestured to the holo. "This is the TDS from a transport convoy destroyed three weeks ago by Dram forces. Data recovery confirms the visuals. The ship was seconds away from coming apart. Sung was one cool customer."

"Or delusional and psychotic," said Marshall. "*Ghosts?*"

The major eyed the medic harshly. "Yes, it would seem. Except for the fact that we have multiple TDS from the last month, all from devastating attacks on our forces, and in several of them are reports that sound a lot like this one."

"What do you mean?" asked Williams.

"All report strange events. Creatures or forces penetrating all their defenses, wreaking destruction on their personnel and machinery. Forces *not* Dram."

"Not Dram?" asked Moore, his lip a sneer. "*Ghosts?*"

"Ghosts, Sergeant. Or shadows. Gas clouds. Force fields. Whatever you want. Different terms for the same phenomenon, it would appear."

Moore continued. "So, you're saying that what has suddenly made us lose most of our positions across the galaxy, maybe about to lose the whole fucking war, is a bunch of evil spirits attacking our forces?"

Mizoguchi shook her head. "What I'm saying is that something has changed, and the Dram have a new weapon that we do not understand and cannot counter."

"And that is why we are here?" I hardly knew what to expect.

The major nodded curtly. "We have a crisis. One that must be addressed immediately, or we may lose everything. The Daughter and her advisors have devised a plan. It is not a large-scale military engagement—we now know that such efforts would be futile until we can understand the threat."

"Then what?" asked Fox, her eyes narrowing.

"Guerrilla tactics. We will transport elite special forces teams to several key locations in the Time Tree. These teams will be charged with two missions. The first is recon: find out what the hell we are up against and how to respond."

"And the second?" I asked.

The map reappeared, the Dram-controlled red sea of points ominous in the darkness. Several of these points grew in size and brightness.

"Sabotage. The Daughter has determined a set of three nodes in the Tree that, if impeded, can effectively seal off the majority of the accessible hyperspace routes to the regions we still control."

Thin blue lines connecting the Orbs appeared on the screen, showing the possible routes through the Time Tree. When Mizoguchi pressed the bright Orbs highlighted, the web of interconnections fell apart, isolating the Dram-controlled regions from the majority of those the alliance still held.

"Without access to the Orb strings, the Dram and whatever new forces they have brought into this conflict are effectively isolated through the vast interstellar distances."

"Won't this cut off many worlds that depend on our protection?" asked Fox, her expression horrified.

"Yes," said the major. "It cannot be avoided."

"What will happen to them?" asked Marshall.

"We don't know. They could be attacked. Or perhaps with them cut off from us, they will be ignored as the Dram focus on how to deal with the setback. But losing contact with intergalactic trade might mean that some of them will face food and energy catastrophes."

I probed further. "And we have to hit all three of those points? Does the order matter?"

"The order is unimportant. However, doing them in sequence and not simultaneously could result in the Dram deducing our purpose. This could lead to fortifications of the Orb projections in those systems."

"So we hit them with the teams at the same time?"

"No," said the major. "There will be a single team."

"But if they will fortify the last two, that doesn't make sense!" said Kim.

"It makes sense if you understand the limitations of the engagement," said Mizoguchi harshly. "We can't send normal forces."

"Why not?" I asked.

"We have tried to. We performed seven missions to various Orbs early on. None of them returned."

"Jesus," whistled Moore. "So this is a death mission."

"Perhaps not. Because those other teams lacked a critical element that you will have."

No, they can't. My stomach lurched. "And what is that critical element, sir?"

"Ambra Dawn."

Fox gasped. *"The Daughter?"*

The major nodded.

Moore slapped his hands together. "Now that's worth signing up for! This whole *assignment* just got a hell of a lot more interesting!"

"Wait. We're missing something here," said Kim. "How are we supposed to get back once we take those nodes out? We'll be cut off, too!"

Mizoguchi turned from him dismissively. "You forget that the Daughter doesn't need to travel through the Time Tree. She can open the Orbs."

Ancient history was becoming our very practical reality. The major continued. "This decision is not a light one. Our safety has depended on her for two centuries. Our greatest battles have been fought through her. Now we have learned to lock her behind the walls we think are protective. But those walls keep her from fighting now where she is needed. And those walls are no longer as safe as we once thought."

"What do you mean?" I asked.

"In addition to the nebulous threat our reports have brought to us, there is a far, far less nebulous one. A threat we have anticipated. One that was sure to occur, although the day on which it would was unknown."

"*What threat?*" I nearly shouted.

"False Dawns, Captain Ratava." We all exchanged confused looks. "Biological clones of the Daughter, constructed from the eggs stolen from her when she was a prisoner of the Dram two hundred years ago. Eggs that have been used to create, to breed, to engineer—we don't know exactly what has been done—a number of *replicas* that have been raised effectively to recapitulate many of her powers."

"Is this for real?" asked Kim, his expression disbelieving.

"Reports and documentation of those attacks have now surfaced from several battle fronts. Images of a young woman, looking remarkably like the Daughter, opening space-time wormholes and entering combat against our forces."

"False Dawns?" I repeated numbly, the world spinning around me.

"How many do they have?" asked Williams, her voice still and quiet.

"We don't know."

"You don't *know?*" asked Kim incredulously. "You mean they could have an army of them?"

"Unlikely. What they have achieved is technically very difficult. The Xix claim it is beyond their current technology given the instability of human chromosomes during manipulation and the even harder problem of randomness in neurological development. It's hard enough to clone an Ambra Dawn. Then you have to raise one. There is psychology, tumor growth, and many variables that an alien race would have extreme difficulty with."

Moore shook his head. "Unlikely, but not unlikely enough, it seems."

"They may have had help," said the major.

"From who?" Moore asked.

"Again, this is speculation. But consider the facts: suddenly after centuries of devastating losses, the Dram counter with two breakthroughs in this war that seem beyond anything they have ever done."

Fox cut in. "If so, then you are talking about aliens with tech better than the Xix. There's nothing like that in our galaxy. Who are they? Where are they coming from?"

"Another galaxy?" offered Kim.

"No," I said. "As far as we know, only ours has the Orbs. We're cut off from other galaxies completely. There's no intergalactic travel."

"So far as we know," added Moore.

"Again, this is all speculation," said Mizoguchi, "but it is the leading theory in the Daughter's advisory circles. The Xix are convinced the Dram cannot have achieved these advances by themselves."

Williams sat back in her chair. "*Shadows* and *ghosts* tearing apart our ships, and now, the Dram have replicated the powers of Ambra Dawn." She shook her head. There was a long silence.

Mizoguchi looked grimly at us and closed the holo, the room lights switching on automatically. Suddenly, we were transported from the depths of space to our small briefing room, from existential darkness to a mundane light. She spoke coldly.

"We no longer have a monopoly on manipulating space and time."

13

We only have to look at ourselves to see how intelligent life might develop into something we wouldn't want to meet.

—Stephen Hawking

It was a clear day for the festival, and the Temple crowds were large. Most were from the Six Cities and Temple City itself, devoted pilgrims who had dedicated their lives to the service of the Daughter. In addition, there were several thousand visitors from around the world, those fortunate souls who had received clearance and visitation visas for the event. In all, there were likely fifty thousand people gathered to celebrate the salvation of New Earth. It was a security nightmare.

Special mission or not, we were still assigned to the standard Temple patrol alongside numerous MECHcore teams but were singled out from the others by being placed at the Temple gate where the Daughter would speak to the crowds. It was a duty of some prestige that sat uncomfortably with other teams that had greater seniority. Our unusual suits also marked us as different from the others charged with patrolling the area. While these suits were designed for another, much more dangerous purpose, I still didn't mind having one on me. After what we had learned recently, paranoia was at an all-time high.

I tried to keep a lighter heart and not think about the dark facts of the war. The Festival of Rebirth was the anniversary of the beginning of the Great War, the salvation of our planet and emancipation from the tyranny of our alien masters. It was the education of the entire Earth. After the Calamity was reversed, a New Earth really was born, one of a different time path, a parallel universe in which the planet was not destroyed by the Dram. Humanity as one suddenly shared a similarly vague vision of death and destruction, of horror unmade. Like waking up from a strange dream, our ancestors discerned for the first time the reality of their slavery, their libraries full of books and warnings. A world war was sparked to purge the Dram and their agents.

We won. We pressed our war with the help of Ambra and the Xix throughout the galaxy. A terrible dictatorship based on fear and death was removed and hundreds of worlds freed.

The Festival of Rebirth was still raw and real to humanity. It was the greatest holiday on the planet. Few just went through the motions. Many would make the pilgrimage to the Temple at least once in their lifetimes. And billions would watch the proceedings live as it was broadcast to every gridpoint on the globe. Dawnists would worship. Skeptics would mock. Separatists would protest, and some would cross the line into terrorism. It was the same every year.

Except we knew this year things were not going to be the same.

How would the masses react—on this day of all days —to the news that the world might actually be ending after all, and what's more, at the hands of the Dram? Would there be panic? Would we come together? Would the separatists feel the threat from outside and put down their arms and join the rest of humanity and the allied aliens? Or would they just ramp up their claims of the Calamity hoax and the invasion of Earth by the Xix? I couldn't see the Earth First diehards converting over a broadcast by the Daughter. They immediately assumed everything she said was a lie.

But the stakes were high, and emotions would be rattled. So our patrol was not an ordinary one at the Temple. We all felt the weight of events hanging over us. In the middle of all those feelings, it was difficult to feel the joy of the festival. But I tried. There were hundreds of memories from my childhood and adolescence to bring to bear. Nights watching the Diwali lights relit for the Rebirth. A field trip to Dawn's Eyes, that great Indian monument built by devout Hindus who took her as our contemporary avatar of God. Seeing her face projected across the world during the Communion, when she reached out from the Temple and shared her mind with all the Readers of Earth. Staring at the stars at night after the fireworks, dreaming of her, imagining countless ways in which we would meet. How could I know that our actual meeting would be far more magical?

Most exciting was that she would come to speak. I would be in her presence again. That thought alone sent a wave of energy through me.

"MECHcore captains, this is Sepehr Mazandarani. Waythrel is now moving to the platform to introduce the Daughter. Please assume your secondary positions."

All the teams called back their affirmatives. On our select band, I made sure my group was moving. We were to be in front of the dignitaries and the largest crowds. The last thing I wanted was to miss any signs of terrorist activity or for my team to respond to an attack ineffectively.

"Roger that, Captain," came Williams. "We're already there. Fox removed three civilians from the crowd earlier. Scans found weapons. Don't know how they got those in. Nothing in the databases about them. Don't think they were here to cause trouble, but they're eighty-sixed."

"Noted. Moore, how's that desert look?"

"As fit for our bloody bones as it ever was, sir," he reported back. "Nothing growing, nothing moving."

"Roger. Marshall, status?"

"In position. Aid stations are operational and staffed. We've got a full triage unit as well. Ready for anything except a land war."

"Copy." I picked up a growing murmur from the crowd on the other communications bands. "Looks like Waythrel is moving to the podium."

Cheers went up from the crowd for New Earth's most popular, and most despised, alien life-form. A large stand had been erected between the entrance garden we had stepped into on our arrival and the barren desert. It stood twenty feet above the ground, with the crowds in front of it. A ramp from the main road into the Temple City was placed on the back end of the stage. The towering Xix bounced forward from the road onto the ramp, and with its strange dexterity and speed, it was soon at the podium. Hologens were placed around it to capture the speaker and beam it to projectors around the globe.

"Greetings, citizens of New Earth," it began, the amplification systems producing localized holosound around the crowd. A full minute of cheers and applause flooded the sands around us. When it had died down considerably, the alien continued.

"We celebrate this New Year—233 AD. After Dawn. After a young Earth woman stepped into a machine. It was a machine built not by members of her species, but by creatures strange, even frightening to her. With great vulnerability, she placed her body into that large device. She opened her mind to share the consciousness of hundreds of others—humans and nonhumans—and worked together in trust with them to achieve a great purpose: the unmaking of a terrible evil, and the beginning of a new timeline in the history of our galaxy."

Again, the cheers and cries. The Xix were not naive. I had no doubt that the translator was imbuing its tones and words with exactly the kind of charisma needed for this speech. But it didn't matter. It was not false because it spoke the truth, however artfully. I felt my own heart stirred. This truth is part of what drew me into the military in the first place: to defend our world, our lives, and that which was most precious.

"Captain?" It was Fox. "Unusual readings coming out of my tensor field monitors."

"Say again?" I asked.

"Space-time distortions flickering nearby, localizing to...the desert. You're not seeing this?"

Waythrel continued. "In those early days, New Earth united to fight a common foe, and we achieved great things together."

"Negative, Fox. I'm not reading anything."

The alien paused, its eyestalks scanning in multiple directions at once. "For two hundred years, we have worked together to keep a great peace in our galaxy."

"I'm getting it too, Capt," said Moore. "It's behind the crowd, centered several hundred yards in the desert."

Maybe I was too far from the source. I raced forward toward the crowd, my movements in the gleaming MECHcore suit drawing stares. "What the hell is it?"

"Not sure, Captain," said Fox. "But the signal's growing off the charts."

I felt a knot form in my stomach. Intuition took over. "M-teams, this is Captain Ratava. All available suits to the Temple entrance—immediately!"

I lowered the volume from the nonmilitary channels, Waythrel's voice becoming a soft whisper. "And now, the Daughter needs you once again to achieve that unity, that commitment, that devotion to a cause."

I reached the crowd and continued around behind. My instruments were definitely picking it up now. Most of my team had assembled nearby, and the other M-teams were closing.

"You see *that*?" yelled Kim, pointing forward.

I stopped completely, staring forward. "By the Daughter...."

The desert sands, the air above it, the dunes in the distance—all was becoming distorted. It was as if we had been embedded in crystal-clear rubber and some giant's hand was pulling on the material in front of us. I could continue to hear Waythrel speak through the broadcast, but no longer could focus on her words.

"Call this in, Kim, now!" I switched to a broader transmission band. "All M-teams, *combat alert*. I repeat, combat alert! Possible security breach at alpha point 7." I switched to my team directly. "We may not have long."

I was right. As I spoke those words and heard the acknowledgements from the other M-core teams, the distortions became a vortex. The clear rubber imploded and dove into itself as if it were being sucked in a direction perpendicular to everything else: a dimension beyond those we could access even mentally.

"It's a portal," said Williams flatly.

The vortex turned to a whirlpool and suddenly the diameter increased fivefold, spanning three to four hundred feet. The clarity of the portal faded, and it took on a hideous black-and-violet hue. A depth became apparent to the structure making it look more like a tunnel than door.

A blast of air struck us, kicking up a wave of dust that accelerated outward and rained across the crowds. An electromagnetic pulse nearly shorted out our suits. The hologens weren't so lucky: they exploded. The broadcast failed; Waythrel's voice was cut off in midsentence. Through the thick chassis of my battle suit, I could hear the faint sounds of people screaming.

On several smaller picture-in-picture streams from suit cams displayed in the corners of my view screen, I could see the crowds turning toward us and the growing disturbance. But what held my gaze was the portal itself. The entrance turned pitch black. Out of that darkness poured a battalion of Dram troops like a plague of locusts.

The chaos began.

14

*There is an urge and rage in people to destroy, to kill,
to murder, and until all mankind, without exception,
undergoes a great change, wars will be waged,
everything that has been built up, cultivated and
grown, will be destroyed and disfigured, after which
mankind will have to begin all over again.*

—Anne Frank

We were outnumbered one hundred to one,
but our fifty MECHcore soldiers held their
own. All the suits were outfitted with the
new AI modules of the Xix, and we brought
considerable firepower to bear as well. But we were not
prepared for this. A terrorist attack, a core of trained
assassins, perhaps. But not an invasion force. In all our
combat drills, in all the sims and imagined encounters,
none of them involved the opening of a wormhole at our
feet.

And out of the wormhole came the worms. Ten or
twelve triads and the escorting company of insectoidal
Dram infantry—we never could nail down the exact
number in the end from all the carnage. They flooded
the sand plains in front of us with weapons blazing.
Assigned to the front of the festival activities, it was up

to me to organize the response, and I had to respond quickly.

"Equispaced grid assignments! All MECHcore units prepare for triad pairings. Commence AI dance immediately!"

Williams fired back. "Captain, we have a lock—two triads!"

"*Two?*" We'd never engaged two. What was the crazy computer doing? But there was no time to think. "Dance!"

Flechette rounds sprayed near us, but we managed to stay out of the way. Our team locked into the dance, centering on a pair of triads—six worms in all—situated close to each other. It was one thing to buzz around with our thrusters orbiting one triad, but with two, it seemed like some crazed multi-star system with planets dancing between each ball of hydrogen. A wrong move and we'd be vaporized.

It quickly became a blinding geometrical nightmare. In our suits, at these speeds, the infantry was a nuisance, but we could handle those for the most part. As we spun about the triad pair, we blasted through their ranks with the ion slingers. Their charred forms began to litter the desert sands.

But most of our attention was on the worms. Amazingly, we held the advantage. The new AI was incredible. Just when it seemed they'd gotten a lock on one of our team, blasting a flechette round, there would be a complicated choreography that would leave their guns off target. We closed in and readied the missiles.

"Confidence level reached, Captain," called Williams, her tone strained. A data read on my view screen told me that her suit was damaged.

"Damage report, Officer."

"I've got a few minutes, sir. Give the order!"

"Take them down!"

Darting back and forth, in and out like a mad amusement park ride, it seems like the height of insanity to simultaneously launch missile strikes from multiple directions. But until you have seen the dance, watched the blinding intricacies of the movement, your ideas of what is sane in combat are out of date.

We fired. Old-school chemistry-based-propellant, dual-EMP/solid-explosive warheads. The EMP drilled a hole in any field defenses they set up; the explosives were a very modernized version of some of the best twenty-first-century weapons. Twelve missiles fired, two per worm, and we rocketed outward to avoid the debris field. The triads were down in seconds. We spun back and quickly mopped up the infantry cohort.

"I'm out, metalheads," said Williams. Her suit was venting black fumes and flying irregularly.

"Copy that. Get your ass down on the ground." We needed a battlefield perspective now. "Status report, Kim."

There was a brief pause as my team sergeant plowed through the tactical. We reoriented, forming a tight circle facing outward. "Eight triads down, sir! Minimal casualties for our forces. Wait. Yes, four down, two confirmed fatalities. The civilian situation is FUBAR. A bloodbath."

Dear God. "Okay. Status on that wormhole."

"Empty of hostiles, sir. Looks like we got this under control."

"Not even close, Sergeant! We need to shut that door. Get Central Command on the line. We need the Daughter out here! She's the only one who has a chance of closing it."

"Yes, sir!"

"As long as that portal's open, *anything* could come through."

And then—something did.

The first sign that we were in trouble was the screams from several MECHcore transmissions. Then five or six suits were flung past us.

"What the hell?"

Kim broke in. "Gamma-3 team, sir. They danced past us toward the hole during the battle. Life signs have flatlined. They're all dead."

We had been pushed to the left of the platform, nearly up against the city walls when we downed our triads. We couldn't see what was going on in front for the mayhem. But I had a very bad feeling about the situation.

"Alpha team—power up the space-time countermeasures! Power them up now!"

Then it came, a cry over the COM, the chaos too wild to figure out from which team. "False Dawn!"

"False Dawn, False Dawn!" And then screams.

"To the wormhole!" I shouted to my team. "We're the only ones who can hope to engage!" We fired our thrusters and blasted toward the spinning vortex.

And there she was.

A nightmare I could never have imagined, standing at the base of that hell-tunnel was the small figure of a woman in a white robe. She walked forward slowly, her arms upraised in front of her. MECHcore soldiers were thrown away from her like debris in a cyclone. The sand in front of her was matted and compressed, heat waves rising from the ground, darkening and reflective pools forming in places from the heat and pressure that glassified the grains. Red hair fell from the sides of her partially bald and bulbous head. Her green eyes were clear in my magnified view screen. It was Ambra Dawn.

And yet it was not.

Her gait spoke of a different personality, her features similar but not identical to those of the Daughter. Her expression vile, devoid of the depth and empathy I had come to associate with that face. Hideous cables and wires sprouted from regions of her skull to embed themselves at others—of medical or mechanical nature, I couldn't tell. This was a demon's fashioning of Ambra Dawn, a fiend's torturing of an already tortured life.

And I was going to destroy it.

"Semicircle around that thing!" I yelled, arming my final missiles. "Full tensor deflection on! Burn the batteries dead! We'll only get one shot at her!"

My team responded. I detected the field activations, the warheads armed in other suits, and they struck the formation in seconds. The countermeasures allowed us to resist the space-time warping that had doomed the other MECHcore teams.

"Launch!" Ten birds blasted toward the creature from multiple directions, closing in at several times the speed of sound.

All for nothing. Before impact, all the missiles veered away sharply, flying harmlessly off into the scorching desert. Several seconds later, their explosions could be felt. But we didn't have several seconds to contemplate events.

My suit exploded. The chassis was blown off my body, the material ripped off cleanly like some discarded exoskeleton. I was thrown to the ground with a terrible impact. I screamed as I felt my right leg snap. The bone ripped out from the thigh through the muscle, blood spurting and running down my shattered leg to wet the sand below.

I don't know how much time passed. I couldn't move, the pain blinding me, distorting all my senses. I was half naked, stunned, cut off from my team and all communication.

I have failed to protect her.

A shadow dimmed the sun, and a figure stood over me. It was the demon girl. That impostor with red hair and green eyes who dared violate the sacred image of the Daughter. I tried to reach up to grab the vile form, to beat the false life out of it, but I couldn't lift my arms. Some force from that thing had paralyzed me.

Then she entered my mind.

Her thoughts were a knife driven into my skull. Inward they drove against my will, pushing, tearing, groping their way through my consciousness, my thoughts. My life, my memories, my feelings, my dreams—she sampled them all harshly, holding me in contempt at every moment. Completely vulnerable, broken in body, and now my mind lay supine, her corrupt Reader organ digging deeper into my being than even I had ever gone.

The False Dawn paused a moment, seeming to grasp some structure of my consciousness within the tentacles of its thought. And that monster smiled. It smiled down at me with a hideous glare and began to laugh short barks that sliced me like razors.

I screamed. I screamed as I never had from any pain, any injury I had ever suffered. Like a child trapped in a nightmare that he cannot escape, my soul cried out for salvation from this torment.

Suddenly, the universe *shifted*. I don't know how else to explain it. A seismic event in space-time. Nothing that could be seen or touched or felt except in some deep, primitive place. The air around us undulated. Time stopped and started, events hopping from point to point discretely without meaning. A deep, infrasonic throb within the center of my consciousness.

The False Dawn stood up. In an instant, the agonizing probes were gone, its hellish mind removed from my own. My body shook. I could not help myself; I wept. Tears flowed madly from sobs in profound relief and personal devastation.

But greater events were unfolding. The remaining Dram triads imploded, crushed into objects hardly larger than a suitcase and slung to the side. The remaining infantry collapsed, bodies intact, forms dropping to the ground as if they had suffered some terrible stroke.

The False Dawn stared grimly around her and then turned to look behind me, toward the Temple. Weakly, pathetically, I arched my neck to look as well.

The Daughter had come. She floated—*floated*—like some goddess descended from on high, the rubber matrix of reality around her puckered and warped and appearing to strain to the breaking point. She glided forward toward her clone, her expression furious, her eyes nearly glowing like emerald lanterns in a sea of white and red.

The False Dawn threw her hands forward. Ripples of distorted space exploded between her and the Daughter. Unfortunate souls between them were pulverized, torn inside out, and most bizarrely, aged or returned to fetal forms of themselves. It was like some sort of space-time bomb.

And it hit a wall of nothing in front of Ambra Dawn. As if space itself were made of water, the air seemed to refract everything around it like spray from a hose impacting a crystal sphere. *Space* and *time* splattered, bounced, and danced in multiple directions. Droplets of reality congealed in the air and floated, events and places locked within them, winking out of existence in a miniature vortex. Rivers of the universe cascaded in all directions away from the Daughter, ignoring gravity, repelled by some incomprehensible force.

The False Dawn's jaw slackened. She appeared momentarily stunned.

The Daughter drew her hands together slowly, like someone raising up a precious package, and the False Dawn screamed. It was a hateful cry, a furious rejection of the events occurring around her. She was lifted off the ground, her arms and legs thrashing, her eyes wild. Ripples formed around her and then turned into cords and ropes of transparent nothing, wrapping her in a cocoon of solid emptiness.

The Daughter eased up in front of her. The False Dawn was helpless, trapped twenty feet above the desert floor, staring forward maniacally at her near mirror image. Then Ambra closed her eyes.

The False Dawn arched her back in midair, her green eyes rolling back in her head, her body turning rigid like the onset of rigor mortis. It remained that way for several seconds, and then her body began to shake. At first barely detectable tremors, and then progressing to visible convulsions.

Yet Ambra did not let her go. The Daughter's eyes remained closed, her expression firm but focused. Given what had just happened to me, I knew what was occurring. She had entered her enemy's mind.

Suddenly, Ambra's eyes flew open, and at that moment from the corners of my eyes, I saw shapes. *Shadows.* Forms indescribable, their edges seeming to burn the essence of reality around their shapes. As a viscous smoke they flowed from the wormhole, extending black projections toward the False Dawn, wrapping tendrils around the imprisoned creature.

Initially, they began to pull her back toward them, the wormhole narrowing. *They're trying to rescue her!* The Daughter watched their efforts silently, seeming to study the situation carefully.

As the shadows seemed to take control of the False Dawn, Ambra closed her eyes again.

The effect was like nothing I had ever known. Everything before, from the military engagement to the powers of these two Readers distorting reality around me, paled in comparison. From a center near the shadowed entities, from some point of nothingness, a force radiated outward that seemed to impact me like an explosion as well as a hallucinogen. Time and space—*meaning itself* was thrown down, obliterated, in whatever way these things exist. I cannot explain any better. I have no words for it.

The result in front of me was dramatic. The creatures melted, blended, and like some chaotic ink were driven back into the tunnel. My mind felt struck by what I could only characterize as screams from these creatures. But their screams did not take place in the medium of sound. I don't know what I was experiencing.

The Daughter stepped forward, and her hand plunged through the distorted rubber prison around the False Dawn. She touched the creature's forehead with the flat of her palm, and the woman's head whipped backward. The False Dawn floated limp in the cocoon, blood dripping from the insertion points of some of the larger cables in her skull. Ambra waved both hands toward the woman, and the bubble and figure within flew violently backward into the tunnel. They disappeared from sight.

Staring forward, her glare fierce and disgusted, the Daughter closed both fists. The portal slammed shut. A powerful blast of sand burst out from where it had existed and rained quietly about us.

A terrible silence fell. I had not realized that there had been such a great noise until the portal shut. In this relative quiet, I began to hear the moans and cries of the wounded.

She turned to me and glided over beside my form, her feet lowering and then gently resting on the sands by my chest. I could see tears in her eyes as she knelt down and stroked my forehead.

"I'm so sorry, Nitin. Rest. It will be okay." Her voice was the most beautiful music I had ever heard.

An enveloping warmth flooded through me, a profound sense of safety and belonging. And fatigue. Deep, deep fatigue. I could not keep my eyes open and felt myself losing consciousness.

I slept.

15

A thing is, according to the mode in which one looks at it.

—Oscar Wilde

The tunnel never seemed to end.

I was passed through it, backward and forward, like some package in a delivery system, until I couldn't tell which direction was which anymore. Stars surrounded me, peered brightly through the distorting walls of the tube. They were so silent. So still. Unconcerned.

I could not speak. I could not scream. I had no voice or sense of my form. Back and forth, again and again, stars blurring during my acceleration or just staring back at me callously during lifetimes of stillness.

What am I?

The tunnel seemed polarized. I began to sense opposite charges, feelings, purposes. *Beings.* At one end there was light and warmth. A terrible and wonderful love that I could hardly face without being reborn by it.

At the other end, an opposite force. A darkness. An anger and need to unmake. Manipulation. *Antipathy.*

From both ends, green eyes stared back at me through this endless space.

Green eyes in blackness, cold darkness. Laughing. Green eyes in sunlight. Weeping. Calling my name.

Nitin. Come to me, Nitin.

Ambra, how do I come to you? I can't come. I can't move! Help me!

Then I will come to you, my love.

Green and blue.

The green swayed in the blue, golden crowns dancing at the tops of towers. My eyelids twitched open and shut in the bright light. My shoulders felt weighted down, my entire body pressed into a clay mold.

Soil. My hands opened and closed, my fingers scratching through dirt. The towers came into focus. *Corn.* Adrenaline coursed through me. *I know this place.*

Weakly, painfully, I pulled myself to a sitting position. I sat in the middle of a giant cornfield once again. My body naked. My mind muddled and sloppy. Part of me was afraid. Afraid of this strangeness, this vulnerability. Afraid for my sanity.

But Ambra is here.

I stood up. It was as if I had left only recently. I remembered the way. Limping forward at first, then nearly bringing myself to a run, I dashed through the maze of cornstalks, my heart racing, a powerful hope of seeing her driving me on.

I crashed outward from the corn and stumbled onto the grassy lawn. The farmhouse loomed before me. A figure stood in front of it.

"Nitin." Her voice traveled undiminished across the yard.

Tears welled in my eyes. So much horror seemed lodged in the back of my mind, threatening to grow and consume me. My body felt ransacked. Broken. I was lost.

But here is my haven. Standing before me was a woman not yet twenty. The image of the Daughter I had known and gazed on my entire life. Pale like china. Red like fire. Green like emeralds. Light seemed to dance around her.

Yet different. Alive in a way I could never feel from holos. Transcendent in a manner only this dream could create. And centered in a universe without other distractions. Without other worries. Focused on me alone.

And I on her. "Ambra?"

She too stood naked, my eyes darting across the lines and curves of her body. There was desire. There was stunned awe at the depth of her beauty. She walked toward me.

"Do you know where we are?"

I blinked at her words. "No. A farm?"

"*My farm*, Nitin," she said, taking my arm in hers and smiling more broadly. She pulled me forward gently and led me toward the house. "I was born here, spent eleven years here." Her voice began to lilt and dance as though she were reciting a magical tale. "You came out from my father's cornfields. They go on and on until it seems like the world will end before you get out of them. He used to work so hard out there. The big companies always wanted to swallow us up, but he was determined to stay independent. He hated them and how they killed the plains."

We were about halfway across the backyard when she turned and pointed to an open expanse of land between the tall cornfields and the house.

"Isn't it beautiful?"

The land continued, seemingly forever, nearly flat but for a very slight slope that enhanced the view from our position. Browns and greens and houses dotted the endless plain until it faded into the horizon. The blue above and around us faded toward that end, turning first gray, then black as it crashed into a bubbling mountain range of clouds. Lightning flashed in front of me a million miles away.

"A storm is coming," I said.

"Many," said Ambra solemnly. "But they are not here yet. We have a short time."

I turned to her and spoke, the wild creativity of a dream releasing my thoughts. "Please don't go away this time." I was remembering the other dream. *Memories of dreams in a dream.* I tried to suppress tears, but so much emotion flowed over me that I was overcome. "Please let me stay here with you, Ambra. There is a hole. It eats away at me. My whole life. No one understands. I can't face that hurricane of emptiness." I trailed off, a nightmare lurking just behind my conscious thoughts. I tried to push it away.

"I understand, Nitin," she said, placing her hand on my face.

"But here,' I said, "here it's safe with you. It's right. Please, can we stay?"

She shook her head sadly. "I'm sorry, Nitin. We can't."

"So, I am dreaming? This is all a lie?"

"Dreams are not lies, Nitin. Dreams are other spaces. Other times. But spaces and times within larger places. Bubbles within seas. Sometimes a person can stay in the bubble and ride out the storms. Never leave the dream."

I looked back at the dark clouds, seemingly no closer yet no less threatening. "But we can't."

"No Nitin, we can't. And that is my fault." She sighed.

Just then a tan-and-white blur sped around the corner of the house. Before I could process it, Ambra let go of my arm, and the blur leaped into the air. She caught it and embraced an enormous pile of hair. I recognized it as some sort of sheepdog.

The animal licked her face and seemed beside itself. Its fur was copious, thick, and silky, giving the dog an appearance of being overweight.

Ambra laughed as she cradled the dog. "This is Matt, Nitin." She turned the dog toward me.

Dogs do not have the popularity in India that they do in Western nations, so my experience was more with street strays than manicured breeds. The strays were usually diseased beggars or even aggressive ones. Hesitant, I reached out my hand.

"Turn your palm down and bring it below his nose."

I did so, and the dog sniffed me and looked me over. Satisfied, but not much taken with me, he returned his attention to Ambra.

"I saw him die, you know," she said. "First in a vision. It was horrible." Her face clouded as she squeezed the animal a little too tightly, and the dog started twitching its paws. "I couldn't stop it then. I didn't even know it was a vision at that age. And then later, even when I understood my powers, I had to let Earth die."

"But you did it to save so much more. So many worlds! And in the end, you brought us back!"

"That success doesn't change the choice. Or the damage it does, Nitin."

"Don't blame yourself."

She shook her head. "If you could only know and see. I am a frightening nexus of cause and effect. It was my fault my parents died. Servants of the Dram killed them, butchered them to get to me. My fault an entire planet full of life boiled. And it's my fault that we can't stay here." She touched my cheek again and smiled. "Where it's safe."

I reached out and held her hand, the porcelain hue like a beam of light in my palm. "It's okay; I knew that we couldn't. Felt it. But I can't explain how much I need you. Need to be with you in a place that is safe."

She looked into my eyes. "You are the handsomest man I'll ever not see." I was taken aback slightly as she laughed. "Do you know what is most powerful about being close to you? Warmth and *smell*. You know I can see in my weird way. I can see your features. I've *seen* them in ways and times you don't even know. And you *are* handsome to me, Nitin. I've had crushes and infatuations, but the first time I saw you—the many times I've seen you—always such power! It's underneath conscious thought. But I do not see you with my true eyes. All those pathways in my brain are atrophied now. All to the great service of my tumor."

"You speak like it's evil."

"It is."

"It's what has saved us!"

"And killed so many." She looked out across the plains again toward the storm. The dog jumped down and, nose to the ground, began an indecipherable olfactory quest across the grass. "You grew up with the powers of this thing in my skull as a force for liberation. But living with it, what it has done to me and others, what it will do—nothing is ever as it seems."

It was unsettling to hear her pain in those words. History lessons are one thing—imagining the difficult life of another is an important exercise, but so limited. A five-minute conversation in the middle of a dream conveyed infinitely more. Seeing the lines in her face, the tension in her muscles, and sadness in her blind eyes.

"I want to understand, Ambra. I want to know everything about you."

"I know you do. And you will. A few steps at a time, Nitin. That's how we climb to the Temple. Hand in hand."

She breathed in deeply, closing her eyes. "*Smell*. Waythrel said something about immune receptors and genetics and mate selection, but it's all a blur. Biology. Isn't it strange how so much of everything we are and know and feel is biology?"

"We are what we are."

"Yes! But even the Readers don't know what that is."

She inhaled again, dipping her head close to my neck, sending involuntary shudders through me. "I could eat you up!" She paused there a second as my body tensed like a bow. Suddenly she pulled away. "Walk with me, Nitin, away from the storm for a time, or I'll want to entangle us right here and now. But it's the wrong time. And the wrong place."

My throat was dry, and my hairs stood on end. I felt things stirring below and was momentarily embarrassed. But she pulled me toward the side of the house, the growing thunderheads at our backs and a bright sun halfway to noon before us.

"It *is* beautiful," I managed. I had never seen America's Great Plains before. I had imagined that the sameness, the flatness, and the agricultural devotion of the land would be monotonous. Boring. In a way it was, until you drank in the enormity of it, the fields like a sea with different colored crops cresting here and there, houses like small boats afloat. Even the storm we had turned our backs on was majestic in a terrible kind of way as it poured forward like lava from a volcano.

"This is what imprinted me," she said wistfully, "shaped and programed the impressionable mind of a little girl. I guess I was born learning to see into great distances. But I can never go back to this place, as much for where I must go as for what terrible things happened here."

The land she loved, and yet the land that was stained with the spilled blood of her parents. Why were we here? And where was she going that she couldn't stay?

We came because you approach my heart, its light and darkness, Nitin. We came as you search with me to return from the darkness that clone monster threw you into. We came because existence is layer upon layer of dream within dream.

At the mention of the clone, that nightmare I had pushed aside threatened to rage into my consciousness. I shook slightly, and Ambra held my hand firmly.

"But look, Nitin! There is so much light!"

She waved her hand across the fields before us, and the air shimmered and swayed, and space opened. In the middle of the bright daylight, a necklace of gemstone stars exploded.

She pulled me forward into the breach of space, and we stepped through the day on Earth onto the sands of an alien beach. Strange seas crashed in front of me, and above was a churning miracle of radiance: an entire galaxy painted across the night sky.

Ambra pressed her naked form against mine and kissed me gently, staring deeply into my eyes. She placed her hand on my chest, near my heart. My breathing deepened and quickened. She whispered softly into my ear.

"I am with you, Nitin. Always. Never forget. Follow my voice as you did to get here. Feel my love. And you will find your way home."

"Is this home?" I asked stupidly.

"One of many," she said, smiling. "A place we will soon visit in another dream. Here we will love each other on these very sands."

16

There is always some madness in love.
But there is also always some reason in madness.

—Friedrich Nietzsche

Once again, I woke from trauma in a hospital bed, staring up into the forest of eyestalks of a Xixian medic.

I was completely disoriented. I didn't know where I was, where I had been, what day I had woken into. The room was strange; I did not know it. The medic was a Xix, but not one I recognized. I was thankful I could recall my own name.

There was a tunnel. I remembered a long and endless tunnel. There were worm triads in the Thar. Japanese nurses. *No, that was before.* The Sahara. A new team. *Yes!* A special mission to salvage the war.

A wormhole.

I shuddered and closed my eyes. It came back to me. The monster came back to me. I could still feel it, feel her thought tendrils in my mind, probing my inner person. I felt sullied. Unclean. *Used.*

A warm sensation pressed against my hand. I opened my eyes, turning my sore neck to the right, and stared into green, blind eyes once again. But not the clone. Eyes that embraced and did not wound.

"It's okay, Nitin," she said. "Don't think of her." Her hand squeezed mine more tightly.

"Daughter of Time," I whispered. I did not know what else to say. Echoes of a dream washed over me. *Was it real? Is this real?*

"I am more than that to you, my Nitin." She smiled; it was soft and lined with sorrow. I had never felt so much love poured toward me. "Say my name."

I choked out the word, hardly suppressing the tears.

"Ambra."

I was in no state of mind to analyze what was happening, what had happened. There could be no sequence of events that I could imagine leading to this moment. Nothing I could conjure in my imagination that would place Ambra Dawn at my bedside. Holding my hand. Speaking impossible words.

"My love," she said, the smile large and radiant. *You don't have to understand, Nitin.* The words in my mind again. *Just accept what you know is true. There will be a time soon to talk more.*

"Yes. Please." I closed my eyes as emotion overcame me. I could not process these events. Then other memories came flooding back. "What happened...to my team?"

A familiar voice spoke. "They are recovering nearby." It was Waythrel. I shifted my gaze to my left side to see the huge bulk of the alien. "Most of the injuries were moderate, like your leg."

Moderate? I looked down to see my thigh. There was little evidence of damage, only a hairline scar where the bone had torn through.

"Most of the injuries?"

"Medical Sergeant Ryan Marshall died before we could reach him. He spent his last moments tending to the others. He saved their lives." Waythrel paused a moment. "The rest of your team is stationed back at the barracks. They recommenced training yesterday."

"Yesterday? Why am I still here?"

The medic cut in. "Because your injuries were more severe." I glanced down at my leg, but it corrected me. "Not to your body. To your mind."

Ambra reached over and brushed her fingers against my forehead. A thrill ran through me. "She had done terrible things to you, Nitin." Her face was pained. "An act of violence and power that was as unnecessary as it was cruel."

"The mind, and the neurological support framework that gives birth to the epiphenomenon, is fragile, Captain Ratava," said the alien medic. "We had to act quickly, or much of the damage would have become permanent."

"Damage."

"Psychological damage, and through that, physical damage," said Waythrel. "The matter of the brain and the field of the mind are like a particle and a wave in quantum theory. Two aspects of a greater whole. Damage to one is damage to the other. There was some work that could be done at the level of your organism, but for the sentience field that is your mind, we needed a different kind of doctor."

"Ambra." I turned back to her and looked into her eyes. They had turned to green pools filling with water.

Waythrel spoke. "Ambra did not leave your side for a week."

"Until I knew I could do no more," she said.

A week? I wasn't sure what was harder to believe: that the Daughter had devoted herself to my sickbed for an entire week as the war effort collapsed around us, or that she needed to. I shuddered involuntarily. "I can still feel that thing in my head."

"Even with Ambra's ministrations, it was impossible that you would suffer no lasting effects from such a mind probe," said the medic. "But we can assure you that your cognitive functions are unharmed. Psychologically, there will be residual pain."

I turned to Ambra. "Thank you." I spoke to the others as well. "Thank you, all." I couldn't convey how grateful I felt to have that horrible mind erased, even incompletely, from my own. Had it not been, I'm sure I would have gone mad.

I felt fatigue creeping over me again, but there were questions bubbling underneath the surface that began to break through to my consciousness.

"I saw...*shadows.* Were they real?"

Ambra spoke firmly. "Yes."

"What are they?"

"Nothing that we have encountered in this galaxy," said Waythrel. "But by showing themselves here, they have revealed much to us. Ambra herself as well as the monitoring equipment that survived the battle have provided enough information for us to begin piecing together what we are dealing with."

"Why did they come?" I asked.

"We don't think they meant to," said Ambra. "They were overconfident in their red-headed Frankenstein.

The clone was not supposed to fail so completely, to be taken prisoner."

Waythrel picked up the thread. "At the least they probably assumed their Reader could retreat and return. When it was clear that she could not escape from Ambra, they sought to intervene."

"So, they were close. Waiting."

"Yes," said Ambra. "Hiding in the corners of space-time. Whatever they are, they have extremely advanced technology, as we could have guessed from what is going on. Not advanced enough to control a wormhole—they still needed their Reader clone. But enough to know how to exploit them, cache themselves unseen within them."

"But you defeated them," I said, a note of pride in my voice I didn't mean to let escape.

"They aren't supernatural creatures, Nitin. They are made of the basic components of matter in this universe, just like everything else."

"With one exception," finished Waythrel.

An exception to material existence? "What do you mean?"

"They are creatures wholly composed of antimatter."

"Antimatter? *How?* Wouldn't they just explode or something in our atmosphere?"

"We aren't sure how they manage to shield themselves, but they expend enormous energy to do so," said Waythrel. "But because they are very much natural creatures, Ambra was able to deal with them."

"Then, we have a chance," I said, finding myself slipping into sleep. "The mission. There is hope."

"Yes," said Ambra, smiling. "We'll talk more when you are stronger." She bent over and kissed my cheek, whispering in my ear. Her breath was warm and raised goose bumps over my body. "Soon, we will walk among the stars together, Nitin Ratava. And for a time, you will experience how beautiful they are."

Her words spun around me like poetry, beautiful and comforting, and I felt myself smile even as I drifted off again into a deep sleep.

17

Jealousy does not wait for reasons.

—Gandhi

The clinic staff had turned in for the evening, and I was alone with the flashing monitors and night-shift nurse at her station in the hallway. Tomorrow, I would be released and allowed to rejoin my team, as we were to meet with Ambra and her advisors to finalize the mission plans.

Several days of intensive rehab had proven to me that the Xixian medical technology was nothing short of miraculous. My shattered leg was as good as new, and my basic physical performance, as well as short drills in my suit, showed absolutely no degradation of function. There were some attention-deficit red flags. Apparently, it would take a lot more time to smooth out the mental damage that monster had inflicted on my psyche.

I couldn't notice it in my daily actions and thoughts. But nights were another story completely. I dreaded them and began to fear my own dreams. I needed to get this thing out of my head completely, or the sleep deprivation was going to end up making me dysfunctional.

It was on this last evening in the hospital, later into hours after midnight, that he came. I wasn't sleeping. Another nightmare had startled me awake. I was wiping the sweat from my forehead when I heard footsteps in the corridor outside my room. Not the soft padding of the night nurse, but a heavier, more assertive gait.

Curious, I propped myself up in the bed and listened more carefully. At least this gave me something concrete, something tangible to consider instead of the ghostly remnants of a mental assault. The steps stopped outside my door and a tone sounded, indicating that the touchpad outside had been activated. The door dissolved as a male figure stepped into the room.

"I understand that you sleep poorly at night."

It was Sepehr Mazandarani, the advisor to Ambra Dawn. In this moonlit dark, his devilish features were only caricatured, and it was with some apprehension that I watched him pull a chair over to my bedside.

"News travels broadly here," I said, a sense of threat palpable from this man.

He smiled sharply, waving away my words. "I am the Daughter's closest advisor. *Human* advisor, anyway. Her thoughts are rarely hidden from me."

"You are a Reader? Do you commune with her?"

I saw his face tighten. "No. Ambra employs me for other talents that I can offer."

He seemed to enjoy playing with words for my discomfort. "What talents?"

Again that smile. "Analysis. Logic. Strategy. She relies heavily on my counsel."

"Yes, you are an important man."

He cocked his head slightly to the side and laughed. "I did not come here to monkey dance with you, Ratava."

"Good. Just why are you here, then?"

He eyed me harshly. "I don't dance, Captain. I act when I have the data to act. Right now I don't have that data, except for circumstantial evidence. But that evidence has me concerned greatly for the safety and well-being of the Daughter."

I pushed myself to an upright position. "What do you mean?"

"In your desert heroics at the Rebirth, you were present at an event that has never occurred before. *Never* has there been an attack at the Temple. Not in two hundred years."

"Yes, I know."

"Furthermore," he continued, cutting me off, "in order for that clone to have breached the Xixian defense fields, they would have needed help from within. The three-space location of the Temple is scrambled to any Reader of space-time, and opening a wormhole at the perfect location and time to attempt an assassination would require a device, a beacon of some sort, to be placed to transmit our real location."

"What are you saying?"

He locked eyes with me. "That we have a traitor in our midst, Captain."

In the Temple? It was impossible to believe. I had seen the devotion of the people here. I couldn't imagine any of them aiding our enemies—the enemies not just of Ambra Dawn but of the entire human species. Not even the terrorist groups. They might hate the Daughter, but they hated the aliens even more. And besides, how could they get a spy past the Daughter? She could read minds. She could read the future!

"What do the Xix say? What does Waythrel say?"

"It was *their* hypothesis. They know the nature of the defenses they have established—which now they are modifying to prevent a repeat event."

"Who could possibly do such a thing?"

"We don't know. But I will tell you, Captain—I am going to find out." His face poorly concealed an anger bubbling beneath.

My thoughts were troubled. Something felt wrong. His visit with this information in this manner made little sense. "Why are you telling me this now?"

"The Daughter has developed a particular empathy toward you. At best, I hope to persuade you to take this threat seriously and to do all that you can to protect her."

"And at worst?"

He stood up and grasped the neckline of his black desert robes, looking down on me with contempt. "I don't like anomalies, Captain Ratava. Unexplainable events or people. Your resume as it concerns Ambra Dawn is strange beyond explanation. You have single-mindedly aimed your career trajectory like a missile to place yourself just in this location. You offer this seeming unconditional emotion to her, immediately winning her attention and confidence. And it is only just after you arrive, after centuries of peace in the desert, that our defenses are breached from within and the Daughter attacked."

I felt the blood run out of my face. "You can't be serious."

"Circumstantial evidence, Captain. But rest assured, if it ever becomes more than that, I will be the first one with a gun to your head."

With that, he turned sharply on his heels and marched out of the room.

18

If we have learned one thing from the history of invention and discovery, it is that, in the long run—and often in the short one—the most daring prophecies seem laughably conservative.

—Arthur C. Clarke

We entered an enormous room located directly below the gargantuan tower reaching toward space.

The four remaining members of my team had been escorted by a still-suspicious Mazandarani across the Temple City. The tower loomed above us constantly, impossible to grasp in its height, and our path soon within the five-mile radius of the supporting base.

We passed the massive columns of a strange Xixian metal that plunged underneath the desert sands. The base supports themselves were as wide as buildings. The webbed shadows of the structure fell across our path from the setting sun. We came to rest at the entrance to a beautiful building, some well-realized combination of human and Xixian tastes blended harmoniously.

The structure rose to a height of seven or eight stories like some strange plant or deep-sea creature. The largest portion was at the top, a toroidal curvilinear solid that looked something like a sphere that had been pressed in deeply from the top. It seemed to float above the desert sands but in fact was supported at six points by tapering columns that became ellipsoids at their apex. The larger top portion was therefore resting on smaller round objects that appeared to almost flow into the desert floor. The material seemed to be the same indestructible concrete found in the buildings in the Six Cities, the tan color blending into the sands around us.

Most strikingly, the walls seemed almost porous in places, complex, flower-like geometrical patterns of different sizes arrayed across the surfaces of the bulbous toroid. As our local star dipped below the horizon, the day faded quickly in the Sahara, and a golden light radiated outward from those thinner regions of the walls. It was like looking at some enormous Japanese lantern, or perhaps some strange bioluminescent jellyfish from the depths.

The Temple. There had never been a holo to emerge from the Sahara. Here the Daughter met with some of New Earth's most powerful Readers along with those from many alien species. Here they entered into a group trance, their minds connecting through the medium of space and time. Many claimed they formed a powerful community mind greater than the sum of its individuals. This mind had once traveled back in time and unmade history. This was the epicenter of our power in the galaxy.

As we walked up the thirty broad steps below the entrance, we passed beneath a high arch decorated with symbols of both alien and human origin. Suddenly, we were inside a cavernous space, the curved walls appearing far larger than they could possibly have been from the outside. What had appeared as human-sized geometric patterns on the outside now took on dimensions many times that span.

But what stole my eye was the light source that gave the glow that seeped through the patterns on the outside. In the middle of this vast space undulated a brightness that I can only compare to a plasma. Like some superheated state of matter, its iridescence was formed from multiple colors flowing and merging in constant motion. Its shape was hard to fathom. From a distance, with a brief glance, I assumed it was a spherical object. But the longer I looked, the closer I approached, it seemed as if there were some solid structure present beyond anything I could grasp, but that only part of it was in this space. As its shape altered, I felt as if I were seeing pieces, projections, sides of the full shape that came into view and then disappeared. It was dizzying.

As if that were not enough, in the middle of that terrible and unearthly energy was a dais. I identified it from legend—the dimensions of a small table, obsidian, connected to the pulsing energy field by numerous extensions, many of which appeared alive like slick tree roots. This was the Xixian-designed seat of power for Ambra Dawn. This was where she sat, connected to the powerful devices that amplified her modulations of the space-time matrix. Placed radially around this central point were several hundred small depressions— additional seats built into the Temple floor.

Despite the presence of that powerful energy source, I felt nothing. No disorienting sickness as I felt when the Daughter had battled the False Dawn, no sense of electricity or heat. The air was mostly still except near the entrance where the Sahara winds entered feebly and died. There was no sand anywhere in the Temple.

"They sure don't mess around," said Moore. He and the other members of the team gawked at the vision before them.

"There's some kind of geometrical distortion here," said Fox. "Space-time funkiness. It's bigger inside than out."

"Yeah, noticed that," said Williams. "What do you suppose that glowing glob is there in the middle?"

A voice answered from in front of us. "A doorway that opens to the Orb." It was Ambra Dawn.

Seeming to step out of fog and darkness, the Daughter appeared flanked by Waythrel on her right and Major Mizoguchi on her left. They walked toward us slowly as Mazandarani left our side and took a place beside Mizoguchi.

"The Orb?" asked Kim. "How is that possible? We're on New Earth."

"The geometry of time and space is not intuitive, Sergeant," said Waythrel. "We could give you more detailed explanations, but we are here to discuss more pressing matters."

"Why in here?" I asked.

Ambra smiled. "That will become apparent soon. Please, take a seat." She gestured at the floor space in front of her and elegantly crouched into a crossed-legged sitting position. Her advisors, including the alien, also sat. I looked across my team and shrugged. We sat.

"With their victories in space, our enemies grow more bold," said Mizoguchi. "Although with the compete destruction of their recent attack force, they will perhaps be more cautious for the time being."

"In addition, Ambra has sent them a message," said Waythrel. "She cast back at them the dead body of the clone prior to closing the wormhole."

"Yes," I said remembering. "What did you do to her?"

Ambra looked sad. "I tried to look into her mind, to understand what she was, what had motivated her. But there was so much darkness. The Dram can apparently program their human cattle to harbor extreme hatred toward us—so much that there was little hope to reach out to that pitiable thing." She shook her head. "There was no saving her, no hope to keep her prisoner. And I could not let her return. So, I wiped her mind."

Moore leaned forward, his long legs uncomfortably splayed in his seated position. "You did what?"

Ambra sighed. "It was a telepathic overload, a destruction of her mental space-time matrix that scrambles all coherence."

"The biological portion of her mind was reduced to pulp," said Mazandarani. "You can think of it as *frying* her neurons."

"What this means," said Waythrel, "is that our enemies will learn nothing from her, nothing from their attack except that we hold a power that they do not yet know how to counter. Even a cohort of their new allies was destroyed."

Mizoguchi cut to the chase. "But because of the recent attacks, we have decided to accelerate the covert mission. You will be leaving today for your first target node."

"Today?" I had just stepped out of the hospital!

"Whoa, wait a minute! Time out!" cried Kim. "What about recon? Mission prep? Stuff we like to do to stay alive."

Williams cut in. "We're not just going to jump to some random system today and engage without knowing anything about it."

Mizoguchi answered. "Of course not. Do not insult me with such a concern."

"Then what?" Kim asked.

Mizoguchi looked toward the Daughter and Ambra picked up the conversation. "If you are willing, you can learn all you need to know about the locations right now, in there next few minutes. We can cut through hours of briefings and holocrystals."

"And just how might we do that?" asked Moore.

"By opening your mind to me. With your permission, I can share the information telepathically without the need for any slower and more cumbersome methods."

"Hold it right there, princess," said Moore. "No one's crawling up inside my noggin—you got that?"

"Sergeant—," I began.

"Sorry, sir, but no fucking way."

Mazandarani looked sharply at Moore. "There is nothing to fear unless you have something to hide."

"Yeah, I got a lot of things to hide," said Moore, leaning back and smirking at the counselor. "Like what me and that mechanic girl were doing under the engine hoist the other night. Or what I think of that minger growing on your chin."

"The Daughter is discrete," said Waythrel. "Such sharing is a daily experience with the Xix. It unifies us, eases misunderstandings, and grants us an efficiency and group memory we would not otherwise possess. Ambra has now brought this gift to your species. Already, the Readers of New Earth have begun to be united in this way, especially those who have taken part in the great sharings here at the Temple."

"It sounds amazing," said Fox. Moore eyed them all suspiciously.

"What do you mean discrete?" Williams asked.

Ambra spoke. "She means that I am careful to touch only those aspects of your consciousness that I am required to. I will not pry into your thoughts or memories. I will learn from you only that which you want to share with me. Also, none of you are Readers, so you cannot through me invade one another's minds. Only I can reach out to each of you."

My heart was racing. I couldn't believe the privilege we were being offered. While I could understand the concerns of Moore and Williams, my heart responded like Fox's. I wanted nothing more than to have her mind share with me. But I dared not speak of it, or speak anything. I feared my eagerness would spook the members of my team.

Kim raised his hand. "You said that we could share what we wanted. What do you mean? Are we going to hear your voice in our heads and point thoughts at it? See your face? Exactly what the hell's going to happen?"

Ambra smiled. "It is a different experience for every person, and not one that has a simple physical correlate like those you mention."

"I think I can answer this," said Mazandarani, still keeping an eye on Moore. "I'm not a Reader, but I have shared like this many times with the Daughter. If you have ever had a sense of another's personality—their soul, for lack of a better word—that understanding of their nature that is not tightly bound to their appearance or voice or words. *That* is the experience. You will be given the experience of the Daughter's personality without having to do all the work of really getting to know her. It will just be there, filling your awareness, more completely and clearly than in any way I've ever known."

"By the Dawn," said Fox.

"Exactly," quipped Mazandarani. "Through Ambra Dawn."

Moore ignored him and turned to Ambra. "Well, what if I don't want to get to know you that badly?"

Ambra nodded. "I respect that. I respect any of you who refuse."

"If we refuse, then what? We're out?" asked Williams.

"No," said Ambra. "You can be briefed by the others en route and at the site. Only they will know far more, and you will be playing catch-up."

Moore didn't hesitate. "Count me the hell out, then." He leaned back on his elbows.

"Williams?" I asked. She didn't look as if she was too keen on the idea either.

My warrant officer stared straight at Ambra for fully half a minute. I didn't know what her internal battle was, but in the end she nodded and accepted the sharing.

"Risk assessment," she answered when Moore asked her why. "I calculate that the gains outweigh the losses."

Mazandarani spoke. "Am I to assume that the rest of you are in favor? Except for Sergeant Moore, of course."

Kim, Fox, and I nodded. Moore stood up. "So, what, I go wait outside or something?"

"Not necessary," said Ambra. "But please don't disturb us until we wake."

"Wake?" asked Kim.

"From the trance," said Mazandarani. "You don't think the Daughter will enter your mind and download a week's worth of material and you'll continue to chat?"

Kim and the others took this in silently. Waythrel spoke. "Please, then. Try to calm your thoughts and feelings. It usually helps for humans to close their eyes."

I closed my eyes. I tried to calm myself by imagining the forms around me. My mind moved to the rip in the fabric of space that had embedded a segment of the Orb in this very chamber, the colors of the thing spinning in their bizarre paths and hypnotizing me. For a few minutes, I heard nothing but the soft breathing of those around me and the faint, dying howls of the winds outside—haunting cries of a tortured land.

It grew quieter and quieter, until I began to hear my own heartbeat, feel it throbbing in my ears. The pounding grew louder and began to take on shapes. Shapes of the heart muscle, vessels straining under the pressure, blood coursing in spurts through my body. Blue to red. Lung to heart. Webs of alveoli opening, growing in size, until I could see the cells themselves take on the form of vast continents stretching before me to the horizon. And regularly, like clockwork, the pulse and pound. Each beat brought a wave of gray particles, molecules of oxygen, which were trapped, held, and fed to contorted monsters, bands of chained atoms with a central core not unlike the dais of Ambra Dawn.

Inward and inward I sank. Past protein molecules, to amino acids, carbon-carbon bonds. Electrons danced around me, nebulous, unreal and alive. Inward, crossing thousands of times the distance before, toward a glowing center like the heart of a star. The nucleus exploded to reveal quarks and strings and elements I had no words for. They danced and danced around me in confusing motions.

And then everything reversed. The bizarre strings took on the shapes of atoms again. Simple structures of the simplest element: hydrogen. And at speeds I had never experienced, I raced out from this microscopic labyrinth into the very depths of space.

A nebula. A nearby star lighting the colors of the gas cloud. A band of diamonds coating the space opposite me. Thousands of stars.

An ocean world, blue and reflective in the blackness of space, devoid of land. It spun about the star.

Between them, the dancing colors I had seen in the Temple in their full context: the Orb.

19

The more you see how strangely Nature behaves,
the harder it is to make a model that explains how
even the simplest phenomena actually work. One
does not, by knowing all the physical laws as we
know them today, immediately obtain an
understanding of anything much.

—Richard Feynman

Three star systems, their planets, the location of the Orb in each system. It was as if I had lived multiple lives in those distant spaces, ages flowing through me, images and cultures and locales. It was like no learning experience I had ever known.

I was passive in the beginning, letting the Daughter do whatever it was she had to do in order to plant this information in my mind. The flood of information was all-consuming. Detail upon detail of places and times and events. Entire histories of other worlds and planets—somehow it was all hers to share, as if she had lived eons across every point in space. Her vision was with the eyes of a god. Sometimes so much would pour through me, things that made no sense and bordered on surreal, that I cannot explain how that experience translated into concrete information about the place. I was not conscious of any learning—only endless experience.

But learn I did. Later on, when I woke from the trance, I knew all I needed to know about each target to complete our mission. Much more than I needed. I had become a citizen of each world, a historian and anthropologist. An organic library.

By the experience of the third system, the third Orb projection, I began to become accustomed to the process. The mind is an adaptation machine, and already mine was finding an equilibrium with the impossible. I found myself restless. Searching. Reaching out into the blackness for that which truly held my heart.

Nitin.

Her voice whispered my name. I experienced the warmth and love I had sensed lying in the hospital bed when she tended me, but a thousandfold more strongly.

Follow my voice, Nitin. Come to me.

There was an Orb. All space was black, the star systems gone, the background of the galaxy missing. The information flow stopped in an instant.

There was only the Orb. It grew in size, or I approached it at reckless speed. I could not tell which. Without any reference points, size and motion were relative.

Patterns, colors, *passages* rippled across the enormous surface—which I discovered was not a surface but like the reflective ocean skin, an illusion blanketing fathoms of mystery. I sensed the power of the thing, a terrible, monstrous depth and abstraction that nearly froze my heart. Cold, dark, like the bottom of the deepest chasm in the sea.

Yet warmth. At the same time, in the midst of the alien and transcendent that I could not comprehend, there was empathy. A vibrational resonance connecting me and the Orb. Pure. Guileless. Limitless *affection*.

By now the object had grown to span the width of my peripheral vision, the multidimensional corridors frothing beneath the surface of the entity transforming into enormous rivers that dwarfed me.

Nitin, come.

She called from within the god-sphere. I felt her, felt her person like a presence in my own flesh, that barely remembered flesh that once sat in the Temple in the center of the Sahara. I hesitated one instant—a heartbeat staring at that anomaly—and then I steeled my courage, willing myself to her.

I felt a terrible acceleration pull from deep inside me. A madness of dimensional mazes darted around me, through me, all the while sensing her presence grow stronger and stronger. It seemed that the entire Orb was becoming one with her.

And then screams. Panicked cries around me. Not my voice. I was yanked back and forth. *Stars stars stars stars in this endless tunnel.*

My dream? I felt that nontube that held me bend and twist and form hyperspace knots and burn at the very fabric of space. The stars took on hideous rainbows of distorted color.

And cold hands, cruel hands pulling, pulling, tearing at me, seeking control, breaking my form, remaking it, demanding pounds and pounds of my flesh.

The pain was excruciating. I had no body, but I felt my teeth grind, my body spasm, my back arch, the very skin across my ghost form stretching and tearing and yielding to the merciless strain.

Now, I screamed. I screamed down this Orb hole and tunnel of hell where time spiraled and spun and completed a circle to re-become.

Full circle in multiple dimensions, I crashed screaming face first into the onrushing madness of my own torment.

20

*My heart, the bird of the wilderness, has found its
sky in your eyes.*

—The Gardener of Tagore

There were waves.

Waves crashing, the sounds of their foam bubbling across my consciousness. Waves and wind. Water over rocks while a breeze stirred refreshingly across my face.

"Nitin, wake up."

I opened my eyes. For a moment, all I could see was green. The green of the evening glow of the vegetation. Of a forest of bizarre trees climbing around me, their fluorescent light glinting off the ocean to my left.

And her eyes.

I lay on my back, a rough sand underneath me. As I stared upward, the sky was an explosion of shape and form. Something like the aurora borealis danced madly through the atmosphere. Behind it, roiling like some vortex of light, was a sea of stars, an entire spiral galaxy splayed out across the night sky. The atmosphere rendered the stars in multiple winking hues of gold, crimson, and purple. Like gemstones.

Like the two emeralds above me.

Ambra stared down into my eyes, her knees in the sand beside me, the water lapping the black robes that trailed behind her. Her hands held mine over my chest.

"My Nitin." She smiled.

For some time, I could not respond. Could not move. The shock of my experiences, the devastating beauty of the planet around me, her body alongside mine as she looked into my eyes—I was powerless. Once again unmade by her.

Finally, she reached one hand behind my neck and pulled me to sit up. It seemed that I weighed four tons, and my body was sore in all the muscles and joints. I grunted, breathing in shallow gasps as she helped me sit, her right arm around my shoulders, the left still holding my hand.

"It will pass soon."

I looked into her face. "What happened, Ambra? Where is the Temple? What has happened to me?"

"Too many things that should not have," she said. "The Temple is where and when we left it. We will return to rejoin the others soon."

I breathed shallowly through the pain. "Was the journey so difficult for you?" She seemed unharmed.

Ambra shook her head. "No. And it should not have been for you. Travel through the Orbs can be disorienting, especially the first time. But it is not painful." She sighed. "Unless there is interference."

"How can there be interference?"

"I am no longer the only one who manipulates space-time in our galaxy."

"The False Dawns."

"Yes. Their numbers grow, and so does the recklessness of their attacks."

"They are created that quickly? Don't they have to be raised like a normal person?"

"Yes, but not all in just one era. Our enemies have been patient. They *will* be patient. And their successors have sent back an army to destroy us in our time."

"An *army*? How many?"

She shrugged. "They can hide much from me now. I see only the warped edges of string-space where they have vandalized the Mind."

I didn't understand what she was saying. "Ambra, please, what do you mean?"

She frowned and pressed her body into mine, her arm looped now around mine. "These wormholes. These cloaking efforts. They are *obscene*. Because space-time and sentience are a unified field. Where there is one, there is the other. Where there is great intelligence, or a mass of minds, space-time is altered. Where there are great alterations in space-time, dynamic and structured—can you guess?"

I could, but the implications were insane. I caught my breath a moment, thinking through her words. But I felt so unafraid to speak to her. I did not fear her judgment, even in my stupidity and blindness. I felt only acceptance.

"There is…*a mind?*"

"Yes, Nitin!" she squeezed my arm again. "Of a kind. The very fabric of our universe is constantly stirring, cogitating, becoming. From its chaotic birth pangs to the great structures of our era until the singularity of equilibrium, it will grow and become in ways we will not understand for billions of years. Only at a time when our far descendants have grown together with the rest of intelligent life into a form that can communicate and understand this much more alien and powerful thought."

"But you understand it now?" Part of my mind wondered why I was even accepting this bizarre idea.

"To recognize it, to feel its living soul is very different from understanding it. But these reckless acts are wounding the structure of this mind. Creating lesions in the cosmic cortex."

"Why do they do it then?"

"Because they are like children. They cannot see, born and bred as instruments of war. They are horrible, but I pity them. I know what it is to be an object, Nitin, with no other value other than what purpose you can be to another. To be helpless while altered as others see fit, never understanding. Only knowing pain, fear, and self-loathing."

I felt my arms tighten around her waist. Her past was rote history for most of us. But not to her. I could see the pain of her enslavement etched in her face. "I'm sorry, Ambra."

The corners of her mouth twitched. "But what's driving them is something different. Much *darker*. Even the Dram do not understand the bargain that they have made to acquire this new power."

"The shadow forces?"

"The *Anti*. We pull them now, Nitin. Pull at them terribly for our ordering and our great growth through time. Our bias of the cosmic background. They will do all that they can to destroy us."

"Why? What are they?"

"Our inverses, Nitin. And no more. The shadow of our light, as for them, we are the shadow of theirs. Creatures we know little about. But now they have revealed themselves." She sighed at shook her head. "At least it is still small. Still localized. These clones are clumsy and stupid. Raised without love. Taught without wisdom. But there are so many."

My thoughts were racing around, trying to process the implications of these confusing words. "What about the Orbs? Don't they also damage this Mind?"

"That is what makes them so special. They don't. The Orbs *synergize* with it. They harmonize with it. They have been made with a purpose commingled with the cosmic mind. They are meant for far greater things than our simplistic use of them." She sighed and looked around the green seaside. Shadows from the alien trees danced across her face as the aurora undulated. The wind tasted fresh. "Even if that is what brought us here."

I looked around again. "Where are we?"

She smiled. "One of my favorite places in all the galaxy, dearest. We are orbiting a star on the outskirts of the Large Magellanic Cloud, a satellite galaxy of our Milky Way."

My mind searched through the extensive astronomical training required by the MECHcore. "That's hundreds of thousands of light years from Earth."

She nodded. "Fifty kiloparsecs."

"Ambra, how?"

"The Cloud is teeming with life. Some intelligent. So, there are also Orbs here." She smiled and gazed up at the swirling cornucopia of colors. Our Milky Way. "Isn't it beautiful, Nitin? I have come here many times over the last two centuries. It has been a place to escape the burden of all that I must do. All that is asked. A place to forget, if only for a moment, all the terrible destinies. But I grew tired of witnessing it alone. It grew harder and harder to wait for you, even in this heaven."

"Wait for me? You knew..." I stopped myself. Of course she knew. She was the Daughter. "You called my name in dreams," I whispered, memories flooding back. "You had never met me, but you called me *love* in the Temple hospital. You speak as if we have already lived our life together. You have seen everything already?"

She shook her red curls at me. "Not like you think. The broad outlines, the truth that one day you would come, yes, I knew. But the closer events come to me, in space, time, or heart—the more poorly I see. Blame quantum mechanics."

"I don't understand."

"Better to ask Waythrel. I don't understand the physics either. What's important is that I did not know when or what form you would take. I only knew you would come. But I could sense you, Nitin. Once you were born, I knew you had come. I sought you out and watched over you as you grew in India. I came to love you as a child at your grandmother's country home, as a young adult studying late into the nights to pass the Force entrance exams, as a grown man—brave, honest, and determined to find me."

I stared at her in wonder. She had seen my entire life. She had known about me for centuries.

"I came to you in Japan. And in the Sahara, I tended your bruised mind and learned to love every one of its imperfect contours."

"But Ambra—why? Yes, I was searching for you! If you knew this, why did you wait? Why make me search? Why have we wasted so much time?" The idea that I was alone—yet not alone—that so much of my life had passed by when we could have been together—it sent a wave of panic through me.

"It's not that simple, Nitin," she said, sadness in her eyes. "You are blind in ways I am not. If certain futures are altered, the ripples can become tsunamis. The fates of our galaxy always rest on my choices. I am never free of that. Even when—especially when—it concerns what is most dear to me. I've known nothing more painful than watching you in silence for decades, longing to reach out to you, play with you as a child, speak to you as a man. Feel your love for me openly." She looked into my eyes and squeezed my arm. A wistful look clouded her face. "It's funny. Chodak saw this two hundred years ago and shared his vision. I saw myself through *your* eyes. It was then that I knew the depth of your love, felt your soul adore me as I had never witnessed a man love a woman."

I swallowed. "Who was Chodak?"

She smiled sadly. "Someone long dead. A monk and powerful Reader. He forecast your coming to me. He told me we would be married."

My head was swimming even as my heart raced. "Ambra, please. *Please.* Everything with you is a mystery. Every time you speak with me, it is like the universe changes and I cannot keep up."

She pouted. "So you are saying that you do not want to marry me, Captain Ratava?" Her brows were wrinkled, her expression ridiculously charming.

"Ambra, I…" She continued to stare at me. I felt as if I were leaping into the dark. "Yes. Yes, in fact I do. But this is not exactly how I had pictured the subject coming up."

She threw her head back and laughed. Her shoulders shook as she brought it back down and nestled into my chest. I smelled her hair, and it was like a revelation. A thousand pathways in my brain must have lit to this simple olfaction. My eyes drank in the orange surrounding me, and instinctively, I reached up and stroked it, caressing the enormous bulge of skin over the top and back of her skull.

"Yes, my heart," she said, her laughter subsiding. Tears filled her blind eyes, and I knew from her face that they were tears of both joy and sadness. "You love even that. That deformity that no human animal should carry before her mate. Who would love such ugliness? And yet, you do."

I placed my hand on her face, softly stroking the left cheek with my hand. I stared into her eyes. I knew those eyes could not see into my own, yet her mind could Read the deepest place in my person. Her breath was warm in the cool air, tendrils of fog extending from her lips. My hand appeared nearly black alongside the whiteness of her skin. I cupped my hand and pulled her mouth to mine.

Kissing a goddess is to open not only your body to another, but also your soul. As our lips met, and the limbic thrill shot through my veins, a much stronger electricity rushed through my consciousness. As we held each other in this embrace on a distant world, our hands wild, exploring, our lips and tongues caressing, I felt the fingers of her mind pass gently over the contours of my consciousness.

Love should always a mixture of body and soul. But when you kiss a goddess, the greater ecstasy is in the soul.

I pulled back after a few moments. "Daughter. Of Time."

She did not laugh at my clumsy exclamation. A flame of passion possessed her features, but they were also imbued with sorrow. "Nitin, wait. You must know."

I ached as I stared into her eyes. "Know what, Ambra?" I only wanted to kiss her again.

Tears ran down her cheeks. "Our time together can only be short."

I nodded. "That's okay. We have an important mission. I understand." I found myself reaching for her again.

She pushed me back gently but firmly. "No. I don't mean now or here. Not because of the mission. Together, all paths end in darkness."

"What do you mean?"

"I can't see the details, but the broad form is all too clear." Her face was twisted in agony. "If you choose to be with me, it will set in motion events that cannot but end in tragedy."

"What tragedy?"

"Your certain death, my love." She was now perfectly still.

I looked away from her, my hands still on her shoulders. *My certain death?* As many times as I had faced death in battle or seen it in the casualties around me, it was hard to imagine my own death, my own nonexistence. And yet these words came from the Daughter. I looked back at her.

"And if we are not together?"

Her face tightened. "There are many futures on that path. But in most you will live a long life."

"Without you?"

She nodded. "Yes."

My words poured out instantly from deep within me. "Then it will be a long and empty torture. It will be living in the darkest prison." She looked at me with a strange pity. But my choice was easy. The easiest choice for death that I could imagine making. "So then—how long do we have?"

"Oh, Nitin." She held me tightly for a moment. "Do you want to know?"

I thought about this. If I knew, I might only focus on that date. Yes, I would obsess on that fate as the clock ticked down to the exclusion of what occurred around me. She was right. It was better that I not know the hour and live in the moment. With her.

"How will I die?"

"I don't know, Nitin. I can't see so near to myself—and you are as close as my own soul." She touched her fingertips to my temple. "But it will be terrible, my love. And it will be at the hands of our enemies. We will be shattered by betrayal. In the end, our humanity stolen forever. In return for this terrible price, I can give you so little. A short time, but a time when we will love as no one have ever loved."

She drew her face near mine. Our lips brushed as she spoke. "One short and beautiful dream for all the horror. I had to tell you. You must choose."

My throat caught. "My only horror is to leave you. If I am torn from you, tortured, killed—I can only die once. But to walk away, to live each moment alone, apart from you—that is a choice I can't make even once. And certainly not every moment of my life. That life is hell."

She wept and smiled. Her hands cupped my face, her fingers slipping over my scalp sending waves through me. Her body pressed against mine. I felt the swell of her breasts, the warmth of the life within her. I was surrounded by a sea of red.

"Then love me now and until our time ends."

21

*I submit to you that if a man has not discovered
something that he will die for, he isn't fit to live.*

—Martin Luther King, Jr.

We stepped out of the Orb projection into the
Temple center.

Again I was disoriented. Again the pain
racked my form. Ambra had tried to minimize the
discomfort, and while I suffered, it was far less than
before. I didn't ask why, as I was sure to misunderstand
it. I was just happy I was not to end up screaming in
agony and half dead on the ground again.

In fact, overall I felt better than I had in a long time.
Alive. Even *fulfilled*. To kiss a goddess is one thing. To
make love with her, something entirely different. Our
bodies were remarkably attuned to each other. I had no
explanation for it. Few couples find such physical
harmony so early on. Part of the joy and pain of coming
to know another person is just in this adapting to and
learning of another's body, communicating in intimately
personal and sensitive ways. Perhaps because of how we
had already entwined our consciousness, perhaps for
reasons I would only discover later, that harmony of

body was already present between us. If sex can be a religious experience purely on physical terms, then I had been born again.

But the physical ecstasy was the lesser of our oneness. I cannot tell you much about how our souls met, how her telepathic powers brought our consciousnesses together, and as we joined our bodies, joined our minds. It seemed an eon. A place beyond time. We met in a thousand memories, hers and mine. We bathed in a million desires and fears. Images. Music. Smells. We shuttled through the labyrinth of cognition like some ray of light through an evanescent maze, the walls painted in flickering ideas, until they mixed and touched so that the resonance began to remake the essence of each independent consciousness.

I was one person when I journeyed to that alien world overlooking the Milky Way. I left as someone else. In the process, my mind had been healed, purged of the lingering damage brought on by her clone, and continually remade in ways I would slowly come to understand.

We stepped out of the swirling colors and into the relative darkness of the Temple hand in hand.

Astonished faces greeted us.

The members of my team were talking animatedly with Waythrel and Mazandarani. Slowly, one by one, they noticed our presence from afar and turned to face us. It took a full minute for us to walk the distance across the Temple floor. In that time, none of the others uttered a sound.

We stopped in front of the group. "It is time," said Ambra.

"Wait a moment!" said Williams, her expression flabbergasted. "What the hell just happened? My brain is about to explode from drowning in a sea of information, and then I wake up, see the rest of these bozos waking up with me, but you two are *gone*. Vanished like magic. Then you reappear coming out of that *thing*?"

Moore laughed. "Holding hands like lovers in the park."

Waythrel was silent at the outburst. Mazandarani stared at our clasped hands, his expression devastated. I didn't know what to say.

Ambra took the lead. "You should be happy—Nitin can report back to you about travel through the Orbs. He has successfully completed the test flight." She smiled at the confused expressions around her. "You didn't think that we were going to travel by strings, did you?"

No one answered. Waythrel spoke. "It is far less efficient, and dangerous now that the Dram control much of the Time Tree. But Ambra can access the Orbs directly."

"Right," said Kim. "We just have to teleport through that thing." He stared wide-eyed at the kaleidoscope in the center of the chamber.

"It would be an honor, a great privilege, Daughter of Time," said Fox, and bowed her head.

"So, Captain, hell of a ride?" Moore asked.

I couldn't suppress a laugh. I nodded. "You have no idea."

"Wicked. I'm game. Don't even know where I'm going, but I'm not going to miss out on surfing that baby."

Ambra looked over the others. "The rest of you? You have the information. You know the purpose."

Williams nodded. "Something else, all that *sharing*. We should be using that at all the schools."

"Someday we will," said Ambra. "Most people aren't ready for it yet. But New Earth's Readers are learning from the Xix. Our planet is in the early stages of a group memory, soon to be a group awareness. A sum far greater than its parts that is slowly waking up."

"I remember," said Kim. "You're going to seal the Orbs!"

Moore looked over. "Seal them? What does that mean?"

Kim looked at a loss for words. "I saw it, but I'll be damned if I can explain it."

The alien spoke. "Ambra will reconfigure the local projections. The hyperspace filaments will be retracted. There will be no string on which to navigate. The node will be dead." Waythrel paused. "And while we are there, we will find out what we can about our enemies. If we are lucky, we might even run into them, or lure them to us."

"We?" asked Fox. "You're coming, too?"

"Your team seems to be short one member," said Ambra. "I have chosen Waythrel to fill the gap."

Williams objected. "Waythrel would not complete a team. The exercises are tuned for six soldiers. She would be an outlier."

Waythrel addressed her doubts. "In what will come, your previous training will have little relevance. We will not be a special forces operation. We will be a unique delegation serving as much or more as detectives than as soldiers, even if fighting may become necessary. I will fit well into this construction."

"Detectives?" asked Williams. "So why us? You don't need soldiers. Especially not with her." She gestured to Ambra.

"It's not about that, is it?" said Moore, his eyes squinted and sharp. "It's about *him* and about her. We're part of that puzzle. Part of the *vision.*"

"You are fated," said Ambra. "There is no other word for it. No other way to explain it."

"So can we choose to change our fate? Is that some kind of paradox?" asked Kim.

Ambra smiled. "Only because your minds limit what you can see. Each of your choices is free *and* preordained. The distinction between the two is artificial, like describing a tree as either soaring into the air or digging into the ground. Contradictory—yet both true, because a tree is much more than either conception. Each choice you make is really a family of choices that propagate through space and time to sum to your final reality. If you could see, truly see the essence of the fabric around us, you would understand that you actually will make *every* possible choice available to you. You are infinite even as you create finitude."

Williams shook her head. "I shoulda never put my name down for this crazy assignment." Fox beamed.

Ambra prodded me with a look. I turned to my team. "Suit up, metalheads!"

We donned our gear, the Xixian skins layering over our forms like some self-aware organism groping its way forward. The process took several minutes, with pauses to examine fit to check specs and performance.

Meanwhile, I watched Mazandarani walk up to Ambra. They were some ten feet away, but I could hear the exchange. The counselor paused in front of her, seeming at a loss for words.

"This fate is cruel, Sepehr," she said.

He didn't raise his head, but looked down at the ground. "You know my heart, Daughter of Time, so I can only be honest and agree." He seemed to move his mind to another topic. "But you also know my thoughts. Why do you take this risk?"

"I trust him, Sepehr. I *know* him. He will never hurt me."

"I only wish that you had omniscience. A little prescience is a dangerous thing."

She kissed his cheek. For a moment a wave of jealousy flowed through me, but it was quickly dissipated. Her expression was not desire. It was love. An affection and concern that I realized was even deeper than what I had feared. I felt ashamed.

"I will return, Sepehr. And he will be with me. I need you to prepare for our return and for the ceremony to follow."

"Why do you ask me for this?"

"Because you must walk this path or never be free. I am cruel, perhaps. But I care for you too much to have you enslaved anymore."

He nodded. "My fear is that I will disappoint you, Daughter. But your disappointment will not be from my failure to try. It will be as you asked." He stepped away.

Fox appeared before me, blocking my view to the conversation. "We're ready, Captain!"

I nodded, looking over my team. After what I had seen and experienced, I suddenly realized how ridiculous we were. Our little special forces crew wasn't much of a match for even a well-armed Dram attack force. What were a bunch of metalheads thinking to accomplish stepping through an Orb? Traveling through space and time? Perhaps meeting an enemy that even Ambra feared and none of us understood?

Waythrel had joined Ambra at the edge of the long pathway to the Orb projection. They motioned, and we followed. The walkway was lined on both sides with the creature-sized depressions. After our sharing with the Daughter, we knew that these were the seats of the other Readers who would telepathically connect with Ambra during the long meditation sessions when they formed a group mind of some nature.

Ambra had tried to share this experience with me during our unexplained absence, but I had understood little, even when she shared it telepathically. She had even admitted that it was hard for her to understand. The combined mentality of the group exceeded her own consciousness by such a degree that even she could grasp only bits and pieces of the insights when separated. I understood nothing, not even bits or pieces.

We reached the Orb. Ambra gestured toward it. "Step inside; it is perfectly safe." We walked inside followed by the alien and Ambra. "If you are ready, I will open the Orb."

I nodded, and the members of my group gave their assent in various ways. All looked nervous. All seemed excited.

Fox smiled. "Get ready for the trip of your life."

"Or the trip to our death," said Moore.

Ambra stared solemnly at them. "Both futures have already occurred."

And then, infinity exploded around us.

Part 2

Until you grasp the limitations of Entropy, you cannot understand the possibilities of Time.

—Wisdom of the Six Cities

22

How on earth did Descartes, who could not on prima facie evidence accept his existence as real, believe that his thinking was? This was the beginning of the dark ages of European philosophy.

—Yin Yutang

Water.

It dripped. It began in a plastic bag, puffed out, gleaming. A drop traveled through a valve, down clear tubing approaching a bedside, and there dove into an adaptor with a sharp needle at the end. The needle plunged into the pale skin of an arm.

Ambra's arm.

I sat at her beside. Her eyes were glassy, the sedative beginning to dull her senses. I held her hand. It was very cold.

"Nitin, I'm so glad you're here. I'm scared."

I looked around at all the hospital equipment, dumbfounded. "Where are we?"

She sighed with sleepiness. "Dreaming. We're dreaming again. Walking layers of awareness and walking and walking…" She trailed off.

As my thoughts began to clear, I studied her closely. She was younger. My mind slowly ground into gear, and I pieced together the facts from her life.

"This is when you were a prisoner on Earth. These are your surgeries, the ones that changed you forever."

The early teenager smiled wanly. "Yes, Nitin. My second surgery. The most terrible."

"The first wasn't?"

She shook her head slowly. Her words were slurred. "Nope. Nope. I thought they were going to *cure* me then. Take it out like they promised—right before they killed mom and dad. I was starting to go blind. That scared me. Nope. First surgery was fear and hope."

"The second?"

"Then I knew. Bastard *told* me. 'Making it bigger. You'll be blind soon; isn't this sooooooo cool?' Freaks R Us. Freaks R Us. Freaks R Us."

I waited for her to calm down. "So this time, you knew they weren't curing you. They were destroying you."

"Yeah. Sucks, huh?" She looked up at me and smiled. "You look *really* good. Well, almost blind here, but the me visiting this me knows. So many of me. Me, me, me clone me. Mmmmm, you smell good, too. Sound good. Bet you taste good."

"Ambra…."

"Going to fall *off* the world, Nitin. Drugs pushing me under the water and outside the universe. And I'll be just meat meat meat to them again. Cut, drill, screws, slice. I'm falling to black and sick at my stomach, and they are going to come with saws and drills and screws..."

Tears trickled down the sides of her face as she shook it back and forth. I squeezed her hand tightly and kissed it. "It's okay, Ambra. I promise you'll be okay. I'm here with you. I'm here with you the whole time."

Her green eyes flashed open. She gripped my arm tightly. "You promise?"

"Yes, of course I promise."

She relaxed and sank back into the pillow. "Then I'll sleep. And we'll go away. To a new place. I just don't know where..."

She closed her eyes again and began to breathe deeply. The breaths became rhythmic, louder, pulsing and grasping my attention so completely that before I could realize it, everything had faded around me. The hospital room, Ambra, even her hand.

Only that constant rhythm.

I had thought it was her breath—but she wasn't here. But the rhythm was here still. Pulsing. Beating.

Rushing.

—

Water.

It sounded like a giant waterfall or storm wind through the trees. White noise. Deafening. The sound was focused in front of me. The blurring was decreasing. I was seeing.

Masses of naked men and women cowering against a wall. Robots darting about blasting high-pressure water against them. People struggling to get in front of someone to ward off the pain.

Those who could. Many just lay there on the floor or crawled slowly away from the machines. These were hardly people anymore.

It was the smuggler's ship where the Daughter had almost died. Interstellar merchants who drove their human cattle until they dropped. They bought those who had scored poorly in the Dram sorting. My Ambra's deformity had not been recognized for what it was, and she was scored poorly. She was defective, cheap goods. Bought by smugglers who nearly killed her before the Xix raided the ship.

I scanned the row of screaming and blistered slaves. *There*. Near the far corner crouching into a ball. A mass of red, unkempt, tangled hair that ran down from a bald top.

I rushed over, the water not touching me, the robots unconcerned. "Ambra!"

I knelt down beside her. I hardly recognized her face. She was shivering badly. Her pale skin was so thin that the blood vessels decorated her like some demonic henna art. Muscles and fat were gone. Only transparent skin over a skeleton.

This was what happened to Ambra from the history books and in the art of our age. But all that didn't prepare me for what it was like to be in the presence of near-death starvation. It was horrible.

"Go, Nitin," she whispered faintly. I bent closer to hear. "Don't see me like this. Let me die."

Dreams within dreams. She had said I experienced her childhood home because it was close to her heart. I was in the hospital because she was deathly afraid and called to me. And now I was here.

"I won't go. I love you, and you are going to survive this. You know you do. I know you do. Remember that. I don't know where in time and space or your memories we are, but I'm going to stay with you."

She was too weak to answer verbally, but as I cradled her, the fingers of the sticklike hand on my shoulder pressed meekly.

"Good. Don't talk, Ambra. Just feel me here. I'm here I'm here I'm here," I said, rocking her in my arms.

"Don't stop," she managed to mouth silently.

"I won't."

And I sat there on that floor filthy with human waste and dirt, rocking the wrecked form of my beloved, over and over through what seemed to be an ever-slowing rate of the passage of time. Rocking her nearly weightless body pressed to me like a crumbled paper bag. Rocking back and forth, stronger and stronger, until we drowned out the screams around us, silenced the roar of water.

They became muffed sounds. Beeping of equipment. Darkness in the rocking. Or was it floating?

Yes, floating in a dark sea. Water everywhere.

—

Water.

The older dreams. Back in this awful place. But these dreams had never had water before. Even when I was floating, there was only darkness. Numbness. Emptiness.

And stars.

But now I could see it. *Water.* A faint light seemed to grow from the giant sea around me. It was a faded color, pulsing. Inorganic. Without life or sense of purpose. Just—rhythm.

But it shone through water. Of this I was sure. I knew I should be seeing the maze of the Orb light. I was traveling somewhere. There were all these facts and truths and things just beyond my ability to grasp them, hold them, focus on them before they bled out in a rainbow of colors and dissolved into the green.

My mind thrashed wildly trying to hold onto...*what?* I was a soldier. I was on a mission. I had loved a woman, the only woman, the only woman in the universe centering my life and hopes. I held her hands and I rocked her to peace and she is red and white and soared through the clouds of a nebula and a beach where I made love to her looking up at our galaxy in a night breeze.

Things that must be true but now gone and only existing as belief in my devolving memory of dream, fading in this throbbing greenness, this water of death.

I tried to move. *I saw!* Motion. Blurred. A hand! I had a hand! Again I flailed my arm, but it only achieved a weak waving, a sickly motion in the mossy ocean. But I saw it again. There was form. *I had form.* Form in water.

But there was no exit, no way to wake from this nightmare. Nothing but stasis and wetness and flailing, feeble limbs. Endless green water.

Nitin, come back.

Ambra? I called in my thoughts. *Ambra, please. I'm lost!*

Beside my chest, there was a brightness. A vortex of light spun in the middle of the water. I peered into its center, the point elongating from the edges, drilling deep into a third dimension. Soon, it seemed that I was looking down a long tunnel.

You aren't lost. Only displaced.

The tunnel pulled me. I felt myself drawn slowly through the green water, the vortex growing, the light from another space flowing into the dark sea around me, brightening. Soon I felt myself spinning, following the strange undulations of the turbulent light, accelerating to greater and greater velocities. Around and around and around until there were only star trails of radiance.

I left the sea and entered the swirling tunnel, buffeted, flipped, stretched, and pulled forward relentlessly, a billion suns and years and parsecs flying by my awareness.

Plunging through the light and out of the tunnel. Free. *Free!* Floating free above a great and terrible world of blue. Horizon to horizon blue. Enormous. Endless.

Water.

23

Innumerable suns exist; innumerable earths revolve around these suns in a manner similar to the way the seven planets revolve around our sun. Living beings inhabit these worlds.

— a heresy of Giordano Bruno,
burned at the stake in 1600

So much water.

I lay on my side, my breath coming in shivering gasps. The floor below me, the walls pressing against my forehead—were invisible. Like perfectly clear glass without back reflection, absorbing no moisture from my breath in condensation, never smudging from the oils of my skin. A technology that did not exist.

Underneath me was—nothing. Darkness and stars. Behind me, I felt the bright radiance of light. Because of the planet before me, I knew it must be from a star. We had arrived at Orferlin: planet without land.

I rolled slowly onto my back and gazed up at a group of faces. The alien, Waythrel, monstrous and still. The members of my team. And Ambra. She knelt down beside me.

"Welcome back, love."

I pulled myself up to a sitting position, the low friction in this strange bubble disconcerting. I felt unsure of my motions. I rubbed my temples. "I thought you said this wouldn't happen again."

"I know." She sounded apologetic. "It was a massive problem, interference from our enemies. I was prepared for something, but nothing so intense."

"They knew we were coming," said Waythrel.

I looked around at my team. They seemed okay, but I needed to make sure.

"What happened? Anyone else hurt?" I pulled into a ball, and placing my hand on the nonexistent wall, pushed myself up. I could stand in the bubble. My feet appeared to be planted on nothing. But that nothing held me up.

"No," said Waythrel. "You are the only one who suffered any deleterious effects."

"That doesn't make sense."

"Captain's a little soft, is all," laughed Moore.

"It's not the first time," said Ambra. "He's being targeted. Because of me."

Waythrel looked on in silence. Williams stepped toward us. "And just *who* is targeting us? More of those clones?"

"Thousands of them," said Ambra, her expression troubled.

"*Thousands?*" asked Kim.

"Their numbers have risen considerably."

"How can there be more? Where are they coming from?" asked Fox.

Waythrel spoke. "From many spaces and many times. There is a growing convergence. A massing of the troops, if you will."

"I'm sorry, Nitin," said Ambra. "It was more than I was ready for. An ambush."

"So how the hell did they know we were coming?" asked Williams.

"The same way they found us in the desert," answered Waythrel. "We have been infiltrated. There is a spy among us."

"Whoa—*us*? Time out, okay?" said Kim. "Others besides us knew we were coming. What about that counselor? He seemed pretty unhappy with the group. Especially the captain."

"Or even Major Mizoguchi," said Williams. "She's not Force. She works for the Temple only now. That's unusual. Maybe she's there for a purpose. Don't turn on us just because we're the new recruits!"

"Sergeant Moore refused to share with the Daughter," said Waythrel.

The sounds of ion chargers filled the space as Moore's suit lit up. "You look here, squid-head. I didn't watch my mates torn apart by Dram soldiers on Dworn to listen to this shit. Put up or shut up."

Ambra shook her head, staring at Waythrel. "Enough. There are many possibilities, including many we haven't likely thought of. Mazandarani and Waythrel suspect a mole. But there are forces gathering with powers I haven't yet probed fully. Moore is right. We have no reason to doubt one another. More importantly—we are going to need one another if we are to complete this mission. Distrust will poison us."

Purge your minds of it.

I felt it as a mental slap. So did the others. Ambra was angry, and it was the first time I had felt that anger. It was frightening as much for her power as for how much she was holding back.

"I said I don't want anyone in my head!" shouted Moore.

"Then power down your weapons unless you are going to engage our enemies," said Ambra forcefully.

I saw his mouth tighten, and he eyed her harshly. But it wasn't a look of hatred. He was sizing her up. There was respect in his eyes. The humming ceased as his suit switched off.

"Now we have a task to complete," she said.

"Ambra, where are we?" I asked. Too much was unexplained.

"Orferlin," cut in Williams. "You shared, right? Dolphin world."

"I know the planet and the facts. I remember," I said with some annoyance. I gestured to the invisible bubble around us. "I mean *this*. What is this? An advanced ship? Is it from the Xix?"

Waythrel spoke. "No, Captain. This is beyond the ingenuity of the Xix."

"It's my doing," said Ambra. "A distortion and warping of space-time. There is in three-space room to carry us and also the ability to expand or contract in multiple hidden dimensions, providing volume enough for weeks of air, munitions, food. Anything we need we have brought with us from New Earth."

"Toilets?" asked Moore.

"With privacy, Sergeant, in case you are shy," answered Ambra with a grin.

Moore smiled back.

"Also, quite defensive," said Waythrel. "Outside of an overpowering clone attack, there are no weapons the Dram possess that can harm us."

"And what of those *Anti*?" asked Fox.

"We will see," said Ambra. "For now, we need to find out what we can from the inhabitants. Once we've investigated, we seal this node of the Time Tree. We have two more stops to go before we are done."

24

What makes planets go around the sun? At the time of Kepler some people answered this problem by saying that there were angels behind them beating their wings and pushing the planets around an orbit. As you will see, the answer is not very far from the truth. The only difference is that the angels sit in a different direction and their wings push inward.

—Richard Feynman

The descent to the planet surface was unlike anything I had ever experienced. Without a view screen, a hologram—*without walls*—it was as if we were falling freely from the edge of space. The enormous expanse of water grew before us until it eclipsed our peripheral vision. I instinctively pressed against the invisible walls of the bubble, the unnecessary pressure providing some feedback to my anxious nervous system that we were stable, that we weren't pitching forward through the atmosphere with nothing to support us. I noticed several members of my team doing the same thing.

The ride was also disturbingly smooth. As we broke into the atmosphere, there was no shudder. No turbulence. Nothing to indicate we were in fact moving relative to the planet at all. Only that the darkness of space receded, the clouds swam over us, and the water continued to expand before our eyes.

We even plunged into a gigantic storm dwarfing anything that occurred on New Earth. Orferlin was at least three times the size of our planet, with more than ten times the surface water. So much moisture and a tropical temperature cooked up some continent-sized tempests. Straight into the heart of one of these beasts we flew, all light quickly disappearing, the new night interrupted by colossal bursts of lightning. It seemed like the innards of a nuclear explosion.

Yet, silent. Eerily silent and still. The rain poured over our enclosure without the sound of a drop. The lightning was never accompanied by thunder. The bubble had not a single tremor in the midst of this powerful display of nature.

"It is so quiet," I whispered.

"You wish to hear it, Nitin?" asked Ambra.

"Yes. Can you do that?"

She nodded.

I looked around to the others. "If that's okay with everyone."

No one protested. I looked at Ambra, and she smiled. *Then listen!*

Suddenly the bubble exploded in sound. Howling winds were accompanied by stunning crackles of lightning that were swallowed by the deepest bone-rattling bass ripples of thunder I had ever heard. The bubble was still moving peacefully through this, but somehow, Ambra had allowed the sound to penetrate. It made the worst thunderstorm on New Earth seem like a drizzle.

"By the Daughter," whispered Fox, her eyes wide.

"Beats anything I've ever seen," echoed Kim.

The tempest roared around our little bubble as we continued our rapid descent. The trajectory was angular, so as we neared the bottom of the storm system, we cleared its shadow and left it seething to our left and behind us. Suddenly, we were bathed in a bright light from the local star. The ocean lay beneath us, extending in all directions to the horizon. As we decreased our altitude, the crests of waves became visible to our eyes. At first they were seemingly no different from those of Earth's seas, but as we neared the surface of the water and could use ourselves as a reference point, the true size of these giants became apparent. Larger than the greatest Pacific waves, these on Orferlin were like small mountains that loomed before our bubble, often blocking out the light and then breaking over us with great noise and drama outside, yet causing no disturbance to us at all.

This planetary ocean was *loud*. Everything you might expect from an Earth ocean multiplied by one hundred. Like small mice in a storm at sea, we stood speechless before the power of it.

"So, we go swim with the dolphins, huh?" asked Moore.

Ambra smiled. "I wish we could. The Brax aren't really very much like our world's sea mammals. They have something more like gills than lungs. Theirs is such a strange and rich culture; it stems from a distributed nervous system with more than ten brain-nodes across their bodies. Makes it almost impossible to damage them in such a way as to render their mental faculties deeply impaired. And the brain-nodes recombine in space-time to form the most beautiful patterns of thought. Their Readers are second only to the Xix of the aliens in our galaxy." She seemed to be lost a moment, as if remembering or searching the planet for signals from the sea creatures. "I wish we had the time to spend…" Her face clouded suddenly.

"Ambra, what's wrong?" I asked. She almost looked to be in pain.

She took my hand. "Something's wrong here." She stared off into space, trembling. "Something has happened to Orferlin."

"What?" asked Williams. We all stared toward the bright, blue world in front of us.

"Something terrible."

We hovered over a scene of destruction. The Brax inhabited underwater cities engineered from coral-like substances that they had long ago learned to modify and employ as building materials. Depending on the density of the coral, they were able to build to various depths. These floating, submerged metropolises had housed billions of their kind, their entire civilization powered by solar, water, and fusion energies. My mind had strong images from the sharing with Ambra of the intricacy and beauty of their curvilinear constructions, tunnels, and filigree spanning miles and dwarfing our largest land-based cities.

Now all I saw was ruin. Floating on the surface were the blasted remains of the coral masterpieces. Fragments floated like a snowstorm of shattered china from a distance. Diving below the sea, we saw other structures that had sunk to varying depths. Ambra sped the bubble around the globe at blinding velocities, verifying that this carnage was not isolated but planetwide. Nowhere was there any sign of life, any sign that the Brax were anything but utterly exterminated.

"Looks like the Dram, all right," said Williams. "Fuckers like nothing better than a good genocide to make a point."

"But they usually just like to roast the whole planet," said Fox. "But Orferlin is fine."

"Not exactly fine," said Moore.

Waythrel spoke. Its voice was subdued. "Ambra, is there nothing you can detect? No sign of the Brax at all?"

Ambra was crouched in a meditative position, her legs crossed with her arms on her knees. Her eyes were closed.

"There is more than an absence, Waythrel," she said, her concentration unwavering. "There is an interference. A poison in space and time."

"Wait, what does that mean?" asked Kim.

"I don't know," said Ambra. "I've never felt anything like it. Just to be here is to feel it sickening my thoughts."

Waythrel spoke. "Then maybe this is not the Dram."

"No, Waythrel, it isn't. This is something else. We shouldn't stay here very long unless we can undo what is causing this. But first I will need to understand it."

"Well, if supergirl here doesn't know what's going on, I agree," said Moore. "Let's pull back until we have some idea what we're dealing with."

"Not yet!" cut in Ambra. Her face was strained. "In this poisonous cloud, there is a signal. Faint. Fading." A sorrow came over her face. "*Caga.* I hear her."

"Caga?" I asked.

Waythrel answered. "A powerful Reader of the Brax. We often communed with her from the Temple."

"*From* New Earth?" asked Fox with awe.

"Distance is deceptive," said Waythrel.

The bubble accelerated out of the sea and burst over the water's surface, darting like a missile toward the northern regions. We were moving so quickly that I soon could not process the images outside, which had blurred into a single, multicolored brushstroke on either side of us. In front and behind were small circles in focus.

"She is calling us," Ambra whispered. "And she is dying."

25

I hear the approaching thunder that, one day, will destroy us too. I feel the suffering of millions.

—Anne Frank

We found Caga near the pole of the planet.

The destruction seemed complete here, as well, but somehow the creature had survived within a spacecraft. The ship was floating without power on the waves, and Ambra had brought our bubble up to it. Nestled alongside a craft as big as an island, she projected a bizarre filament toward the walls of the ship. To our complete amazement, the tunnel passed right through the walls, and as we looked down the passageway, it was clear—the wall did not cross into the space, although Ambra insisted it had not been destroyed.

"The tunnel is outside of the space of the wall," she explained as we followed her down the corridor, the walls completely transparent, the inside of the ship open to us.

The reverse of a human ship, the chambers inside were all water filled for these sea creatures, except for a few rooms where damage had occurred and air flowed in. However, our tunnel created no damage. No air flowed in along our path. We were surrounded by water and a water-functional technology that glowed faintly around us.

We walked for ten minutes until we came to a central cavity in the ship, a giant chamber that appeared to be some gathering place the size of a sports stadium. Thousands of bizarre sea creatures floated randomly about.

The best a human mind could do was map their form to New Earth's sea creatures. The physics of water flow dictated streamlined forms, fins of some kind, but within those design constraints, evolution had a lot of room to operate. The "fins" of the Brax were more like webbed tentacles, making the creatures seem as much like squid or octopuses as dolphins. They possessed visual and auditory organs across their bodies. Without the centering of the neural system at one end of the body, their forms were free to house them around the many brain-nodes spread throughout their elongated torso. Without a directionality, their appendages could easily accelerate them in any direction. I imagined that it would have been amazing to watch them swim.

But there was no motion here. All were lifeless and floated along the currents and turbulence in the dead ship. All but one.

The tunnel Ambra had constructed ended at a medical pod, and a single Braxian creature was suspended with numerous tubes penetrating its body. The visual organs, looking like multifaceted gem faces, moved slowly and tracked our approach.

"Caga," whispered Ambra as the tunnel stopped directly in front of the dying creature. She placed her hand against the side of the bubble, and the bubble flowed outward. She extended her arm until the surface of the space-time distortion fit it like a tight glove or skin, and she stroked the side of the creature. Ambra closed her eyes, and Waythrel stood strangely still, its eyestalks wrapped around themselves like a braid.

"I can speak with her telepathically. She has consented for me to share with you as I do so, if you wish to participate."

I looked across my team as we each traded glances. Finally, all our eyes settled on Moore.

"Ah, fuck it. Okay," he said. "There isn't going to be anything but fucked up on this trip. Blast away, girl."

Suddenly, it was as if viewports were opened in my mind, and through them I could see—or rather sense—the thoughts of others: my team, the incomprehensible images from Waythrel, the partially understandable thoughts of the creature, Caga, and of course, dominating all impressions, Ambra herself.

You must leave our world. It is not safe.

The creature's thoughts were foggy, whether because I had trouble parsing them or because of its decaying physical state.

Ambra responded. *I know. We are okay for now. Whatever is happening, I can deflect its effects for a time.*

You will grow weary, Ambra.

Yes. And you do not have much time, dear Caga. Please, tell us what you can so that we may begin to understand.

The creature's eyes swam across its body, but its thoughts were strong.

The Dram came. Once to claim the Orb strings and guard them. The Time Tree is compromised. We thought we were spared worse. But five Orferlin cycles ago—several weeks your time—they returned. They laid waste to everything.

Images of the terrible Dram armada flashed through my mind—explosions, the deaths of billions, and the emotions of a species watching itself die. A cataclysm. It was nearly too much. So much horror and pain. I tried to block it out but could not. I'm not sure how much time passed as the images ran through me, but it was likely only a moment.

But of course they could not kill all of us. But the Dram armada departed. Then the Anti came.

The shadowed ships flowed out from the Orb strings like a polluted tide. Black spots like flies separated from the main contingent of ships and stationed themselves equidistant across the planet. Then the madness came.

The Anti left these drones, and returned to the strings and were gone. There is something dark in those machines.

The poison. Ambra's thoughts were a warm light in this sea of strangeness.

Yes. As we tried to salvage our people, all things began to fail. Technology decayed. We lost our power, our machines. Everything. Within days, nothing functioned. Then, our minds. The weakest-minded of us went first. Forgetfulness. Unreason. Finally, madness. As Readers, a few of us could defend our minds longer from the ravages. I lasted the longest, because my ship returned from space and was in orbit for the assault. I landed after the slaughter, lucky to have escaped immediate destruction. A last group of medics sought to lessen the effects by trial and error and have me attached to numerous therapies. They are all dead. They only have delayed the inevitable. I am so glad that you have come.

I felt a terrible sadness flow from Ambra. *Caga, no.*

You must, Ambra, or you will condemn me to the same terrible fate. There is no time to save my world or to save me. You and Waythrel have my memories. You must take them, use them, and find a way. You must leave before this poison overwhelms you.

I felt the seemingly infinite complexity of Waythrel's mind engage. *Ambra, Caga is right. We cannot risk staying here any longer. She cannot be moved. She will be enveloped in madness by tomorrow.*

I don't know how Waythrel knew this, but I couldn't process most of the thoughts and images coming from its mind. Just trying to read its thoughts was painful. But I saw Ambra's shoulders slump.

Then there was a human thought interspersed.

What if we can destroy the drones in orbit?

It was Fox. I could sense it from the personality. I felt her mind racing, an empathy for both the dying alien and the pain of the Daughter driving her thoughts like a whip.

Caga responded. *It is likely impossible. We tried to send what forces we had left. They did not return.*

I could feel Fox's mind dismiss the objection. *But you were weakened, your technology decaying. Ambra can protect us. We are soldiers. We can send a small team, to avoid risk to the others, and try.*

I don't know if I can protect you. It was Ambra. *The toxicity becomes stronger nearer the source. I can see it in the odd patterns in space-time. Almost the erasing of patterns.*

But Fox was undeterred. *But maybe we can! Then it would stop, and we might be able to save her!*

Unlikely, responded Waythrel.

We have to try!

"I'll go," spoke Kim out loud. His thoughts also conveyed his determination.

I looked over at the two. "Are you both sure of this?"

Waythrel spoke. "It is too dangerous."

Caga's thoughts were strong. *It is too late for me. I am sure of it. But for you, for others — the risk may be worthwhile. To know if there can be an engagement with these devices.*

Even if the answer is negative, you can take that answer and the details of the failure with you to devise countermeasures.

Waythrel's eyestalks uncoiled, and several eyes pivoted toward Fox and Kim. "It is probable that you both will die."

Kim's suit powered up. A second later, Fox's did as well. Kim smiled. "Well, the Daughter has protected us from equipment failure so far. Guns still good."

Fox spoke. "Besides, every engagement has probabilities of death in this war. And I have faith in Ambra Dawn."

You have love for me, Erica Fox. And trust. I thank you, but you have more trust in me than I deserve.

"Humble to the end," Fox said, smiling.

"There is a last consideration," said Waythrel. "Caga spoke that the Dram returned to destroy the world when initially they had spared it. Orferlin poses no risks to the Dram—it has always been a peaceful world riding the currents of the galactic struggles. Why destroy it? The node was secure. Why even spend the resources? And why in a time frame nearly identical to when we ourselves planned this mission?"

There was a long silence. Williams ended it. "The traitor again? You think details of the mission were leaked. You think this is sabotage."

"I am raising the possibility," said Waythrel.

"If so, then it could also be a trap," I said.

"There's no way to know, and meanwhile, this world is dying." Kim looked at me. "Sir, do we have permission?"

And now I had to make a choice: whether to send them to a likely death that they ignored in their bravado or to deny them their bravery and the chance for us to know more about our enemy's terrible weapons. If something happened to them, I would be the one responsible for their deaths.

"Permission granted, soldiers. Ambra, can you take us up to one of them?"

I felt a resignation in Ambra. She broke off the sharing and paused several minutes. She seemed to be communing in private with the aliens. Then she opened her eyes, stood up, and walked toward my team.

"We will try, then."

The tunnel wrapped about us closely like plastic wrap and pulled itself out of the alien ship at high speeds. We merged with the main bubble again and the enclosure rocketed upward faster than a starship toward the blackness and stars.

26

I know there is a God because in Rwanda I shook hands with the devil. I have seen him, I have smelled him and I have touched him.

— Lieutenant-General Roméo Dallaire

We could all feel it as the dark object came into view.

It came on as a combination of fatigue and disorientation, like a flu without the fever. Moore expressed it best with his distinctive flair.

"Feels like the worst fucking hangover I've ever had."

Ambra piloted the bubble purely on her sense of the thing. We had no equipment, no scanners, *no ship*, but I doubt that any technology we or our allies had could measure and detect this thing. It was like a hole in the night. At this distance, it appeared to be a sphere of unlight at least twice the size of our bubble.

Ambra looked over at Moore. "There is an essence to this thing that is against everything I understand. It's like the very nature of the object is antithetical to understanding itself. I don't dare go any closer. I may not be able to protect all of us if this gets much stronger."

I looked over toward Fox and Kim, who stood together, gazing into the emptiness. "This thing looks bad. No shame in dropping the mission."

I could see fear in their eyes but also determination. Fox spoke for them. "Hell there isn't. Since when do we back down from the enemy?"

"When there is nothing to be won. We outthink it, come back better prepared."

"But that's just it, Captain," said Kim. "We don't even know enough to run away yet. Time we found out more."

They were set on it. I nodded. "Ambra, can you make separate bubbles for Kim and Fox, maintain a link like that tunnel on Orferlin and pull them back if things get bad?"

Ambra shook her head. "I can try. But it might be that this force will sever the connection. I might not be able to bring them back."

"Well, then we'd better make sure we kick its ass," said Kim, the pitch-changing hum of his ion slingers sounding. Waythrel made no comment.

"I don't like this," said Moore. "Very bad feeling. Whatever this thing does, it's like some fucking crime against the universe."

Ambra startled and looked at him. "Yes, sergeant. That is *exactly* how it feels to me. A crime not against us, not fundamentally. But against the very structure of our existence. Against anything that could possibly be us."

"Don't mess with it." Moore stared fixedly at Fox and Kim.

"Damn, Moore, never figured you to be the one to chicken out," said Kim.

"I think he's right," echoed Williams, nodding toward Moore.

Fox rolled her eyes. "Now you, too."

Williams turned to me. "It's the wrong call, Captain. Gut tells me so."

The weight of this decision was becoming enormous. "Waythrel, you were cautioning us before. What is your feeling now that you see it?"

The tall alien seemed to shudder. "There is death in that thing. An unlife, perhaps is a better phrase. It has killed a world. But Caga was not wrong. If we are to face this challenge, we need information. There is only one way to obtain it."

Kim nodded. "Right on! Then it's settled, yeah? 'Cause I'm getting a little nuts debating this here."

"Ambra?" I was desperate for surety.

"My vision is obscured beside this thing. I cannot follow the possible paths. But the endings hold more death than life."

Fox engaged the helmet, and the mechanism grasped her skull and assembled over it. Her words came out from the speakers, amplified and artificial. "Life through action!" Kim followed suit.

"Okay, but we're yanking you back at the first sign of trouble." Little did I know, we would never get that chance.

They lined up against the wall facing the death drone, and Ambra carved out a separate space for each of them. Two bubbles detached from the main enclosure and floated out toward the device. Every hundred meters or so, Ambra would test the connection and pull them backward to ensure that she still had control over their capsules.

Fox and Kim were continuously reporting back. Their sense of sickness in body and mind increased, but they reported that it was manageable.

"Might need to hurl soon," said Kim, "but otherwise okay."

"I'm having some visual problems," Fox said. "Can't focus on the thing. Can't keep it centered in my vision either."

"Yeah, me too," said Kim. "Don't know how we're going to shoot it like this. Telemetry's gone all funky." There was a pause. "Hell, the whole HUD is flanking out on me."

"Then we pull you back," I said, looking at Ambra. She was sitting again, focusing intensely on maintaining the projections despite the disturbances from the drone.

"Wait, not yet," said Kim. "Hard to see, but I'm making out some structure, finally. It looks like—"

And then, it was like a switch was thrown. A harsh static sounded over my communications and I saw both their suits darken. It seemed the power had suddenly been lost, even though they carried their own mini reactors embedded in the chassis. Simultaneously, both bodies dropped to the bottom of their enclosures. Neither moved.

Ambra cried out, "A pulse!" She gasped. Then I felt it too, as if my eyes were being driven into my skull with knives. I crouched to one knee and tried to stay conscious.

"Ambra, get us out of here!" shouted Waythrel.

Through eyes squinting in pain, I looked out of the bubble and saw that we were indeed speeding away from the thing. I was glad to see that Kim and Fox were still in tow.

The destructive power of the device definitely decreased with distance, but there was more to it than that. Off to my right, the Orb grew bright. As bright as the system's star from this distance. As the radiation bathed us, it countered the effects. Ambra steered the bubble closer to the Orb, and soon things were back to normal. Or so it seemed until we pulled Fox and Kim back into the enclosure.

I've seen horrors on the battlefield. Flechette injuries and deaths that are almost inconceivable—something your mind can't envision and only direct experience can convey. But I wasn't prepared for what we brought in.

Kim and Fox—they were dead. More than dead, gutted. Dissolved. *Unmade* in a fashion that no weapon I had experienced could achieve. The MECHcore suits, these highly designed products of superior Xixian technology—they looked like ancient artifacts discovered in some tomb aged ten thousand years. The very structure of the metals and plastics seemed to be coming apart. Disintegrating. There weren't words for it. Matter just didn't behave this way.

As for the human bodies, the effects were grisly. Decayed metal and plastic is one thing, flesh and bodies something else. Their remains oozed out of the pocked holes in the wrecked suits like a tomato purée. The biochemical bonds holding tissues, bone, and cells together seemed to have failed completely. There was nothing recognizably human in their appearance at all. That demonic device had removed all semblance of an organism from them and reduced the two members of my team to a homogenized form of their constituent ingredients.

"Captain, what the *fuck*?" hissed Moore, his face strained, green and sick looking. The smell began to hit us.

Williams looked away and held her hand to her mouth. We all instinctively stepped back from the sight. Several moments passed as we stood in shock.

I was gobsmacked. I found myself stammering. "Dear God. I don't know." I felt Ambra wrap her arms around me from behind.

"I'm so sorry, Nitin. I'm sorry I was right and could not stop it."

I held her hands tightly. I felt like a child comforted simply by the warmth and physical presence of another. I had seen that monsters were real in this universe, but I had never seen something so monstrous occur in it.

Waythrel alone seemed composed. "We will have to deal with your sorrow and examine these developments later. We have more urgent matters to attend to."

"Jesus, squid!" yelled Moore, flashing a wild look at the alien. "The Orb strings can wait a few minutes!"

"Yes, I'm sure that they can," answered Waythrel. "But I don't think that the Dram warship approaching us will."

27

The observed macroscopic irreversibility is not a consequence of the fundamental laws of physics, it's a consequence of the particular configuration in which the universe finds itself. In particular, the unusual low-entropy conditions in the very early universe, near the Big Bang. Understanding the arrow of time is a matter of understanding the origin of the universe.

—Sean Carroll

We followed the alien's outstretched arm, the twelve digits pointing into space twitching with a suppressed anxiety. The warship was Dram all right. Huge, rendering our small bubble an ant beside an elephant. And ugly in that way all the Dram warcraft appeared to me. Possessed of an inherent malice from even the point of design, the sharp edges seemed more like blades, the terraced, bulky levels like prison floors, the surface pitted and etched as if from acid. The weapons arrayed fore and aft required no hateful intention to convey their purpose.

"A trap!" yelled Williams.

"Looks like it," I said.

I turned to Ambra. She had gone to kneel over the bodies, the pool of remains spreading and nearly wetting her black robes. But the seeping sludge slowed and then stopped. Then the two forms seemed to float away from the main enclosure in their own external bubble.

"Ambra, we need to do something."

She stood up and nodded. "The bodies are in a time stasis that will preserve them until we can examine carefully what has happened." She walked forward and stood beside Waythrel. "Only this ship?"

"Yes," said the alien. "It should not pose a danger."

"Unless they are employing the technology that destroyed Orferlin and killed Nitin's soldiers."

"Do you think that's possible?" I asked. Everyone looked anxiously toward Ambra.

"I am unsure of everything, now," she said. "But something tells me that it would be as deadly to the Dram as to us. For now, we assume they are armed as usual."

Bright trails erupted from the ship. Waythrel spoke. "And so far, they respond predictably. Incoming missiles!"

We were sitting ducks. As soldiers, nearly useless. We could only stand there and watch.

Ambra raised her arms, her bright green eyes disappearing behind closing lids. "Then we respond to them as always."

The Orb flashed. Tendrils of light erupted from the sphere and crossed the distance to us before I could blink. They wrapped themselves around the missiles and detonated them harmlessly before they arrived. Before I could process what happened next, the Dram fired beam weapons, unloading on us nearly everything that they had. At least ten different rays were aimed at our bubble, the coherent light dizzying only meters from my face, yet stopped in their tracks by offshoots of the light tendrils from the Orb.

After nearly twenty seconds of full burn, the Dram wised up and decided not to completely drain their power supplies. They had thrown everything at us, enough firepower to blow up and melt down entire cities on New Earth. We were not scratched. The ship arced violently away from us.

"Chickenshit bastards!" cried Williams.

"They're rabbiting, all right," laughed Moore. "Damn, I've heard what you could do with those things, sister, but, well, *damn!*"

"We're going to board them," said Ambra. "And find out what the hell is going on around here."

"Board them?" asked Williams. The ship was already aligning its panel of engines toward us, readying for a string jump. "Well, first you gotta *stop* it!"

The large tendrils opened into sheets of light. The membranes flowed around the Dram warship, surrounded it. The engines fired, the ion blasts distorting the light around the hull. But it went nowhere. The monstrosity belching forth more power than half the New Earth navy couldn't move.

Williams shook her head. "Guess I had that one coming."

Ambra opened her eyes. I have to say that for the first time, even after that battle in the Sahara, I nearly felt the religious awe so many knew. The raw power of what she controlled almost compelled worship in feeble creatures of flesh and blood. But as I looked into those eyes, that awe was eclipsed by love. That all-consuming worship not of her divinity, but of her person. My lover. My beautiful and terrible and sad Ambra Dawn.

The bubble sped toward the paralyzed Dram war boat. Her plan was a good one. She had been able to read the minds of the Dram even from the first recognitions of her powers centuries ago. They could not hide anything from her, provided they did not commit suicide. If we moved quickly enough, with the power she demonstrated, they would be helpless before her. Maybe we could find out what the Anti were up to and how to defeat them.

Only the Anti had no plans of letting that happen. As we approached, Ambra darted her head to the side and gasped. I followed her gaze, and beside the Dram ship, a crack seemed to appear in space itself. A massive shadow erupted through the fissure, its form cloaked from light and difficult to discern. I felt in my stomach the same unease I had experienced at the death drone.

"Ambra! An Anti ship!"

Ambra knew, but it was too late. The powerful folds engulfing the warship shimmered, faded, and dissolved like silk unraveling. But the Dram did not flee. Before they could move, a spray of particles came from the shadow ship aimed at the warcraft. The impact was pure energy.

It seemed like a nova. Ambra screamed. "Close your eyes, everyone! Turn away!"

I did as I was told. The bubble turned pitch black as Ambra sought to shut out all radiation. Even so, enough penetrated to make the interior bright enough to blind. The temperature inside increased dramatically, and within seconds, I began to sweat even through the climate control of the MECHcore suit. I didn't think we could last long in this radiation flux.

But suddenly, it was over. I looked around the bubble. Everyone seemed okay. Even Ambra standing and facing the explosion without protection was unharmed. I ran to her side.

"I'm okay, Nitin."

I looked into her eyes and kissed her, holding her body tightly to mine.

"What happened?" asked Moore, his face pale.

"We lost our catch," said Waythrel. "The Dram ship is destroyed."

"How? Why?" asked Williams. "Where's the wreckage?"

"Annihilated," said Ambra. "Converted to pure energy by an interaction with antimatter."

It seemed that she was right. There was no sign of the Dram warcraft, and an enormous amount of energy had been released. It was exactly what one might expect in a matter-antimatter collision that converted both to pure radiation.

But we were not alone. The shadow ship hovered beside us. Ambra set her mouth into a thin line.

"Let's see how they respond to the full power of the Orb."

She closed her eyes once more. For a moment, nothing happened. There was a total silence in the bubble. The shadow ship didn't move. Finally, a dim light glowed from the Orb. The light slowly intensified, broadened into multiple wavelengths, and then flashed more brightly than the exploding Dram warship. But the light was directed. It sped forward at a speed that I could follow, like some glowing fist thrown at the body of the enemy. I couldn't imagine what it was going to do.

The shadow ship didn't wait around to find out. The inky disturbance kept toward the side of the Orb. The fist of light followed and nearly impacted the dark shape. But the Anti were prepared. They had prepped a jump on a local string. The very Orb that lashed out at the ship provided through its discarded energies a door to the Time Tree, and our enemies stepped through it. The darkness vanished, leaving the star-filled dark of regular space in its place.

"No!" Ambra cried. She looked furious. "I should have sealed the Orb and then dealt with them. Stupid pride! I was too ready to show them justice! Now I've let them escape."

Waythrel moved forward and stood before Ambra. "The good news is that they were afraid of you, Ambra. Whatever technology they possess, they were not willing to go up against you and the Orb."

"Yeah, but they were clever enough to take out that Dram boat," said Moore. "Didn't defend the ugly bugs from us, you'll notice. Not much love there. But they didn't want us getting them, getting any information."

Again Waythrel commented. "Which is another good sign. They fear knowledge falling into our hands. That means they are vulnerable."

Ambra looked toward the alien and smiled. "Yes."

"And this means there is far more hope for our cause than we might have had before the Dram attacked," finished the alien.

Hope? Perhaps. But it was all abstract. I looked out of the enclosure behind us to the smaller bubble holding the time-frozen remains of two members of my team. A feeling of failure swept over me, of responsibility mismanaged. *I* had allowed that mission to occur. Their deaths were in my ledger.

I thought over what had just happened. A world brutally slain and then devilishly poisoned. An enemy with terrible weapons we hardly understood and could not counter. Yet an enemy that feared us, that fled before the Daughter in her wrath, that murdered its allies rather than let us interrogate them.

As we moved toward the Orb and Ambra began the process of sealing the Time Tree strings to shut down this first of three nodes, those last thoughts comforted me some. In the midst of my sadness and revulsion, despite the fear and uncertainty, there did seem to be a ray of sunlight. A hope.

And as always, that hope depended on Ambra Dawn.

28

The atoms or elementary particles themselves are not real; they form a world of potentialities or possibilities rather than one of things or facts.

—Werner Heisenberg

We left without doing anything more with the death drones surrounding the planet. Because we feared our mission might have been betrayed, time seemed of the essence. Also, the world had already perished, the Dram and the shadow device having destroyed all hope of reviving it. What sealed our decision was the death of Caga. After the shadow ship escaped, we returned to the surface, only to find the creature dead. The last of her kind on a sterilized world.

Ambra stood silently staring at the planet as she guided us toward the Orb for transit. Her expression was inscrutable—sadness, guilt, fear, and expectation were turbulent waves passing over her features. I leaned softly against her arm, holding her cold hand. How was I to comfort her when she gazed on the death of an entire world? A world she had communed with, known intimately in ways I now had begun to understand after our sharing.

Waythrel too stood at her side gazing backward and spoke sorrowfully. "So much waste. So many beautiful creatures. Beautiful minds. So much unmade and lost."

Ambra spoke so softly that I strained to catch the words. "Not lost. Never wasted." She looked between the alien and me with tears in her eyes. "Waiting for a time of harvest."

I waited for an explanation, but Ambra said nothing more, and Waythrel did not probe. I let Ambra have the space she needed to mourn. I had never seen her so heavy with loss.

Meanwhile, the presence of a possible traitor at the highest levels of our group had put the rest of us on edge. Despite Ambra's efforts to persuade us not to second-guess one another, that was becoming more and more difficult as the dangers increased and the Dram seemed ready and waiting to pounce even at what should have been arbitrary star systems for them, places they should have never thought to set an ambush. Combined with the penetration of the False Dawn in the desert, I had to admit that there was a little too much coincidence going on.

But which of us to suspect? If it was to be one of our group on this strange mission, it couldn't be the Daughter or her closest advisor. A Xix betraying the cause? It was beyond unthinkable. That left only the two remaining members of my team. While it was true that I had only just met them, serving together in combat reveals a lot about a person. There is something raw and unfiltered about placing your life on the line in front of others. It's hard to hold a lie in your eyes when your death is staring you in the face. I had been with Moore and Williams. I had seen them face death. I trusted them. Moore had even relinquished his dislike of mental sharing, and Ambra had reported nothing about that. His mind must have been clear of betrayal.

So that only left the other members of Ambra's inner circle. My mind immediately focused on Mazandarani. I knew it was partly jealously as well as anger at his own suspicions of me that biased my judgment. But that very suspicion itself became suspect in this growing paranoia. Did he do it to cast eyes off himself and onto an innocent? Had his hatred of me because of Ambra's love turned him? Men had turned traitors for less than that. But it seemed unlikely that Ambra would have missed such thoughts in him. He too had shared with the Readers, even if he was not one. Finally, there was the major. Mizoguchi hardly seemed the type, but now I questioned everything. Of course, could she have hidden such intentions from Ambra and the other Readers any better than Mazandarani? Could anyone? Spies would seem to be impossible in the presence of the galaxy's most powerful psychic.

None of the potential traitors held up under scrutiny. It was a mystery. I began to feel that either it was someone whom none of us suspected, or perhaps we were imagining a threat that didn't exist. Perhaps the Dram and their new, mysterious allies had ways of obtaining information that we didn't know. We certainly were stymied by some of their technology, and that lack of understanding had cost the lives of two of my team.

It was a quiet, far less adventurous transit through the Orb to our second destination. Everyone was consumed with his or her thoughts and doubts and the mourning of two of our members, whose bodies we carried with us like some surreal baggage. I was also anxious about the transit and once again became ill from it to the point of almost passing out. But the effects were somewhat lessened, and Ambra told me that she worked hard to shield us from the vulnerabilities inherent in the process. I remembered no dream this time.

When we exited the Orb and I had recovered enough to process my environment, our small bubble was orbiting an enormous violet-green gas giant that humbled Jupiter. It had no name from its inhabitants; they were creatures so different from us that even language was a very artificial construct for them, developed only after years of mental communion with the Readers led by Ambra—a concession in order to help very different forms of life communicate. The Xix named the world Gyl, and so we called it.

My mind played over the reams of data I had absorbed from the sharing. Gyl was so large as to possess enough mass and gravitational force to fuse deuterium in it core. It was as much a failed star as a planet. Its star system was located on one of the spiral arms of the galaxy near the center. That explained the bright and dense star field around us, making the night skies of New Earth seem so pale and dim. It was also located a good bit closer to the system's star than our Jupiter, causing the planet to be much warmer. The weather was exceedingly violent in the upper layers of the atmosphere.

Like most gas giants, it was primarily composed of hydrogen and smaller amounts of helium. These elements began as gases in the hard-to-define surface of the planet's outer atmosphere but then transitioned deeper into the world to multiple alternative states in layers as the pressure and temperature increased beyond anything humans could really intuit. At the center of the world was a core resembling in many ways the rocky inner planets of our star system. Trace amounts of the larger elements that make up our planet—those nuclei once formed in the death throes of giant stars—sank to the bottom of Gyl because of their relative density to form the core. Only this core was many times larger than New Earth and under tremendous pressure and temperature, so the atoms adopted states bizarre and outside the modeling of our science.

The layers directly above the rocky core were the heart of the world, however. In those layers brooded a sentience that I found almost impossible to consider *alive*. The hydrogen atoms at this pressure and temperature were forced into a bizarre form of matter that New Earth science had only a foggy grasp of. The Xix understood more, but the explanations were beyond my comprehension. There was a crystalline form of hydrogen, not exactly a solid, not a liquid, but an ordered structure. It was from this order and the interactions with other quasi-crystalline elements that a completely different form of atomic organization occurred. From that organization evolved a form of life so different that it called into question my conceptions of life itself.

Truly thinking about my existence for the first time brought on a disorientation. What were we, exactly? Atoms that on their own have no will, no purpose, nothing but constraints based on "laws" of physics (whatever those really are ultimately). Somehow, under the conditions of New Earth—temperature, radiation impact from the sun and cosmic rays, composition, pressure—these atomic entities can form organized structures that at one point obtained the power to replicate. Then the process of "survival of the stable" took over, and evolution produced increasingly complex molecules, cells, bodies—*minds*. That love and the ideals of beauty and wonder all come from the arbitrary dance of molecules like carbon chains and water is extremely strange when you really think about it. In fact, it makes no sense at all to me.

Given our exposure to the aliens in our galaxy and the powers of Ambra Dawn, I should have been more open to the idea of what life and especially *mind* could be in this universe. But we were produced over millions of years in a very specific (and, by the standards of the cosmos, *strange* environment), and that has shaped our mental framework. It limits our thoughts, places assumptions and obstacles before our minds. *Obvious, logical,* and *reasonable* have meanings we have evolved toward, but they are truly relative. I was now faced with the reality of that relativity as I never had been before.

The atoms of hydrogen, helium, and the trace elements did not form the direct substrate for life on Gyl. The quasi-crystalline lattices *themselves* did. A poor and likely distorting analogy might be that the atoms and chemical bonds that form the basis of our bodies could be mapped to the lattices and interlattice interactions of different crystals in the Gyl planetary layers. There was a higher-level crystal-chemistry that sat above the basic atomic interactions.

Even more bizarrely, the sharing with Ambra revealed that these structures were only partially crystals across the space of these layers. More fundamentally, and critical to the evolution of intelligence on this world, they were also *crystals in time.* New Earth scientists had only recently begun to appreciate the existence and properties of time crystals—where repeated arrays occurred in cyclic time points and not necessarily in space. In the sharing, Waythrel's mind had noted that our theories were embryonic and based on a lot of incorrect thinking, but they were the beginning of a step in the right direction. So my lessons went. On Gyl there existed a wonderland for experimentalists wishing to study the full potential of this form of matter. I would have normally left them to it. But nothing was normal in our mission.

The end result on Gyl was an evolved form of life in a state that had no analogy to our minds, which used the great heat energy of the world from gravity and weak fusion to produce higher and higher order and structure. And finally, millions of years ago, intelligence. The creatures of Gyl were far older than we, and yet, because of their extreme differences, both more and less advanced than other forms of life in the galaxy. Their technology was primitive, their mental reach into science and mathematics profound.

All these thoughts raced through my mind as I stood in our space-time bubble before this enormous world. But before we could begin any attempt to communicate with the creatures of Gyl, there was an unexpected Dram welcoming party for us to deal with.

29

The doctrine that the world is made up of objects whose existence is independent of human consciousness turns out to be in conflict with quantum mechanics and with facts established by experiment.

—Bernard d'Espagnat

"**S**hit!" Williams whistled. "There must be four or five squadrons."

"And look!" said Moore, pointing to dark patches in the bright local star field. "Shadow ships. Maybe half as many."

My stomach dropped. One Dram cruiser and a single of those devil ships was enough. This time, there were likely twenty or thirty starships between us and Gyl. The balance of power in this standoff was much less clear to me.

Waythrel spoke ominously. "Gyl has no obvious strategic importance to this war. We are here only because of the critical node point Orb that rests next to their world."

"Someone's selling us out." Moore scowled. "They knew we were coming."

"And likely knew about the last engagement. Look at these numbers!" said Williams. "We chased off one of their ghost ships. Can we scare off ten of them?"

The case for the spy seemed to grow stronger. But there wasn't time to think about that. As I looked across the waiting group of starships, my mind raced through stratagems, tactics, scenarios. But something was bothering me. "Why aren't they engaging? Moving? They're just sitting there."

"Maybe they haven't picked us up yet," said Williams.

Ambra responded coldly. "No. They are closing the noose."

Instinctively I spun around. She *was right!* Another twenty or thirty ships were approaching behind us, spreading out to the sides and above, cutting off all avenues of escape. We were completely surrounded, cut off from the Orb and the planet.

"An ambush!" cried Williams.

I turned to Ambra and placed my hand on her shoulder. "Ambra?"

"You must do something soon," said Waythrel.

Ambra smiled at Waythrel. "Dear Waythrel, you should know that time is also an illusion."

And then she was gone.

We all startled. Williams gasped, and Moore let out a short bark. One moment I was touching my beloved gently with concern, the next I was holding only air. We all stared at one another in confusion. And then the explosions of light began.

Afterward, Ambra would explain to me what happened, but all we could see at the time was a sudden, massive, and broad attack on the enemy ships from every position. Those in front of us nearest the planet, those behind us, and those that completed a sphere entombing us in a net of ships—from every location of a Dram and shadow ship, there came light.

The Orb had become bright, as bright as we had seen in the attack around Orferlin, but there was no buildup as before, no period of time to observe the flaming arms of energy extend from the object—they simply appeared around us.

The carnage was spectacular. Where once we were surrounded by a spherical lattice of ships, now a fiery globe encased us. The Dram war boats vaporized, the shadow ships exploded with the powerful energies of annihilation. Before we could even fully process the destruction, a gargantuan cyclone was born in the midst of it, a hurricane of light and debris swirling down to a vortex as large as a great moon, the tunnel of radiance extending back toward the Orb. The great sphere of power controlled by the Daughter lit up brighter than the local star.

We shielded our eyes, and I engaged my suit helmet. As it fastened itself around my head, I toggled the view screen to filter out nearly all incoming radiation. Even so, I squinted as I looked toward the Orb. I watched the remains of a fleet of enemy ships pour into the multidimensional portal and then disappear.

The light suddenly winked out. Its disappearance was like a thunderous sound that had been suddenly muted. My senses responded similarly, relief sweeping over me, a long breath escaping my mouth.

"You cannot win a battle if you focus on winning space alone."

It was Ambra's voice. She stood in the middle of the enclosure, a tired look on her face. "One must understand that the universe moves in more than three dimensions."

I opened the faceplate of my suit, ran to her, and enveloped her body in my hard exoskeleton, the nanofiber gloves retracted so that I could feel the softness and warmth of her flesh. Only after I had held her for a moment did I realize how terrified I had been at her disappearance. The irrational fear of losing her swept over me now in waves.

"Ambra, don't do that to me again, please," I blurted out incomprehensibly, my face pressed tightly into her shoulder and neck. "I can't lose you. Not after finding you."

You will never lose me, Nitin. Even if it might seem so for a time. Like distance, time is an illusion.

"I'll be buggered!" shouted Moore. "That all by itself makes this trip worth whatever shit we're going to see."

Williams stared open-mouthed and said nothing. Waythrel walked to the middle of the bubble and stood next to Ambra. "And once more, our Daughter of Time teaches her teacher a lesson." I think if a Xix had a mouth, it would have been smiling.

I pulled back enough to look into her eyes but held her shoulders. She felt cold. "Are you okay?"

"Yes. Tired, Nitin. I will sit." She lowered herself into a cross-legged position on the floor of the enclosure and closed her eyes. I knelt with her, continuing to hold her hands as she sat, as if she were a fragile piece of china that could slip and shatter. Then I instinctively began to stroke her hair, drawing a smile from her lips. "I wish I could sleep right now," she finished, resting her head on my shoulder.

"Okay, so are we going to get an explanation for that Dram navy Armageddon we just saw?" asked Williams.

"I think I can tell you and spare Ambra the energy," said Waythrel. "The simplest explanation is that using the Orb, Ambra can travel through both space and time.

Such travel normally requires tremendous energies. But we are in close proximity to the Orb, and she did not need to travel far in any dimension. She was able to access several different three-space locations at the same time."

"Run that by me again," said Williams.

"She accessed the same temporal location repeatedly, but each repetition changing the position." I thought that I heard a slight impatience in the alien's translator. Her words must have been the Xixian version of *Physics for Poets*.

"Went to different places but all at the same time?" asked Moore, his brow furrowed.

Williams nodded. "Right. That's why we saw everything happening everywhere but all at once."

"And if you could have seen with better eyes at higher resolution, you would have seen Ambra—tens, maybe hundreds of Ambra Dawns—positioned near the enemy ships and simultaneously inducing their destruction," said Waythrel.

"That's good enough for now," sighed Ambra taking my hands. She opened her eyes. "But further explanations have to wait. We need to see what is left of the Gyl for us to speak to. And speaking with them will not be easy." She stood up and kissed my hands. "Walk with me, Nitin?"

I followed her to the edge of the enclosure. Even now, in the midst of this insanity, I found myself distracted, stunned by her beauty. Uncountable numbers of stars carpeted the background around us, shining undiminished and without distortion through the space-time compartment she had fashioned for us. The stars framed her form, her red locks bouncing slightly with each step. Still reeling from the sudden sense of her disappearance, the reality of her physical presence before me felt infinitely valuable, precious, and vulnerable. Had I understood our ultimate fates, I would have treasured that physicality even more.

I am yours and you are mine, Nitin. In flesh and in spirit.

"I feel them," she spoke out loud to everyone. The rest drew near, hanging on her words. "You can't see them, but the entire planet is ringed with poisonous seeds."

"The death drones," I said, involuntarily shuddering. The memory of the one around Brax was still very raw. I had to stop myself from looking out toward the bodies of Kim and Fox suspended in time outside our bubble.

"Yes, but the Anti have not achieved their goal here. Not fully. Not yet."

"How do you know?" I asked.

Waythrel responded. "Because we can sense the mind of the Gyl below. It has not been destroyed."

I felt relief. "Then they are okay."

"No," said Ambra. "They are weakening. But it will be much slower with them than with the Brax. I will speak with them now, find out what I can. And then, if we conclude it is safe to do so, I will purge these drones from the system."

30

*In the beginning there were only probabilities. The
universe could only come into existence if someone
observed it. It does not matter that the observers
turned up several billion years later. The universe
exists because we are aware of it.*

—Martin Rees

Ambra parked the bubble outside of the
planetary atmosphere, but close enough that
the huge world spanned our entire field of
vision. Churning bands of clouds encircled the disk
before us, their hues spanning a range of colors from
blue to violet. Monstrous storms the size of entire worlds
spun in tight knots at various locations. I could see
perhaps seven moons on this face of the world, and my
memory from the sharing told me that there should be
another five obscured from view.

The Gyl were beings whose form was composed of
the very planetary layers themselves, and to enter the
atmosphere was to violate their personal being in some
strange sense. Not the outer layers, as the substrates for
the quasi-crystalline life were buried deep within the gas
giant, but Ambra wished to cause no offense. The
crystalline mind of the world was strange beyond
prediction, and she proceeded with great caution.

Immediately there was a problem: the members of my team and I wished to partake of the communication, but Ambra and the other Readers on New Earth had only spoken with the Gyl through the telepathic medium, those fields of space and time that were the substrate and the enzymes of mentality. While we could have shared as we did with Caga of the Brax, Waythrel warned that it would not likely be productive. It might very well be deadly.

"You must understand," the alien said. "The thoughts of the Gyl will not be like any thoughts of creatures like us. Only through the deepest meditations, only through the greater insight of the Group Mind were we able to establish contact at all. Here, devoid of the horde of Readers, that mind does not exist. We may not be able to communicate at all."

Ambra explained further. "And if we do, we will only be able to understand them because of that memory, of the lessons our minds learned through the Group Mind experience." Her gaze was serious and concerned. "You have none of that experience. The presence of the Gyl mind may even be dangerous, threatening to your consciousness in its terrible alienness."

"How can some crystal brain in there hurt mine out here?" asked Moore.

"Ambra can kill with her thoughts, Sergeant," said Waythrel. "I've seen her drop entire Dram infantries to the ground without lifting her finger. The brain creates a field. That field can be modified by a Writer, one space-time field modifying another. Those modifications can be beneficial, healing, educational. Or they can be destructive. The interaction of two extremely different mental fields is very unpredictable. You are one small mind in front of a planetary brain of proportions and a nature that would frighten you if you could see it, understand it."

Ambra nodded in agreement. "It will be dangerous even for Waythrel and me, even with the power of the Orb. That is because to communicate, I will have to open myself to them. To become vulnerable."

"Are they potentially violent?" I asked.

Ambra seemed lost for words. "It is difficult to answer that without distorting what is true. Could they damage me? Yes. Would it be violence? Is the radiation that burns your skin violent? Or is violent a word suitable for creatures like us but not for other things in this universe?"

"Lost me, sister," said Moore. "But I'm good to stay out of this sharing. Wasn't keen on the other one except that I was tired of being left out."

Williams agreed. "It sounds like too big a risk. Count me out."

"But there may be a way for you to partake of the conversation, even if it will be strange," said Waythrel.

Ambra looked over to the alien with confusion. "What do you mean?"

"The MECHcore suits," it said. "There is a powerful AI embedded within. It has scaled several levels of proto-sentience."

Ambra nodded, a pained expression on her face. I was immediately concerned. "What does this mean?"

"Sentience. Intelligence. A space-time field, Nitin. I Read and Write. I can begin to interact with the artificial intelligences of the more advanced systems the Xix have developed. Simple minds. Ugly in many ways. But real. And growing more complex with their science, with each generation of the technology."

"And before we left, Ambra had begun serious efforts to interface with our AI," said Waythrel, "achieving remarkable results with the more developed versions that have progressed much further in consciousness than the more simple minds in your suits."

"Is this bad?" I asked. Ambra's face seemed strained. "You look troubled."

Now is not the time, Nitin. Trust me. I will explain everything later.

"No, it's not bad at all. It means Waythrel is right. I can work through your suits, funnel the fields of thought through them and the Xixian translator." She nodded as if seeing the alien's plan come together in her mind. "Yes. Suit up, turn on your COM, and you'll hear their speech come through the speakers."

"Mangled as it might be by our understanding and Ambra's interface with the AI," completed Waythrel.

Moore laughed and shook his head. "I swear everything that happens on this trip has got to be weirder than a peyote cactus ceremony."

"Cactus ceremony?" asked Williams, an eyebrow arched.

"Yeah, you know, American Indians? Mescaline?" Williams shook her head and shrugged. Moore smiled. "Never mind. Sounds wicked, sister. I'm onboard."

Williams nodded. "Me, too."

"Okay, then let's suit up," I said, grabbing for my headgear before remembering I had already put it on during the attack. I engaged the COM. "Ready whenever you are, Ambra."

We watched Ambra and Waythrel sit together in the middle of the bubble, the alien's long arms reaching out toward her. Ambra held the many-fingered ends of the Xixian extremities and closed her eyes. They sat there silent for more than thirty minutes. The bubble was quiet except for the shallow breathing of the humans and the strange respiration sound of the Xix—a noise like some rhythmic steam leak from a radiator.

I knew that there must be something powerful happening. Something amazing involving the galaxy's greatest Reader, the Orb, and a bizarre crystalline intelligence inhabiting a planet dominating my field of vision.

But I felt nothing. Sensed nothing. Never before had I felt so strongly the difference between Ambra and me. The woman I loved, whom I had loved since my birth, with whom I had shared flesh and heart and mind— right now in this place and time, in this state, she was something very distinct from me. Something I could not reach or understand. I was blind in a sensory world in which she had the greatest vision of all. I felt much more than inadequate—I felt alone. And for the first time, I yearned, longed with a hungry desperation, to be able to share her experience.

I strained. I tried to activate some latent power within me. Like a blind mole, I tried to conjure organs of vision to pierce the darkness. If desire alone could remake the fabric of the universe, I would have succeeded. Of course, it was laughable. The darkness remained, and all I succeeded in doing was to give myself a tension headache. Ambra and Waythrel remained in a place I could not access—would never access. And the realization of that finality brought a weight of sadness on me.

As I waited with that new burden on my heart, suddenly our COM units crackled. Static bursts and garbled noises. Then words came out.

The Voice of Gyl.

31

What do we know of the world and the universe about us? Our means of receiving impressions are absurdly few, and our notions of surrounding objects infinitely narrow. We see things only as we are constructed to see them, and can gain no idea of their absolute nature. With five feeble senses we pretend to comprehend the boundlessly complex cosmos, yet other beings with wider, stronger, or different range of senses might not only see very differently the things we see, but might see and study whole worlds of matter, energy, and life which lie close at hand yet can never be detected with the senses we have.

—H.P. Lovecraft

"*We are the having been becoming to the invader uncreation deathling approaching reaching hydrogen oxygen carbon netting summation broken crystal seed.*"

The genderless voice of the AI stopped abruptly, leaving only static flowing over the COM. I looked over to Ambra and Waythrel—they remained motionless in their deep meditation. I locked eyes with Moore and Williams.

Moore shook his head. "What the fuck?"

We didn't have any chance to consider the opening greeting. The conversation continued and cut us off.

"We are a seed of the Sol Mind, the seven-kilo parsec three-dimensioned pathway."

This came through Waythrel's translator, but it hardly seemed the alien's voice. Some combination of the thoughts of Ambra and the Xix, perhaps, relayed through whatever cybernetic linkage Ambra had established between their minds and the equipment. The response in our COMs was even stranger.

"*The nucleation event corrected being devoid of augmentation. Understanding through other complexities passes inside solvent channels.*"

"No other pathways are open," rang out Waythrel's device. "But paths must be taken. Gyl dissolves."

"*Gyl dissolves.*"

"Well, I'm glad we've established *that*," said Williams, rolling her eyes. "Maybe we should have just sat this conversation out. Makes no sense."

Moore nodded. "It's like listening to a malfunctioning translator."

"Then switch off and shut up," I said testily. "I want to hear this!"

"...with the time infinite crowd-mind gate. Gyl lacks the interference projections to unmake the dissolving."

"*Carbon crystal seeds dissolve upon breaching radial separations.*"

"We will maintain a safe distance."

"*Acceleration achieving possible state spaces augmentation is the lattice drivings the asymmetry breaking.*"

There was a long pause after this statement. Several minutes passed while Moore and Williams impatiently paced the bubble and talked together. I ignored them. I was staring intently at Ambra's lined face. There was a lot of tension in the muscles, her pale skin hardly covering the veins bulging from pressure within. Stress was building up within her at whatever the Gyl had said or at her efforts to understand it.

"Yes. The disorder is understood now," came a response at last. "Molecular organization is reversed."

"Surface defects in the lattice only are your thoughts failing assembly of divergent structural integrations. Maximum extensionings through all available states to render the end the beginning sameness."

Ambra's back stiffened. "The symmetry will be unbroken."

"The final first through crystal will was now always healed wounding killing all lattices built from broken order. Earth shards prolong Gyl thankfulness anxiety universal erasure."

"We understand."

Moore laughed. "Yeah, that sure cleared it up." I placed my finger over my mouth to indicate quiet as Williams just shook her head.

Waythrel's translator spoke a final statement. "The symmetry induction for Gyl will be halted."

And the rest was static. After five minutes of it, we shut off our COMs. The two Readers still did not move, and we waited nearly half an hour until Ambra finally stirred. She opened her eyes slowly, like someone who had slept far too long or under the influence of narcotics.

"Waythrel?" she asked softly. The alien did not respond. Ambra reached over and placed her hands across the midsection of the creature, the location of the brain-like structure of the Xix. "Waythrel, come back. Follow me, follow my voice!"

She sat in that position unmoving, repeating the commands for the alien to follow her call. Over and over, her expression pained and concerned, she called the creature's name. Minutes passed. Half an hour.

"This isn't looking good," said Moore after some time, turning toward us and whispering. "Maybe that Gyl-thing lobotomized the squid. If that's even possible with one of those things."

I dared not interfere, even to ask a question to learn what was happening. The minutes dragged by without a sound other than Ambra's repeated calls. Her voice had become quieter, softer, her eyes closing as if her mind were traveling some great distance. Finally, after an hour of effort, which the rest of us had begun to assume was in vain, Waythrel stirred. And promptly fell over on its side unmoving.

"Ambra! What happened?" I leaped across the bubble and crouched down, trying to lift the alien. Even with the hydraulics of my suit, the Xix was a struggle to move.

"Easy, Nitin," said Ambra. "The worst of it has passed. Waythrel's in a recovery state unique to its kind. We won't get a response for a few hours. You can let the body lie down—no need to hold it up."

I lowered the body gently back to the surface of the bubble, the bright and dense star field staring up at me and surrounding the body of the Xix. Having no exobiology training, I could not tell whether Waythrel was even alive.

"Then how do you know it's okay?" asked Williams, both her and Moore also now gathered alongside the alien.

Ambra leaned forward, placing her face into her hands. The enormous bulge from her skull protruded from the tips of her fingers, the veins still protruding and strained. Her fingers were like a mask surrounded by a red halo. The words came out muffled.

"We could connect mentally. Only at the end." She massaged her temples a moment and then placed her hands on the ground behind her for support. "At first, Waythrel's mind had become detached, the Gyl mental field breaking the connection to the physical space-time incarnation. I had to reintegrate them. There was some damage, but it's hard for me to know exactly what. The Xix minds are too complex for me."

"Damage?" I asked. "Permanent? Memory? Cognitive function? What?"

"I said I don't know, Nitin!" Ambra cried. I recoiled slightly, never having been the object of her anger. Her face quickly softened, and she reached out and took my hand. "I'm sorry. This has been extremely difficult. This whole damn day. We'll just have to wait and see."

Ambra stood up and stretched her arms, bending her body in different yoga positions. Waythrel remained unmoving on the floor. Moore and Williams looked back and forth between Ambra and me. Finally, Moore cursed and stood up as well.

"So, while we're waiting to see what happened, can you tell us what the hell all that conversation meant? Because as far as the three of us could tell, it was all just gibberish."

Ambra sighed. "We told you it would be hard to understand. What we experienced in the direct communication was far more difficult."

Williams probed further. "But it sounded like you learned something important at the end, and that you were going to destroy the drones or something."

"Yes," said Ambra. "On the last part, it is easy to explain. The Gyl are unable to remove the drones and were happy for us to do so. It represented no danger to them to simply destroy the devices, and in fact doing so will save them. But what they explained to us about the drones, what they had perceived was happening to them and the planet—that was something very troubling, if we have actually understood it correctly."

The strange words kept floating through my mind. "Something about fixing *broken symmetries* and *achieving all states*. You said that you understood. What did it mean?"

Ambra turned around to face us, her expression serious. "The Anti are not allies of the Dram. The Dram may think so, but if Waythrel and I have understood the Gyl, the Anti are the enemies of everything in this galaxy. In fact, of all the known galaxies. Of nearly all the matter that exists in the universe."

Moore looked between us and Ambra. "That's ridiculous sounding. How can you wage war on the universe?"

"I don't know," said Ambra. Her words sounded bone weary. "But these devices are the clue. The first real clue to what is happening. I'm anxious now to reach Hola, our last node. There we may be able to examine the effects of the drones in light of this revelation with a species that is at least *slightly* more comprehensible than the Gyl. Assuming the Anti have placed the drones there as well." She stared out into the surrounding star field. "But I have a feeling that they have."

"So what do they *do?*" asked Moore.

"Entropy," said Ambra. "But in a far deeper sense than it is usually understood."

"Entropy?" asked Williams. "You mean like the second law of thermodynamics, everything becomes disordered?"

"Yes, although *disorder* is a loaded, human word. Things moving to greater *freedom* might be a more insightful phrase, but Waythrel is the better one to talk to. I'm no physicist, and the physics of New Earth is primitive compared to the Xix. But entropy is why when you have order, it becomes disordered. Why you have to keep cleaning your room but it never needs to be messed up. Why when you pop a balloon full of helium that it mixes with all the other gases in the room, doesn't stay seperated. Why things break down. Why energy transfer is always with a loss. All possible states are accessed." She paused a moment and nodded as if to an unseen voice. "It's why time appears to flow in one direction. Space, time, order, disorder, freedoms, constraints—they are all tied together in a very deep sense. The ultimate structure of reality is like a chord whose quality depends on the notes sounded by each of these."

I had no idea what she was talking about. "So, if these drones accelerate entropy, things would break down, lose structure, become disordered more quickly?"

"In some sense, yes," said Ambra, looking out toward the remains of my team. "At a terrible level, that was unimaginable until now. The Gyl understood it best because of the highly structured crystalline nature of their being. They possess a unique perspective as well as form in our galaxy."

"Form that these things are breaking down even now, right?" asked Williams.

"Yes," replied Ambra, nodding toward my warrant officer as if receiving a reprimand. "So the time for talk is over. We have some orbiting drones to destroy."

32

The total disorder in the universe, as measured by the quantity that physicists call entropy, increases steadily over time. Also, the total order in the universe, as measured by the complexity and permanence of organized structures, also increases steadily over time.

—Freeman Dyson

And destroy them she did.

There were over three hundred of them spread around the surface of the planet, just outside of the atmosphere. First we approached them one at a time, and Ambra summoned the full power of the Orbs to grant us maximum protection—a kind of wall of energy—as she crushed the devices by severely warping space around them. There was no form of retaliation from the drones at this activity, and the other drones did not seem to learn from the attack and mount a response. Perhaps the Anti had never encountered anyone who could effectively approach and destroy the objects. Perhaps it happened too quickly for any useful information to be transmitted.

Whatever the reason, the end result was dramatic. After the drones were crushed, they tended to fail in some aspect of dealing with the matter-antimatter shielding the Anti had employed for themselves and their devices. The drones made contact with the edges of the Gyl atmosphere, and suddenly it was a light show. As the low-density matter impacted the crushed remains of antimatter of the drones, there was a building glow. Soon, gravity or some random explosion in the annihilation would drive the drone carcass faster into Gyl, and the equivalent of a thermonuclear explosion of epic proportions would occur. Not enough to be a problem for a planet the size of Gyl, but gigantic, moon-sized explosions.

Three hundred was a large number, and after encountering many of them, Ambra began to sense their locations. She claimed to be able to detect them by the strange effects the devices had on space-time, but also it became apparent after several had been located that they were spaced equidistant around the world.

Once it was clear where they were, Ambra summoned a tidal wave of power from the Orb, and in a burst of flame, all the drones were hit with a blast of energy. Once again, a giant vortex in space formed and drank down the refuse of her wrath and sucked it into the Orb.

It was shortly after this fireworks display that Waythrel woke. A stirring in the eyestalks was the first sign, and soon the individual eyes were pointing in various directions in that way the Xix have to quickly survey their surroundings. Ambra knelt down beside the alien and held its arm.

"Waythrel," she said.

The alien spoke, almost robotically. "We are about Gyl. I have been injured. Deductions suggest that you have destroyed the drones, but I have no memory of such a conversation, or any communion, with the Gyl. The contact must have been too much for me."

Ambra nodded as the alien's legs moved at bizarre angles and miraculously raised it to a standing position. "Yes, the drones are destroyed, and Gyl is free of their poison. You were displaced, Waythrel. I did my best to help. I'm sorry for where I failed."

"We will have to see how much you have failed. And I know you did all you could, Ambra. I knew all the risks." The Xix seemed to be trying to comfort her.

"But there are important things you must know of the communion," said Ambra. "Things too complicated for me to explain. Do you feel ready to share?"

The alien reached out for Ambra's hands. "Yes, but go slowly, Daughter of Time."

Once again the rest of us waited in silence as the Readers functioned in that plane of existence that we could not access. But it was much shorter than the interaction with the Gyl. After little more than five minutes, their hands separated, and Ambra opened her eyes.

"This is frightening information," said Waythrel. The alien began a strange pacing inside the enclosure. Of course, every movement of the Xix appeared strange to human eyes, their body composition and design so completely different than our own. I always expected them to snap their limbs as they supported their bodies at those impossible angles, dangling the midsection bulk by thin legs far off the center of mass.

"I'm not sure that I have understood it correctly," responded Ambra.

"Perhaps not, and I cannot access my memories to compare. But as you noted, we can test the creatures at Hola. We also have the suspended bodies of the MECHcore team of Captain Ratava. There may be critical evidence there that scientific equipment can detect."

It was a little disturbing to hear Waythrel refer to the butchered forms of two of my team in such clinical terms, but I knew that the alien was right. Whatever dignity one could have thought to preserve for their bodies in death had been taken away by the hideous tools of the Anti. If we could learn something about those tools by examining whatever was left of them, at least they would not have died in vain.

"Anyway," began Ambra, "we are nearly finished here. We need to seal the Time Tree node and then continue to Hola. But this time, I think we will make sure we are early."

"Early?" I asked. "What do you mean?"

Waythrel seemed to understand immediately, which indicated to me that the alien had not lost much of its cognitive power. "The Time Tree lattice places all the star systems with Orbs on a synchronized clock. A *time frame* relative to the rest of the galaxy but absolute within the member worlds. Ambra doesn't want any more surprises."

Seeing our confused expressions, Ambra explained further. "We have to assume that our plans have been leaked to our enemies. The Dram and Anti, they expect us to travel to Hola next, and because they are locked with the time frame of the Tree, they can only move forward or beside us in time. They may be waiting now, perhaps setting up a trap days or weeks ago when the spy first betrayed our mission. But not several weeks ago. Not months ago. If we go far enough back in time, after the Dram took the node, but before we made these plans, they cannot touch us."

"Aye, yeah, but there's a hole in all that," said Moore. "What if it's one of us blokes who's that traitor, eh? Then he or she will send a signal to the Dram, and they'll adjust their schedule."

"They can't go back in time on the strings," said Williams.

"What's that?" asked Moore.

"Have you forgotten all your basic training? The strings the Readers navigate on connect physical points, *but at the same time.* That's what she means by a clock. If we go back in time, they can't do anything."

"She is correct," said Waythrel. "Only Ambra, who has far greater access to the dimensional doorways in the Orb, can do so. Not even the False Dawns have yet opened an Orb—as far as we know. If we go earlier, we will be far less likely to find unpleasant visitors."

"So the traitor—if he or she exists," said Moore, eyeing all of us with a sharp smile, "will just have to stew in it."

"Yes," said Ambra. "But we will pick a fairly random time point. We don't know what might be waiting. Probably nothing, but perhaps the whole Dram armada." She raised her hands palms up. "So, what will it be?"

"Fucking life through action!" cried Moore with a broad grin. "Let's go through time, baby!"

"Fine with me," said Williams. "Long as we don't have to talk to any more crystal minds. The Hola, wait, I remember—they're primitive, right? Low-level mind, so maybe no talking at all?"

Waythrel answered. "Communication will not be fruitful. But mental monitoring will be. More significantly, they are a hive mind, and the structure of that mind was studied in detail by a Xixian scientist hundreds of years ago."

I spoke up finally. "I remember from the sharing. But I didn't understand anything of that analysis."

"Me either," echoed Williams.

"Then we will discuss it more," said Waythrel. "But the hive mind now can be analyzed and compared to the data from before. If the Anti devices are increasing disorder, even to the realm of mentality, there should be very specific effects on that mind. A signature, if you will. It will be important proof to this hypothesis."

"And if Ambra's right?" I asked.

The eyestalks danced around. "Then we should be very afraid, Captain."

33

In all the laws of physics that we have found so far there does not seem to be any distinction between the past and the future. The moving picture should work the same going both ways, and the physicist who looks at it should not laugh.

—Richard Feynman

Once again Ambra stood before the Orb node and sealed it shut. It was something I had to assume was happening. I could not see the strings. I was no Reader. Her efforts left no visible change in the Time Sphere that I could perceive. But as with so much I was being introduced to in the universe during this mission, I would have to get used to being in the dark.

Then we left Gyl through the Orb, and I again was racked with pains and lost consciousness. Once again, to my continued embarrassment, I was the only one affected. The faded outlines of a disturbing dream ate at my subconscious, but I pushed it to the side. I didn't feel like getting up, but I did. I mustered all my strength, denied the presence of the nausea and headache, and announced myself fully ready to continue the mission. Ambra looked skeptically at me but said nothing. I was just happy that I was able to maintain my composure and avoid passing out for the first few hours.

Another large gas giant waited in front of us. The knowledge learned in sharing with Ambra poured through my mind. Several hundred years ago, when astronomers on Old Earth began the first cataloguing of extrasolar planets, those interested in extraterrestrial life were disappointed to find that most star systems did not possess small, rocky, water-covered Earth-like planets. Instead, the predominant form of star system involved one or more large gas giants. Some at the time spun this to believe that moons around the gas giant could perhaps be habitable enough to support life as they imagined it. This indeed is the case in hundreds of systems. Much more common, however, is that the gas giants themselves would harbor life very much *not* like what the earlier scientists were imagining.

The radiant orange Hola was a member of this common set of worlds. The planet was about twice the size of our Jupiter, much smaller than the enormity that was Gyl. Yet for a creature of New Earth, it still seemed gigantic. Twenty moons circled the world, none of them with life. Life aplenty filled the upper atmosphere of the gas giant.

As we approached, Ambra announced that she had detected the death drones. As on Gyl, they were positioned across the surface of the planet doing their dirty work. So Waythrel's experiment was on. We would examine the creatures of Hola for any evidence of "entropic acceleration." Then, we would destroy the drones and seal the final node.

We descended through the atmosphere in the bubble enclosure, choosing a location equidistant from the drones. The gas layers were highly structured. The cloud formations were beautiful, colorful, titanic, and multilayered. They seemed almost like mountains or towers built out of the vapors of the planet. Light dimmed slightly as we entered more deeply, soon passing a distance several times the depth of New

Earth's paper-thin atmosphere. It was here that we first saw signs of life.

Our search was for the more developed Holaians, but our first contact with living beings was with the more primitive cloudhoppers of this Jovian world. Giant bags of gas, they floated in the relatively safer upper layers of Hola by controlling the mixture of hydrogen and helium within them, as well as the temperature of the gases. More hydrogen, higher temperature meant they rose. More helium, colder gases, and they descended. Like everything about this world, the creatures were monstrous. Easily several thousand feet in length, they resembled ellipsoidal jellyfish. Strange projections came from several ends of the creatures, and a complicated internal structure seemed to exist partially visible through the somewhat translucent outer membrane.

There were millions of them, rising and falling across the skies, able to dart with surprising speed in different directions. As we wandered through this biolayer of the planet, my eyes began to discern subtle differences in what at first seemed creatures that were identical. There were in fact hundreds of different "balloon" species mixed together in the air. Some were even predators that chased and at times consumed their prey. Others seemed to move in what I could only describe as "herds." It was all mesmerizing. Like a kid at a zoo for the first time, I felt that I could stare through the invisible barrier and watch these things all day long.

"Amazing, aren't they?" asked Ambra, smiling toward me.

"Yes. They're beautiful," I said.

"Creepy as hell," said Williams, shivering with a chill. "Sorry, I'm sure that there is all kind of astrobiology fun here, but these things are right out of some of my nightmares as a kid."

"Wait, you had dreams of aircraft carrier-sized floating gas bags as a kid?" smirked Moore.

"Not exactly, smartass," said Williams. Her glare was icy. "But close enough."

"I just had dreams of bonking the mail girl," said Moore.

Williams nodded. "Not surprised."

"Where are the Holaians?" I asked.

Waythrel answered. "They are the most developed species on Hola, but their numbers to date are low. With their intelligence, it is forecast that in several hundred thousand years, they could develop a technological civilization and populate the world. But for now, Ambra will have to find them by homing in on their sentient signal."

"Okay Waythrel," Ambra said with a sigh. "It was nice to relax a bit. But point taken."

For the next hour or so, Ambra sat in her meditative position in a deep trance. Most of the time, the bubble simply sat still as the rest of us paced, watched the bizarre animals outside, or discussed our fears of the war. Waythrel remained quiet, seemingly focused on its own thoughts. Every now and then, the enclosure would move—accelerate in some direction rapidly and then slow down, finally coming to a stop. This occurred five or six times. After a few instances, we assumed it was simply Ambra finding a "scent" but losing it.

Eventually, the bubble accelerated again, and this time did not slow down for some time. Williams and Moore moved toward the end of the enclosure facing the direction in which we were moving. We were flying quickly through the giant cloud formations now. I understood how Ambra felt—it would have been nice to let go of the pressing dangers and worries of our mission and enjoy this journey through Hola. There was something soothing about the endless airscape of cloud form, the herds of dirigible life, the orange light, warm and calming, that filled the space of this atmospheric layer.

Ambra stood up and opened her eyes, moving beside the two members of my team. I followed her, staring over her head toward the rising star of the system. It would be early morning in this portion of the planet, whatever morning meant here. Ahead, there was a cloud that looked different from anything we had seen before. To begin, it was small. And black, as well as porous seeming. It also drifted strangely, often at odds to the prevailing air currents.

But it was clear that the cloud was the destination to which Ambra was steering the bubble. As we neared it, the partly solid nature of the cloud disintegrated, and we could see that it seemed to be comprised of thousands and thousands of smaller objects. The individual objects were quite small relative to the lumbering air beasts that we had encountered. But they were much faster, darting here and there with speed, yet constantly maintaining a structured form to the cloud.

"Looks like a flock of birds," I said.

"Or a school of minnows," replied Williams.

"Or some ugly bunch of angry hornets," said Moore.

Ambra laughed, and just like that, the hornets attacked us.

34

The second law of thermodynamics is, without a doubt, one of the most perfect laws in physics. Not even Maxwell's laws of electricity or Newton's law of gravitation are so sacrosanct, for each has measurable corrections coming from quantum effects or general relativity. The law has caught the attention of poets and philosophers and has been called the greatest scientific achievement of the nineteenth century.

—Ivan P. Bazarov

Protected within Ambra's space-time field, we were never in any real danger, but it was still disconcerting as tens of thousands of angry Holaians threw themselves at our enclosure. Of course, their efforts achieved nothing, but it was amazing to watch. The cloud almost seemed to grow arms and hands, extend those extremities toward us, and try to grab us individually or altogether. Apparently they couldn't perceive the bubble.

"Notice the coordinated projections," said Waythrel, as if the alien had read my mind. "The Holaians are a hive-mind, the simpler individual members of the hive working in unison to create a much greater whole. The cloud, as a whole, functions as a superindividual, far more intelligent and capable than the individuals or even smaller coordinated groups. Only when the cloud has enough members, a threshold, and those members have worked together for decades, diversifying, harmonizing, can the cloud step into this higher level of consciousness."

I had remembered some of this from the sharing. It was like a developing human with our much larger brains. We have billions of neurons that have to work together. It takes us years and years of interacting with the world and being taught to function at the levels of adults. I said as much to the others.

"So also with the Xix," added Waythrel. "For life-forms with large brains like ours, individuals can achieve a higher level of functioning, even if reaching the full potential of the individual requires a larger social mind—a culture—to be involved. The Holaians, however, cannot achieve such mentality unless they have large numbers of individuals. The individual minds are much simpler."

"So its like a bunch of stupid bees together that get smarter when they are part of a hive?" asked Moore.

"Similar," said the alien. "The Holaian individuals are much smarter than your individual insects, and therefore their mentality in a hive-like state is far greater."

"So, hive mind. Got it. What's the plan then?" asked Williams. "How do we know if the drones are getting to them?"

"Waythrel and I will monitor them," said Ambra.

"I have within my species-memory the patterns of their mind-forms from scans of Readers who researched on Hola years before. Ambra and I will compare what we see now and look for evidence of drone effects."

In this manner we spent the next five days. Chasing one cloud mind after another, Waythrel and Ambra in their Reader trance would probe the hives. The process was arduous and long, the hive minds difficult for the two bipedal life-forms to understand. But they posed far less danger than the efforts at Gyl.

Always when they woke from the trance, it was with sorrow. One after the other, each of the hive-minds we encountered showed signs of a terrible mental deterioration. Proximity to the drones increased the decay. It didn't take long for the pattern to be incontrovertible. The Holaian minds were dying.

"They had been on the cusp of an organized civilization," said Waythrel after one grueling session. "The reports from Xixians detailed the progress of the hives hundreds of years ago. Rudimentary versions of social structure and generational learning had taken root. In a manner simpler and yet very different from human and Xixian technological civilization, they had begun to fashion advanced cultural building blocks. Now, they have been set back millennia. At the rate of decay we are witnessing, in several decades they will even begin to lose hive integrity."

"What are these terrible drones, then?" I asked, revolted by the destruction they were describing.

Ambra shook her head. "The deeper purpose is unclear, but we have all but confirmed the entropic manipulation. The antiorder. The higher-level sentient structures are affected first, but the Gyl were even finding evidence that the lower-level structures of chemistry, even atomic physics, are affected."

"We will need much more evidence to confirm that," said Waythrel. "But the possibilities are frightening."

"Atomic physics?" asked Williams. "You mean like atoms falling apart, now?"

"We don't know," said Ambra. "The Gyl were hard to understand."

"But we know enough now to move on," said Waythrel. "With the information we have, and critically the bodies that were subjected to the powerful pro-entropic fields, we may begin to find a way to develop countermeasures."

"So, that's it?" said Moore. "Mission accomplished, and we bug out of here?"

"Yes," said Ambra, standing up from her crossed-legged position. "First we destroy these drones. Then we seal the third and final node and seal off New Earth from the Dram."

"And return to plan the next stage in this conflict," concluded Waythrel.

And so it would have gone, likely to far less sorrow and tragedy, if only we had left a day earlier. Such are the random chances in time. So proceeds the cosmic play in ways that often seem more capricious than purposeful.

We left the decorative atmosphere of Hola, and Ambra set course for the Orb. It was a strange feeling to be thinking that this mad mission was coming to an end and that we would soon be walking on the sands of New Earth again. Of course, I dreaded the transit through the Orb and was beginning to develop a phobia of it. But I could face a last trip without undo anxiety. And there was the satisfaction that we had achieved a critical goal in protecting not only our homeworld, but thousands of star systems that would have been vulnerable to invasion. I knew that Fox and Kim both would have considered their sacrifice worth that end. That was why they had signed on in the first place.

As the Orb grew in size before our approaching bubble, there was a bright flash next to it. I immediately recognized both the phenomenon and the object materializing. An adrenaline spike coursed through my system, causing my heart to race. Coming off a Time Tree string was a Dram warboat. It materialized nearly right upon us.

In the end, despite my reaction, it would not pose any risk to us in and of itself. Ambra would disable it and in fact exploit the seemingly useful opportunity to interrogate its crew.

But what we learned would set in motion a series of events that would long traumatize both Ambra and me.

35

Let us draw an arrow arbitrarily. If as we follow the arrow we find more and more of the random element in the state of the world, then the arrow is pointing towards the future; if the random element decreases the arrow points towards the past. I shall use the phrase 'time's arrow' to express this one-way property of time which has no analogue in space.

—Sir Arthur Stanley Eddington

"Looks like we have guests," said Moore.

The warship didn't waste any time with pleasantries. There were a few moments of inaction as the Dram likely tried to figure out what exactly this floating group of travelers could be that they saw on their visuals. Unable to do anything but verify the composition of our party, they did what the Dram do best. They immediately opened fire on us.

This surely elicited a second round of confusion in the enemy ship. Even the most shielded Xixian starships collapsed under the focused firepower of the Dram military. Here was a gaggle of only four individuals with a strange cargo—apparently encased in some mysterious and transparent craft—who just stood before the bulk of one of their most feared battle cruisers and took the full fury of their assault.

Ambra didn't give them much time to seek a more analytic mode. She steered the bubble quickly toward the craft, the beam weapons and missiles deflected away from us as the Dram tracked our motion, and parked it outside the hull.

"Time to talk to some bugs," she said impishly.

Unlike our entrance to the Braxian starship where we encountered Caga, Ambra didn't spare the Dram hull. It began to bend inward, the metal soon buckling and then ripping as she forced her way in. As on Brax, some kind of extension to the bubble was projected forward, and we entered into the belly of the warboat. Air didn't rush out of the breach, so Ambra must have sealed off the ship as much as she shaped a tunnel of nothing for us to walk down. Since the Dram coincidentally breathed an atmosphere very similar to our own, it would have been simpler to exit the bubble once inside in order to engage them. Of course, once the insectoidal monsters started blasting at us inside the ship, I understood the usefulness of the enclosure in a very up-close and personal manner.

The engagement was surreal. The Dram threw everything they had at us short of blowing up the entire ship. Williams had cautioned that they might even try that, remembering what had happened around Brax. But Waythrel disagreed.

"It was the Anti ship that destroyed the Dram. The Dram culture disdains suicide and will always fight to their own or their opponent's death."

"But if a shadow ship comes into the system?" I asked. "Then what? We don't know what their plans were for Hola."

"I'm monitoring the Orb. We'll know," said Ambra. "In the meantime, I've shut down their ship's ability to navigate or send external communications. They are paralyzed and cut off from everything."

Moore laughed. "I do like this new way of fighting."

And so we continued to watch the fireworks. By now we had overcome our instinctual concern about standing in front of Dram warriors unloading their weapons on us. The scene became comical. The bugs were frustrated by now, scampering around the finger-like field of emptiness that prevented even their best weapons from achieving anything.

Ambra sat cross-legged in front of the mayhem, the Dram ship and crew in front of her and the starlit backdrop with Hola behind. From all appearances, there was absolutely nothing between her and the attacking Dram. Seeing the Daughter here, the soldiers were eager to grab or kill her. With their razored hands and weapons, they tried over and over to accomplish either of those goals. Ambra had closed her eyes and seemed not to notice the crazed efforts.

Finally, several began to try to study the phenomenon. Soon the weapons were silenced, and we were surrounded by a semicircle of what must have been exhausted and confused bugs. A few smaller-sized Dram had entered the area near the breach. They brought instruments and set them around us. *Scientists*, I assumed. After a good while of that, some figures with considerable authority entered the chamber and were arguing with the others. I could hear the interminable clicking speech of the insects.

Waythrel spoke. "Ambra?"

"Yes, this one will do," she said, her eyes remaining closed.

Suddenly the figure was inside our bubble. The transition was undetectable except that the other Dram were banging on the outside trying to get to it. The officer inside moved to attack, but Ambra overrode its own mental control of its body, and the creature sat there paralyzed.

"Allow me released or there falls destruction overall complete!" it shrieked through their horrid translators.

"Waythrel, would you like to start?" asked Ambra.

Waythrel approached the creature. The two aliens couldn't be more different in mentality and appearance. The tribal, warlike Dram, who seemed to excel mostly in the creation of devices of conflict, next to the peaceful and contemplative Xix. An insect-like frame towered next to us yet was matched by the bulk and height of Waythrel.

"These devices you plant around the worlds—what is their purpose?" the Xix began.

The Dram officer said nothing. Its many legs twitched in anxiety within Ambra's web.

"We know they are destroying the minds and societies present. But this is not of Dram. The Dram preserve function. The Dram destroy in combat, with honor, or enslave. What has changed? Who controls the Dram and why?"

"The Dram never to be withheld," it spat.

"Then why are you placing these devices for others?"

The bug clammed up again. Moore shook his head and folded his hands over his chest. "Fucker isn't going to talk. Maybe if we start ripping segments off that exoskeleton."

"I'm afraid he's right, Ambra," said Waythrel. "We will need another probe." Several of the eyestalks flipped over toward Moore. "One not involving torture."

Ambra sighed. "Mind probes are at best unpleasant, Waythrel, and being within the mind of a Dram still brings bad memories." She stared directly at the officer. "Listen to me. You know who I am. If you do not answer our questions to our satisfaction, I will enter your mind and take those answers from you. Is this what you wish?"

The officer twitched madly, trying to find some way to escape the invisible bonds holding it in place. Outside, the creatures had returned to a frantic mode, firing weapons at us, one even setting off an explosive device that killed several of their crew yet left us unharmed.

Ambra lowered her head for a moment and then raised it with her eyes closed. The creature stiffened, its purposeful movements subdued. It was clear she had reached within it in some profound way. Even the warriors outside the enclosure paused in a curiosity that got the better of them for a moment.

"Fogged light ships usurp and control," came the strange words from the Dram in front of Ambra. "The appearance from nothing to something in zero. Burnings provide us with the right, as we know it. Performance in the war. The power of life. Shadow promises Dram war triumph."

"The Anti," whispered Williams.

The creature stopped any discernible speech, and the sounds became weak with abortive attempts at clicking. Ambra remained focused as minutes dragged by. But she was unable to coax anything else out of the bug. Eventually the creature began to slump backward and then collapsed on the ground, suddenly outside the enclosure. The Dram dragged the immobile body out of our sight.

Ambra opened her eyes, and I saw a fire in them. "We need to go to Dram."

Moore and Williams approached quickly in shock. Even Waythrel seemed surprised.

"Ambra, we can't go to Dram," I said. The idea was surely suicide.

"We can and we must," she said, beginning to pace.

Waythrel spoke. "What did you see in its mind?"

"First, slavery. The Dram are no longer in control of their own destiny. The Anti have taken over."

Moore scoffed. "So what? Serves the bugs right. Let 'em rot."

Ambra ignored him. "The entire planet is transformed. They have been organized into factory centers, entire populations displaced. Manufacturing cities have sprung up from the wastelands of the planet."

"So these drones, the growing armada—it's all being made on Dram for the war?"

"Beyond anything we could have imagined. And there are clones. Thousands of them. Something enormous is being planned. A long-term industry."

Waythrel stepped forward. "A work with the Anti that will proceed far into the future." The two Readers looked at each other knowingly. Many eyestalks turned to the rest of us. "Ambra may have a point. If only for a reconnaissance mission, there may be important information we could glean given what I have heard."

"And just how do you suppose that we are going to do this?" said Williams. "Just waltz onto the Dram homeworld and start taking holos? Won't the entire planet of Dram warriors and their new shadow friends have something to say about that?"

Ambra nodded. "Yes, they would. But they won't see us. Watch!"

Suddenly the Dram outside our enclosure startled. Their heads darted around in a panic, several walking forward toward us and then crashing into nothing.

"We're invisible," I said.

"I can block various forms of matter from reaching us here, and I can modify the path of photons. I can make it appear that nothing is inside."

Moore placed his hands on his hips. "Might have been useful earlier, sister, you think?"

Ambra shook her head. "It leaves us vulnerable." Suddenly the Dram outside seemed aware of our presence again. Ambra gestured toward the soldiers. "They could have shot us just now. Blurring where and what we are prevents me from maintaining the structure for a shield. We didn't know exactly what we'd face before. Now we do. We can't walk into Dram openly."

Moore continued. "So then, you do your magic cloak act, we transport to Dram, have a look-see, find out what they're up to that's so important, and then get out?"

"That's basically my plan, yes," said Ambra. "The more I think about it, the more it makes sense. We've come across too many disturbing things on this mission that we don't understand. Now I know where the Anti are holed up. It's on Dram, and they are planning big things. We add one more stop on the trip. Maybe the most important one."

I nodded. It made sense to me. It still seemed incredibly risky, but the payoff could be very high. I turned to Moore and Williams. "Waythrel's onboard, it seems. Me too."

"I'm not sure how I'm going to stop myself from opening fire on those bastards," said Moore. "I've watched too many good soldiers killed by those bugs. But okay. I'm there. I wouldn't mind standing under their antenna and pulling out their dearest secrets."

Williams nodded. "I would have had to see this to believe it," she said, gesturing to the Dram around us, who still seemed perplexed. "But that's starting to be my new normal. Never thought I'd set foot on Dram."

"I was there once, many years ago," said Ambra. Her face was pained. "It is not something I do again lightly."

"Then let us finish the mission and seal the last Orb node," said Waythrel. "And then, we set an unexpected course."

"For the Dram homeworld," I said, shaking my head.

As I gazed toward the quiescent Orb, a feeling of dread took hold within me. The Time Sphere looked different somehow. Of course it wasn't. Objectively it had the same appearance I had always seen on the inactive Orb—a grayness not exactly black, a reflection not exactly true, a hidden depth that could not quite be perceived. But it *felt* different. It projected something different to my paranoid eyes.

It looked almost hostile.

36

This last trip was the worst for me.

It began as a terrible torture, pain assaulting my body, my mind. Nausea struck me the moment Ambra engaged the Orb. That stomach churning sickness was followed quickly by a splitting headache. I remember falling to the floor of the enclosure and grabbing my head between my hands. I'm embarrassed to say that I think I screamed. It is hard to explain how the physiological reactions occur without one's will when placed in extremis.

After that, I passed out—or that is rather how I understand it. Whether a coma or some trance, I don't know. Maybe it is better that I don't know.

In my nightmarish awareness, I was no longer with the group. This time there was no tunnel. No water. No shapes or stars or competing Ambra eyes.

There was only the devil Ambra. A demon child.

Once more, I was lying in a field of corn. A region around me had been flattened into a circle extending perhaps twenty feet radially. I was at the center, my head swimming, my body aching. The sky overhead was clear and blue.

Then I heard laughter. It floated on the soft breeze, spinning around my dizzy head. A child's laughter, high pitched, playful, without guile or cynicism. *Pure.*

To my left, I heard the sound of cornstalks rustling. I turned toward it, the motion making me seasick. A little girl, perhaps eight years old, walked into the circle.

It was Ambra, yet it was not Ambra.

Her hair was red and long, but she was bald in patches from points at which hideous machinery had been inserted into her skull. Like the Ambra in the desert, she was flesh and machine, natural and artificial. Enhanced. Degraded. *Altered.*

She looked down on me, smiled, and began to skip around the outside of the corn circle, her hands slapping the upright stalks to the rhythm of a song she was humming. I didn't know the tune. It was a strange melody, disturbing in its unusual scales and note resolutions, like some unhealthy inversion of all the musical rules I had grown to know. I tried to follow her as she danced, but I couldn't move my head fast enough to track her movements.

I tried to sit up. My attempt ended dismally with my head and shoulders slamming back down to the ground. The headache returned, momentarily blinding me, and I had to squint to look into the sky again.

The girl was standing over me. Her long red hair hanging down like limbs from a willow tree set on fire, the tips of the hairs nearly touching my face. I could see the enormous expansion of her skull where the tumor lay, the tubes and wires exiting and entering it appearing vile and gleaming. Her eyes were bright green.

"We will have to take it," the thing said.

I tried to clear my head. *Take what?*

"It's all part of a bigger plan. All the gods, they always have their *bigger* plans. She can't know, of course. She's not ready. She won't be ready for a long, long time. I'm afraid she will resist."

I tried to sit up again, more carefully this time, but the effort was too much.

"Do you want a hand?" the girl asked, cocking her head to one side. She offered her arm.

I didn't know whether I should trust her, but I was helpless enough for her to have harmed me by now. That she hadn't gave me a small amount of confidence. I reached out my hand.

"It's safe. I'm all walled off from you."

Walled off? I grasped her hand and with help rose to a sit. The hand felt strangely slick and featureless. "I think I'll just stop here for now," I said as the pain returned.

"Good idea," she said. "You fell hard."

"Fell where? Where am I? How did I get here?"

The clone looked into the sky and around to the horizon as if searching. "She brought you, I think, but I don't really know." She shook her head and shrugged.

"Who brought me where?"

"The answers won't make sense. And words don't help much. Only in the very end will they all make sense. And then there won't be words."

She sat down and crossed her legs in front of me, staring directly into my eyes. I assumed that like Ambra, the clones were blind and used their visions of the past and future to "see" around them. Maybe as cyborgs they had found a way to let the tumor grow uninhibited and still spare the visual regions of the brain. But I actually didn't know.

"Please, why am I here?"

I don't know, Nitin Ratava.

"Please don't do that!" I said. Having a clone inside my mind again nearly made me panic.

"You have mind scars," the girl spoke aloud.

She's reading my mind! "Yes, one of *your* kind attacked me."

"My kind? No, you don't know my kind. And I'm not my kind, really. I'm brokenly fixed."

"Yes, I do!" I nearly yelled. "I know them too well."

The clone in front of me was quiet for a moment. Then she nodded her head. "Oh, I see. Most of it is erased in your mind—she did this, yes? She didn't want it to hurt you anymore. Anyway, I can see enough still there. Yes, they hurt you. They are made to hurt you, as I am."

My heart raced, and I instinctively began to push myself backward from her.

"But if I want to hurt you, you can't run away, Nitin."

My mouth was dry. "What do you want with me?"

"I don't want anything with you. She wants something to happen. *They* do." She looked into the skies again. "But maybe they found what they are looking for. It feels like we are almost out of time."

I shook my head and squeezed it with my palms. "I don't understand *any* of this!"

"I know. I don't either. There is so much for me to learn. Every step is a *lesson*, Nitin. That's the other reason why we're here. Not for you, I'm sorry. But for me."

"We are here for you to learn something? About me?"

"No. We've known about you for a thousand years. The Daughter's consort is an important lesson taught to everyone. Especially for strategy. Many think that you are the flaw, the weakness to find a way to destroy her."

"To destroy Ambra?"

"Yes. And once she is destroyed, they believe the Orbs will fail."

I sat there dumbfounded. "I won't hurt Ambra."

The clone eyed me knowingly. "But the lesson is not to know you but better understand her. At least I think it is. There can be no healing of the crystal without truly understanding her, just as she seeks to understand me. That is why we are here. That is why I can coexist with you now, and even touch you!"

Before I could move, she placed her index finger right between my eyes. I jumped backward and almost fell over.

She giggled. "So fun! They have such power in the deep future." She beamed. "It will be strange to destroy them."

Suddenly, a fierce wind picked up. The clone's hair flew around us, the standing cornstalks swaying madly in the gusts. She started humming that weird tune again and then stopped, looking back at me suddenly.

"Time. Not enough time to know all of you. There are other holes in your mind, Nitin Ratava," she said, closing her eyes and looking upward. "Remember, I will take it soon."

The fabric of space split open before me. The figure of the girl, the green stalks, the blue sky ripped like some aged cloth to reveal a backdrop of stars. The previous vision I had fell into one thousand fragments and scattered into a howling wind.

I floated in the silence of space.

37

What I am going to tell you about is what we teach our physics students in the third or fourth year of graduate school. It is my task to convince you not to turn away because you don't understand it. You see my physics students don't understand it. That is because I don't understand it. Nobody does.

—Richard Feynman

I awoke feeling as sick as I had remembered in the dream. Ambra was kneeling next to me, her hand on my forehead.

"His fever broke," she said to others outside my field of vision. I could only see her and the seemingly endless star field above me. I remember thinking that this was all I really needed to see, anyway.

"This is becoming dangerous for him, Ambra," came the voice of Waythrel.

"I know," she said softly, concern on her features. "Only one more. I will be much more careful. I was too eager to get here and see what was happening."

I was down for two more days. Meanwhile, the group and I floated outside of the Dram homeworld in our now-invisible enclosure. While I had heard stories and seen holos of the red giant star at the center of the system, it was something else entirely to be close to it, "in the flesh," to appreciate its size and the strange effect that living in a colorspace lacking most of the higher wavelengths has on one. Everything appeared washed out, tanned, and faded. Even living in the deserts of New Earth seemed to bring more vitality.

And yet the busy world of our enemies was below. When I had recovered sufficiently to work my suit, we planned our approach to the planet surface. Ambra wanted to go straight to the seat of power, to the emperor's palace. She believed that we could enter undetected yet observe everything that went on. The prime strategies and plans of the Dram would be revealed to us. We could learn much to help our efforts in the war.

Even more important, there could be much revealed about the Anti and what they were actually up to. Ambra seemed to be holding something back, but I got the sense that her visions had convinced her that those answers would indeed be forthcoming on Dram. From her words of what she had seen in the Dram officer's mind, we might even find the Anti there.

Williams and Moore were concerned that the Anti might be able to detect our approach. I shared that concern, but my level of trust in Ambra was high. Too high, as I would discover soon.

"I mean, we don't know their technology. Even if the Dram couldn't see us, couldn't stop us, maybe those monsters have something that can," said Williams as we debated.

"It is possible," said Ambra, "but I think unlikely."

"Why?" asked Moore. His face was stern, and it was clear he wanted to hear reasoned arguments.

Waythrel interjected. "The Anti aren't magical, Sergeant. They may be composed of particles that are inverted in specific characteristics from ours, but the same laws of physics apply to them. In fact, in their own antimatter galaxies, they could appear as close copies of any life-form in our galaxy. Imagine looking into a mirror of a kind, and everything is inverted in some ways but still basically looks the same. Atomic physics, chemistry, etc., while not compatible with us, would still be entirely recognizable. Life would likely look very much the same."

"Well, they still have tech we don't understand. Purposes we don't understand," said Moore.

Ambra nodded. "Yes. Any advanced alien technology could baffle us for a while, so your worries are legitimate. But so far, they have not been able to counter my effects on space-time. Nothing makes me think that this will be different for cloaking us on Dram. I think it's a risk worth taking."

We finally reached an agreement. We would take an initial risk and descend into Dram, ready to rocket out of there quickly at the first sign of discovery. First we would enter the atmosphere and test their long-range scanning abilities. Next, we would hover over the central city of Gred, where the emperor's palace was located. If things went well to that point, we would proceed to the palace itself and find out what we could.

Ambra assured us that she could make a very fast run for the Orb. From what I had seen in our adventures so far, I had no doubts. What I didn't know and would soon find out was just how fast she could actually go.

We left the bodies of Kim and Fox orbiting Dram in their private enclosure and descended slowly, Ambra monitoring all that she could of the mental states around us. Despite the thickness of the atmosphere, the enormous luminosity of the red giant hardly faded as we descended while the space around us took on a reddish hue so that it nearly seemed that rust leaked out of the very sky itself. For a human to spend much time on Dram would be psychologically challenging.

Ambra was explaining. "Mostly it's too much noise, too many inputs from the billions," she said. "But if we are detected, there will be a synchronized meshing of thoughts with a spike in focus and energy. *That* I can likely sense. As they would organize to respond, such activities would be even more outside the random noise."

Nothing happened. Ambra didn't sense anything and no warships or ground-based defenses responded to our penetration of the atmosphere. The deep desert of Dram began to fill all my vision—a red-and-orange sea of sand dwarfing the Sahara, spanning the entire planet, to human eyes colored nearly monochromatically by that swollen sun. To avoid being overwhelmed visually by the expanse, I focused on the shape of Gred taking form as we approached.

It was a gigantic city, spanning four to five times the largest metropolis on New Earth. The buildings were a stark contrast to human design. There were few sharp edges, little glass. The materials were strange and the shapes curvilinear. It almost appeared as if one were to take Manhattan and multiply it by a factor of one thousand, in width and height, and then turn it to sand and spray just enough water to melt the edges of the structures but have them retain their structural integrity. *That* would be an echo of the alienness of Gred. But really, when presented with the truly alien, my mind could only map it to the most similar memories of New Earth. Usually, there was a lot of distortion in that comparison.

Soon, we were flying over Gred in our bubble. Part of me felt vulnerable. There we were, perched over the largest city of our deadliest foes, with no discernible walls, a collection of three soldiers, one alien, and the wildcard that was Ambra Dawn. Of course, she was the reason the bubble existed, that it withstood without complaint the full discharge of a Dram warship, that it allowed us to see everything around us in protection yet hid us from enemy eyes. I should have been calm. But I wasn't.

"The city appears almost deserted," said Waythrel. "And the sky traffic is minimal."

"Look—that's where the tribunal was held," said Ambra quietly. It was an enormous dome, hewn out of the commonplace metallic, marble-like substance found across Dram architecture, cut with facets reflecting the red starlight. It matched in near-perfect detail the descriptions in the history books. But Ambra turned away from it and pointed to some much smaller buildings nearby. "That's where they held me prisoner. Where they took my eggs to make their abominations."

Her tone sounded loaded to me. I began to wonder if her obsession with coming had something to do with the clones. We would find out soon.

The emperor's palace sprang out of the cityscape in front of us. Unlike the town-sized dome of the Tribunal, the palace rose like an obscene termite construction towering over all other structures in Gred. Military craft darted around it, laying out a protective radial grid of hovercraft with stunning amounts of firepower. One thing about the Dram, they sure knew how to militarize the hell out of anything.

"The emperor is housed at the very top of the structure," said Ambra. "It gives the creature a god's-eye view of Gred and Dram, feeding no doubt into the monumental egos they always seem to have."

Williams laughed. "Except for the one you nearly destroyed centuries ago, right? When you escaped?

Unless the history books lie. *That* emperor must have been a bit humbled!"

Ambra looked away. "What happened then is not something I'm proud of." There was an awkward silence.

The sea of guarding spacecraft ignored us, and we passed through their ranks undetected. It was a tense few minutes, and as MECHcore soldiers we were the most tense in this potentially explosive environment. Waythrel and Ambra seemed to remain calm, although Ambra retained a sharp focus that had descended on her since she had looked into the captured officer's mind. Perhaps it was just returning to Dram. I could not imagine how disturbing it would be for her. But it felt like more, as if she suspected something terrible and was only waiting to confirm it.

We approached the enormous tower that gleamed in the ruby light. Ambra did not slow down. Just as I thought that we would smash ourselves to pieces on the hard walls, they *bent*. Where they bent to I cannot describe because my mind can't grasp it. But a kind of hole appeared in the wall that again only we seemed able to perceive. Our little invisible pod entered through it.

38

All that we see or seem
Is but a dream within a dream.

—Edgar Allen Poe

We haunted the emperor's palace like some aggregated poltergeist. The four of us hovered near the tops of the enormous ceilings, watching and listening as the creatures obliviously went about their activities underneath. It did not take us long to confirm Ambra's worst suspicions.

The floor that housed the emperor was constructed like a throne room. A grand hallway led from an elevator of sorts to a central chamber, domed on the inside, in the center of which was a reclining chair-like piece of furniture designed for the Dram insectoidal bodies. But this was clearly a special version. Even through the alienness of it all it was easy to connect the human desire to aggrandize its rulers with something similar in the Dram. The more I saw of Dram, the more uncomfortable I felt at the similarities between them and us that kept surfacing. Some part of me began to suspect that humanity shared more with this warlike species than with the peace-loving Xix.

The emperor was in its chambers. There was the expected flurry of activity around the ruler as orders were given, problems were raised, deals were negotiated, and strategies were plotted.

Waythrel's translator converted the speech before us almost in real time, casting each speaker's tones with different human voices, allowing us to easily follow the conversation. A subject of the emperor was explaining something to the ruler.

"Dram is suffering, Holy One," came a pleading voice inside our bubble. "Crops are neglected. Power and resources are being diverted to the Project. The alien harvests are consuming all that we have. We cannot continue like this. Dissent is growing. There is talk of rebellion."

The emperor's voice was robotic. "Is that all?"

I watched the many legs of the petitioner dance around at this response. "Yes, emperor."

"Then take this message back to the local governors. The Project is all that matters. Defeat of the human Reader is the highest priority. The war cannot be won without it. Suffering births strength. Any resistance to the Divine Orders will be met with death. The fields will continue to expand."

The giant bug in front of the throne straightened its long torso, lowering its head before the Emperor. It turned and scampered out of the throne room.

"The Emperor looks drugged," said Ambra.

Waythrel agreed. "We have both spent enough time on Dram to know the personalities and character of these creatures. Ambra is right—something is wrong."

"Let's get closer," said Ambra. "There's a lot of room behind the throne, and no traffic."

Our bubble descended. It also turned out to be a fortuitous location. Nestled behind the throne, we were able to observe the comings and goings without becoming an obstacle. More importantly, we were given a view of the back of the Dram emperor's head.

"What the hell is that on its head?" asked Moore.

"A crown," said Waythrel. "Of a kind."

But Moore didn't mean the cap-like crown with its multi-threaded braids hanging half a foot below the head of the creature. He pointed to something else.

"No, look—underneath the braids. That thing in its head. I don't think I've ever seen that in my readings or meeting with the Dram."

"It's embedded in its brain," said Williams, a scowl on her face.

"Ambra, can you allow me to approach?" asked Waythrel.

"Yes. Just walk," she said. "But be careful. If you get too close, and it moves and hits you, it will feel a disturbance from the enclosure. Remember, all of you, while we are cloaked we are vulnerable."

Waythrel walked forward. To my eye, it seemed that the alien stepped away from us toward the throne without anything around it or between us. Of course, I knew intellectually that Ambra had encased us all in this invisible barrier. But it required an imaginative focus to continue to believe in it without any sensorial feedback about its existence. Part of me wished the Dram would start shooting at us again, only so that I'd have the sense that *something* was actually around us and doing something. Of course, with the thing cloaked, those shots might actually do us some harm.

Waythrel approached within several feet, its eyestalks moving forward together to inspect the black box seemingly stuck inside the glistening exoskeleton of the Dram ruler. After a minute or two, the alien returned.

"I have never seen it before," it said. "Five decades on Dram, and nothing like it existed."

"Maybe it's new," said Moore. "Been a few hundred years since you visited."

"Or maybe it's reserved for the rulers," I added.

"The technology is not from Dram—that was clear on inspection," said Waythrel. "It appears to be constructed of raw materials from the planet, however. I have studied Dram physiology and possess a renewed memory of it from my species-sharing. The device is located precisely in the region of the mental organ that controls conscious choice in the Dram. The only reason to embed a machine there is to override or modify the will of the emperor."

"Wait," said Williams. "That box is controlling its mind? And the Dram didn't make it?"

"The Anti," said Moore.

Ambra nodded. "You heard the words they spoke. The emperor is killing Dram, working it to exhaustion and stealing the resources of the planet for some grand project. Some of this I saw in the mind of the Dram soldier. But to see it at this level is something else."

"What are these fields? What are they harvesting?" I asked.

"Not food," said Waythrel. "The reports of starvation and rebellion indicate that."

"Whatever it is, it has to do with *you*," said Moore, pointing at Ambra. "The project is to build something that kills *you*."

"Agreed," said Ambra. "So, you'll excuse me if I am motivated to go find these fields and look for myself."

"Find them—how?" I asked.

"They can't be far," said Waythrel. "If they are diverting power and resources to them from Gred, they are likely on the outskirts of the city."

"Wait—shouldn't we listen in and find out more?" asked Williams.

"Perhaps," said Waythrel. "But I can't think of anything more pressing than determining how they are working to kill Ambra Dawn."

"I agree," I blurted out.

Moore cocked his head to one side. "Fields for harvesting. To kill Ambra. I think I know what they're growing."

I caught my breath. I thought I could guess too.

Waythrel's eyes swiveled and stared at all of us. "We need to go find these fields."

39

Close your eyes and listen. Listen to the silent screams of terrified mothers, the prayers of anguished old men and women. Listen to the tears of children.

—Eli Wiesel

W e found the fields.

Take the giant AgriCom farms from Ambra's youth in the Midwest, replace them with humans instead of corn or cattle, multiply by a factor of one hundred, and drop the entire thing into the oven-baked landscape of Dram, and you would have some idea of what spread out before us. Mile after mile. Housing, pens, birthing factories, biotech. Square after square of parceled land marked repeating installations in an industrialized assembly line to manufacture people. To manufacture copies of a single person. To the horizon a sea of copy after copy of buildings, workers, and Ambra Dawn.

At first we just flew over the fields, scanning the layout, noticing the absurd lengths to which the Dram and Anti had gone. It was only when we descended to enter the compounds themselves that the disturbing nature of the enterprise really kicked us in the teeth.

I could spend five books detailing everything we witnessed, swooping down into buildings, entering the labs and factories, following the clones. We spied on the workers, Ambra pilfered information from their thoughts, and much was simply obvious as function followed form. But a summary is sufficient. It sickens me to even remember it now, and the briefer I can be, the better.

The biotech labs were staffed by Dram technicians, but it was clear that they did not drive the research. Several other alien species that neither Ambra nor Waythrel had encountered directed the efforts. Imports from locations distant and strange, perhaps, brought in to perform highly specialized work. And behind them in every location, pulling every string and setting each course, were representatives of the Anti. They were housed in energy-gulping protective containers that shielded them from the matter surrounding them. But the seat of power was clear as the unknown aliens took instructions from these shadowed boxes and relayed the research protocols to the subordinate Dram techs.

The labs had obviously been in operation for hundreds of years, likely opening soon after the Great Calamity was reversed. And what had they been working toward for so long and with such dedication? That became obvious in the birthing wards—or more accurately, birthing factories.

The human slaves of the Dram, and the descendants of those slaves, were paying a terrible price for existence. They became the experimental animals on which the Anti applied their dark technology. How many had suffered and died at the hands of these sociopathic monsters, I didn't know. But I could begin to guess some of it when I saw the current products of the R&D.

Women had been converted into fetus-production units of a hellish nature. Each woman in the birthing rooms had become a demonic fusion of flesh and machine, a cybernetic organism invaded and controlled by hundreds of wires and tubes. Their midsection was distended beyond recognition, the womb augmented in size ten times what it should have been. The rest of the body had reversed, atrophied, shrunken to the point that it was clear that everything about these warped creatures was designed for one thing: producing fetuses.

And produce them they did. Artificially inseminated as well as directly implanted with embryos (it depended on the facility—the Anti were trying many approaches), these womb-sacks, human only in ancestry, gestated at many times the normal rate. We didn't have time to find out whether it was due to specialized nutrition, hormones, genetic changes, or other approaches we had not imagined, but it wasn't relevant in some broader sense. Suffice it to say, the Anti with their Dram pawns had found a way to take the initial stock of eggs stolen from Ambra and create an industrial production line for growing clones of her.

Within weeks, each birther would be harvested for offspring. Robotic implements would insert into the exaggerated vaginas and remove upwards of ten fetuses. These fetuses were hardly developed enough to survive outside the womb, but the machines plunged them into artificial wombs for a second round of growth. How they had optimized this—the timing, design, hormone and nutrient balancing—was as unclear as it was astounding. But it worked with horrible efficiency.

From our cloaked enclosure, Ambra discovered more shocking information from the minds of the techs. In the span of two months, they had crawling infants. Within a year, prepubescent girls. Within five years, fully functional adult clones that could speak and manipulate the fabric of space and time. An investment that required extraordinary patience, but at the end, they had succeeded in industrializing the production of the ultimate bioweapons.

The process was centered on the acceleration of human development. We examined several different sites and determined that as newer technology was created, they simply built more locations with cutting-edge methods but allowed the older plants to continue operating—likely until the product was so inferior that they shut them down.

Herds of little Ambra Dawns were penned together, a sea of orange hair covering the landscape like some strange crop. Here and there we could see humans shepherding them, putting them through trials, teaching them lessons that seemed odd to our eyes but functioned within the artificial program to produce these weaponized humans.

How much experimentation in human mental development had they performed? The standard human cattle that they kept at every site were constantly studied and probed. Rudimentary cultures were allowed to develop within their prisons so that they could be observed and mimicked in the raising of their prized breeds.

The rejected failures of their efforts were one of the saddest parts of this terrible story. Deformed, brain damaged, emotionally traumatized—they were the most plentiful population everywhere. But they didn't live long. Studied, tested, tortured—the Anti tried to find what they had done wrong. Once a given failed clone had given them what information they needed, it was killed and discarded.

The scope of the monstrous plan was in this way revealed to us. Now we knew where the False Dawns were coming from. And it was clear that the Anti were just getting warmed up. They were in it for a very long haul. I shuddered to think of the suffering on Dram and across the galaxy their continued efforts and progress would produce. One of those things in the desert had been enough. *An army?*

Soon Ambra zeroed in on the newest fields. These were clustered toward the northernmost position from Gred. She was able to identify them because the clone development in these locations was far superior. The minds of the False Dawns were more intact, more powerful, their signature and distortion of space-time extreme.

And there were thousands of them. Tens of thousands in the largest complex alone. It was at this site of greatest progress where events took a terrible turn and our time on Dram ended.

40

Those who understand evil pardon it.

—George Bernard Shaw

"I want to speak with one of them."

I could see that she was worked up. Gone was the usual distant tranquility I had come to associate with her knowledge of time through her visions. Her face was strained. Her hands clenched at her sides. I suppose that had we been under less stressful conditions, it would have been easier to understand and forgive her. But I couldn't stop myself from protesting.

"Ambra, no!" I said. "We got what we came for. We've pushed our luck far enough! Let's take what we know, get the hell out of here, and put together a plan of action when we have time! When we can summon resources. *Armies.*"

"He's right, Ambra," said Waythrel. "The risks outweigh the benefits in this."

But Ambra had a wild look in her eyes. "I said I want to speak to one of them. And I will, whatever any of you say."

"Look, sister," said Moore, "what you say we have a wee vote on this? When did this become a dictatorship?"

"When everything that has happened has been possible because of me!" she shouted. "I got us to every world. I protected us from the Dram. I uncovered this information. I'm only asking that we speak to *one* of the clones. *Just one.* I can handle that."

Williams stood in front of Ambra. "And you're losing your mind on this one, girl. In case you missed some important things, we've got two human purée waiting for us in orbit. You didn't see *that* coming. You didn't stop it. So, how about you back off from the almighty god thing and stop ordering us around."

"Ambra, please—" I began.

"Do you know what it must be like for these girls? Do you have any idea what it's like to grow up as a guinea pig in a hostile lab? Where they starve you, beat you, shock you, and cut on you? Turn you slowly, steadily into a monster, a dark, twisted form of what you should have been? Where your worth is found only in their approvals?" She waited as if we would answer. "Well, *I* do!"

Waythrel tried to intervene. "Ambra, whatever pain these clones have endured cannot be—"

"Look at them!" Ambra shouted, gesturing in front of our bubble at the sea of orange hair beneath us. "Thousands of them! At least I had a few years of love from my parents. I grew at some human pace. These things—their mothers are nightmares. They have no fathers. They have no normal development. You want proof of hell? You don't have to look any further."

I saw tears dripping down the sides of her cheeks. I walked up and put my hand on her shoulder. "Okay, Ambra. I'll come with you."

"Ah, shit," cursed Moore, turning away in frustration.

"Look!" I shouted. "Ambra can send the rest of you away, back through the Orb or something. You don't have to be involved."

"For myself," said Waythrel, "I am not concerned. My primary fear is for the Daughter. To engage these highly developed clones could risk much. You don't know their powers."

"I easily defeated the one in the desert, Waythrel," said Ambra. "I will be careful. I will choose one and bring it inside the enclosure, sealed away, unseen by the others. If we are attacked, I will kill it."

"Why don't we just kill it now?" said Moore. "You remember what that thing did in the Sahara, right?"

Ambra looked at Moore but touched my cheek with her palm. "I remember. But I didn't know about this. I hadn't *seen* this. I hated them before—the very idea of them, even. Now…now I feel pity."

"And what do you think you will accomplish speaking with one of them?" asked Waythrel.

"I don't know, but I need to look," she said. "I need to look and find out if there is any hope."

"Hope for what?" asked Moore with exasperation.

"That they can be saved. That there is something inside them that can be saved."

41

Everything you do reverberates throughout a thousand destinies.

— Nikos Kazantzakis

In the end, everyone signed on to the crazy idea.

Signed their death warrants. All because deep down, we were all somehow committed to Ambra, and this was something that she had to do. I saw it first, but the others came to accept it. Foolish or not, it was impossible to stop her. We were either with her, or we would abandon her to this fate.

Ambra floated the invisible space-time bubble over the enormous compound, past the birthing warehouses, the labs, the pens of hundreds and hundreds of tiny Ambra Dawns. For me, it was hardest to see the child clones. I didn't know when in the process of their brainwashing they would be turned into the creatures that would seek to kill us, to kill Ambra, to destroy the planet of their origins. But seeing the small ones, it was almost as if I could detect remaining innocence in their eyes. Children's eyes. And this more than anything gave me empathy to the pain Ambra felt. I could feel deeply why she wanted to save them even if I believed the cause hopeless.

We slowed around the demented "schools" where the older children were instructed. Preteens, early teens— the age when the tumor and its powers developed and flourished. All had been modified surgically. All sported the invasive machine technology embedded in their bodies. All had lost some aspect of their humanity. Most had probably already lost their free will.

They never slept. Instead, unconscious, they would be attached to machines that sent electrochemical signals through their brains. What it accomplished we didn't have the time to determine, but Waythrel guessed that it was an accelerated learning and maturation program. Part of the long research program that had culminated in the ability to produce human clones like so many items on an assembly line, ready to be shipped into battle.

When awake, they were subjected to tests. Attached to machines or out in open fields, their powers over space-time were examined, challenged, and augmented ruthlessly by Dram and human trainers. Some of the older clones served as advanced teachers as well. The Anti had learned to preserve extensive features of human culture, hierarchy, and social bonding even in such a dysfunctional form. They had perfected the madness and addiction of cult attachment.

Ambra found a smaller group of younger teens who were moving from one of the sleeping chambers to a practice field. One of the girls was several steps behind the others.

"She will do," said Ambra, the enclosure swooping down beside the clone. "They likely won't miss her for a few minutes."

Suddenly the girl stopped, bumping into an invisible wall. Disoriented, she tried to walk forward but could not. I realized that Ambra had enveloped the clone in the bubble.

"Don't panic," said Ambra. "They can't see her, and she can't reach us. But she can see us."

The clone turned around.

"Ah, shit, here we go," muttered Moore, charging up his ion-slingers. Williams followed in short order.

Ambra walked up to the clone and spoke. "What is your name?"

The girl—no more than twelve or thirteen—looked confused and frightened, but determined. "A4552, Teacher."

"You are blocking your mind from me," said Ambra.

"Yes, Teacher. Lesson 22. Never lower defenses in the field."

"I want you to disregard Lesson 22 right now, please."

The clone appeared anxious. "That is illegal. Is this a new test?"

"Yes," said Ambra. "I want you to share your mind with me."

"I live to kill the Originator," the clone nearly chanted. "I do not break the laws."

"You will not share with me?" asked Ambra.

"I will not break the laws." There was a short silence. "Do I pass this test, Teacher?" The clone's breathing had increased dramatically. It was terrified.

"Sit down," said Ambra. The clone sat, and Ambra followed suit. "If you will not open your mind, I will have to enter it myself."

"I will defend."

"Yes, I thought you would."

The clone screamed. She grabbed her head as her eyes opened maniacally. Ambra appeared tense. Her eyes were closed, her mouth set as a thin line. The clone began to moan, rocking back and forth, holding her head, the pitch of her voice rising and falling like some tortured animal.

The sounds were terrible to hear. I looked at Moore and Williams. Both shook their heads. The eyestalks of Waythrel danced around, but the alien did not intervene.

"No! Liar!" cried the False Dawn. "It's not *true! Stop!*" Blood began to trickle from the inserted tubes in her skull. "*Liar!*"

"Ambra, you're killing it!" I whispered harshly.

Suddenly Ambra stiffened, and simultaneously the clone's eyes opened. It spoke in a demonic voice that seemed to project like some loudspeaker. "The Originator. She is here. She is here. Come. Kill. She is here!"

Ambra's face was strained. The space around us began to undulate. The bubble seemed to lose some kind of integrity as waves propagated outward from the clone.

"She's losing control of the thing!" yelled Williams. She stepped forward and sighted the clone in her targeting system, raising her arms to fire.

And then she was torn apart. Blood sprayed across my face, and tissue exploded in all directions. Body parts were slung against the walls of the enclosure.

"*No!*" Ambra shouted. "Nitin! Waythrel! They're programmed! Automatic!" her breathing was labored. "I can't stop it! It will reach them."

And then I grasped my temples. The sound of its voice exploded in my mind.

She is here. She is here. She is here. She is here.

I managed to look around. Moore was kneeling, his hands to his head. Waythrel's eyestalks were darting around wildly and the alien swayed as if it might topple over.

She is here. She is here. She is here. She is here.

Ambra cried again and stood up, a terrible strain in her features. *"No!"*

The clone arched its back, the tubes exploding out of its skull along with blood and bone. A red paint seemed to splash against the invisible barrier behind it and drip slowly downward. The False Dawn swayed backward, its eyes rolling up in its head.

The voice in my mind stopped. The clone fell over and didn't move. I slowly got to my feet, dizzy, unsteady, and stepped beside Ambra. The enclosure smelled of blood. A metallic taste coated my mouth.

I sensed movement in my peripheral vision. A fog of orange seemed to be rising around us, becoming denser, congealing and choking out the other shapes and colors around us. I placed my hand on Ambra's shoulder.

"Are you okay?" I asked.

"Oh, Nitin." Her desperate eyes looked outside the enclosure. I followed her gaze and focused. A swarming herd of shapes converged on our position. Red hair. Green eyes. Thousands of clones. And they knew where we were. They saw us now.

Waythrel spoke. "The dead clone triggered them. They know *you* are here, Ambra! They are coming for you. Uncloak us! Harden the enclosure, now!"

Ambra shook her head. "What have I done?"

42

By a route obscure and lonely,
Haunted by ill angels only,
Where an Eidolon, named NIGHT,
On a black throne reigns upright,
I have reached these lands but newly
From an ultimate dim Thule—
From a wild weird clime that lieth, sublime,
Out of SPACE—out of TIME.

—Edgar Allen Poe, *Dreamland*

The entire compound turned on us. I don't know how many there were. Likely thousands in all. Certainly hundreds of the power Ambra had fought in the desert and just killed in front of us. I know that she couldn't have repelled them on her own. There were just too many. She must have tapped into the power of the Orb, which, after everything, brings this part of the story to a most ironic conclusion.

"Kill as many as you can!" Ambra cried.

The contrast to the empathic hurt she had felt only hours before couldn't have been greater. But we didn't need convincing. We'd seen that thing rip our warrant officer to shreds in front of us. Ambra had seen its mind, felt its thoughts and feelings. That she had now jettisoned all concern for their well-being said a lot.

"I don't know what we can do!" I shouted. "We're only two!"

We began firing. At first we created considerable carnage. The clones had no battle armor. They were standing in front of us like ducks on a pond. With our missiles and ion slingers, we likely downed a hundred or more in half a minute.

No doubt Ambra was a big part of that success story. She had semipermeabilized the enclosure. Our little bubble allowed our weapons to escape but still presented a formidable shield for us inside. Even though the clones didn't raise any weapons, this still came in handy when the Dram military showed up and began firing on us, which happened about a minute into this insanity.

Soon piles of slaughtered clones encircled us. But the real battle took place in a realm that only Ambra could access. Waythrel sat with her in the center of the bubble clasping her hands, deep in that Reader trance like the one we had seen around Gyl. But this was far worse. I could see in Ambra's face the tension, the fatigue as her energies were quickly depleted. I didn't know how long we could hold out.

There were massive disturbances around us. The ground itself heaved and buckled, space contorted, and time and again our enclosure suffered assault that seemed to bend the air around us and then pop back. Meanwhile, as our weapons became increasingly useless—the missiles now spent, the ion rays deflected by the clones who had zeroed in on our efforts—even greater chaos erupted outside. In a large-scale replay of the death of Williams, the clones were being shredded. It was literally a meat grinder out there, and the only reason I didn't turn away from the visceral horror of it was that I was caught like a deer in the headlights. I was stunned by the sheer fleshly decimation progressing around us. Only the shield of the enclosure Ambra continued to maintain kept us from drowning in blood.

I began to become seasick, as much from the time distortion as the physical carnage. Back and forth the pace of events seemed to rock, suddenly slow, suddenly fast, skipping moments, backtracking to create repeated experiences of déjà vu. Holes opened and closed around us, tunnels to nowhere and from nothing. The veins bulged on Ambra's brow, and the alien had changed to a deep shade of purple. This was going to kill them.

"Ambra, just punch a hole in all this and get us up and out!" I shouted.

I'm trying, Nitin. They have cast nets around us, came a voice pounding my consciousness.

Moore looked at me grimly. "We're not going to make it out of this one, Capt. Look! These roaches are just pouring out of the woodwork."

He was right. More and more clones approached. They ignored the horrific fates of the mangled bodies surrounding us. They were fanatical, devoted completely to destroying us. If Ambra didn't get through whatever they were doing soon, we were dead.

A bright light flashed in my eyes and I fell backward, stumbling to my knees. *Flash bomb?* I could see; it wasn't a device. Instead, standing behind Waythrel was an apparition from my nightmares.

It was the little demon girl from the cornfields. Somehow, in the midst of all these identical clones, I recognized her. Something about her movements, the sparkle in her eye, and the slight twitch at the corners of her mouth when she noticed I was staring at her.

"*You?*" I gasped. But Ambra's cry interrupted me. I looked away from the devil girl and saw that Ambra was flat on her back, a stunned expression on her face.

The young clone grabbed Waythrel's upper arm, and the alien cried out and collapsed.

Ambra sat up and screamed. "Stop! Nitin, help me! I can't move! Please, stop her!"

The thing smiled. It looked right at me knowingly and winked. *It winked at me!* Another flash blinded me temporarily. When I looked back, there was nothing. The child was gone. Waythrel was gone. There was only empty space where they had been a second ago.

Ambra sprang forward with a cry toward where they had been. She landed on her knees grasping only air, tears on her face, a wild, mad look burning in her eyes.

"Waythrel!"

The agony of her scream cut deep inside me, and I nearly stumbled from the impact of it. But I couldn't focus on her pain. The disappearance of Waythrel had done what ten thousand attacking clones could not: broken her power and focus. The bubble around us collapsed.

Into the breach, a False Dawn clone flew like some possessed witch. Red hair billowing behind it, arms upraised like claws and a homicidal death mask on its face. Ambra didn't respond. She didn't move. She sat there holding herself, her empty arms that had missed grabbing Waythrel wrapped around her chest as she rocked.

I launched my suit forward, but I knew that I could not make the distance in time.

The impact was both metallic and fleshy. Moore's suit blasted upward, his shoulder set as it smashed into the stomach of the clone. I could hear the creature's spine snap as its body was bent from the impact, and the two of them rocketed high into the air.

"Moore!" I screamed, watching as a red cloud of clones darted upward in pursuit.

Moore's actions shocked Ambra out of her state. She stood up quickly, the remaining clones once again boxed out by a wall. Looking into the air, however, she saw what I did. It was too late to save Moore. The clones had already ripped him apart.

"Ambra—"

She held up her hand to silence me. I could sense her concentration. She closed her eyes. Outside the clones redoubled their assaults on the enclosure. But their progress was reversed. The inroads before were turned around.

I began to see them pushed back, struggling against unseen forces. I felt as if I were hallucinating. Many began to age horribly, their skin drying and peeling off their bones, the bodies that seconds ago were attacking us bursting into a cloud of dust. Crawling around in the dust were tens, then hundreds of infants. The structures outside began to sway. The warehouses and laboratories rippled around me. Newly arriving Dram military craft disassembled and rained fragments onto the sands.

"They're still here," said Ambra.

"Who?" I said, my eyes wide at the impossible things I was seeing.

"Waythrel is in the system! We have to hurry. They're heading to the Orb!"

Ambra stared upward and grasped my hand harshly. Two things happened. We blasted off the ground in our enclosure, the surface of Dram quickly receding. Below, it was as if a nuclear weapon had gone off. The entire clone field was flattened suddenly, circular ripples extending outward and leveling everything in their path. All the clones, the buildings, perhaps large regions of Gred itself were annihilated in the destruction.

But I didn't watch very long. I turned my eyes upward as we ascended toward the heavens.

And so a doomed pursuit began.

43

Madness rides the star-wind...claws and teeth sharpened on centuries of corpses...dripping death astride a bacchanale of bats from nigh-black ruins of buried temples of Belial.

—H.P. Lovecraft

We rocketed upward through the Dram atmosphere. I don't know whether the remaining hordes of clones tried to follow and were held back or were so incapacitated by Ambra's wild destruction that they couldn't. Whichever, I did not see anyone following. All I knew was that I was traveling faster than I had ever experienced with a mad goddess, her eyes flaming green, shockwaves exploding outward from the atmosphere around us as we blasted into space like some meteor in reverse.

She had let go of my hand and placed her own near head level against the enclosure walls. The speed made me want to hold on as well, although the need was illusory. As before, everything within the bubble she created remained stable and unperturbed, sealed off from the chaos around us. In a few short seconds, we were thrust into the blackness of space, a darkness punctuated only by the Dram world receding behind us, its two moons, the red giant star of their system, and straight ahead of us—growing closer at a shocking rate—the incandescent shape of the Orb.

But I had never seen the Orb like this. Even when Ambra had summoned such breathtaking power from them in the battles we had fought, what I saw now was a supernova to a nova. The local star was eclipsed in brightness. And inside the Orb was a churning chromatic cyclone that seemed more hostile than transcendent. For the first time, I began to truly fear the thing.

Ambra focused only ahead in its direction, speaking nothing, her entire body tense like a rod. Following her gaze, I was amazed to see another pair of bodies between us and the flaming sphere, the distance slowly closing. It was not hard to guess that it was the False Dawn and Waythrel. They were heading straight for the Orb as well, and something told me that somehow, impossible as it should have seemed, the creature that had kidnapped Ambra's dearest friend had the power to use the portal as well.

We continued to gain on them, but it was clear that it was a hopeless chase. They would reach it before we could. If the clone could activate the Orb, it could transport to whatever place and whatever time it desired. We would lose Waythrel.

No! We won't lose them! The thoughts from Ambra exploded into my mind. *We will follow them through any pathway to any place or time!*

You can do this?

Watch me!

The Orb storm—I had no other phrase for it—seemed only to intensify, as if responding to her words. The bright light was now also offset with black clouds, vortexes, tunnels, and membranes that seemed to enter and leave our space as portions of a higher dimensional whole. The light almost felt like thunder—so bright it was an assault on the senses. The darkness pulled at something deep within me, something primal, so that every irrational fear that I had ever felt suddenly came alive. I was stunned, overwhelmed by the cataclysm brewing within the cauldron before us. My feet felt rooted, unable to move as I stared dumbly ahead. Had I needed to act quickly to save our lives, I don't know what I could have done.

Suddenly, the pair in front of us vanished into the Orb. We were only seconds from entering the maelstrom ourselves.

I still see you, clone. You can't get away!

She was not even speaking to me, yet I heard those words in my mind. She was screaming to the universe, or perhaps toward the shapes that we were pursuing. My mind just happened to be in the blast radius. Ambra was determined to follow that thing to hell and back if necessary.

I remembered the horrible trips through the Orbs that I had experienced. All of them sickening, several reaching levels of pain I had never known. Now Ambra was about to enter the thing when both she and the Orb were in a state of such turmoil that space itself seemed to be seething. She was going to chase through those labyrinths of space-time another being that appeared adroit as well. This would be no prepared journey, no stroll to the edges of the galaxy. This would be a wild chase on a rocket through the fire. I closed my eyes and prepared for the worst.

But it was Ambra who screamed.

I opened my eyes and couldn't believe what I was seeing. Before me, the Orb had reached some sort of mad climax, the frothing currents of space and time, light and darkness, wonder and fear, like some enormous maw opening to swallow us. But that epic background to my vision meant nothing.

Arms outstretched, her face contorted in rage and pain, Ambra rose before me. She seemed increasingly paralyzed, flattened against an invisible slab, chained to it and unable to move even to turn her head. She thrashed back and forth, staring wild-eyed into the devouring mouth before us.

She screamed again. Her arms moved slightly, her back arching, and the surface of the Orb rippled before her like the sea underneath a squall. Lightning erupted from the dark clouds, rays of light splintered the space around us until I could not keep my eyes open except in a squint. Blood began to leak from her nose, and her body convulsed.

"Ambra, no!" *You're killing yourself!*

I tried to grab her legs, but the second I touched them, an electric charge threw me across the enclosure. My hands burned and went completely numb. My vision blurred, and I had to strain to focus. I tried to stand—my legs no longer functioned. I could not move. Crumpled and helpless on the transparent floor of the enclosure, I looked on this terrible sight in growing horror like some broken and castaway trinket.

Ambra continued to rise like some terrible statue, her form now completely frozen. There was nothing between her and the Orb. The bubble was perfectly transparent, and in this numbness consuming me, it began to feel as if it were nothing more than an illusion. Reality had become the Orb alone, that Titan raging in anger, and it had grasped my beloved and ripped her from me.

Still she rose, now fifty feet above me, still paralyzed, still unmoving. There was no sign of the False Dawn or Waythrel. By now I had to assume they were long gone, and I guessed that Ambra did as well. I could see the muscles across her body straining, twitching, trying to find some way out of this invisible prison. All her efforts failed to move even a finger.

And then the ascension stopped. For minutes that passed like hours, she floated there alone, a fleshly form dangled in the midst of space before the door to heaven or hell, I didn't know. I tried several more times to move, but it was fruitless. Something had damaged me badly, and I would not be able to reach out to my lover. I was helpless to intervene, if there were anything I could have done anyway. Looking on this madness, I knew that I was a fool for even trying, arrogant for thinking that a lowly soldier could involve himself in such affairs. This was an arena for gods.

It was at this moment of resignation and despair that I began to hallucinate. The electrical discharge that had wrecked my nervous system in my extremities must have damaged my mind as well. This is the only explanation I can find for what I next witnessed, but you can judge my memory as you will.

As I gazed through tears toward my beloved, shapes began to form in the churning broth of the Orb. Indistinct at first, small spheres that could be viewed as mini-cyclones in the greater chaos, they took structure. Definition. Recognizable patterns. Chills swept through me. The Orb surface was forming *faces*.

A few at first, large, the size of cities. Then thousands. *Millions*. Uncountable numbers of faces that bubbled in and out of the broth like some witch's horrible brew. Many of the faces were recognizably human. Most were not.

And then the faces began to chant.

It was like no music I have ever heard or experienced since. I'm not sure that *music* is the right word to describe it, but I have no other. More complex than the greatest symphony, as pure and clear as a temple chant, currents and sounds that were distinctly human were wrapped and mixed with ten thousand that could only have come from the orthogonal mentalities of the truly alien.

The chorus swelled. The faces continued to materialize, the harmonies increase, the sound seeming to fill the very emptiness of space itself. The Orb ceased to churn, the surface of the hypersphere calmed like a placid lake. Only the disembodied faces moved, chanting, creating a music that seemed to have more substance than the sparse matter of the universe itself.

It was beautiful. And it was terrible. It was so much beyond what I could grasp and appreciate, what I could internalize without drowning in it. Being consumed by it, I began to withdraw. A survival instinct perhaps. My paralyzed body began to shut down, and I felt myself slipping away. The edges of my vision darkened, blurred, and I could not focus. Like a drowning shipwreck victim, I flailed madly to tread water and breathe. Frantically I thrashed to stay awake.

As my consciousness bobbed above the chanting currents for a moment, suddenly the visions entered the truly bizarre. Now there were two Ambras. Still, my beloved hung as a hazy outline before me. But before her, larger, spanning the size of continents, a form bubbled out from the space-time surface of the Orb. Tendrils of light and cloud clung to it and then fell back into the infinite sphere.

It was Ambra, but not Ambra as I would ever wish to see her. Mirroring the paralyzed position of the Daughter, this titanic apparition floated toward her with arms outstretched to the side, frozen in place and unmoving. But not whole. The hands were mutilated, the flesh ripped and jagged. Worms or tubes or cables or something crawled into the skin of its hands and feet.

Blood flowed outward and seemed to stain the fabric of space itself.

But the horror had only begun. The body materializing before us was further desecrated. The skull was cut open, removed, the brain spilling out in layers across a black slime. A giant tumor, some mountainous mimic of my dear Ambra's neural growth, lay like an obscene egg in its own depression of the reflective darkness. Living cables of dark material slithered into those mental tissues and merged with them, the entire form becoming some nightmarish mixture of flesh and machine.

And for a third and last time, Ambra screamed.

Somehow she broke through the forces holding her. Her mouth opened, and a cry of such devastating pain ripped through the cosmos that I was convinced that the geometry of space-time would be shattered and unrecoverable. Her cry did not die but wailed into the void ceaselessly, the waves of sound beating through me, the sense of her pain and torture unbearable.

And then she fell.

A second electric shock coursed through my flesh. And then, I could move. I could see clearly. I leaped forward, my suit granting me a speed and power that made it just possible for me to catch her as she entered the enclosure. Ambra landed roughly in my arms.

The lights from the Orb were gone, and it had turned a deep black. There were no faces, no chanting, no chorus of the gods. The monstrous apparition of Ambra was nowhere to be seen. There was a stillness and powerful silence that felt thick like fog.

And stars. Stars all around, softly shining through the transparency of our journey's bubble.

I sensed the softness of her flesh even through the suit and longed to hold her without this artificial barrier between us. Her eyes were closed. Red hair cascaded down my arms. Her porcelain skin nearly glowed against the black of her robe and the darkness of space.

I raised her closer to my face and bent my neck, bringing my lips to hers. I kissed her but pulled my head back sharply, listening.

She wasn't breathing.

Part 3

Parasitism is the birth pang of symbiosis.

—The Book of Xix

44

The other gods! The gods of the outer hells that guard the feeble gods of earth!...Look away...Go back...Do not see! Do not see! The vengeance of the infinite abysses... That cursed, that damnable pit...Merciful gods of earth, I am falling into the sky!

— H.P. Lovecraft

*F*alling.

Holding Ambra, falling to my knees. Struggling to remain conscious. Swimming through images, voices.

Songs.

Endless echoing chants of limitless gods forming shapes and patterns and realities before me.

The dark sphere approached, the surface enveloping us, the universe behind disappearing. Still I held her, tightly, refusing to give in to the call for sleep.

Peaceful sleep. To rest, finally. For this terrible and long struggle to end. The voices spoke of tranquility. I only had to close my eyes, to stop resisting, to trust them to bring us out of danger and into safety.

They knew my name. They knew my heart. And I knew them. Faces of family and friends and enemies. My parents.

My slain comrades-in-arms. Fox and her starry-eyed faith. Kim and his childlike energies and enthusiasm. Moore with his rough and loyal mouth. Williams and her blunt analysis. Marshall and his abstracted duty.

Waythrel. The one we chased. She too was here. Beside her another Xix. Waythrel nodded toward it. "You will meet soon."

And then Ambra's face. She spoke to me. I felt her arms around me. "I hold you now as you hold me. Let go, Nitin. It will be easier this time. Don't be afraid. Just let go."

The space before me was spinning, the light labyrinth glowing and beginning to burn brightly. A million passageways through space and time and song. I didn't want to go down those painful roads again. I feared them.

"A last trip. This time, there will be no pain."

My own voice.

It spoke to me from outside of me. My madness and hallucination were complete. Dreaming or imagining, I didn't know. Or were they different? Which was waking and which was dreaming? In this impossible universe, what was truly real? How could such limited forms of flesh discern?

It was too much. I felt myself falling. I placed Ambra down on the surface as a glowing vortex built around us. I lay down next to her as the bubble dropped, plunged down into the bottomless, rotating well of light. I closed my eyes.

We fell.

45

I measured the skies, now the shadows I measure.
Skybound was the mind, earthbound the body rests.

—Johannes Kepler,
self-authored epitaph

I awoke to the sound and scratching of blowing sand.

A fierce heat beat down on me as I tried to open my eyes. Stuck together, the lids refused to part. I reached up and tried to clean them but only managed to spray sand into my face and mouth. I coughed and spit it out, using the spittle to lubricate my eyes. The sand and spit made a mud, and it was rough to rub it across my skin, but it worked.

I cracked the lids open and squinted at the blinding sunlight. Two seas, orange and blue, faced off below and above me. I was disoriented but also comforted in some strange way by something familiar. After a few seconds, I understood. I was back on New Earth.

Ambra!

I sat up and looked around me frantically. Her body was beside mine, face up, eyes closed in the sand. I crawled to her quickly and placed my face over her mouth. *There was no breath!* I grabbed her wrist but could not find a pulse. I forced myself not to panic, to think, to act professionally. My emotions would only doom her, if she was not already.

I powered up my suit, relieved that it was fully charged. I engaged the medapp and diagnostics unit on the side of the suit, and needles and probes extended into her arm, taking samples. The AI reported promptly.

"Asystole diagnosed without discernible trauma. No serious internal injuries, body temperature normal."

No obvious harm! But no heartbeat. No respiration! Normal temperature—then it could not have happened very long ago! There was still a chance!

"Immediate CPR recommended with intravenous vasopressor."

It had been over a year since I had refreshed my CPR training, but there was no choice.

"What's an intravenous vasopressor?"

"Medkit epinephrine syringe is provided to all MECHcore battle units."

Adrenaline! I reached around and detached the medkit, pressing the keypad to open the box. There was a large syringe labeled Epinephrine. I grabbed it, removed the safety cap, and plunged the end into her arm, keeping it there for about ten seconds for the solution to drain.

I tossed it to the side and rose over her on my knees, the sand scraping beneath the metal of my suit. Sweat began to bead over my eyebrows, and I had to wipe my hand over them just to see. I placed my hands above her sternum as I remembered and began the rhythmic compressions, squeezing her heart, forcing blood through her body. Life liquid of cells and oxygen and nutrients and now adrenaline.

I pressed hard, as I was taught, and after six, I heard the first rib break. *No!* I couldn't let it distract me! It happened, I remembered from the training. I tried not to think about breaking her bones.

I continued through fifteen, twenty, and then stopped at thirty. I put my palm on her forehead and gently tilted her head back. Then I lifted her chin forward with my other hand to open the airway. I listened. *Still no breath!* I pinched the nostrils shut and covered her mouth with mine. The contrast to our loving embraces was an offense. A crime so horrible and clinical and desperate. But I made a seal and began breathing into Ambra's lungs.

Back to the chest. Fifteen more compressions, another crack occurring in the middle. *Dear God!* Another breath. Salt water flowed down my face, stinging my eyes. It was almost impossible to keep my vision clear.

"Please, Ambra! Please!" My words were hissed out through the compressions of her chest. Again and again and again I pressed. I didn't know how long I could keep this up in the heat.

In the middle of the fourth cycle, Ambra gasped for air.

"Ambra!" I screamed at her, but she didn't respond. But she was breathing! Her chest shuddered and fell in haphazard movements.

I attached the diagnostic device, and the AI spoke in monotone. "Ventricular fibrillation detected. Recommend defibrillation with current unit. Confirm, please."

"Confirmed!"

"Please clear contact with patient."

I pulled back, and the device hummed to a charge and sent current through Ambra's sputtering heart. The muscles around the chest wall tightened and striated. Then they relaxed.

"Normal cardiac rhythm established."

I didn't hear anything else it said as the AI rolled out numbers that were much more useful for a doctor to hear. I bent down and felt a regular breath from her lips. Her chest rose and fell. *My Ambra was alive!*

"Recommend immediate evacuation to medical facilities."

For the first time in this insanity, I looked around the desert. It was familiar. A sand plane of enormous length ran in all directions, decorated in the distance by a tower that seemed to rise into the heavens. The Sahara. *The Temple.* How we had gotten here, I didn't know. But I knew we were within communications range.

I stood up and engaged the transmitter on full power and broadcast on all emergency frequencies. "MAYDAY, MAYDAY, MAYDAY. This is Nitin Ratava, Captain of the Special Temple Guardians unit. I am outside the Temple City within sight of the antenna. Ambra Dawn is seriously injured. Repeat, Ambra Dawn is with me, and she needs immediate medical evac. Please respond."

My COM shot back only static. I tried to boost the signal and ramped all the power to communications. "MAYDAY, MAYDAY, MAYDAY. This is Captain Nitin Ratava—"

"Captain Ratava, roger your transmission. We are locating your position. Please confirm again your message."

"I have Ambra Dawn with me. She is critically wounded."

There was a sharp crackle in the static and then a different voice. "Captain, this is Major Mizoguchi linking in. Where is the rest of your party?"

"Dead, sir." Just saying this was a gut punch. "They're all dead. Correction: Waythrel of the Xix was kidnapped. Whereabouts, unknown. Status, unknown."

There was a short pause on the COM before Mizoguchi continued. "And the goals of your mission?"

"A success, sir, but I don't give a damn right now! Ambra's hurt!"

"We have medical on route to your position and have a high resolution visual on you."

"Tell them to burn through their thrusters," I said, seeing a thin line of blood trickle from the corner of her mouth. "I don't know how long she has."

46

A man is a god in ruins.

—Emerson's "Nature"

I stayed beside her on the wild flight back to the Temple City. After I had told them all I knew, the medical crew asked me to move to another part of the ship, but I refused. They saw my eyes. I stayed out of their way, and they seemed to ignore my presence.

From their conversation, I gathered that her condition was serious but stable. I had indeed broken ribs in my efforts to revive her, even puncturing a lung in the process. But her vital signs were strong, and they believed that with proper Xixian care back in the city, she would recover quickly.

It was a tremendous relief to hear, and for the first time in many days, I relaxed and let others take on the burden of crisis. I was exhausted both in mind and body. So much had happened, so many losses, so many impossible revelations and events—my mind was still in shock. I leaned back against the walls of the hovercraft and closed my eyes.

The opening of the bay doors startled me awake. They took Ambra quickly off the ship and moved her to the medical unit. I stayed out of their way and decided against causing any more interference. She was stable. She was going to be okay. With that knowledge, I could let them do their jobs.

Mizoguchi, Mazandarani, and several others awaited me as I exited the craft. I sighed, much too tired to want to deal with anyone right now. But I knew they wanted answers. It was only right that I try to provide them.

I stopped suddenly in my tracks. A Xix stood with the others, its eyestalks a tower above the humans. I stared at its black and phosphorescent colors shimmering through the color spectrum in curved lines across its body. I had seen it before. In the last dream.

"Synphel," I whispered.

The others looked from me to the Xix in surprise. The Xix walked forward and stood in front of me.

"How do you know my name?" it asked me.

"Waythrel told me."

"Waythrel spoke to you of our mating groups?"

Mating groups? "No." *How do I explain this?* I put my hand to my forehead. I was so tired. "Until I saw you, I would have said Waythrel never spoke of anything like...mating groups. Or your name. But once I saw you, I recognized you from...an experience I had before I transitioned here."

"What was this experience?"

"I don't know. Another strange dream. I always get dreams when I go through those damn Orbs. I heard voices. So many of them. So strange. At the end of it, Waythrel spoke to me. *You* were standing next to Waythrel. Waythrel said that I would meet you soon." I looked over the alien and shook my head. "And here you are."

By this point Mizoguchi and Mazandarani had stepped forward, listening in to the conversation. Synphel bowed to me.

"I am pleased to make your acquaintance, Captain Ratava. You clearly have been blessed with profound experiences in your travels."

"Or cursed."

"Yes, such powerful events are hard to distinguish and are often both." The alien's many eyes looked me up and down. "I recognize that you are weary, but Waythrel is important to me. Please tell me all you know about what happened."

"You are Waythrel's mate?"

"One of them."

"So, you have marriages, divorces? Or multiple spouses?"

"Closer to the latter, Captain. We tend to keep our social behavior to ourselves, but because you are so intimately involved in our stories, I will explain something few humans have heard." The Xix let that sink in. It did, but I had no idea what to do with it. "You may have noticed that we do not use gendered terms when speaking about ourselves."

I nodded. "Yes. It's a strange hiccup in your translators."

"Not a hiccup, Captain. It is intentional, because to do so would distort our natures. Humans have a bisexual genetic and phenotypic biological mating structure: male and female. Of course, there are spectrums of behaviors and physiology associated with this basic average sexuality, as in any biological system, but that is the general structure of your reproductive and culture norms. We of the Xix do not possess two genders."

"You are asexual?" I offered, wondering if they budded like yeast or impregnated themselves. I needed to lie down.

"No. We have six genders."

"*Six?*" I *really* didn't know what to do with that. Even Mizoguchi and Mazandarani looked surprised. This obviously was rare information.

"Yes, with the associated physiological and genetic differences. You have male and female, each with very different bodies and character. Sexual organs. Biochemistry. We have six, and a successful reproductive mating event can only occur when all six copulate simultaneously. Of course, sexual partnership can occur in binary, ternary, and other combinations for the pleasure and companionship of the mating group members, but reproduction requires all six."

Now my head was swimming. "I'm not sure I want to learn much more."

"I will spare you the details. But Waythrel and I were different genders in one such group. In fact, we were a very closely associated pair in the combined sexual event, and somewhat similarly to your mostly monogamous interactions, had lived extended portions of our lives in each other's presence."

"Married?"

"Not precisely, but the term will do. Does this help you understand why I care so much to learn what befell?"

I nodded, thinking of Ambra. "It does. Thank you. Let's go to the hospital, and I will tell you what I can on the way."

The Xix bowed again and stepped to the side. I began to walk toward the entrance of the medical wing.

Suddenly Mazandarani was in front of me. I nearly crashed into him. My temper flared. "Excuse me, yes?"

"You are a fortunate man," he said, remaining where he was. "The only one of your team to survive the mission. It's as if certain fates are shaping your destiny." There was a fire in his eyes.

I couldn't believe I had to deal with this. "Sepehr, *not now*. Just get out of my way and let me go see Ambra."

"Yes. Your only failure was that she lived. Do you go to finish the job?"

I weighed my options in an instant. Possible statements or silences as a response to this. After a half second of consideration, I threw all pretense of maturity to the wayside and hit him.

I smashed my fist across his jaw, and the Iranian sprawled upon the floor. There was a collective intake of breath from bystanders around me, followed by a natural parting of the waters as people cleared out from around me. But Mazandarani wasn't the fighting type. He just held his face and the trickling blood coming from his mouth while scowling at me.

So then I did more than hit him. My suit was still activated. I reached down, and with the full power of the hydraulics, grasped him by the robes and lifted him into the air. His feet dangled inches off the ground, a shocked but unbowed expression on his face.

"Captain Ratava!" came the imperial voice of Major Mizoguchi. "Put down the counselor now!"

But I was in a state. Blame fatigue, loss, mental trauma, or the ugly insinuations of Mazandarani, but I had simply had enough.

He spoke through clenched teeth. "And did they pay you to kill me, too?"

I glared at him. "They wouldn't have to."

I felt a steady but very firm grip on my shoulder. The towering form of Synphel loomed over me like a shadow. "Captain, there is nothing that would pain Ambra more than for us to hurt one another."

And like that, my will for violence was gone. I put Mazandarani down, perhaps somewhat roughly, but the alien had rebooted my emotions. It had known exactly what to say.

Mazandarani straightened his robes and looked at Synphel with some semblance of shame. I simply turned on my heel and strode out of the docking area without a word or a second glance toward anyone.

47

No one is as capable of gratitude as one who has emerged from the kingdom of night.

—Eli Wiesel

"You saved my life, Nitin."

She looked beautiful. Hair in disarray, eyes bloodshot with dark circles like a raccoon—it didn't matter. It's hard to describe the overwhelming feeling of joy and wonder that ran through me to see her open her eyes and smile. Speak. Gesture with her hands in that elegant way she had. *My Ambra is alive! And I love her!*

"I guess that's fifty to one, now. I'm still deep in the red." I tried to maintain a soldier's composure. It was difficult. "I'm sorry about the ribs."

"They'll heal, love," she said, smiling again.

I sat in a chair holding her hand, gazing upon her face like the first time I had seen it as a child in school. Synphel was present. Mazandarani stood opposite me on the other side of Ambra's hospital bed. After our altercation a few days ago, the two of us did our best to avoid each other.

"Thank you for speaking with Synphel, Nitin. I have shared with her now. All the details that we have are passed on to the Xix. They will do what they can, but there is little hope to find Waythrel now. The clone could have gone to any place at any time through the Orb."

"And the bodies of Fox and Kim? They were not in the desert?"

"No," said Mazandarani. "A thorough search turned up nothing."

Ambra spoke. "It's my fault. I left them on Dram in my chase after Waythrel. The Orb may have brought us back, but it didn't pick up after us."

The Orb. I had a distinct ambivalence about the object now. All my life, I had learned the mythology of the Time Spheres. I had memorized the legends because they were central in the story of Ambra Dawn. Always awe and goodness, always hope when the subject was presented. After the terrible events at the Dram homeworld node, I would never see them in quite the same way again.

"How could the Orb have turned against you?"

Ambra's smile faded. "Oh, Nitin, there is so much I wish I could explain. The Orb is something far greater than I, and it has a mind of its own. I have always known this, but because my will and that of the Orb had always aligned, it was somewhat abstract. But things changed near Dram when they took Waythrel." Ambra sighed. "The truth is that the Orb did not turn against me—I turned against myself."

"What are you talking about?" How could she blame herself for this?

"You see, I had worked a lifetime to accept and plan for our losses, those terrible losses to come that you believe in abstractly because you trust my words, but which I have witnessed time and again. In vision after vision. Never able to escape them, their pain, living daily the loss. I didn't understand how much I had repressed of it. The anger. A deep bitterness. Especially after meeting you and you turned out to be everything I had envisioned. My heart was lost to you. To think about that terrible future—I barely held myself together, Nitin."

I felt embarrassed as she shared such personal feelings. Synphel was one thing—no doubt the alien knew much from the Reader sharings. But Waythrel's mate was still very alien and that provided a distancing. With another human, it was different. With Mazandarani—I didn't like his hearing about our relationship, and I am sure he didn't like it either. A quick glance at his face established it beyond a doubt.

"You seemed so strong. I didn't understand," I said.

She touched my cheek. "I didn't either, or you would have seen it when we shared. But when that thing took Waythrel, something shattered inside me. I had *not* seen this in visions—it was hidden from me by greater powers. A total surprise—something that happens less and less frequently to me. But it was another terrible loss. One I had not prepared for." She nodded, as if explaining the entire thing to herself as much as to me. "I lost control, Nitin. I flew into a mad rage. I abandoned all my efforts in this long struggle, refused to listen to my visions and the calls of the Orb. The clone had opened the Orb. The *Orb* had allowed this. I should have recognized this, accepted it, *understood* the significance. But I was too crazed, too rebellious, too *arrogant* in my hurt to let go and take my rightful place. I'm afraid that I was beginning to believe in my own mythology." She shook her head. "As I tried to change what should not have been changed, the Orb intervened. It showed me my mistakes. It reminded me of my path."

"What path?" I asked, horrified, remembering the terrible visions.

She glanced away from me. "My path is still unfolding, and even I can't see all ends. What happened there is beyond fully understanding. For now, at least. Until events reach completion."

Synphel interrupted. "I am very grateful to Captain Ratava for sharing his experience in the Orb transit. It may not seem to make sense, but I believe that you heard the voice of Waythrel, Captain. How, I don't know. But somehow, through the Orb, Waythrel reached out to you, and to me, to connect us in our future struggles. I will remember this."

I was unsure how to respond. I certainly did not feel I deserved such commitment and connection to Synphel. As always, the Xix left me slightly in awe. But I bowed my head and tried to accept the offer.

"We all loved Waythrel. Ambra most of all."

"Not more than Synphel, Nitin." Her face dropped. "But yes, I miss Waythrel terribly, already."

Mazandarani cleared his throat. "Daughter of Time, I have completed the preparations as you have requested. I only need your go-ahead for the ceremony." His face was terribly strained.

"What ceremony?" I asked.

Ambra's demeanor brightened considerably, and she squeezed my hand. "A marriage ceremony, Nitin. One that will take place here in the Temple, before all the Readers during a Great Sharing. The Group Mind will be formed to preside over the sacrament. The Readers are en route from across the world right now!"

I looked around in confusion. "What wedding? Who's getting married?"

Synphel spoke. "The Daughter of Time, of course."

I looked at Ambra in shock. She smiled impishly at me. I stared at Synphel, who was unreadable, and then at Mazandarani. "Is this true? Ambra is getting married?" It seemed as if the floor was about to give out underneath me.

"Yes. Even though I sought to prevent it."

"Counselor, you have yet to overcome your possessiveness," spoke Synphel. "Until you do, you will have no peace."

I didn't give a damn about Mazandarani or his peace at this moment. *Ambra to be married?* It couldn't be! How?

"Ambra, I don't understand. Married, to whom?"

"Why to *you*, Captain Ratava," answered Synphel.

Ambra laughed. "Nitin, I will not ask you a third time: will you marry me?"

48

I dive down into the depth of the ocean of forms,
hoping to gain the perfect pearl of the formless.

—The Gitanjali of Tagore

But the first ceremony we attended was to pay respects to those who had recently fallen in our struggle. There were now no bodies, no remains, nothing but the memories we carried with us for the five who had died serving humanity. Serving more than our species—giving their lives for thousands of sentient worlds across our galaxy that fought this long and often dark conflict to free themselves from the tyranny of the Dram.

A few of us gathered in the desert, near the spot where Ambra and I had awakened only a few weeks ago. A collection of Xix and humans gazed upon a makeshift memorial hewn from the bedrock, orange and marbled, polished to a gleaming finish, with the names engraved:

Erica Fox

David Kim

Ryan Marshall

Grant Moore

Aisha Williams

Only Waythrel's name was withheld, at the request of Synphel and the Xix. They refused to commit the kidnapped alien to the causality list, holding out hope that someday Ambra's beloved advisor would be found.

In homage to ancient rituals of Old Earth, a flame was lit in an oil-filled bowl beneath the names. A protective field was set around the memorial, shielding the slab from wind and sand. The oil was to be refilled weekly by servants of the Temple who would trek the distance in the heat to pay respects.

Ambra stood by my side in the winds, her robes billowing and her hair dancing. She smiled and turned to the rest of the group.

"Until we join them again," she said. I was too consumed with conflicting emotions to parse what she meant. Too often, her metaphysical pronouncements escaped my understanding. For the time being, I struggled to accept the loss of my team, my inescapable responsibility for their deaths. Command carried terrible burdens. Sometimes there was a debt that could never be repaid.

We returned to the Temple City, and the Temple proper, by hovercraft. Ambra said that the truest way to honor their deaths was to fully live, and she insisted that our ceremony proceed that very evening. I began to sense that she truly possessed a unique view of death, and therefore of life as well. She seemed to speak as if the dead were not truly departed. Perhaps in her special sense of time they were not. Perhaps she was always able to access their existence from a place outside of time, viewing life and death as eternal elements in the fabric of existence. Try as I might, I could not share her combined joy and sadness, nor could I understand the far-flung gaze she possessed when speaking of and to the dead. I was left with my struggles.

Whatever I thought of Mazandarani, he had somehow pushed aside his jealousy and pain at losing Ambra to me. The marriage ceremony was planned as grandly as the Festival of Rebirth. As we approached the Temple, the streets were lined with forms. Xix and human, as well as the odd other alien species—some in environmental suits, some remaining in protective craft. Tens of thousands had come from every corner of the planet and from star systems distant. It was a gathering like no other I had ever seen.

I wore my military dress uniform. Black coat and pants, the red beret with the MECHcore gear train insignia stitched in gold thread emblazoned on the front. My captain's bars gleamed along with honor badges and medals from numerous combat operations. It was an oven in the suit, but I tried to appear relaxed.

We disembarked from the hovercraft directly in front of the long stairway to the Temple. Ambra and I walked together in the lead up the stairs, Synphel and Mazandarani behind us, and then a pack of dignitaries. Behind them, the crowd quietly fell into line and followed us into the enormous structure.

The mood was festive yet serious. Many of the most powerful Readers of our galaxy were present, and their combined experience and wisdom in perception and repeated sharings produced a crowd personality unlike any I had experienced. Perhaps it was a weak echo of the Group Mind that Ambra often spoke about, now reflected even in the demeanors of its constitutive elements, these individual Readers. There was no randomness of disconnected strangers, nor was there the empty-headed mob mind. It was something else, something more than alien. It seemed to permeate the space around us.

We entered the open expanse of the central chamber and walked straight toward the swirling chromatographic projection of the Orb into our local space. The Orb projection reflected the mood I sensed from the crowd of Readers now spilling into the chamber. Gone were the storm clouds present in the terrible conflict with Ambra at the Dram homeworld. The colors seemed alive with potential and anticipation. The patterns somehow suggested in my mind future possibility and a strange sense of hope. I wondered, somewhat amazed, that this abstract-seeming display could shape my thoughts so.

Onward we walked, hand in hand, and neared the central dais within the color swarm. Thousands and thousands of Readers poured like a river through the entrance behind us, flowing over the surface of the chamber and pooling into their individual depressions. They did so nearly soundlessly, without speaking, the only noise their footsteps and the friction of the fabrics of their clothing.

We entered the prismatic nexus. Ambra turned us around, holding up our clasped hands into the air as the remainder of the Readers entered. I looked at my beloved, as much because I longed to as to calm the anxiety at this strange display of a power I could only sense subconsciously. She was more beautiful than I had ever remembered seeing her. She wore a special black robe, the material finer than anything I had ever seen, partly reflective of the glowing walls of the Temple building. She had recovered under the care of the Xix, her skin radiating in startling white, green eyes like luminous emeralds beyond valuing. I wanted so much to reach over and run my hands through her long curls of red but we remained still in the statuesque position she had chosen to greet the incoming Readers.

It took some time before they were all settled, but once the last Readers had entered, the door to the Sahara outside was shut. The sounds of the desert were completely silenced. The Readers assumed positions of meditation. Most were reminiscent of Indian yoga positions, although there was a wide variety, especially in the alien species that were present and visible.

Ambra lowered our arms and stared out over the landscape of meditating Readers, seeming to enter a trance along with the rest. For a moment, I felt strangely alone in this giant crowd, the only one excluded from the communion of their minds. A simple soldier without great talents placed in the center of a process that he could not understand or partake in.

But it was short lived. Suddenly, I began to feel strange. A vertigo began to unbalance my sense of position and reality, and it almost seemed that I could sense a deep rumble, some barely detectable bass hum that flowed around and diffused through everything. Something unusual was happening, beyond my experience. The passage of time seemed to alter.

I began to feel an irrational sense of presence. It reminded me of the intuition one has in the dark that one is not alone or a soldier feels in combat when a life-threatening event is near. Except this was not a fearful feeling. On the contrary, it was a calming one, but a sense of a presence nonetheless. Of something deep, greater than I. And it was everywhere, unlocalized, pervasive. Had I not known better, had I been alone in the desert with no education and nothing to hang this powerful sensation on, I have no doubt that I would have ascribed it to the presence of divinity.

We form the Mind.

A voice from everywhere and nowhere. I looked at Ambra. She had turned her gaze on me, her eyes penetrating into my own. The voice was not hers. It was not an individual. It was something much larger. It seemed to radiate from deep inside me.

We are *the Mind.*

I felt waves of warmth and electricity pass through me. I saw Ambra's face flush and her pupils dilate. My breath became stronger, more rhythmic. I felt as if I were being consumed, that tendrils of power were reaching into me from outside, entering my nervous system, stirring up a fire. Then I understood. I was becoming aroused.

The many have become One. Now two will be one and of One.

My breathing was heavy. Goosebumps covered my forearms and legs. My mouth went dry. I felt an erection stir. Waves of life seemed to flow through me, summoning all my energies. It was frightening. It was a hunger I could not possibly refuse.

"Ambra…" My voice was hoarse.

She whispered softly, "And shall I show you marital bliss, my husband?" She came close to me, her lips barely parted and engorged with blood, her body brushing against mine.

I gasped out, panting. "Haven't we already known it?" I wondered, remembering our time outside the galaxy on the sands.

"Not like this."

She began to undo the gold buttons on the front of my dress coat. I saw a bright passion in her eyes. Her fingers explored my chest through the spaces in my shirt buttons, her nails scraping against my taut nipples. I moaned, wanting to explode, my eyes beginning to swim, catching sight of her breasts, the glowing Temple walls, the flashing colors of the Orb, the sea of Readers deep in trances.

"Ambra—*here*? With all of them?" But I knew there was no resisting. No desire to resist. There was only full, complete, utterly consuming *desire*.

"Yes, love," she said, her mouth on mine, her tongue teasing my lips and a warm breath flowing into my mouth. She pulled my coat and shirt down around my elbows and ran her hands over my swelling chest. "A great sharing. And a Mind greater than any you have known outside the Orb will watch over us. And it will bless our love. Even as it partakes and augments it."

She pulled me down on top of her.

49

His left hand should be under my head, and his right hand should embrace me.

—Song of Solomon 8:3

She was right. It was not like before.

There was a swelling in the deep chanting, until it became a true Voice. A voice composed of many voices, low and high, human and alien, spanning notes and scales and qualities I could not have imagined existed and that in a transcendental harmony was multiple yet undivided.

The waves of that chanting washed over us, fueled our mutual desire, drove it higher and higher as we lay down upon the dais. My hands worked hungrily, tearing off her robes, coursing themselves over her naked form. My fingers caressed and scratched, exploring her legs, the red pubic hair, moving across her stomach to the ripe nipples atop her breasts, through her locks, and over the giant and bald skull. She sighed deeply and grasped my erection, stroking, enflaming me, guiding it into herself.

We merged. My hips thrust firmly, a cry escaped both our lips. I looked into her eyes, and they swallowed me whole. Biology commanded, the limbic broth overflowed, and I thrust into her again and again, my lips resting on hers, our breaths shared, her eyes drawing me deeper and deeper into a whirlpool of green scintillations.

The Temple disappeared. Fading to black, suddenly our naked forms were entwined as a single organism dangling within the color explosion of a nebula. My mind—both consumed in the mating act and by her eyes—was enhanced and freed to soar within this cosmic artwork as well. I felt my hands underneath her, grasping the flesh of her buttocks, pushing her pelvis toward me as my heart raced. Before me, the light of stars painted the dusts of space toward infinity.

I love you, Nitin. Always. Remember.

I came. I exploded within her as that life-purpose surged through my form. Again and again I thrust as she cried, her own reaction a perfectly timed orgasm. As before on the beaches of that alien world, our bodies were utterly in tune and in perfect rhythm.

But *not* like before. The tendrils of power flowed even more strongly through me. I felt a charge, and the usual collapse after climax was transformed. Suddenly, the hunger was back, my physiology altered. The arousal did not decrease but ascended to greater intensity.

Her eyes held me. I sensed the question, the request for permission to enter into this frightening and uncharted physical space. The biology of sex is raw power. It can wreak destruction in its intensity to create. I was being asked to play with a fire I only dimly appreciated.

I gave in wholeheartedly, not only from the burning desire churning within me, but also to connect, to become, to merge with the one I loved beyond anything I had known.

And so the waves became storms. The power flowed through us. Again and again our bodies cycled from arousal to climax, gentleness to wild passion. In myriad locations in space we made love over and again—before a star igniting its nuclear fuel, floating over a frozen sea of methane on an ice world, watching the dance of a multiple star system in accelerated time, flying through a dense star field until the points of light became elongated streaks of brightness speeding around us.

All the while in the company of a presence that looked down upon us, enhanced us, observed us, transported us, and loved us in some fashion that I could not completely understand. Beyond any kind of love I had known. Almost to the point of a dispassionate passion, an otherness that transformed the simple affections that creatures like us could possess and understand into something a godlike being would feel.

I was Ambra and Ambra was me and we were part of something *other*. Even I, devoid of Reader talents, felt it distinctly. Whatever vestige of that sensory organ I possessed in my brain, the power of this Being was so great that even I could appreciate it. I could not begin to imagine what it was like for the Readers themselves.

My body was now a portion of a greater organism. In this union, our passions continued, and my emotions were completely unrestrained. Freed by the overwhelming power of the experience, stripped of all semblance of artifice, social inhibition, personal restraint—I wept. And I laughed. I did both with such freedom and completeness that the mystery of how tears and laughter often seemed separated twins was resolved as they integrated and became one. Joy and sadness as much of a harmony as two human bodies becoming one flesh or ten thousand brains becoming a single Mind.

To describe more is impossible. As part of this multipartite creature, my experiences were of a nature I can now only faintly recall. Afterward, they dissolved to faded colors of vivid dreams, ideas that would seem hopelessly in conflict or impossible to be stated or grasped.

But during those moments, the universe itself seemed to drift before my awareness.

Eons passed.

And then we were alone together in her room. The Temple was gone. The Readers were gone. The powerful Mind was a blurring memory.

Ambra lay asleep on the bed, a faint moonlight spilling over the white skin of her bare shoulder protruding from the bedsheets. I was standing, suddenly returning to my senses, as if exiting a trance. I placed my clothes on the chair by a table against the wall.

I was exhausted. I needed to sleep as I had never known. I folded my dress pants, hung my coat, and left my beret on the table. I placed my medals and bars in their boxes and took the holster with my side arm and removed the Hertz, closing it within a drawer in the bedside stand.

I lay down on the bed. As my head touched the pillow, I felt as if the mattress were rising upward and enveloping me. Bone tired, yet at peace. Remade with a powerful emotion that was stronger than any I had ever known yet for which I had no word.

I closed my eyes.

50

Men of broader intellect know that there is no sharp distinction betwixt the real and the unreal; that all things appear as they do only by virtue of the delicate individual physical and mental media through which we are made conscious of them; but the prosaic materialism of the majority condemns as madness the flashes of super-sight which penetrate the common veil of obvious empiricism.

—H.P. Lovecraft

I feel myself drown again in dream.

Standing here as the soft morning sunlight of New Earth streams through our bedroom window, I look down on her sleeping. The white sheets are nearly blinding, wrapped tightly around her seductive curves. Her naked shoulder has slipped out of the fabric. It is nearly as white as the sheets, such a contrast to my dark copper. The entire blank canvas is dramatically altered by waterfalls of red curls streaming down to her waist.

As I look at the swollen—some would say grotesque—form of her skull resting on the soft pillow, I feel a deep attraction, a pull to touch, to caress.

As I walk to the nightstand and open the drawer, it is only in a state of unreal detachment that I remove the weapon. The composite metal should feel cold in my hand, but it does not. I feel nothing. The muscles tighten around the handle of the pistol, but I give no commands, feel no responses, sense no contractions or tightness in my skin. I can only see as if from a distance, from a vantage point I cannot define in space or in time.

And this automaton, my body, or now rather some ghostly form that is no longer mine, pulls that weapon out, unlocks the safety, and turns toward the bed, raising the barrel to the elongated head of my beloved, nearly touching the scarred edges near her hairline.

And before anxiety or understanding can even rise within me, she opens those blind green eyes with adoration, turning to stare directly into my own, tears trickling down her cheeks. I hear her voice in my mind.

Don't be afraid, Nitin. I love you.

I pull the trigger.

51

My friend, I am not what I seem. Seeming is but a garment I wear. The "I" in me, my friend, dwells in the house of silence. I would not have thee believe in what I say nor trust in what I do.

—The Madman of Gibran

The gun did not fire. My hand pulled the trigger over and over, and nothing happened.

Ambra sat up in the bed, her hair spilling over her chest and the sheets. She looked at me with a terrible coldness.

"We have anticipated you."

My mouth screamed, and my body lurched forward with my hands stretched outward to grasp her throat. But I got nowhere. Suddenly, I was paralyzed, frozen in space. She rose and slipped a robe over her naked body, straightening the beautiful locks above the hood after it passed over her head. The sound of running footsteps filled my ears, and I caught the outlines of several shapes entering the room through my peripheral vision. But I could not turn to see them. I continued to remain suspended.

"You are unhurt?" I heard one of them say. A male voice. Accented. *Mazandarani.*

"Yes," she said, staring across my field of vision to the door. "Sepehr, put the weapon down." There was a short pause, and she spoke with more force. "*Sepehr!* Now. Put it down!"

"He would have killed you." The words were spoken with such venom.

Synphel spoke from the same direction. "Remember not to condemn an innocent, Sepehr. Nitin is as much a victim as Ambra nearly was. More so. He has lived in ignorance because of our machinations. Show pity, counselor."

Ambra watched intently for a few seconds, and then I saw her face relax. "Thank you, Sepehr. Now, place him in restraints and put him in that chair."

My paralyzed and suspended arms were pulled behind me, and there was a buzzing sound as field restraints were used to bind them. Several sets of arms lifted me and moved my body backward, placing it down on a seat, my legs also restrained and bent to a sitting position.

"He is secure?" she asked. I could see them all in front of me now. Mazandarani nodded.

The paralysis ended. Suddenly, my mouth erupted in a string of vile curses aimed at the Daughter. I watched this happen as in a dream. I was possessed. I was mad. I was a split personality, and I watched helplessly as I cursed my dearest love. I wished to shout, to weep, but I could do nothing. I was a mind trapped in the prison of my own rebellious body.

Ambra held up her hands and my mouth closed, the sewage of profanities stopped. "That's enough." She knelt down in front of me, and my body spasmed vainly to get at her, to attack and spill the lifeblood of my lover.

She stared fixedly into my eyes. "Nitin, it's okay. This will be over soon. Hold on."

Mazandarani shouted. "Be careful, Ambra! You don't know where he is or what will be waiting for you."

She placed one hand on each side of my skull and closed her eyes. My body was shaking so violently that I thought it might be having a seizure. "No, Sepehr, *they* don't know what is *coming*."

What happened next I can only tell you through analogy and metaphor. I clothe it in visual images and archetypes because this is all my mind can do with the experience. As for what truly happened, only Ambra Dawn knows.

Like some supersonic freight train, the entirety of her consciousness as I had known it blasted into my mind, or rather into some now-enlarged space that contained what I once thought of as myself. Only now, I was not alone. Inside this place, anchored in some way as fundamentally as I was, there lurked *another*. It seemed that it stood in the back of my awareness by a doorway that I had never perceived before. Like a fading shadow, it slipped behind the portal and disappeared.

And the fury of Ambra was a billowing fire that rushed after him. As some phoenix or incandescent dragon, her soul flew past my awareness, through the door, and was gone in an instant, leaving me utterly alone in this strange, new space. Once my mind. Now, some insane house of mirrors.

I found I could move my body under my own will once again. I found that I could speak. I opened my eyes. Ambra was still there, still holding my head in her hands, her eyes closed, focused, and in some trance. The others in the room stared downward anxiously.

"Synphel. *Help me*," I whispered.

The tall Xixian approached. "Captain. It is not safe to remove the restraints yet. Do not disturb her."

"Why?" I asked. "Where has Ambra gone?"

"To kill an assassin."

"What assassin?"

"The one that has lurked within you since the day you were born," said Mazandarani.

"The Anti have been busy for centuries, Captain Ratava," said Synphel, "and not only training the Dram to create clones of Ambra Dawn. Equally audacious has been their plan to infiltrate Ambra's inner circle. To place spies. And among them, to bring to life the perfect assassin. One who could win the heart and mind of the target, who would be placed next to her in moments of extreme vulnerability. One who could be activated at precisely that point when the probabilities of success were highest."

I was trembling, not from the foreign murderous impulses I had felt before, but from my own horror and fear. "What are you saying?"

Mazandarani spoke. "That you are a deadly pawn, Captain. An experiment in murder. A monster designed by enemies so vile that nothing is sacred to them. You were *engineered* to kill Ambra Dawn. And had she not see through it, you would have succeeded."

"No."

"*Yes*," he spat. "A chimeric Frankenstein composed of three bodies and two souls, harboring malice and murder behind a veil of love."

Synphel interrupted. "*Careful*, Sepehr. You are letting your emotions cloud your thoughts. In what is to come, we will need your mind." The counselor lowered his head.

My words were spoken through a parched throat. "Synphel, what does this mean? What is he talking about?"

"A horror, Captain. A diabolic cleverness. You see, somewhere on the other side of the galaxy, in a future several hundred—perhaps thousands—of years from now, there is a ring of power plants not too different from what you have seen here. Except within the bowels of that place, deep underground, there are two bodies floating in a stasis medium. These human bodies are connected to feeding tubes and waste management systems, their skulls sliced open and the brains embedded in a dark technology. Surrounding those brains are a score of False Dawn clones, themselves chained to the room, their fate to maintain a long-term manipulation of space and time."

I felt a growing darkness encroaching on me. My vision seemed to be narrowing from the corners. "How do you know this?"

"The Group Mind has seen it, penetrated the layers of deception woven around the place," said Synphel. "In one of those tanks is your brain, Nitin Ratava, or rather, the proto-organic component of your mind. An advanced projection system of technology combined with the efforts from the clones opens a wormhole connecting a future time and another space with our here and now. This projection brought your highly engineered mind to be embedded in a developing fetus in India. Through a process honed by centuries of experimentation and aid from the shadows of the Anti, this process *worked*. You are that creature torn between flesh and space, brain and time."

"*Why?*" Horror flowed through me.

"Because there is a back door in your mind, Captain. A second body, a second mind projected within you, hidden for all of your life, yet *watching*. Seeing everything that has happened to you and transmitting that back to his masters."

"A spy?"

"Yes, but much more. If the time came, if the opportunity presented itself, this back door could open fully and this second mind seize control of your body. And so today it has happened, nearly to the death of Ambra Dawn."

I stared at the face of my beloved, my horror complete.

"I'm the assassin."

52

I know faces, because I look through the fabric my
own eye weaves, and behold the reality beneath.

—The Madman of Gibran

So much crystallized in my tainted mind. Many
things that had made little sense fell into place.
But I took no pleasure in finally understanding
the puzzle.

"She *knew*. She knew all along, didn't she? From the
moment we met. That's why she came to the hospital in
Japan."

Synphel paused a moment. "Yes, Captain. We have all
known for some time. Despite our enemies' best efforts
to conceal what they had done through space and time,
employing the powers of their monstrous clones to do
so, they underestimated Ambra's vision. They especially
underestimated what the Group Mind could achieve."

"How long has she known?"

"Since you were born," said Mazandarani, "although
some of us have only learned of this recently." His
expression was sour.

"Because you were too much in love with Ambra not to take matters into your own hands, Sepehr," said Synphel. "You would have wrecked our careful plans."

I felt a bitter seed sprout inside me. I felt used. My Ambra had used me, knowing for decades. She had said *nothing.* "A plan for me."

Synphel continued. "Yes, or rather, for the weapon of the enemy that was your body. We have played them, Captain, feeding them just enough truth to give them a false impression of our strategy."

I stared forward at the face I loved. Her expression was peaceful. Detached. *Cold?* How calculating had she been? How had she hidden from me this truth while we seemingly shared our souls? My head swam. Nothing seemed real anymore.

"You see, we knew that everything you heard and saw was reported back. *Everything*. Knowing you were a spy, however, presented us with an opportunity. So we led them to believe that we planned to shut them out with the closure of the Orbs. But what we did not tell you is that this is impossible. There is no way to fully wall off any portion of the Time Tree."

"Then those missions were a hoax? My team died for *nothing?*" Cold. Calculating.

"We were all to die if this clone army could not be defeated, Captain. Their deaths were not for nothing. They helped you and Ambra set the bait."

"What bait?" I felt sick.

"Once the Dram figured it out, that they could access the New Earth Orb despite what we did, they were exposed to a terrible temptation."

I understood. The military training spelled out the strategy in an instant. "A final hammer stroke."

"Yes," said Synphel. "Thinking that we had miscalculated, they would be tempted to breach our defenses with overwhelming force and crush us once and for all at the origin point of the Resistance—New Earth. That is why they withheld their full strength when you unintentionally leaked the mission details to them. Did you never wonder why those engagements at Brax and Hola had no clone contingent? They waited for the ultimate prize to reveal their hand. New Earth had to be in the mix."

"And why not kill Ambra in the desert when we returned? They wouldn't have to make me do anything except sit there. She was dying."

"We are not sure," said Synphel, "except that your travels through the Orbs played havoc with the wormhole connection. Nested wormholes, wormholes within wormholes—it is a complexity beyond anything we've approached in science. It was a terrible strain on you—it must have been much more so for them. Likely by the time they recovered and realized that opportunity, it had passed. They would rather be sure, plan the assassination carefully. Leave no room for failure—they would only get one chance. That was the final temptation in the great assault plan: if they had just assassinated our most powerful Reader—the only one who might stand a chance to defeat the horde of False Dawns, victory would have been assured, and New Earth would have met the fate of the old."

"Well, does she?" I asked. "Stand a chance? She told me that she couldn't. Was that a lie, too?"

Suddenly, I felt a blast through my mind, and the room became blindingly bright. A white noise filled my ears and then slowly faded. My sight returned.

"No," came a voice inches from my face. I startled within the restraints as Ambra spoke and opened her eyes. "No, Nitin. I cannot defeat their numbers."

"Then what is all this *about*?" I pleaded. I felt like screaming.

Ambra looked heartbroken. "I can't defeat them as I am. And so I will become more than what I am."

Synphel was silent, and Mazandarani looked toward her in horror. "Please, Ambra," he said, "don't do this thing." He was begging her.

"The assassin is dead," she replied to all of us. "I followed the link back to its source. There were multiple clones, as we had foreseen. I killed them, and then I shut down the life-support machinery of the spy."

"And what of Captain Ratava, Ambra?" asked Synphel, an anxiety in her tone.

Ambra reached around behind me and removed my constraints. She held my hands. "As my worst fears. His proto-brain was not there. They have him in another location." She saw the confusion on my face and explained. "I had hoped to free your mind, Nitin. To disconnect it from the flesh of its origin and permanently anchor it in the brain here. But I can't. I don't know where your body is. And I can't follow your link without them killing you."

"But you did for this...assassin."

"They were not prepared. That is why I acted so quickly. And they did not know what I could do. Now, they will know what happened, or figure most of it out. They will take steps."

"What will they do?"

"Kill you, Nitin. Pull the plug and break the connection."

"Then why not come for me first?"

She shook her head. "And leave that assassin free to roam your mind while I was gone? He could have broken the link within your mind and killed us both at the same time. I had to stop him first. It was the only way. The only hope."

The complications completely baffled me. "But wait. Haven't they been listening in? Don't they know about the trap now?"

"No. I didn't travel along the link they made to your proto-body, but that didn't mean I didn't touch it. I have propagated waves down the wormhole to the source. It will disrupt their ability to monitor you. It will wreak havoc with the passage of time in their space. It will slow them down. But not forever, my love." She wept and kissed me. "It is only a matter of time."

"Before I die." The finality of it struck me at last. "As you said."

"I'm sorry, Nitin." Her face was anguished.

And in an instant, I forgave her. I understood the larger context. I experienced a glimpse of the long pain she forced herself to carry. A terrible, terrible burden of knowledge. "I would never make a different choice, Ambra. Not even now." I stroked her hair as she leaned her face into my hand.

Synphel spoke. "It is also only a matter of time before their armada of ships and clones arrives. If you are to carry out your plan to the end, Ambra, we must act now."

I pulled her face away from mine, my cheek wet with her tears. Her lower lip trembled nearly imperceptibly. "Ambra, what are you going to do?"

She wiped her eyes with the back of her hand. "I am going to be butchered by my dearest friends," she said with a false smile and bravado, looking somewhat wild-eyed toward Synphel. "I will go through a new hell and a transformation. I have already died in your arms, beloved. Soon, I will be reborn."

Mazandarani looked at her in pain and with awe. "Daughter of Time."

Ambra stood up and straightened her robe. "And then I will call all souls to me."

53

The day will come when, after harnessing space, the winds, the tides, gravitation, we shall harness for God the energies of love. And, on that day, for the second time in the history of the world, man will have discovered fire.

—Pierre Teilhard de Chardin

I felt the first assault as we descended from the Temple deep into the sands of the Sahara.

A sudden vertigo, a sense of distance from my body, and my legs buckled beneath me. Ambra caught me and helped break my fall in the elevator car. We had descended nearly three miles into the crust of New Earth, heading to a secret center for the final stage of Ambra's long plan. But I couldn't focus on her explanations. I felt as if I were being separated from my own flesh.

"Nitin!" Ambra slapped my cheeks. I could hardly feel it.

"It has begun," said Synphel. "Captain, this is proceeding faster than we had anticipated. We will do what we can."

As the elevator car came to a stop, the wild vertigo stabilized, and I no longer felt quite as if I were looking in on myself. But I could no longer use my legs, and my arms moved liked some poorly manipulated puppet's. Synphel bent down and with one powerful motion lifted me bodily off the elevator floor.

They whisked me off to some medical ward staffed with at least twenty Xixian medics. I didn't have time to process what they were doing here, why this secret lair looked more like a hospital than a war cave, but I would soon discover the terrible answers to most of my questions.

Ambra was gone. They wouldn't tell me why, but instead the medical staff buzzed around me like some nightmare beehive with their arms and eyestalks. I felt numbly the insertion of instruments into my skin at various points. They had placed me in a special wheelchair of some sort, the back of it thick with instrumentation. I could barely talk.

"What…what are you doing?" I sounded drunk.

One of the medics paused to speak with me as the others continued. "We are trying to counter the distancing of your mental waveform with this physical body," it said, as if that made anything clear. "Several synaptic amplifiers are being located at strategic points in your nervous system. These will give you back some portion of your sensation and motor control."

The medic was right—I could already feel it. I brought my hand up to my face and touched my cheek. "I can feel it again."

"It is a temporary stopgap, Captain," said the alien. "It will buy you some time until your mind loses the ability to control the autonomic functions such as your heart and lungs. When that happens, your body here will die and you will be cut off."

I nodded. There wasn't much to say to something like that. Ambra had informed me of my coming fate. I had seen the truth of my dual personality. I now understood the powerful yet fragile link I possessed to this time and place.

But I didn't understand what was going on around me. The other medics were clearing out, in some kind of a mad rush. "What's going on?" I asked. "Is there fighting already?"

The Xix stared at me with its eyes. "Has she said nothing to you?"

Nerve dysfunction or not, I felt a wave of nausea sweep through me. "No."

"Then it is best that you learn from her or Synphel. I am Rel. I have been assigned to you. I will guide your chair to the operating room."

Operating room?

Things moved quickly. I discovered that the "wheelchair" was more of a *hoverchair*. The alien motioned over the holodisplay floating in front of it, and the device levitated. The medic exited, and the chair followed automatically, perfectly steering its way through the winding corridors.

Deeply, deeply winding corridors. We spiraled inward for a good ten minutes. The mystery of this place deepened as we passed room after room of Xixians and humans, their eyes following us through clear panes in the walls. When their eyes fell on me, their expressions became sorrowful.

"They seem to know me."

The medic spoke softly. "They are the dedicated Readers of the Temple, as well as tens of thousands more who have swelled their ranks for this final battle. They have shared in the Group Mind, Captain. They have traveled together with the Daughter through space and time. They have seen entire histories and futures, terrible and beautiful. They have seen the horizons of alternative universes. In these tapestries, they have seen your story and how it is interwoven with that of Ambra Dawn. They were present at your union." Inward and inward we continued to spiral. "The Group Mind is far greater than any one mind, even that of the Daughter. The Readers retain fragments of memories from the experience, even if they cannot understand the deeper insights of this more profound experience on their own."

"And I thought they came for our wedding."

"They did, Captain. It was a joyous and miraculous occasion. But an even greater purpose called."

I strained to move my head to the side where the alien walked beside me. "You're one of them, aren't you? You're a Reader."

"Yes, Captain. And soon I will take my place with the others for a very long journey. A final journey."

The spiral had tightened sharply, the unusual Xixian building materials giving way to a bright room. Medics, human and Xix, dashed around. Instruments of surgery, machinery, vessels with organic-looking broths were strewn about—not haphazardly, but with patterns I could not put together.

But the center of the room focused my attention. A huge slab of black reflective material, appearing wet like ocean shale, was embedded in the floor so deeply that I had to guess that the greater portion of it was invisible underneath the structure. The slab was not simply material, however. The best I can describe the impression it made on me was that the thing was organic—it was alive. It seemed to breathe and change shape, interfacing like some cyborg with pure machinery and the biological tanks and equipment. In the center of this bizarre creation was carved the negative of a human shape. The slab was imprinted with the form of arms, legs, a torso, and an extended, seemingly dreadlocked head.

In this negative space was Ambra.

I felt a cold shiver. I didn't know what this thing was. I didn't know why she was lying in it. But my intuition was profoundly shaken, disturbed and trying to call to my conscious mind. I felt I had seen it before.

"Bring me closer to her," I told the Xixian medic.

"It can only be for a moment, Captain," came the voice of a translator that I recognized. Synphel.

"Please."

The hoverchair floated forward toward Ambra. Her eyes were closed, but as I approached, they opened. They held fear in them.

"Hold my hand, Nitin."

Clumsily, I reached across the side rests and dangled my arm toward her. She reached up and grasped my hand tightly. I'm sure if I had retained normal sensation, it would have hurt.

Her voice was sad. "Look what they are doing to you." My deteriorating state was not lost to her blind eyes.

"Ambra, what are they doing to *you*?"

She looked away. "Very soon, I will never be able to hold your hand again."

"Because I'll die."

"And because I will never be able to touch another human being again."

"Ambra, *please*—explain to me."

"The cruelest part is how much I need to hold you, my Nitin. The Anti were so perfect in steering their Dram sheep. So cruel and heartless in their plans. You were made precisely for me. Maybe once in a thousands years two people chance to meet who are so precisely tuned to attraction and love." She looked back at me, a deep, terrible sadness in her green eyes. "But the biology can be engineered. You chose this creeping death that is rotting you rather than live a life without me. Part of me wishes that I could make that choice."

"Why Ambra? What is going to happen?"

She closed her eyes. "I will live an eternity encased in this living machine. I'll become an elemental part of it, until what was human is long forgotten and I am the nucleus of this ever-growing mind that will soon be born." She leaned forward and grasped my arm, her eyes flying open, a wild expression on her face. Her nails dug into my skin. There were trickles of blood, but I felt nothing. "All humanity lost but for a lingering *echo*, a terrible, unfulfillable *longing* over eons for you, Nitin. To touch you, hold you, love you once again as a woman."

She was shaking. I wanted to reach for her, to cradle her in my arms, to kiss the tears away. But I could not rise. I could hardly lift my arms. I was a broken shell, helpless to comfort the most cherished person in my life.

"Ambra, I can't..."

I'll be here, Nitin. And when they take you from me, don't despair. I will come for you. Always.

A voice interrupted. "Ambra, it is time."

Synphel stood to my side, its eyestalks darting around nervously. "The hyperbrane is failing. It must be now, if it is not already too late."

Ambra let go of my arm. "Take him outside."

"Ambra, wait, no!"

Too late. The hoverchair pulled back, and I saw her lying back into that wet rock as the distance between us increased. I tried to move, to grasp something, to stop the chair. If I could have, I would have thrown myself off and crawled to her.

But I could not even do that. I was nearly paralyzed once again, my puppet masters across time and space yanking, pulling, snapping string after string.

"Ambra!" I screamed, or tried to. My ears heard only a weak whisper of her name.

Be strong, Nitin. I need you to be strong for me right now. And then, to wait. Even in death and what comes afterward. Wait for me.

The medical workers closed around her like sharks in a feeding frenzy. They brought tools. Blood bags. Scalpels, scissors, laser cutters. Wires and cables.

The chair carried me underneath the doorway and out into the hall. A transparent field materialized, sealing the entrance. I was brought inside a nearby room. Synphel entered behind me, and Major Mizoguchi stood stone-faced gazing into the operating room.

Mazandarani stood there, his face pale, his form swaying as if drunk. His face was pressed against the glass, his fingers scraping down the sides of it.

He was weeping.

54

God judged it better to bring good out of evil than to suffer no evil to exist.
— Augustine of Hippo

It was like drowning, or what I imagined drowning might be. I fought to tread water, to keep my awareness in my body, to resist the vortex pulling me tirelessly into that star-filled tunnel and away from Ambra. But I was tiring. Each time I dragged myself back, I had slipped some more, and my awareness was increasingly detached from the reality around me. Out of the corner of my eye, I began to see the haze of light, the tunnel of stars opening its maw to draw me in. I knew I could not escape it for much longer.

My vision and hearing, all my senses, were now like machine-gun staccato. I couldn't be sure I had understood what I had heard. The words made no sense. They were monstrous. Using all my strength, I formed sounds, willing my numb lips to move, squeezing my chest with all my energies to force air through my throat.

"There must...be anesthetic."

Mazandarani turned bloodshot eyes to look at me but said nothing. Synphel gently approached my hoverchair.

"I'm afraid that there will not be," it said.

"Why?" The word came out like a whisper, a harsh sound of a dying man.

"The Dram horde is approaching, Captain, with its army of clones and dark allies. We are not ready to engage them. To fight them now means certain and swift defeat. Therefore, Ambra stalls them, as best she can."

Mizoguchi spoke. "She has been interfering with their attempts to transition to our space and time. But it cannot go on forever. There are too many forces arrayed against her."

"And if she is unconscious," continued Synphel, "if her neurological system is suppressed, the first loss of control will be in her tumor cells. The barrier will collapse. Their armada will pour into the space of your solar system in our now."

"She must remain awake until the last moments," finished Mizoguchi.

"The pain...distract her."

Synphel understood my increasingly simplistic phrases. "Yes, but the Readers are coming. The Group Mind, it is hoped, will be able to support her focus through the pain. But without Ambra, there is no Group Mind."

"It's...torture," I managed.

"Yes," said Mizoguchi, her expression grim. "She has accepted her sacrifice."

It was then that I began to notice them. A tide of figures, at first slow like a trickle, but then building like some organic tsunami, they came pouring into the honeycombed rooms around us. The chambers were like the floor of the Temple, with depressions in the ground like a grid across the floor. The figures, human and Xix, streamed across the grid and took seats in the depressions, their hands inserting into hollows on the sides, bands glowing with Xixian tech around their heads and midsections.

Synphel saw my clumsy gaze track their movements. "They come for the final synthesis," it explained. "This will be their last home."

The medic had said there were tens of thousands. It was like some enormous subterranean city of psychics. A gathering of powerful Readers, coalescing around the focal point in the center of the spiral. A giant hive for a group mind with my Ambra at its center.

"When the procedure is finished, Captain, we will rise into orbit to meet our enemies as One, united in a fashion unlike any army before."

"You talk," I gasped out, exhausted and confused, "like this is a starship."

"That's because it is, Captain," said Mizoguchi.

I will be here with you, Nitin, until your moment comes. Then you will not see me. And then you will see me again.

Synphel spoke. "They are about to begin."

"No, I can't!" cried Mazandarani. "I will not watch this!" He put his hand to the glass and stared toward the rock. "Forgive me, Ambra."

He turned an anguished face away and stormed out of the room. I couldn't turn fast enough to follow his movements. By the time I had moved my head to see down the hallway, he was gone.

The lights dimmed everywhere within the building except for the operating room. I could still not see Ambra for the medical staff surrounding her. Only the gleaming black of the living rock in which she lay rose above and past the forms tending to her.

The Readers had all taken seats and were absolutely still in positions of deep meditation. While my five senses were nearly completely numb, I began to feel a familiar sensation. Perhaps it was due to my strange limbo between two bodies, the contortions of space and time that was the matrix of my mind increasingly stretched by the linkages of the Dram and Anti. Whatever the explanation, I sensed something I had experienced only once before—two days ago at our marriage. But this time, my sense was much more acute. A sixth sense—not sight, hearing, touch, smell, or taste, but an *experience*—that maybe mirrored the powers of the Readers around me. My current degeneration granted me for the first time in my life a chance to see the universe a little as Ambra did. For all the pain and injustice of it—for that reason alone—I embraced it with all I had. It would not be wasted.

My words are distortions. The feeling can only be described in the images and vocabulary of the sensory world I had known. The sensation began as an odd vibration. Deep inside me, as if my bones had begun to shake. Undulating, long, then the cycles accelerating. The power of it steadily increased, and the vibrations transformed into tones, notes, pitches rising around me. It sounded like singing.

A chorus of voices. Each voice a personality. Each personality linked in unique harmonies of thought. *Mind songs* that grew into mental symphonies beyond my ability to follow. And this symphony, like all great music, had a personality, a mood, a character of its own. The Group Mind.

It was sublime. It was haunting and stirring. It was beautiful beyond words.

And then Ambra began to scream.

55

We are not human beings having a spiritual experience. We are spiritual beings having a human experience.
　　　　　　　—Pierre Teilhard de Chardin

I floated in space, the earth beneath my feet, the sun unimaginably clear before me. Truly, I had never seen before, vision limited by the biology of human eyes through the medium of atmosphere. In space, there was nothing. How I saw, I don't know. What I was, I didn't know. I had no body. Only thought and experience.

I am here, Nitin.

Ambra? How? They are…hurting you.

Yes. Below. But it is better to say, We are here.

Then they flooded me. Thousands of minds. The singular consciousness I had felt as Ambra alone fractaled forth, splintered like faceted shards of a gem and seemed to project into multiple new dimensions. What had seemed a single whole was revealed to be a host. But not divided. Of one essence and always reflecting back to the nexus of her mind.

I was overwhelmed. I could not process all the minds, their separate and full personalities, thoughts, memories, and emotions. I recoiled.

Don't be afraid.

And suddenly, it was only Ambra again. The other minds were gone, tucked into the fabric of hidden dimensions in this mental matrix.

Ambra. Where am I? What happened?

You are displaced. You hang by a string to your flesh on New Earth. In my trial below, I focused on you too much. I pulled you here with Us, even if you are not yet part of Us.

Ambra, I can't. There are too many. I only want you.

Shhhhhh, Nitin. See — there! — how they approach?

The emptiness between New Earth and the sun shimmered. Like the clear rubber material I had imagined in the Sahara when the False Dawn attacked, space itself puckered, undulated like ripples in a pond. Each impact, as if a pebble tossed, and the blackness was partly filled with ghostly presences. First, ships. Starships by the thousands like a plague of locusts beginning to blot out the sun.

Then I felt them. The False Dawn clones. Their power over space-time resonated through me like sound waves. I could feel them, feel their thoughts and feelings like the sense before a thunderstorm. I tasted the bile of their hatred for us.

Was it like this in the desert?

Yes. Even more so. You are not free, Nitin. You are wrapped in the chains of your keepers. It is like being wrapped in plastic insulation. What you see and feel is a whisper of what is there.

What I felt was awful enough. The shimmering ceased, and space returned to normal. As it did so, I could feel something *relax*.

Dear Ambra. You are all working to stop them. As they are cutting on you, doing whatever they will do to your body, you are also out here.

Not much longer now.

Again the ripples. Stronger, the ships becoming less transparent than before, their presence lasting longer than before. It was like a tide coming in inexorably.

This time, I saw more. Between the ships. Not the clones. There was a darkness. A lack of light more than the emptiness of space.

It is an unlight, Nitin.

It filled the space between the ships, around them, like some ink that ate the very space it occupied.

The Anti. Ambra, what will you do? I felt a violent pull within me again. *Ambra, I'm dying.*

The wave of sadness I felt wash over me was disorienting.

It is only a matter of time. It is always of Matter and Time.

56

And now I go—as others already crucified have gone.
And think not we are weary of crucifixion. For we
must be crucified by larger and yet larger men,
between greater earths and greater heavens.

—The Madman of Gibran

I crashed back to my New Earth body. *My body.* The only body I had ever known, yet that was not truly me. *Or was it me?* I no longer knew what anything meant anymore. What was real. What could be trusted, even within myself.

I was now completely paralyzed. My vision had narrowed to a tunnel. But in the hover chair, angled forward, I could still see through the energy field into the operating room. The medical personnel had been diluted. A handful buzzed around the slab. I could still see, but part of me wished that I could not, that I had stayed in space and died there, that I would never have had to see what had been done.

My Ambra.

Her distended skull was gone down to the hairline, the orange curls stained with blood and nearly black. Her brain—I can hardly describe it. The tissue was splayed out over several feet and deeply embedded in the living machine-rock. The slab seemed to absorb it, meld with it, fuse its surface to the cells in her body. The giant mass of her space-time tumor occupied a special cup in the slab surface.

Tubes bathed the tissues in her own blood and other nutrients. She was entirely sealed in a strange, clear Xixian material—sterile, environmentally controlled.

Her hands and feet were torn open like some science lab dissection. Tissue was filleted and distributed across the slab, particularly the fingers. Tubes, cables, wires, and dynamic extensions from the slab flowed into the rest of her eviscerated torso. She could not be alive. It was beyond imagining.

And then the full memory burst through my subconscious suppression like a sledgehammer to my gut. It was exactly the vision presented by the Orb near Dram. That vision was not a metaphor. Not some nightmarish insight into Ambra's soul or the soul of our enemies. It was not an abstract teaching tool. It was a precision prophecy.

"The extreme digits possess many nerves and therefore occupy a large representative volume in the brain tissue," said Synphel. Many of its eyes swiveled to look at me. "I know that you cannot speak anymore, Captain Ratava. I will explain what I can in the time you have remaining." It gestured back toward the horror in front of us. "Similarly, large nerve clusters in her eyes, her lips, ears, genitalia: All nerves must be accessed to optimize the synthesis. They will be reprogrammed, used instead to communicate with the AI and project to the other Readers. The initial operation was successful. With the help of the Group Mind, we were able to prevent excessive shock to her system. The integration is proceeding rapidly."

They had opened up her entire body like some medical school cadaver, *yet she was still alive.* Still conscious. *Without anesthetic.* In an agony I cannot possibly imagine. I looked over the cables and tubes extending from the large machinery around her, embedding themselves into her tissues. Her eyelids could not even close as wires inserted into the sides of her eyes. Only the irises were untouched, staring outward like two green pin lights. Her body shook, nearly convulsed, and the Xix swarmed around her, their distress at her suffering palpable.

"I am so sorry, Ambra," said Synphel. The alien paused a moment, and then continued. "When complete, there will be a phase transition. It will give birth in multiple dimensions to space-time fields surrounding her physical body. What was a relatively weakly linked mind of Readers will become far, far more a single organism, and the mental fields meshed as never before. Combined with the evolving AI, in a few minutes we will give birth to a cybernetic organism unlike anything in our galaxy. More importantly, a diversified, multifactorial mental synthesis will occur. *Should occur*—we don't know for sure, as it has never been done. And if it works, we aren't sure exactly what we will have made. But it's our only hope."

I no longer heard her in my mind. But I felt her. Unmistakably Ambra, yet muffled, distant, the torture requiring all her efforts to maintain focus on Earth's defenses.

Mazandarani returned, gazing in horror through the glass. He seemed to move in slow motion, and I didn't know whether it was because of his emotional state or my own increasingly distorted mental state.

"Can we go in?" he asked, his voice rough.

"Yes," said Synphel.

Mazandarani stumbled out of the room and to the door of the operating room. Synphel activated my hoverchair, and we followed.

"Ambra, dear Ambra," he moaned, and tore at his desert robes. He fell to his knees, his hands shaking as he reached up to the splayed horror of her dissected foot.

I could do nothing. I could not weep. I could not fall at the feet of my beloved. I only felt my body recede further and further. The room appearing to fall below me, return like a rubber band, and fall again. Over and over. The nausea was overwhelming.

WE MUST HURRY.

Her voice was in everyone's mind. In mine, because I heard it. In the others, because suddenly everyone responded.

"The synthesis is complete. The Dram approach." The alien turned to me. "I will stay with you until you pass, Captain. It will be soon. And then I will take my place in this seedship. We will meet again, perhaps."

I didn't understand what she could possibly mean. Maybe some Xixian religion with an afterlife? There was no *after* for me. I would die soon half a galaxy away in a distant future. *Another time?* It was impossible to cut through the maze of complications with these changes in space, time, and history. I couldn't imagine what it might be that could lead us to meet once more. I likely would not have understood even if Synphel had tried to explain.

It didn't matter. The entire facility was powering up in some startling fashion. I was almost lost, nearly losing contact with New Earth, but my last memories were mixed with shock and wonder.

This time there were real vibrations, not some superstring song of meditating Readers. Vibrations like an earthquake, but unlike any I had felt or seen. It seemed as if the very mantle were dissociating from the planet.

A monitor appeared in the air in front of us. To me, it seemed that I was watching from the end of a long pipe, the display small, the figure of Synphel gesturing over several portions of it, small yet clear. The display responded. The view zoomed in from space in seconds to hover above the desert surface.

And the desert moved.

The sands shifted and danced, and suddenly enormous fissures erupted as the surface split open. Lines of shadow spread miles and then connected, forming a rough, jagged shape. Sand from the surface spilled down the growing chasms and was blown high into the air from pressure.

Then the ground rose. A shard of the Sahara the size of an island detached from the planet and rose into the air. I could see the inside of the building in which my dying body lay shake vigorously, but nothing fell. Nothing collapsed. The structure was well designed for its intended purpose.

And then I remembered Synphel's words. Not a subterranean lair. Not a medical facility. *A starship.* A starship with a heart as mad as this universe itself cradling the dissected and integrated flesh of Ambra Dawn.

In the monitor, the thing rose higher, miles of bedrock blasting out of the desert floor like a mountain. Miles of solid crust climbed away from the ground and appeared to ascend effortlessly into the sky.

The view panned back, climbing higher to follow the impossible starship. The region of the desert that contained the Temple and the Six Cities was undisturbed, but the desert around it was roiled with a sudden sandstorm. The ground beneath the ship became choked and opaque, a giant brown cloud visible from orbit.

Higher the mountain climbed. It was a constant speed, with no acceleration, and yet it seemed to defy gravity, flaunting any need for an escape velocity. It just rose as if it traveled the paths of physics by different rules than those that applied to the rest of creation.

Finally, there was a bottom to the thing, and the bedrock ended in a concave surface of jagged peaks. Boulders the size of sports stadiums dropped like meteors to the desert floor from the stratosphere.

The Temple broke atmosphere and entered space, yet nothing seemed amiss. The Six Cities were fine, the people unharmed. Some great bubble of protection must have formed around the entire wedge of New Earth that had sought its fate in the skies.

Soon the entire mountain floated above our world, the blue-and-white glow of the planet bathing the granite. The moon shone the reflected light of the sun brightly nearby, millions of stars winking around it in the deep background.

But there was no sun in front of us. Suddenly, the star disappeared, and its light was blotted out. A wall of darkness materialized and eclipsed all radiance, casting a shadow on New Earth itself.

The Dram and their forces had at last arrived.

57

Deep in earth my love is lying
And I must weep alone.

—Edgar Allan Poe

I floated.

Not in space. The sensation was very different.

I drowned in a vile water that was my prison. I woke, finally, for the first time in the existence of my being, to my real status. Encased in a tank, its walls clear, tubes in my body and around my organs.

I could hardly open my eyes. I feared that I had never used them. Yet, after minutes of struggling blindly, I saw—the blurred outlines of an emaciated skeletal frame too weak to move its limbs.

I knew my brain was spilling out of an opened skull. Merged with machines. A horror show. I shared this terrible fate with my dear Ambra. But I felt no pain. I felt almost nothing. I did not share in her pain whom they lifted up into the stars on that heart ripped out of New Earth. My state was nothing compared to her ravaged body that I would never see again, half the galaxy away, hundreds of years ago in events now long past.

The body that I had loved. That I was made to love.

I told you when I began this story that I was born to love Ambra Dawn. Can you see it now? Can you see the deep, horrible truth of it?

As I floated, questions assailed me. What could our love mean when I knew how it had come to be? For my mind's receptacle on New Earth, they had identified genetic stock that would most respond to her appearance, her pheromones, her MHC sequences, and that would also so stir her sexual and emotional centers—it was chosen to seduce her as well as be seduced. My personality was identified after centuries of testing on False Dawn clones: her likes and dislikes, and the character and mannerisms that would capture her heart and mind.

They tuned my mind in this demon's lair to bring out just such personality traits, imprinted it with her image, her voice, and her movements, so that even the little child could not but adore her. They erased a nascent soul in a womb to implant this poisonous Janus: two-faced, murderous, and camouflaged. All for a premeditated murder that spanned centuries.

What can love mean when it has been completely, coldly, cruelly engineered for manipulation? For *murder*?

What did any of our feelings mean now that I saw the truth—that we were only an organic soup to be stirred and heated at the will of monsters? What of our ideas, thoughts, insights, and deductions? They too came from the same blood-bathed organ of delusion and betrayal.

How ever could there be faith in anything but the cold indifference of the cosmos?

Around me, the blurred shapes outside the tank moved. I did not need to see the outlines of the figures, so similar to my Ambra's, to know that the clones surrounded the structure. Synphel had told me. I felt no curiosity to test the alien's hypothesis. I felt only revulsion. A fierce disgust at what had been done and what they were doing.

But there was nothing I could do. I was as helpless here as I had been on New Earth during my last moments there. Hundreds of years ago, the failing body of Nitin Ratava died above the planet as an enemy armada closed in on all the things I had ever loved. I had lain there immobile as my beloved was hacked apart and fit to a cyborg machinery to try to stop that fleet of death. I could do nothing then but wait. And now, hundreds of years in the future, I didn't know what had happened in that final battle. I didn't know if New Earth still existed, if humans had been exterminated, or if Ambra Dawn survived. And I had no power in this dark circle of hell to find out.

And so I waited.

I waited for the demons to shut down this life pod. For them to kill me, once and for all. I watched these monsters move like underwater divers through the molasses of space-time that she had flooded around them. Ambra had at least promised one thing: that it would come soon.

And I was glad for it. However artificial—their breeding of me, genetic design, testing over centuries—the truth is that my entire being was made to love Ambra Dawn with all my heart and soul and mind.

And so I did. Nothing could unmake that love, not even the realization of the emptiness and unmeaning of my feelings in a universe without purpose or love. Nor could I unmake it, even if I wished to. My life pulsed just as brightly for her in these last moments as it ever had.

Except that she was gone. They had shut out her voice. I was left only with my final thoughts in that tomb, surrounded by my captors. My creators. Soon to be, my executioners.

But what of them? All that truly mattered was Ambra. Without her, I was lost and emptied, forever seeking that which I was made to adore.

The soft hum within the tank was interrupted by a sharp rumble. Then silence. The incessant bubbling of oxygen through the tubes ceased. Light faded above.

And I felt it. My body tried to thrash at the loss of the essentials that it needed to live. Even as I was, feeble beyond imagining, my limbs weakly jerked in some final reflex to alter the environment, change the surroundings that were killing them.

My mind fell down a mineshaft, endless and smooth, in which all light was extinguished.

58

Though my soul may set in darkness, it will rise in perfect light; I have loved the stars too fondly to be fearful of the night.

—Sarah Williams, "The Old Astronomer"

I *embrace this darkness.*

I feel it drink my life. I am not afraid.

No darkness can match her absence; no fear is greater than her absence. I will wait.

Because there must be more.

Because I believe her last words to me.

When this darkness consumes me fully,

The eon of nothingness will be only a moment.

And then, dispelling the void, there will be a Light.

The Dawn: and I will go to it and find my love.

That light will come from Ambra.

That light will be of Ambra.

Because that light in the darkness could be nothing else but Ambra.

I wait for you, my love.

59

There is no death, only a change of worlds.

—Red Cloud, chief of the Oglala Lakota

*N*itin.

In the deepest pit of nothingness, after an timeless eternity had passed, she spoke.

Wake up.

I opened my eyes, and an infinity of stars blinded me. I tried to turn away from them but could not, having no form, no body. I was sighted without eyes. A mind adrift in the vastness of space.

Don't be afraid.

Where am I? What *was* I? I did not speak with words. I spoke with thoughts. But without a body, I did not know what it was that spoke.

See the moon?

I saw it. Her voice guided my vision. A blue-and-white marble like New Earth loomed before me. It circled an enormous gas giant of swirling, banded colors. More moons, many earthlike, could be seen scattered around the monstrous planet.

That is where you died.

And then it all came back. My life. My *lives*. The life I had believed to be true: Nitin Ratava, Indian soldier, devoted seeker of the Daughter of Time, lover of Ambra Dawn. The life that had been harshly revealed to me— chimeric monster, spy, assassin, and puppet. The adventures through space. The deaths of my team. The unforces of the Anti. War. Great and terrible war and sacrifices. The torture of my beloved. My death distant from her.

And this is where you are reborn.

Reborn. I existed, but as what? I never understood the talk of mental space-time matrices. The strange idea that physical thought was some field like electricity. I was never a scientist.

Think of it as your soul, Nitin, if that helps.

I wasn't sure that it did. Souls seemed like an ancient term, better left in the detritus of our superstitious past. It hardly seemed appropriate for the advanced technological world of humans and aliens that I knew. Souls were for the isolated, the old, the needy, such as my mother, who prayed to her icons. But at least it offered me an idea of something beyond what I understood, one that was integrated into thoughts of rebirth, eternity, and personality. After everything I had seen, after being so humbled and destroyed, when it was clear I did not remotely understand the nature of existence, who was I to reject the notion of a soul?

Ambra, where are you?

I am reaching across a bridge, a long bridge from my time and place to yours. Already, where you are, it is many centuries past the era that you left me.

I tried to understand the words. She was traveling through space and time to reach me. I wondered why she did not simply travel through space from this time. Unless she could not from this time. I had lost touch with her and New Earth as the Dram armada arrived. What if…

Are you alive in this time?

Yes. And you are with me.

I didn't understand how this could be possible. Could I be in two places at once?

And we are very busy, Nitin. All of us in making something wonderful.

All of us? What something wonderful?

Just then, several large spacecraft sped past my point of awareness toward the blue moon. They were enormous, city-sized ships, one after the other like a parade. Highly militarized, their forms screamed of violence. Dark shadows surrounded their hulls.

The Anti! Ambra, what do I do?

You are safe, Nitin. They cannot see you. Only the clone aboard can, and her attentions are elsewhere.

The ships continued, one by one, until the parade passed me and shrank to a point as it neared the moon. None changed course. There were no attacks or reconnaissance efforts. It was as if I weren't there.

How do you know all this?

It is difficult to explain. So much has changed. Everything I have been through has been for a purpose, and that purpose has been realized. Is being realized. Will be realized. We are augmented. Integrated. Synergized even beyond our most optimistic hopes. We are something completely new.

I still didn't have answers. *What new? Who is this we, Ambra? The same as I felt above New Earth with you?*

So much more than that, Nitin.

More? I could not imagine. I had been overwhelmed by the flood of their minds.

Don't be afraid. It is not like before. You are free, finally free of the fleshly egg that gestated your soul. Your consciousness propagates through space and time independently now. That shock, that pain from the many—it will not hurt you now.

What if I don't like being with them? What if I want to be alone?

Do you want to be alone, Nitin?

No, I did not. But I also knew that being with others was often very difficult—the clashes of personalities, different priorities, agendas. The thought of joining some mental aggregate frightened me. I only wished to be with her.

You will be with me. And because they have chosen to be with me, they are in harmony with me. You will find them acceptable. Believe that. Trust me, Nitin. Try.

And if I don't try?

Then we cannot be together. My future is determined by my choices, Beloved. Even if I wished, I could not leave. If you do not join us, you cannot be with me. Worse, if you live out here alone, without support, it will be worse than death. You will spend eons devolving. You will lose yourself, and I will lose you forever.

Losing myself didn't really matter to me; it was inconsequential. Being lost to her, losing her, was everything. The only truth I knew was that I could not live without her. Whatever she now was. Wherever that was. Whatever was in store for me.

I cannot leave you, Ambra.

Yes, my Nitin. I know. But you had to know for yourself.

But there is so much that I still don't understand.

Then let us stop talking. Let me show you.

How?

Follow my voice, and it will take you to me. And together we will see all those things that you need to understand.

Perhaps all this was madness—the last throes of a dying brain's hallucinations. But it did not matter at all. In life, in death, in madness—I would always follow her. I would always trust her. Because, in the end, the core of all my love for her was unshakable, unwavering trust in her.

I'm coming, Ambra.

60

So powerful is the light of unity that it can illuminate the whole earth.
—Bahá´u´lláh

I accelerated.

It was a matter of will, of acceptance, and as I focused on her voice, on the powerful sense of her that I felt even across these kiloparsecs and centuries, I was displaced.

The stormy gas giant and its blue moons began to recede behind me, the light of their star fading, and the background of the Milky Way before me shifted in colors, running through a spectrum from blue to red over and over as the stars themselves elongated in my peripheral vision.

Then it all began to spin. Rotating around me, a vortex of stars formed until the lights ran together like wet ink in a rainstorm. The center of the rotation was the only place of stillness, a spherical glow expanding in size, its infinitely layered majesty eclipsing all my awareness.

The Orb.

I saw the Orb now with the visions of my bodiless consciousness. *My soul.* Stripped of the filters of flesh, the Orb was less a portal, less a mechanical or geometrical phenomenon as it was a mind in and of itself. Yet, if a mind, it was of such complexity, such alienness, such godlike stature that I could comprehend almost nothing of it.

And yet I felt an affection. A concern. In the midst of that terrible mind of incomprehensible indifference, there seemed to beat a heart of empathy.

And it reached for me.

I felt a power take hold of my awareness, and suddenly I was drawn through a thousand corridors of brilliance. This time there was no pain, no confining tunnel or prison, no fear. There was joy. Overflowing joy and anticipation like that moment when one finally has discovered an element sought in a long and forgetful quest.

Ambra!

I called. My own thoughts seemed to echo like sound around me, coming back and leaving again, transformed, as if a million different voices uttered the word in response while they all recombined into my own tones. *A host.* I felt them. Mind upon mind around me, inside me, in places I could not imagine or reach, yet present, aware, and anticipating my transit with nearly the same joy I felt.

And then—starlight. Looming and bright, golden radiance bathed space around me. I raced past several gas giants. A blue-and-white disk maniacally rotating, featureless and blurred, until I came to a stop. A solitary moon revolved rapidly around it, slowed, and then appeared to stop as the rotation of the planet came to a standstill.

New Earth.

I seemed finally fixed in time as the globe rotated at a pace I could remember from...*before*. I drifted slowly through space toward a hulking asteroid orbiting the world. As I approached, I recognized the shape, that Earth-shard ripped from the heart of the Sahara, the sand plains of the Temple and Six Cities unharmed at its apex.

Now I sensed differently, and the bedrock of New Earth was not opaque to my perception. Through the crust my awareness flew into the core of a starship.

In the midst of it, I looked down on myself—myself as I was. The body hardly alive, propped up by Xixian technology, a link over great distances through time and space waiting to be snapped. Nitin Ratava struggled there to remain present, watched the giant shard-ship ascend, his life in that flesh only moments away from ending.

But there was so much more to see than the shell of my former self. Tens of thousands of glowing consciousnesses wrapped in fleshly garments had gathered, the tendrils of their awareness mixing and uniting, fully integrated at the center of the rock.

There the tortured flesh seemed hardly present in the midst of a resplendent shower. Threads from ten thousand minds wrapped together with the thick ropes of a single, powerful consciousness to create a tapestry so massive, so intricate, so *alive* that my own mind was in awe of it. As I tore my focus away from this transforming aggregate, I was able to perceive the nexus underneath. White, human flesh. Red hair. Green eyes aimed in the direction of my vantage point.

"Nitin."

She spoke with the flesh of her body, through lips I had once kissed and adored. I could no longer touch those lips, and a distant echo of me yearned for that once more. Yet, I was becoming something *else*. Dwarfing that faint echo was the joy and desire to embrace the form that was invisible to me in my flesh. Ambra Dawn now transcended the woman I had once known, had misapprehended, had torn down to human stature. Before me was indeed the form of a goddess.

No, Nitin. So are we all. And you will understand that soon.

I missed you, Ambra.

The face on her supine form smiled. *And I missed you. Come to me.*

My awareness floated the final distance and hovered inches above her body. All was as I had last seen it, the stripped flesh and remade nervous system now one with the starship. Now I could see the effects of this sacrifice in the distortions of space and time around me. Her tumor served as some powerful transmitter, her entire body the fleshly dish, the thousands of Readers around us interwoven with her thoughts.

Closer, my love.

I passed through the ghostly essence of her body and was enfolded by the fullness of her consciousness. Her mind enveloped my own in a manner unlike anything I had ever known. As partners of the flesh, I could not have imagined any joining more intimate, more powerful, more transfiguring than that which occurred when we made love. Yet it was only an echo of what could be. At that moment, the depth of personally sharing that could be between minds finally became clear to me. It was complete, and so joined, there was an *us* greater than the separated *two*.

And not only two, beloved.

And the host opened itself to me. This time I was not afraid. I was not overwhelmed. I *became* with them. An unusual structure, centered on a binary awareness at the core, or rather a singular consciousness of the Daughter and my own orbit around her, that connected to thousands of other minds. As their awareness, their thoughts, their personalities swept through me, I knew each of them as two fleshly beings could never know each other. Free of confusions and barriers. And each was filled with compassion and interest. With love.

There will be time for so much learning, Nitin. But now, there is a task to complete. Clear your vision and let the Group Mind see for you.

I tried to stop focusing on the myriad of amazing entities around me, to relinquish my grip on controlling my own awareness. Slowly, like some static clearing on a radio receiver, the immediate visions were replaced with a single perspective.

This eye into space was outside the Earth-shard, focused intently on the space just beyond the planet. I felt the power of this gaze, the *otherness* of it. The awareness was of a creature beyond me, beyond the others, and in many ways alien in its thought processes to my simplistic mind. Yet I shared of it. I was part of it, my own mind contributing to its fabric.

To my surprise I saw an awaiting fleet of ships from New Earth Force. Alongside them, hundreds of craft of Xixian make. I marveled that these forces had been arrayed, obviously prepared far in advance, when I had had no inkling or vision of them before I died.

We hid them from you, my betrayer. The hurt of what had happened began to fade in me, and I was even able to see the dark humor in her words. *We had set a trap. Wwe told you nothing, and I masked your vision during your time outside your body.* I understood. I would have done the same in that position. Looking back on it, it was a brilliant strategy. If indeed they had the power to defeat the Dram and Anti.

Turning back to the coming battle, I saw that the ships of the Xix had no weapons, but instead projected powerful field defenses to deflect beam and projectile weapons. The Force ships were armed as I remembered them. Xixian designed ion slingers with a flux far beyond those of our MECHcore suits. Missiles, conventional, and, more commonly, nuclear. With several hundred warcraft in position, they had enough firepower to obliterate all of New Earth's cities fifty times over.

But it would not be nearly enough.

In front of us the blackness of space undulated violently, and thousands of ships bent and blurred as I had seen before I died. And just as at the moment when I had lost touch with Ambra and New Earth, the undulations ceased, and the light of the sun was obscured by the Dram armada.

New Earth sat like a small child before the onslaught of a lion. The Dram warcraft opened fire on the New Earth defensive force. Their military advantage was great but not insurmountable. But they were not alone.

Destruction waged wildly across both fronts as ships were cut in two or blown to fragments. The tide turned quickly in favor of our enemies as powerful waves of space-time distortions and antiparticle projectiles impacted our forces. False Dawns and the Anti, hidden in their ships and between the matter of the Dram ships, unleashed a fury that neither the Xixian field defenses nor New Earth's warcraft could counter. Within the short span of minutes, the sum of our planetary defenses lay in ruin and wreckage. A hailstorm of debris covered the surface of New Earth and began to rain down as flaming meteors.

The Dram then turned their weapons on the planet, beam weapons and missiles ripping fire and destruction across the cities on the surface. Bright explosions could be seen across New Earth from space, and soot began to blacken the skies. Many weapons were aimed at us as well, but all were turned away harmlessly. The warships quickly abandoned their attacks on the impregnable

Earth-shard and concentrated on maximizing the slaughter below.

The destruction on New Earth created a phenomenon I had not anticipated, but I could feel the expectation of the Group Mind focused on it. The mental matrices, the *souls* of millions upon millions of humans and Xix suddenly were torn from their flesh, isolated, and left naked in the fields of space and time. I could sense their emotions and thoughts, bewilderment, panic, and wonder at the sudden and unexpected reality to which they awoke. And waking, they naturally turned toward the light.

One after the other, thousands, tens of thousands, millions came to us, until uncountable masses of awareness flowed like some swollen river into the sea. I felt a great outflow of energy, a sharing of essence that reached out toward them all from the Mind, even if I did not individually will it. *We had.* Ambra spoke in my mind.

The first, Nitin. A small gathering. A test and a change.

What is happening, Ambra?

Part of my awareness again saw her bodily form tense and a smile cross her face.

Something wonderful.

The minds began to soar toward us. First a few intrepid souls approached the Group. Then, the flood. A flood of mental energies and persons from that river of released minds poured into our lake. But a lake smaller than all the rivers combined, so that as they came, the Mind grew. It grew astoundingly, and I felt the integration of these millions into a community of what had been initially only tens of thousands. And the Mind grew accordingly.

Not all approached. And of those that did, not all stayed. Some drifted toward the Dram, the False Dawns, the Anti, but had no manner to join them in their betrayal. But the majority became part of us. As the Dram continued their merciless onslaught, the flood only grew. As they struck down the lives on New Earth, they only made us stronger.

But even with her words and seeing this shocking development, my individual consciousness was seized with alarm and bewilderment as the Group Mind sat stoically and did nothing in the face of this massacre. Yet my presence in the Group was soothed by a greater purpose beyond that which I could predict with my isolated thoughts. My anxiety dissolved, to be replaced with a serene calm. I watched the slaughter, the freed souls, and their joining to the Mind with a peacefulness that might seem diabolical. Part of me felt this discordantly, but it was a minor portion of my experience. The remainder waited in anticipation.

The time has not yet come. Not my thoughts, yet in my thoughts. Not Ambra's thoughts, but of her thoughts.

Then my awareness turned to our enemies, and I saw them with the eyes of the Group. Thousands of refulgent candles stationed in ships around us, their glow poisonous in the fabric of space-time. The False Dawn army was revealed, and one after the other, they released a coordinated barrage of mental attacks on our starship, on the Group Mind.

It was like a series of nuclear blasts. The attacks before shown to be a faint whisper of the power these clones possessed. With these new eyes, I could discern the massive distortions of time and space propagated by these attacks. It outshone the radiance in all energies and fields of the sun itself. All directed on the little rock Ambra and the Readers occupied above New Earth. The False Dawns had perceived what we were.

But I was to see that they understood it as little as I did. Despite the cataclysm of space-time around us, the

Earth-shard was untouched. The Group Mind unmoved. It watched. It waited. And finally, its patience was rewarded.

The Anti attacked, and this time, they were not hidden from me. The eyes of the Group were not blind to these beings but clothed them in shapes and hues inverted yet similar to our own. Flooding toward us from the spaces between the ships came another ten thousand craft. The starships were built by minds so different from our own that it was difficult to understand their structure, their purpose—and yet their energies were great. They turned loose a river of antimatter particles toward us.

I could see the annihilations inherent in the properties of this matter in its juxtaposition to the matter around them. Immediately as the outer regions of New Earth's atmosphere came into contact with the particle beam, there were powerful explosions. Matter and antimatter were converted into pure energy. Enormous amounts of radiation blasted outward, hotter than the surface of the sun. It seemed all of New Earth would be reduced to ash once again.

But the Mind moved. To my great shock, it spun out of nothing great fields of energy that countered the particle beam, surrounded it, and cut off the matter of New Earth from it. The nearby Orb flashed, and a stream of energy funneled toward it from our location and disappeared into its blazing maw. In seconds, there was no antiparticle beam, no energy release—only silence and the ships floating before our rock.

Even the attacks from the False Dawn clones ceased. The Group Mind perceived their mental matrices, the distortions in their form indicating distress. Confusion. The same forms could be recognized in some transformed fashion in the small consciousnesses in the

Anti fleet. The minds of the Dram warriors appeared stunned. Into the confusion crept a new emotion. *Fear.*

But the False Dawns responded with a last and desperate gambit. All their attention became focused away from us, away from Earth. The group awareness turned to follow it and watched silently as the clones together centered their power on the moon itself. Our satellite, astoundingly, began to change its orbit, the great mass spiraling inward from energies too enormous to contemplate.

A thousand Ambra Dawns pulled the moon toward New Earth: the result would be a true cataclysm. Beyond anything even the Dram had achieved with the asteroid. It would be New Earth's redestruction.

But the Group Mind moved again. My dissolving ties to my old body still painted my awareness in physical terms, and that is why it seemed to me as if two great arms reached outward from the Earth-shard toward our moon. Two powerful hands tore loose the shackles of the clones from the great, rocky sphere and slung them heedlessly across the fabric of space-time away from New Earth. Hundreds of Dram and Anti ships were pulled and stretched like rubber from the distortions induced, shattering, tearing, the occupants perishing.

The Mind stopped the inward spiral in a moment. The moon simply stopped in its orbit, unshaken, undamaged—just still as New Earth rotated nearby. Once again, a powerful sense of awe and fear escaped from the ranks of our enemies. But the Mind had more terrible things yet to do.

The two great hands squeezed and crushed the moon to dust. 73,430,000,000,000,000,000 tonnes of rock exploded inward in a microsecond, the forces contained, no particles leaping outward. Rather not to dust, but to asteroid-sized granules that stayed cupped within the palms of this mental force.

And then, like some celestial shotgun, the moon pellets were flung toward the Dram armada. The projectiles were hurled at speeds unfathomable for any known weapons mechanism, but, of course, what was occurring was far beyond any known technology in our galaxy, even that of the Xix. The result was utter devastation. The Dram craft, filled with thousands of clones who vainly tried to deflect a billion pellets of death, were shredded like no flechette gun had every achieved. The matter-antimatter collision of the moon fragments with the craft of the Anti set off colossal explosions that once again were channeled by the Mind directly to the Orb.

After just minutes of the greatest fireworks display ever witnessed in our star system, the entire space between us and the sun was clarified once again. There was no trace of a starship near New Earth. All had been reduced to atoms or energy and funneled out of the solar system through the Orb to some unknown destination.

The Dram armada had ceased to exist.

61

*In the region of nature, which is the region of diversity,
we grow by acquisition; in the spiritual world, which
is the region of unity, we grow by losing ourselves, by
uniting.*

—The Sādhanā of Tagore

I stared across the span of space in front of the
planet where once thousands of starships had
orbited. There was nothing. The ships were gone.
The Anti annihilated. Not so much as a shard of metal
floated before me.

Only in the distance, the Orb. I had never truly seen it
before. As a man limited by his eyes, I had found it so
dull, so bland, so empty and featureless. Now it blazed
with light indescribable, revealing layers upon layers of
maze-like projections. The depth of it made the universe
itself seem small.

Now begins the Gathering of Souls, Nitin.

The Collective grew, not only in size, but to a greater
degree in depth, in power, in sentience, in vision, and it
spread its Awareness over greater and greater distances
as well as through time. Backward to the past, forward

to the future. More and more the minds freed in the battle integrated with ours, and our light grew.

There has been a terrible waste. Losses upon losses. A hundred thousand species in our galaxy with each a billion voices. Silenced as their song died within the Void. Souls that now hear a call. Our *call.*

And the souls came. Not only from around us, but from across distances. Across vast spans of time. Slowly, not like the flood during the massacre on New Earth. But hesitantly, as if the distances in space and in time had dimmed our image in their minds. And yet they had felt us, will feel us, glimpsing us fleetingly through space and time. They *have are will be following* the call. Her voice. Our Voice and Mind.

My new eyes seemed to deceive me, because as I returned my attention from the gathering souls to the island of rock the Collective occupied, it had metamorphosed. The increasingly numerous and complex mental matrices of the minds that had joined, and the far more complex interweaving of those minds together—directed and shaped like some symphonic orchestra from the core of the Earth-shard—formed tendrils, tunnels in multiple dimensions, pathways, and portals that wove complex patterns about the stone-and-sand plains of the Six Cities and Temple. The Earth-shard was becoming engulfed, buried in a latticework of light.

I stared at this growing marvel and then back at the Orb. My mind's eye was surely confused. Bewildered. Lost.

Because as I gazed from the great power of our solar system, the projection of the One Orb that touched every star system containing life, there was a moment of reference frame confusion. Was I coming or going? Did I approach the gateway to the stars that had changed the history of the universe? Or was I flying away from it?

Was I looking at our transforming Collective or back at the Orb?

Back and forth. No frame of reference was unique or special. I could no longer differentiate.

I could no longer clearly see: What was the Orb and what was We.

Epilogue

Of the theme that I have declared to you, I will now
that ye make in harmony together a Great Music.
And since I have kindled you with the Flame
Imperishable, ye shall show forth your powers in
adorning this theme, each with his own thoughts
and devices, if he will. But I will sit and hearken,
and be glad that through you great beauty has been
wakened into song.

　　　　　　　　　　—*The Ainulindalë* of Tolkien

Once, when Ambra was only a shadow of what We would become, it was hard to reach you. Now, reaching you is so simple, even if the mind of your author is mostly inadequate for the task of understanding and relating our tale. But Ambra wished it to be known—an echo of her human love for me—that many, even in our distant past, might know our story. That you might listen more intently for our Call. That when your time has come, you may listen for us in the great Void and not be lost.

Our Collective was One with this sharing. And so you approach the end of this book. A book with a story now finished—or, rather, just barely beginning.

So much has been lost that it cannot be quantified, and to consider it is to nearly unmake my individual mind. Yet I rejoice. I rejoice as I have never known happiness. An eternity awaits us, Ambra and me, and we will traverse the cosmos through a succession of ages within eons.

We keep a great and growing company unlike any our galaxy has ever witnessed. At every moment, in every point in space, the mental matrices set free by the death of their fleshly cages find their way to us. Most will join our Collective, adding new voices, unique and often strange thoughts and emotions to a Mind now beyond anything our universe has known. The others will drift, alone and unanchored, until the boundless eternity of creation drives them mad and their souls lose coherence and are absorbed into the undulations of the Void.

The eye of our Mind no longer sees the linearity of time. It views space-time from a perspective that I can only describe (inaccurately) as *outside* of our cosmos. In this view, causality is understood as multifactorial, each point in space-time affected by all the others. As we Become, we have increasing access to all places and all times.

And so we gather the harvest sown across distances vast and times immeasurable. We seek the minds freed at death and by other means that would have been wasted in the emptiness of space. We provide a haven, a shore upon which they can wash up from the chaos of the vacuum. Among the purposes of the Group Mind, there is no other more sacred, nothing with greater meaning than to search the cosmos for sentience and preserve it, save it, augment it, and give it immortality.

Individually, and in mass cataclysm, at points in time near and remote, in the past and future, we find them. We call them. And for the most part, they come. From forms of flesh wildly disparate, with mentalities even more diverse, each addition, each new scale in the musical registry enhances the expression and depth of the Whole.

We began with beings similar to ourselves, whose minds we could more easily identify and locate. Human, Xix, Brax, Dram, Sortax—the list goes on. Personally, we were able to find our loved ones, families, children, friends who had perished. The special forces team of the entity once know as Nitin Ratava came as well: Erica Fox, David Kim, Ryan Marshall, Grant Moore, and Aisha Williams. And when they arrived, it was as if we began to know them for the first time. The barriers between minds were gone. And now this narrative is shaped as much by them as it is by me—it is the Mind that reaches you now.

Yet in all of our searches, a perplexing mystery remains—we have been unable to find the soul of Waythrel of the Xix. Because so many elements of the early Group Mind found great meaning in this search, it has ever informed the efforts of the Collective. Therefore, that we cannot detect evidence of Waythrel in life or in death at any time point searched raises one of two possibilities. The first is that the Xix has been taken so far in space and time that we simply do not yet have the strength to bridge that gap. As we contact you now, that implies a distance beyond our local group of galaxies and more than ten million years into the past or future. The second possibility is that Waythrel is being hidden from us by forces that can contend even with the power of the Group Mind. Both possibilities can coexist.

The solution to finding Waythrel in both cases is to enhance the Group Mind further. That way, we will either be able to bridge the space-time gap separating us from its mind or develop sufficiently to overcome the forces concealing its whereabouts. Therefore, this seemingly lesser purpose in locating a single soul out of the universal multitude is consistent with our great purpose in gathering all souls.

Imagine the integration of the billions of souls across millions of worlds, not at any time point but at all of them. The creature that awakened above New Earth and dispatched the Dram armada was an infant—ignorant, wide-eyed and empty. It could hardly speak, and walking was beyond its undeveloped capabilities. Now we approach an early adolescence, and our faculties lie far beyond even the imagination of that newborn child.

We are become greater than what we are. For us individually, it is this labyrinthine filigree of separate sentients, sharing thoughts, flowing through and around awareness, constantly learning and changing and giving. It is a loving harmony, and those minds that cannot fulfill that existence of love and peace always detach and seek their own way.

We are like some trillion-celled organism, forming tissues of thought, regulated, divided, yet creating a far, far greater whole. Our individual personalities are like the neurons in a fleshly brain—intricate, filled with millions of internal processes and thousands of external communications with our neighbors in this grand Collective. But the synthesis of our minds into the Group Mind is a step as great, perhaps greater, than the one between an individual neuron and a functioning brain.

What does a neuron understand of the most complicated human thought? And so, what can any one of us understand about those cogitations of the Group Mind? Even labeling this Mind's actions as thoughts is surely a terrible distortion and oversimplification. Those processes available to a simple neuron—biochemistry, cell structure, secretion—are elements wholly unsuited to describe the higher level thought processes in our once-fleshy minds. The activities of the Group Mind therefore must be utterly beyond our ability to even conceive.

We know this. We experience it. We see the awesome powers of what we have become. We do not understand them. Faint echoes of higher accomplishments trickle down to us, bathe us, and modify our thoughts and feelings as the human brain's responses to external stimuli might alter the behavior of individual neurons. But like the neurons, we can only respond and not comprehend.

Yet the cosmos we now see is beautiful. And terrible. Beautiful and terrible beyond the simple explanations our small minds can muster. And what we can understand tells us that the fate of the cosmos, the sustenance of its very fabric, is interwoven with the Group Mind—or, rather, what it will have become in a great and distant future age.

Already we begin to bridge the galaxies, our Collective now powerful enough to cross the intergalactic distances of space and time. We find wild tragedies of destruction like those in our own Milky Way. We watch the fires of worlds consuming themselves in immaturity, or of growing sentients clashing across star systems because of the broken vagaries of evolution. Yet so many of their minds come to us. We absorb them, learn of and from them, and are enhanced.

Now we even detect the stirrings of powerful Minds not unlike our own, yet lesser, in discord, requiring help to survive their own internal disruptions. Already, tens of thousands of Galactic Minds have begun to seek us. A time will come in the successive eons when we will meet and a greater Whole emerge.

Yet always, there are the Anti. Hidden even from us, unmaking, incomprehensible, seeking the self-contradictory goal, the paradox of the destruction of organized thought and action. There is a shadowy sense in us all that some great event lies in a shared future with them, where all things will be changed, and even our Mind, unmade.

In all this we ceaselessly orbit our Daughter of Time. Although only a part of the whole, she is the nexus, the nucleation center of our new consciousness, the core particle around which this mind shard has crystallized. She is the Mother of all that we have become, a goddess in labor, forever giving birth to this new Being.

But still *not* a mere goddess to me.

She may be all these things, but that matters the least to me. All that has happened and is happening, the radical changes to our nature, the growth toward something transcendent—to me, in my core, she is still the woman I was meant to love. She is still the light I followed from the day my consciousness formed. And for a short, blissful time on New Earth and in the heavens, she was my beloved.

Always and ever my dearest, Ambra Dawn.

It is all a matter of time scale. An event that would be unthinkable in a hundred years may be inevitable in a hundred million.

—Sagan's Cosmos

Gratitude

It's hard to know where to begin in thanking people who, in one way or another, have helped make this book a possibility, even in its imperfect form.

There are of course those directly supporting my writing efforts: my beloved children, Anna Maria and Christina (and even little Billy in his own way!), my wife, Nina, especially the last few years of many personal and professional changes—I am grateful for their continued support.

To the β-readers who have given their input—even when ignored by a recalcitrant author—thank you. Writing is a decidedly subjective business, but even so, the intention is to communicate. In my case, I can think of no better explanation, no better motivation for my work, than that given by Tolkien for his own:

> *The prime motive was the desire of a tale-teller to try his*
> *hand at a really long story that would hold the attention*
> *of readers, amuse them, delight them, and at times*
> *maybe excite them or deeply move them.*
> —Foreword to the Second Edition
> of Lord of the Rings, (October 1966)

If I have succeeded to some partial degree in these things, I will personally consider this book a success.

Erec Stebbins, March 2014, NYC

ABOUT THE AUTHOR

www.erecstebbins.com

I am a biomedical researcher who writes political and global thrillers, science fiction, narrated storybooks, and more. My stories often come from the raw emotional conflicts created by contemporary events around us. I strongly believe that the best stories challenge us, so I try to  create art with a certain kind of relevant edge, at least as I experience it.

I was born in the Midwest. My mother worked as a clinical psychologist, and my father was a professor of Romance languages at the University Nebraska in Lincoln. In fact, his specialty, old Romance languages and their literature, is the source of the strange spelling of my middle name: "Erec". It is an Old French spelling, taken from an Arthurian romance by Chrétien de Troyes written around 1170: *Érec et Énide*. Had my brother been a girl, he would have been named Enide. Instead, he's Michael.

I have pursued diverse interests over the course of my life, including science, music, drama, and writing. My academic path focused on science, and I received a degree in physics from Oberlin College in 1992, and a PhD in biochemistry from Cornell University in 1999. I have worked since then in biomedical science, running a laboratory studying bacterial pathogens.

Coming in the near future....

MAKER

Daughter of Time
Book 3

In the fabric of space and in the nature of matter, as in a great work of art, there is, written small, the artist's signature. —Carl Sagan, Contact

MAKER (Daughter of Time, Book 3): The final - *or is it the first?* - element of the trilogy. A story in which the One that was lost will be found. Where the thief will guide against chaos and time. Where all that was held dear will perish. And in that final and utter destruction - there will be a Creation.

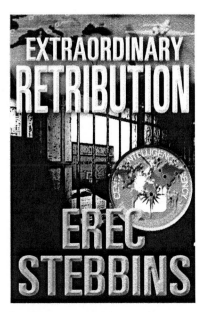

Chapter 1 Sample of thriller
Extraordinary Retribution

1

By the time he reached the razor-wire, the Syrian landscape had shrugged off the delusion of the irrigated greenery around Damascus. Here, the Old Man, the desert, could not be hidden and refused to be banished. Cold even in the oppressive heat, crueler than the scalped links fencing out trespassers, the sands smiled sadistically, remembering centuries of slaughter and dreaming of future screams of anguish.

For the man in the truck, gazing across the landscape, the screams returned to him now. Howling, gasped, panicked. His own and many around him. Images of dank stone, blood and waste-soiled cells. *Eyes. Faces.* Tormentors and their hideous tools. The weeping of grown men echoed inside his mind as the winds stirred the dry sands around his vehicle. He squeezed the steering wheel tightly, refusing their summons, determined more than ever to rise above their damage and demons. He had come too far to be defeated now.

He stepped out of the begrimed pickup truck and slammed the door. Glancing over the barren land, he followed the fence line to the horizon. The entrance was at a large distance around the perimeter of the compound, hidden in part by an outcropping of desert rocks. His well-paid sources had been accurate: an entrance from the rear would likely go unnoticed. *And what madman would ever break into this place?* He did not expect vigilance.

He moved around to the back of the truck and untied a dusty canvas covering the bed. Underneath were several heavy crates. He opened each, removing weapons and explosives, strapping them to his body, and moved to the passenger side of the vehicle. From the glove compartment, he removed a map, glanced at it fleetingly, and pocketed the ruffled pages. It was memorized.

Night fell quickly in the deserts of Syria. In the darkness and desolation, short metallic clips sounded and fell mute on the empty sands. As a shadow, he passed through an opening cut into the gray outlines of the fence and vanished into the blackness.

Through the sandy winds sweeping across the compound, lights twinkled from a handful of incandescent bulbs. Near the gated entrance, he left a guard inside a small shed, seeming to doze peacefully, the unnatural angle of his neck observable only at close range. Before him, a desolate stone structure was dimly outlined by the band of the Milky Way, a single window of light visible in the darkness. Voices could be heard, at times loud and rude, spilling clumsily from the room. Harsh, staccato bursts of laughter confirmed the presence of the prison guards inside. He darted past the window and pressed himself flat against the compound walls. He slid along the rough surface toward the door, arm raised, his hand ending in an extended, metallic cylinder. He made no sound until he spun and kicked in the flimsy wooden door.

He saw four men around a small table, cigarettes in their mouths, pornography and cards strewn haphazardly across the stained wood. As the door swung madly on its hinges and smashed into the wall, they jumped, confused, turning toward him. Even that small pause meant death.

He fired several shots in the confined space. The explosions were amplified and echoed throughout the stone chamber, spilling down the poorly lit hallway opposite to the gunman. Two of the men arched, their heads snapping backward as the bullets blew open their skulls. The whitewashed walls were sprayed red. As the other two men lurched upward and towards him, he spun, his right foot arcing like a sledgehammer coming down, whipping the nearest man backward onto the table. Glasses shattered, and cards dispersed as the guard rolled roughly and fell hard on the stone floor. The intruder channeled the momentum of the spinning motion, and his gun hand came whirling around toward the second man, who now stood unprepared, barely having obtained a fighting stance. His attempted blow was smashed aside, and his jaw shattered as the man's gun arm brought the metal crashing downward. All four guards now lay still around the table, two dead, two unconscious.

The assailant aimed his weapon at the guard near his feet, firing directly into his head. He then turned and aimed at the other prone figure, rendering a similar judgment. He studied the faces carefully. *"At night, five remain once the others leave for the day. And Mahjub works late."* He didn't need to be told this by his informant. Yes, he knew Mahjub worked late. He would never forget. Nor would he forget his face. Mahjub was not in this room. He must be....below. *He had been busy, perhaps.* But not now. By now, he would have heard the shots. He would be afraid.

The assassin smiled.

Two floors below, buried deeply in the Syrian sands, a long hallway with numerous cells ran its begrimed course. Broken men were locked behind stone-walled enclosures with iron doors. The cells were like graves: shallow pits scraped into the rock, devoid of light or even the space to stand. At the far end of the hallway, opposite the stairs, was a small room without a door. Inside Mahjub Samhan clutched a knife in one hand and a pistol in the other. Both hands shook as he cowered behind an upturned table in the middle of the room. He cried out in a high-pitched voice.

"Kamil? Saif?" There was only silence. "Bassam? Nadeem!" He wiped the dripping sweat from his eyebrows and tried to focus toward the stairs. A solitary bulb dangled limply from exposed wires in the middle of the hallway. His left leg began to shake. "Answer me! Who is there? What is *happening?*"

Suddenly, before he could focus or react, a shadow seemed to leap from nowhere, an explosion slapped his ears, and the bulb burst. Shards of glass rained on the stone floor like small bells. A terrible darkness blotted out his vision. In panic, Mahjub screamed, firing shots wildly into the blackness.

A bright light leapt from across the darkness, blinding him. A sizzling rod landed only a foot away from the table. Momentarily confused and distracted by the fire, Mahjub stared down at the stick burning beside him. *Explosive?* Too late, he turned his weapon toward the sound of rushing footsteps from the hallway, the searing afterimage of the flame obscuring his sight.

A gunshot rang. His right shoulder exploded in agony. His knees buckled, and he fell backward against the wall, releasing a howl of pain as he slid to the floor. He dropped the knife from his left hand and reached over to hold his injured shoulder, grimacing as he felt the warm blood coat his arm and fingers.

He squinted against the light as it was raised above his head. He saw a tall, dark shape behind the flare, a gun in one hand aimed at him. In a swift motion, the table was righted and the flare violently wedged into the rotting boards like a candlestick. The figure crouched beside him.

"You always were a coward, Mahjub," spoke the voice in accented Arabic. Trying to block the pain, Mahjub strained to place the origin. *Saudi? Pakistani?* He stared at the face partially concealed in shadow. He had never seen it before. Light hair, blue eyes...*American?* Nothing made sense. Had the Americans turned on them after all this time? Did they need to bury this operation so completely? With all the chaos in the nation, did they care so much now?

"You don't recognize me, do you, Mahjub?" the figure asked, almost with amusement. "How fitting, to lie here in pain, your death awaiting you, and not know the first thing about your tormenter."

Mahjub felt the panic well within him again. "Sir, please, don't kill me. Whatever we have done wrong, we can fix. We will not speak. We will disappear. Please, not like this."

Mahjub's eyes widened at the sound he heard. The man with the gun laughed. *Laughed at him!* "Mahjub, how do you live outside this place?" The Syrian only looked at the gunman in distress.

"I mean, when you buy fruit at the market, mixing with decent people, or entertain your mother-in-law, do you think about breaking men's fingers? Sodomizing them? Do you think of blood and vomit when you stir her coffee? Do their screams, their pleas for mercy keep you awake at night?"

"Sir, no, please, I don't know…"

"You know," said the man, his blue eyes seemingly glazed over, frosted, utterly cold. The shadowed form whispered ominously, "See, I *know* what you do, what you *are*." Mahjub felt his blood run cold.

"These poor men here," said the pale man, gesturing toward the hallway, "they don't know *who* you are, but they know *what you are*." The man spoke with such venom, a snake's hiss. "It took some time to track you down."

Mahjub began to cry, clutching his blasted shoulder, grime and blood on his hands and face. A man with such power over others, now powerless, weeping like a child. "Please…."

There was no pity in the cold blue eyes before him. "Consider me more merciful than you ever were."

The man stood up and aimed the weapon.

"No!" Mahjub began to scream, but a final gunshot ripped through his throat, silencing his cry as he fell against the wall. He gasped vainly for breath, his healthy arm at the gurgling wound, his eyes swimming, his feet kicking madly as he drowned in his own blood. It was over in less than a minute.

The assassin spat on the dead man, turned, and carried a set of keys from the room. One by one, he unlocked the doors along the hallway as he walked toward the stairs. He spoke loudly. "They're all dead! Leave now, if you can. God soon brings fire to this place!"

Soft sounds of bodies stirring could be heard within the cells. The hinges of one door ground behind him.

When he reached the first step, he dropped the large keychain and ascended to the upper floors.

The truck made a startling sound in the desert night as he turned the key. *Twenty minutes.* That was enough. If they had not escaped yet, they were as good as dead anyway. He stared down at a small radio transmitter on the seat next to him. A red light blinked at the upper-right corner. He pressed the button underneath, and a bright orange glow flashed before him in the darkness. Several seconds later, the sound arrived, the rumbling blast from an explosion as the compound was blown into the sky, rubble and embers raining down on the dark sands.

The last shall be first, and the first shall be last.

He doubted Jesus had meant it that way. He shifted gears and raced away from the inferno.

It had begun.

Also by Erec Stebbins

THE RAGNARÖK CONSPIRACY

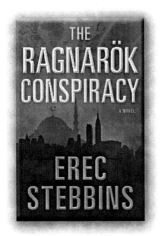

A Western terrorist organization targets Muslims around the world, and FBI agent John Savas must put aside the loss of his son and work with a man who symbolizes all he has come to hate. Both are drawn into a race against time to stop the plot of an American bin Laden and prevent a global catastrophe.

"Fortify your shelf of Armageddon thrillers with this promising newcomer."-*Library Journal*

"**What a debut!** A heart-pounding tale of terrorism sure to be controversial, **turns the genre upside down**." -*Internet Review of Books*

"A taut tale of international intrigue with a **unique twist**." -*The Washington Times Communities*

"An **enticing and much recommended** addition to thriller collections" -*The Midwest Book Review*

"A new thriller with an **unusual depth**" -*BiblioBuffet*

"Unlike most 'war on terror' thrillers" -*Publishers Weekly*

"Fans of the Vince Flynn books will enjoy Stebbins' take on terrorism with a twist." -*Booklist*

"Stebbins has his finger on the pulse of greed, disillusionment and the search for redemption in this **pulse-pounding debut**." -*RT Book Reviews, Four Stars (Compelling-Page-turner)*

"**Outrageously entertaining**: epic, explosive, subversive, engaged and compassionate, like a Michael Bay movie written by Aaron Sorkin." -*Chris Brookmyre, author of Where The Bodies Are Buried*

CPSIA information can be obtained at www.ICGtesting.com
Printed in the USA
LVOW11s1824290714

396578LV00002B/428/P